D1648139

THE INCREDIBLE EVENTS IN WOMEN'S CELL NUMBER 3

KIRA YARMYSH

THE INCREDIBLE EVENTS IN WOMEN'S CELL NUMBER 3

A NOVEL

TRANSLATED FROM THE RUSSIAN BY ARCH TAIT

Grove Press
New York

Originally published as Невероятные происшествия в женской камере № 3
by Corpus Publishing in Russia in 2020.

Published simultaneously in Canada
Printed in the United States of America

This book is set in 12-pt. Arno Pro by Alpha Design & Composition of Pittsfield, NH.

First Grove Atlantic hardcover edition: February 2023

Library of Congress Cataloging-in-Publication data is available for this title.

ISBN 978-0-8021-6073-7
eISBN 978-0-8021-6074-4

Grove Press
an imprint of Grove Atlantic
154 West 14th Street
New York, NY 10011

Distributed by Publishers Group West

groveatlantic.com

23 24 25 26   10 9 8 7 6 5 4 3 2 1

CONTENTS

THE INCREDIBLE EVENTS IN WOMEN'S CELL NUMBER 3

DAY ONE

If you asked Anya which day in prison had been the most trying, she would say the first. It had seemed both insane and endless. Prison time was elastic: it stretched out interminably, only to then fly like an arrow.

It started with her waking up on a clammy, impermeable mattress in a detention cell in a Moscow police department. She had been arrested the day before, but her efforts to outrun the riot police, her journey in the police bus, and her registration at the police department had kept her busy enough to all but overlook how it had ended. The reality of being in police custody struck her only once she was locked in that cell.

She had spent the night tossing and turning on the mattress, trying to pull her top down to avoid her body coming into contact with the oilcloth. The mattress was on the floor, there were no pillows, no blankets, and it was impossible to get comfortable. Either the arm under her head went numb or she got pins and needles in her side. She could only tell that she had managed to get some fitful sleep when she jerked awake, which happened many times.

What the time was, she had no idea. The cell was windowless, with only a dim light bulb above the door, which stayed on night and day. Her phone had been taken from her. Each time she woke, for want of anything else to do, she entertained herself by inspecting the wall in front of her: the peeling paint that looked like crushed eggshells; the suspicious streaks whose origins she preferred not to think about; the graffiti: LEX, UP BIRYULYOVO!, ALLAHU AKBAR. Waking up one last time with a jolt, Anya realized she was not imagining it: she could feel a tremor under the floor, the metro must be open, morning had arrived.

The police department began coming to life, as Anya could hear through her cell door, which had been left ajar overnight. A kindly, older cop had not locked it but left it open a handbreadth. (A chain on the outside ensured she opened it no farther.) She lay, listening to the police arguing among themselves in the reception area, the telephone ringing off the hook, the rasping of a door lock, water flushing in a toilet she was eventually taken to visit. A policeman let her in and stayed outside to keep the door shut.

Anya dithered and looked around her. A scene from *Trainspotting* came to mind, where the main character goes to "the worst toilet in Scotland." He had clearly seen nothing like the one in the Tverskaya police department, with its chipped tile floor awash with murky fluid. A rusty chain hung from the water tank, and as for the toilet itself, it was a hole in the ground. Anya decided against going anywhere near it. Running the faucet for appearances' sake, while avoiding all contact with the squishy remnant of soap on the filthy edge of the washbasin, she emerged, and the policeman took her back to the cell.

Time passed with demoralizing slowness. Her cell door was now shut tight and did not allow in any outside sounds. She ran her eyes over the walls, which were barely visible in the dim light, but it was an unrewarding pastime. She felt heavy and clumsy from lack of sleep, and thoughts stirred sluggishly in her head. Anya could not tell how long she sat like that. Her heart seemed to begin beating more slowly

2

and she felt she was sinking into a trancelike state; perhaps, indeed, suspended animation. When the door opened and a policeman came into the cell, Anya was startled, not sure what was happening.

She was taken through to the reception desk and told to sit on a bench next to a sad-eyed woman who looked Roma, a young guy who was drunk, and a man with a large black eye. The fatherly cop who had left her door partly open took the box of her belongings out of a closet. "Get yourself together," he said. "You have to go to the court hearing." Anya turned on her phone, quickly checked her messages, put her belt back on and laced up her sneakers. (The laces had been taken from her before she had spent the night in the cell.)

"Don't make too much effort," the cop advised. "You're going to court."

"Why, aren't laces allowed in court?" Anya asked in surprise.

"They are, but you'll have to take them back off at the special detention center," he explained considerately. Anya was touched.

Her appearance in court took less time than she expected, contrary to what she'd hoped, because it was at least light and airy there. Her friends had brought coffee and a Caesar salad for her, and she was allowed to keep her phone.

The judge, whose punctuality Anya was regretting, was a severe-looking, gray-haired man. The hearing began on time, the breaks lasted precisely as long as he said they should. This might be a good sign, she thought. If someone looked as stern and unassailable as a rock face, she was sure the decisions they made would be just and fair.

Anya's crime was to have been within reach of a riot policeman at a protest rally. She had been randomly plucked from the crowd and shoved into a police bus, where it was hot but rather lively. Lots of people besides Anya were being arrested, and they were all talking, joking, and laughing together. There was a party atmosphere. This was the first time she had been in a police bus, so it was an adventure. She had no doubt that when they got to the police station they would all soon be released.

She and the others were taken to a conference room. It was a large space with rows of chairs, a bit like a schoolroom. By one wall was what looked like a desk for the teacher, only it had a portrait of Putin to the right of it, one of Medvedev to the left, and the flag of the Russian Federation in the middle. Anya's fellow detainees were called up to the desk one by one. They each signed some papers and were then released. It was getting dark outside, but still Anya was being kept waiting, until finally she was the only person left and the darkness had become impenetrable. An electric light up by the ceiling was making an irritating buzz. A policeman came in and told her she would have to spend the night in an "ADC," which was decoded for her as an administrative detention cell. She could not see why she was the only one being treated like this, and began arguing. The policeman said she was facing a more serious charge than the others and would have to stay in the ADC to await trial.

Lying on the floor in her cell she had found it less easy to suppose everything was going to end well, or soon. The court today was at least clean and orderly, and there was even a bolt on the toilet door. Anya's hopes of a happy ending revived slightly. When the judge invited her to address the court, she was reluctant to stigmatize him in case he was about to release her and she would find she had been unjustly rude to a good-hearted person. The judge heard her out, retired to deliberate for half an hour, emerged exactly on time and, with a wholly just and absolutely unassailable expression on his face, ruled that she should continue to be held in custody.

Anya was duly transferred to a special detention center. The two cops transporting her were in a hurry to get home, so they put a flashing light on the roof of their car and sailed past the Moscow traffic jams. Racing through the streets with the siren wailing, Anya felt like a big cheese in the criminal underworld, but this part of the day was also disappointingly brief. She looked out of the car window as apartment buildings flashed by, and reflected that even the most uninspired five-story blocks appear unbelievably appealing to someone on whom a sentence has just been pronounced.

Arriving at the special detention center, Anya's guards found that their speeding had been to no avail, because a whole line of police cars with detainees was held up in front of the gate.

Another long wait followed. The cops at first took turns getting out of the car to smoke, then they both got out at the same time, then they let Anya out to join them. Inevitably, the discussion turned to politics. The senior cop sententiously pointed out what a lot of trouble Anya and her comrades were causing the police by organizing unsanctioned rallies. After delivering this reprimand, he moved on to complain about a judicial system that was putting Anya in prison for nothing more serious than her idiotic rallies, and thereby obliging him to drive her all over Moscow. Next he excoriated the government for its thieving: police salaries were dwindling, but the number of rallies they were called on to disrupt was not. Anya tried to point out tactfully the possibility of a connection between government thieving and protest rallies, but her guard was not looking for a debate partner. After deploring the chaos around him, the policeman started on the director of the special detention center, who was keeping them in line in this heat and thereby proving himself to be his most powerful and perfidious foe. The cop ranted and railed, his buddy tacitly concurring, until finally the three of them were allowed inside.

Anya was so worn out by the day's waiting, she was almost looking forward to quickly getting into her cell, but this was not to be. Her guards handed her over to the police at the center and made themselves scarce. Anya embarked on the process of being booked.

The registration procedure consisted of several stages and was thoroughly ridiculous. First, the police gutted the bag of goodies that Anya's friends had brought to the court. She had no idea what was in it herself, so she studied the contents with no less interest than the officers did. It was even rather fun, like picking presents out of Santa's sack. The rubber flip-flops and sliced sausage might not be particularly wonderful, but after the ordeals of the day she was not going to be picky with gifts.

Everything was opened, sliced, or shaken out. About a third of her items were confiscated, and some she was advised to leave for now in the storage room rather than taking everything with her into the cell. The bag itself had to be left in storage because its shoulder strap "represented a risk." Anya could not see how it could, so she naively asked the question. A pompous cop with fat cheeks, who she decided must be in charge, gave her a chilling look and said, "You might hang yourself." Anya shuddered and asked no more questions.

In addition to the shoulder bag, other items deemed impermissible were: a pencil sharpener (a blade!), a packet of sunflower seeds (husks!), hair conditioner (due to its nontransparent packaging), a pillow and blanket (also nontransparent). And much else besides, for reasons at which she could only guess.

When she was instructed to discard several oranges, she broke her resolution and tentatively asked, "What's the problem with oranges?"

"Might contain alcohol."

"Really?" Anya asked in bafflement.

"People inject alcohol into them with a syringe," the fat-cheeked cop explained wearily. "Soft fruit and vegetables: impermissible. Only apples, carrots, and onions are allowed. And radishes."

After Anya had put the plundered remains of her belongings into a plastic bag, she was taken for a medical examination. This was performed in a small closet adjacent to the reception area. There were no onlookers, but the fish-eye of a camera in the corner of the ceiling hinted at less than complete privacy.

The doctor was a chubby, bespectacled, fairly young woman, who might have seemed likable but for the expression of withering contempt on her face. She eyed Anya disparagingly, as if unerringly able to recognize an incorrigible case when she saw one. She ordered Anya to take her clothes off.

"What, everything?" Anya asked, with a sideways glance at the camera.

"Just your shirt and jeans. Now show me your back. Were you beaten at the police station?"

"What?!"

"I'll take that as a no. So why is there bruising down your spine?"

Anya tried twisting around to look but, needless to say, could see nothing. "What bruising?" she asked anxiously. "Perhaps it's from lying on the mattress there . . ."

"Some mattress! Right, and what's this bruise on your leg?"

"That's definitely from when I fell off my bike the other day."

"She fell off her bike! Any complaints?"

"No!" Anya said quickly, and the doctor instantly snapped shut her book and made for the door, managing to convey disdain even with her back turned.

It was time to have her fingerprints taken, which was called "finger rolling." A sheet of A4 paper with squares was placed in front of Anya, in which she was to leave prints of the pads of her fingers and, in two larger squares, prints of the whole of her hands. A blonde policewoman of middling years started running a roller with glossy black dye over Anya's hands. "It's really very good, washes off easily," she told Anya, noticing her look of concern. It was unclear whether she was bragging or offering reassurance.

When it was all done, Anya assumed she would at last be taken to her cell. However, the pompous cop brought another tome out of the side room. Anya groaned inwardly. Sitting down heavily, he put the book in front of him and opened it. He looked intently at Anya and said, "We need to list your valuables." "Fine," Anya agreed. "What valuables?"

"That's for you to tell me. There's usually a phone. Do you have one?" Anya nodded. "Put it here. And where's your ID? Yep, there it is. Your national insurance card? That's another valuable for the list."

"Should I get witnesses?" the blonde cop asked. The pompous cop nodded and started writing in his book in ornate, painstaking handwriting. The blonde left the reception area, clanging her way through a succession of doors. Anya counted three before she heard her say, "Okay, girls, this way. You're needed as witnesses. We've got a new cellmate for you." Anya did not hear the reply, but shortly afterwards heard flip-flops slapping along the corridor as someone approached reception. She readied herself.

How did Anya picture her future cellmate? The images in her mind drew on American TV series and Russian news items, so she was expecting a hybrid of a pretty, athletic blonde in an orange jumpsuit and an abject, ground-down woman in a headscarf. She felt the tension building as the flip-flops approached, and when the first figure came around the corner, she almost fainted.

Two women came into reception immediately behind the policewoman. Anya stared at them in disbelief and felt her heart sink, leaving behind a gaping, shuddering void. Athletic blondes clearly end up behind bars only in America.

The first prisoner looked as if she had just been brought up out of a dank dungeon. Anya was struck by how pitifully thin she was, her bony shoulders sprinkled with purple pimples, her rib cage skeletal. She was wearing a tank top with spaghetti-like shoulder straps and, in the presence of cops uniformed up to the ears, seemed almost naked, which made her appearance even more dreadful. She looked like a skeleton in a biology class rather than a live human being. The woman's gaunt face was yellowed. Thin curls straggled over her forehead and through them she glared out at the cops and at Anya with fiendish hostility.

The prisoner following her looked better, but only because of the very low baseline. Anya found her troubling too. The oddest thing was her dull, disoriented expression, as if she were not all there. A further peculiarity was what she was wearing because, in contrast to her half-naked companion, she seemed to be wearing too much. All of it was denim, from her pants to her shirt buttoned up to the throat, to her jacket.

"What is it n-now?" the first one demanded, looking venomously at the police. Anya thought the stutter made her even more sinister.

"We need witnesses," the pompous cop replied without looking up from what he was writing. "Cell phone, black, Apple. Model?"

"It's an iPhone 7," Anya said, continuing to peer surreptitiously at the women.

"Seventh series, case with Apple logo, charger for it . . . for it? . . . white, damaged at . . . what's that called? . . . well, let's say, the base. National insurance document, 133-8096156 . . ."

The cop wrote down the final digit and pushed the log across to the half-naked woman. "Check it," he grunted.

The woman reluctantly bent over the table and ran her eyes down the page. Anya shuddered at the sight of her shoulder blades, which seemed about to tear through her skin. Denim woman stood meanwhile staring blankly at the wall and paying no attention to the proceedings at all.

"S-seems all right."

"Sign it. First name, surname, signature."

The half-naked woman signed. Denim woman did not move, as if she had not heard, but after a poke in the ribs from her cellmate, stirred herself and also scribbled her name in the book.

The first prisoner suddenly turned to glare at Anya, who was so taken aback she stopped breathing. For a while the woman stared at her, completely unembarrassed, before breaking into a smile and saying, "D-don't be scared. All the girls are fine. Nobody's going to hurt you."

Anya stared back at her. She wasn't sure what surprised her more—this sudden flood of goodwill or the fact that one of the woman's front teeth was missing.

"Thank you very much, but I'm not scared," she murmured.

"Don't be scared!" denim woman suddenly repeated very loudly and, looking somehow past Anya, also gave her a happy, childish smile. Anya counted three missing teeth.

"All right, let's go to the cell, girls," said the policewoman. Hearing this, the half-naked woman adopted an expression of deep displeasure, but turned on her heel and walked to the door without another word. Denim woman made no move and carried on smiling blissfully.

"Move, moron," her friend hissed, tugging her sleeve. She swayed, almost losing her balance, but then obediently flip-flopped in her wake, the smile never leaving her face.

"So, how many people are there in the women's cell?" Anya asked after a moment of silence, glancing at the door through which the women had just disappeared.

"Five, plus you," the pompous cop replied, placing Anya's valuables in a striped bag with the number 37 printed on it. Only then did he look up, and something in Anya's expression made him take pity, because he added, "They're all perfectly normal. No drug addicts, no hardened criminals."

Having encountered two of her future cellmates, Anya's impatience to get to her cell had dissolved but, for better or worse, her registration was now complete. Clutching a plastic bag containing what was permissible for her to take inside the cell, she left the reception area, guided by a boy of a policeman with a solemn and serious expression.

Beyond the door leading into the depths of the detention center was a second, and beyond that was a green-painted corridor with no windows and only searingly white fluorescent light bulbs that ran the length of the ceiling. Anya felt she was walking through a sunken wreck on the seabed. On both sides of the corridor were metal doors festooned with bolts and locks. Strange, identical, meter-high pipes with yawning mouths were fixed to the wall by the doors. Anya glanced into one as she walked by but saw only darkness inside.

"What are those for?" she asked the boy.

"That's not for you to know," he replied severely.

There appeared to be only one women's cell, which was exactly in the middle of a row and numbered 3.

"Stand there," the boy said, and started sorting through his bunch of keys. They were so enormous they looked like stage props. It seemed incredible that they could be used to open actual locks rather than serving a purpose only in school plays. Selecting the requisite key, the boy first looked through the peephole into the cell, then looked sternly at Anya, and finally, with a rasping sound, unlocked the door in front of her.

Anya assumed her most independent air, drew herself to full height, took a deep breath, and . . . immediately succumbed to a coughing fit. Clouds of cigarette smoke billowed out of the cell and her eyes were instantly stinging. Her spectacular entry had been ruined, but there could be no turning back. Blinking, spluttering, and firmly clutching her bag of possessions, Anya stepped unseeing into the semidarkness. The door was immediately slammed shut behind her. A silence ensued.

It took her a few moments to get used to the smoke, but when she finally managed to open her eyes and looked quickly around, she saw . . . them.

Several women were sitting far inside the room, looking at Anya. Light from a small window fell in broad swathes on their shoulders and brows, which made them look not like living people but statues hewn from stone. They were silent and motionless, and seemed suddenly like idols arranged on the bunks. A dense fog of cigarette smoke in the cell blurred their features, as if she were looking at them through glass covered in condensation. Seconds ticked by but still the stone idols remained immobile, and Anya felt everything go cold inside her.

"Well, tell us your name, then, and how long you're in for," said the nearest.

The spell was broken and the women seemed to come to life. The one asking the question took a long drag on a cigarette, which, Anya now noticed, she was holding. A ribbon of smoke rose towards the ceiling. All her fellow detainees started moving at the same time, one coughing, another changing position. They were all perfectly normal, and Anya felt a prickle of embarrassment at having almost panicked seeing them all. The women inspected her quite openly, and under their lively, curious gaze she felt herself thawing out.

"I'm Anya. I'm in for ten days," she said.

"Much like the rest of us," said the woman smoking the cigarette. "Driving without a license too, were you?"

"No, actually I was at a protest rally."

"A friend of mine went to a rally once!" another girl chimed in. When Anya turned to look at her she was taken aback for a moment, because the girl was dark-skinned. That was completely unexpected, as if part of Anya's daydream about American prisons had suddenly come true.

"Er . . . may I sit here?" Anya asked, recovering her poise and pointing to a vacant bunk.

"Sit where you like," grunted the smoker.

The cell was spacious, and much less gloomy than Anya had thought in that first moment. The walls were painted a delicate peach color, nothing like how she had pictured such places. There was music coming from a radio somewhere. Looking around, she spotted a mesh-covered recess above the door. The floor was wooden, and the furniture consisted of a lopsided locker in the corner piled high with packets of tea and biscuits, and four narrow bunks. One corner of the room, where the walls were tiled, comprised the "bathroom," with a washbasin and a small cubicle that obviously served as a toilet. Its walls extended to shoulder height on Anya, and on its diminutive door a sheet of paper torn from an exercise book urged, "Run the faucet when using!"

"W-want some tea?" her half-naked former witness asked hospitably.

"If I may." The woman stood up and started rummaging in a pile of blankets on the top bunk. Anya looked for any sign of a kettle, although she would have been surprised to find one, given that she had not been allowed to bring even a pencil sharpener into the cell. In the meantime, the woman extracted a misted plastic bottle from under the blankets, poured hot water from it into a plastic cup, and dropped in a tea bag.

"I'm N-natasha," she said, handing Anya the tea with an encouraging smile. The tea was just short of lukewarm. Anya mumbled something suitably appreciative and took a hasty sip, feeling it important to show enthusiasm and not give offense. She had no way of knowing how she was expected to behave here.

The other women said nothing and carried on looking at her.

Anya hesitantly inquired, "What's your name?"

"Katya," responded the girl with the cigarette, exhaling. She said it in an offhand manner, almost grudgingly, as if to make it clear the question was of no interest and she was replying only out of politeness. At the same time, her gaze was so intrusive and watchful that every time she looked at Anya it made her feel uneasy. Katya's eyes were a striking feature, light blue, almost transparent, and Anya was perturbed by the disconnect between the way she spoke and the way she stared. She was not repellent, but Anya had a sense it might be wise to keep her at a distance.

"My name is Diana," the black girl said. She was tall and monumental, wore a flared black dress, and had a springy bun on top of her head. Taking the cigarette from Katya, she inhaled elegantly and returned it.

"How did you all come to be here?" Anya asked tentatively.

"The two of us," Diana said with a nod towards Katya, "are in for driving without a license. A ten-day stretch. Separately, but on the same day."

"And I s-swore at a cop," Natasha said, pouring tea for herself and settling on her bunk.

"Can you get sent to a detention center for that?" Anya asked, surprised.

"Of course you can. I was standing with my husband outside a store. He was holding a c-can of beer. Unopened, mind you! Up come the filth. You're drunk, they say, come with us. I know all about them. I've been through it all before. I said, we're going nowhere with you . . . and a couple of other things. So, like, they arrest me for obstructing the police in the performance of their duties."

"Have you done time in a detention center before?" Anya asked.

Natasha smiled indulgently: "Yeah, I've done time—but not in a detention center."

Anya nodded quickly, trying to look blasé, even though a siren was wailing in her head. She was curious to know why Natasha had been in prison, but not sure she wanted to hear the answer.

"Natasha's our old hand. She can tell you tons of stuff it's good to know," Katya said sardonically, stubbing out her cigarette. Looking around at her fellow inmates with those cold blue eyes, she paused at denim woman, Anya's other witness. "Ira here is our exotic case. Isn't that right, Ira? She's in for not paying child support."

They turned as one to look at denim woman. Until now she had been sitting, silently huddled in the corner of her bunk, but their attention revived her instantly. She smiled and started nodding. Anya was fairly certain she had not heard the question. Ira's strange condition made Anya no less apprehensive than Natasha's criminal record, but again she did not want to inquire further.

"I'm here for driving without a license too," said the fifth girl, who was sitting on the bunk next to Anya's. When she was sure she had everyone's attention, she added, "Only I had a license." Anya looked at her and could not believe that there was a fashion model in the cell with her. To be truthful, Anya was uncertain what exactly her profession might be, but only because she had never seen such women up close, having previously encountered them only in photos on Instagram. The girl had that photoshopped look even now, sitting a meter away from Anya on a crumpled prison bed. Her eyes were blue, her hair purest silk, her bust an F-cup. She batted her extraordinarily long eyelashes and pouted her lips flirtatiously.

"You mean you actually had a license?" Anya asked, continuing to look her over almost impolitely.

Diana, who had obviously already heard the story, snorted and then responded for her: "It was out of date, for Chrissakes."

"Well, yes, but I never had any trouble until then!" the fashion plate said, immediately explaining to Anya with a friendly smile, "My license was revoked eight months ago but I didn't hand it in! Why would I want to do that? Oh, and my name is Maya, by the way."

"Delighted to meet you."

"For this I was sentenced to five days, and before that I was held overnight in a police station. Can you imagine it?"

"I absolutely can."

"I tried to commit suicide there. They didn't take my bag from me and it had a chain on it. I wound it around my neck and tried to strangle myself."

Anya's eyes widened. "Oh my god!"

"I even lost consciousness for several seconds," Maya boasted, clearly satisfied with the effect she had achieved. "Then I started scratching my veins open. I was just so completely stressed out!"

"Goodness me . . ."

"Look!" Maya thrust her arm under Anya's nose. There was indeed a thin, dotted line of dried blood on her wrist. "But never mind, the cops got what they deserved! When they tried to arrest me, I bit one of them! And then at the trial they started hinting that if I gave them a bribe I could be let off, would you believe such a thing?"

Anya nodded just in case the question hadn't been rhetorical. She was startled not so much by what Maya was saying as by how she was saying it, so full of herself.

"Well, I said, no way. I make it a rule never to give a kopeck to these twats!" Maya concluded with unexpected vehemence, only for her face to light up again the next second in a smile.

"You should be thankful you only got f-five days," Natasha said, sipping her tea. "You're lucky they didn't send you to the funny farm as a suicide risk."

"Could they really do that?" Maya said, sounding appalled. Her expression and tone of voice changed with the swiftness of a cartoon character. In the course of a minute she could appear hurt, scared, flirtatious, complicit, sweet, and incensed.

"You b-bet they could, and you'd have liked it a whole lot less there," Natasha assured her.

Maya became subdued, clearly reflecting on that scenario. They were all silent for a time, the only sound coming from Natasha slurping her tea.

Katya eventually set aside the plastic cup she had been using as an ashtray, slapped her thighs and said, "Right, we were just playing Crocodile. Are you in?"

"I think I'd rather just watch to begin with," Anya responded swiftly. It was not a game she liked, and she had no wish to make a fool of herself in front of five strangers.

"Suit yourself. By the way, do you smoke? Got any cigarettes?"

"No."

"Shit, we've only got three left," said Diana, lighting up all the same.

"It's okay, we'll bum some from cell 5," Katya promised. "And if one of you makes me act out the word 'investment' again, I'll kill you."

They both laughed. Katya started looking for the bag they were using for the game, which they eventually discovered Ira was sitting on. She continued to radiate pure bliss, even when the others began holding their noses and shouting, "Yoicks, Ira, you've farted in it!" As the game organizer, Katya shuffled the pieces of paper in the bag and held it out. The others each helped themselves to a word.

Natasha went first. Standing in the middle of the cell, she raised her arms, clasped her hands above her head, and gazed expectantly at her cellmates. Nobody had the least idea of the answer. She looked at them severely, raised her arms again, and then imitated splashing something around. Her expression was so grim that everybody started giggling, and the longer nobody guessed, the more furious Natasha became. She stared daggers at the others, as if knowing for a fact they had long ago worked out the answer and now were only pretending not to know, out of spite. Finally she gave up and just pointed up at the ceiling, even though pointing at things was against the rules.

Maya shouted, "A light bulb!" which, to Anya's surprise, turned out to be right. She got off her bunk.

Standing with upright posture, she again surprised Anya by having such a diminutive body that her huge breasts looked downright intimidating. Maya was wearing platform sneakers, and stepped forward a little unsteadily, like a newborn fawn. Taking center stage, she squatted gracefully, stuck out her butt and put her fingers to her head, as if they were horns.

"A bunny rabbit!" Katya yelled, jabbing a finger at her. Maya looked pleased with herself, got up and sashayed back to her bunk.

It soon became obvious that Crocodile was not Katya's game. She waved her arms about pointlessly, cursing under her breath at first, then very loudly. The others were in fits of laughter. Katya shouted, bellowed with laughter, swore, and called them a bunch of idiots. She bounced up and down but failed to bring the others any closer to the answer. Finally, when she was in a really foul mood, Diana took pity on her and announced that the word was "Big Ben" and that she had been the one to put it into the bag.

"How can you do a charade for 'Big Ben'?" Katya demanded furiously. "That's even worse than 'investment'! Ooh, I could kill you!"

Clearly undaunted by the threat, Diana shrugged and said, "You only needed to point to your T-shirt."

Everyone looked at Katya's T-shirt. She pulled it forward to take a better look at it herself. There, taking up the entire front, was a picture of Big Ben. Katya yelled angrily and plumped herself down on the bed, crossing her arms and legs.

After Diana and Ira took their turns, the game concluded, and it was at this moment that Anya realized how hungry she was. The Caesar salad her friends had brought to the court had been the only food she had eaten all day.

"Do we get an evening meal here?" she asked hopefully, to nobody in particular.

"We've already had dinner," Katya responded.

"And what about taking a shower?"

"Water's off." Anya gave a deep sigh, and felt it was odd she could have imagined this long, tiring day ending any better than this.

"Is it completely turned off?" she persisted, just in case. "When is it likely to come on again?"

"Only the hot water is off," Katya explained patiently. "For maintenance. You can ask to be taken to the shower. They usually do take newcomers there—but with the cold water it's really freezing. Thursday is the official day for showers."

Anya did not immediately take in what she meant. "What, only once a week?"

"D-did you think you'd come to a holiday resort?" Natasha growled, scowling. "Get used to it. Prison is like this too, you know."

Anya was about to quip that getting used to being in prison was not part of any future she envisaged for herself but, wary of Natasha, asked instead, "So what's the daily routine?"

Natasha, clearly the cell's specialist on prison life, took on the explanation. "First there's breakfast, but g-girls don't usually go. Want us to w-wake you up?"

"You can try," Anya said uncertainly. Hungry as she was, the thought of breakfast in a communal cafeteria was a horror. Ever since nursery school Anya had been firmly convinced such places were best avoided if at all possible.

"Then there's the m-morning inspection," Natasha continued. "After that they take you for phone calls in the afternoon. That's f-fifteen minutes. Then there's exercise. That's an hour. There's also l-lunch and dinner. After that there's the evening r-rounds and lights-out."

"And what about the rest of the time?"

"The r-rest of the time you sit here."

"I thought we'd be made to work . . ."

"Come on!" Natasha said with a laugh. "This isn't a labor camp."

That statement, coming so close on the heels of the other, that everything here was "like prison," struck Anya as inconsistent, but she decided against trying to be too clever.

"Katty!"

A muffled exclamation came unexpectedly through the window over to one side. Katya, who was smoking again, quickly passed the cigarette to Diana and in two bounds was up on the windowsill. The windows were close to the ceiling, so the sills were a meter and a half from the floor. Katya had been nimble and moved like lightning. While lounging on the bed she had given no sense of her strength, but as soon as she leaped up there Anya felt the power in her.

"What?" Katya asked in a loud whisper.

"How you getting on?" the voice outside asked, accompanied by chuckling.

"It's D-dimka from number 5," Natasha said excitedly, half getting up off her own bed.

"Ask him for smokes," the ever-practical Diana prompted. She got up too, more reluctantly, straightened her dress and rather grandly took herself across to the window.

"Got any smokes?" Katya asked in a businesslike whisper. There was a brief pause.

"Yep," the unseen Dimka from cell number 5 confirmed.

Everyone, apart from Maya and Anya, jumped up from their beds and joined the conversation.

"Then give us some!" Katya said, shushing her cellmates with an imperious gesture. Ira and Natasha obediently fell silent and even sat back down. Diana, in a display of independence, stayed where she was.

"What ya got to swap?" Dimka asked after a further pause.

"We can give them the apples!" Natasha whispered, in the excitement losing her stutter.

"We can swap you apples," Katya communicated out loud.

"Okay, done. You send us apples and we'll send you cigs."

The girls immediately rushed away from the window and got busy, Natasha rummaging through plastic bags, Diana collecting the apples. Next Katya went over and hammered her fist on the cell door. The peephole opened almost immediately and Anya glimpsed someone on the other side.

"Can you take some apples for us to number 5?" Katya asked brusquely. Anya couldn't make out the answer.

"Oh, ple-ease," Katya whined, trying to ingratiate herself.

A small hatch in the door opened with a clatter and the blonde policewoman who had fingerprinted Anya peered into the cell.

"What's that, apples?" she asked, sounding bored. Katya ceremoniously passed the bag of apples through the hatch. The policewoman looked in it suspiciously and said, "No notes, I hope."

"Oh yes, we're really going to be writing them letters!" Katya replied tartly. The policewoman sighed and closed the window.

Several minutes elapsed. "Perhaps the bastards have cheated us," Ira speculated, looking, for the first time so far, not just vacantly happy but actually interested in something.

"Oh, get lost!" Natasha exclaimed.

After a moment, the hatch clattered open again and the police-woman's face reappeared.

"Number 5 said to give you these cigarettes. But just so you know, girls, this is the first and last time you use me as a postwoman."

"Yes, yes. Thank you!" Katya exclaimed, rushing to the door. When the hatch slammed shut again, she added, "It's a joke, the way she says that every time."

It struck Anya that the detention center was a bit like a summer camp for dysfunctional adults. When she was little she used to go to children's camps every year and loved them, because they were like a simulator of independence, a model of the adult world she wanted to move into. She had even then been full of contempt for children who were sobbing for their mommies on the first night. Anya herself had been entranced by the prospect of being away from her parents for a whole month. She had liked everything about the camps: singing songs while someone played a guitar, late-night ghost stories, the fare-well campfire, all the entertainments and competitions. Even the two-tier bunks, an invariable attribute of the dormitories, had struck her as yet another novelty. To her they seemed all part of a great adventure.

The student dormitory where Anya had lived for five years after moving to study in Moscow had been the next step on her path to adulthood. Although it was a step closer to the real world, everything about it was still redolent of summer camps—the sense of together-ness, the illusion of grown-upness, even the iconic two-tier bunks. It did not yet feel like real life, only a demo version of it where, in a safe environment, you could learn skills you would be needing later.

Anya believed that her long-awaited adulthood had begun when she graduated from university and moved into an apartment of her own. That was the moment when she had finally grown up, and she never imagined anyone could regress from that state. Now, however, in this special detention center, she felt exactly this, that she had regressed, as she sat once again on a two-tier bunk surrounded by roommates. It was as if she were being drawn back into the time in her life when she was only playing at reality. If the summer camps and student dorms had brought young Anya closer to the world of adults, this detention center was demoting her back to the status of a child, where freedom was curtailed by instructors, romantic relationships conducted by exchanging notes, and the main currency not rubles but apples.

A key again rattled in the lock—the doors seemed to make an extraordinary amount of noise—and the pompous cop came into their cell.

"Are you going for a shower?" he asked Anya sternly.

"Is there only cold water? If so, no thanks."

"Up to you. Here's your bedding." With that he handed Anya what looked like a table napkin that had been folded over many times.

"Is that the bed linen?" Anya asked in bewilderment. The cop became even more stern.

"It's single-use. You'll be brought the standard-grade bed linens tomorrow." Anya turned the table napkin over in her hands.

"They won't," Maya told her as soon as the cop had left.

"What do you mean?"

"They only say that. They haven't yet brought anything different to any of us." Only now did Anya notice that all her cellmates had the same strange table napkins on their mattresses. She unfolded hers. Her "bedding" consisted of two pieces of material: one long and narrow, which must be the sheet; and a second, like a square envelope, the pillowcase. Both were made of a material Anya had only previously seen in hospitals, where it was used for shoe coverings. With a sigh, she made the bed. More precisely, she laid the "sheet" over the mattress and reached for a blanket in the heap at the foot of her bunk.

"I wouldn't use that one," Katya said emphatically.

Anya stopped short and looked at the blanket apprehensively: "What's wrong with it?"

"It stinks!" Ira exclaimed joyfully, continuing to radiate blissful happiness but appearing now to be reacting a little more specifically to her environment. Anya decided to sleep fully dressed.

Her cellmates also got ready for bed. Maya popped under her blanket without a moment's hesitation, and Anya reflected enviously that she had clearly managed to dial down her expectations in the past couple of days.

"Oh, girls, I would so love to go somewhere warm, somewhere in Dominica maybe . . . " Maya murmured dreamily.

No-nonsense Natasha, ensconced on the top bunk, warned Ira, who was on the lower one, "I'll k-kill you if you keep tossing and turning. I wake up in the middle of the night because the b-bunk is shaking and every time it's you t-turning from one side to the other!" Ira continued beaming as if all was well with the world.

"What do you keep poking me with?" Katya asked Diana. They occupied the bunk farthest from Anya and against a wall, with Katya on top and Diana below. Diana was currently lying with her legs raised and purposefully trampling the underside of Katya's mattress.

"My feet. Want me to stop?"

"Well—no. Carry on, I like the massage."

"Do they ever turn the radio off?" Anya asked. She became aware that all this time extraneous voices had been tangling with the thoughts in her head, and only now realized that the radio was never silent.

"They turn it off after the evening rounds," Katya told her. "Although they've forgotten a couple of times and we've had to bang on the door."

"When do they turn it back on?"

"After the morning inspection."

Anya had no recollection of the evening rounds, because she fell asleep as soon as her head hit the pillow. At some point, somewhere in the distance, she heard the clanging of a door and voices, then it suddenly became darker as the main light was switched off. Sometime after that, the radio was finally turned off and there was dead silence so suddenly it almost woke her up fully again. She could hear Maya wheezing in the next bunk. Anya suddenly had such a sense of peace; it was as if she were sleeping not in a detention center cell but in the softest bed in the safest of sanctuaries. This endless day was finally at an end and all her fears were left behind. However odd Anya's cellmates might be, they posed no clear threat, so at last she could relax. With that thought, she opened her eyes to look one last time around the cell, and froze.

Ira was not asleep. In the pink light of the only light bulb, Anya could see her, but she seemed unnaturally tall. Anya remembered for a fact that Ira was short, but now, sitting up in the bunk, the top of her head was almost touching the upper tier. If she had looked like a giantess Anya would have been less unnerved than she was by this barely perceptible, but wholly inexplicable, impossible differentness. Ira was muttering something. Anya could see her lips moving feverishly but no sound came from them. It was as if she were reciting a prayer or an incantation, and Anya felt a panic surge through her. What she was seeing seemed totally, quintessentially insane. At that moment Ira moved her hands and something glinted. Anya was paralyzed in her bunk. Scissors. Abnormally, phantasmagorically large scissors. They could not possibly have found their way into a detention center cell, yet here they were, gleaming in Ira's hands. Horror engulfed her like wildfire and she could not breathe. Ira turned slowly towards her.

Only this was not Ira. It was a woman who resembled her but was a thousand times more terrifying, so old that a patina of wrinkles made her face almost indiscernible. Like in an icon, it had worn away to a dull, dark stain. At first Anya thought in horror that the woman had no eyes, but then saw they were closed. Anya stared at her, rooted to the spot by absolute terror. She wanted desperately to screw up her eyes and stop seeing that face, but she could not. There was an impenetrable silence. The monstrous face with its closed eyes was still turned to Anya and its lips were moving impossibly fast. She suddenly understood that all this time the woman had been looking at her, somehow seeing her despite the tightly closed eyelids. The realization was blinding, as if she had suddenly been dragged out from behind a curtain onto a dazzlingly lit stage. Emitting a terrified, bloodcurdling scream, she woke.

DAY TWO

The next morning, Anya was shaken out of sleep by the clanging of a door. She found herself staring at a low, patterned ceiling and was not immediately sure where she was.

"Breakfast!" said a woman's voice.

The drowsy haze in her head was dispelled in an instant. She was in a cell, in a detention center in Moscow, and looking at the floral pattern of a mattress on the top tier of a bunk.

She sighed, closed her eyes again, and felt a strong urge not to get out of bed. Somebody—Anya guessed it must be Natasha—jumped down from a nearby bunk, grumbling to herself. Only Natasha could already be so grumpy first thing in the morning.

Water flushed, the toilet door creaked, then somebody blew their nose and hissed, "Ira, you i-idiot, you kept me awake all night again!"

Anya smiled to herself, but just for a moment. The moment she heard Ira's apologetic murmuring, memories of the past night flooded back.

She shivered, and everything went cold inside her. Through half-closed eyes she looked around the room. Natasha was in the middle, tying her hair up in a ponytail. Dopey Ira was sitting in her bunk trying inexpertly to button her denim shirt, looking so completely ordinary

27

that just the sight of her made Anya's fears seem ridiculous. Anya tried to detect even a hint, some faint echo of the demonic being she thought she had seen, but found nothing remotely menacing about Ira. She tried to recall what happened after she screamed, but could not. She must have gone out like a light. The hours between the end of her nightmare and her unceremonious awakening were as oblivious and muted as if nestled in cotton wool. Anya supposed she must have roused everyone with her shrieking, but in the half-light of morning the cell looked so unperturbed it was hard to believe there could have been any great commotion during the night. And if no one had heard her yell, surely she must have dreamed the whole thing from beginning to end.

The cell door was flung open. "Breakfast!" said yesterday's police boy. "And bring out the trash."

Natasha was approaching Anya's bunk, but she closed her eyes tight and pretended to be asleep. "Are you coming for b-breakfast?" she whispered, to no reply.

Anya sensed Natasha waiting by the side of her bunk for a while before moving away. A plastic bag rustled and Natasha said, "Bring the water bottle, idiot," before she and Ira finally went out.

When their voices in the corridor could no longer be heard, Anya took several deep breaths. She needed to calm down, clear her head, and have a good think. One obvious way to tell whether she had imagined everything was to search Ira's bunk. It would be no simple matter to hide an enormous pair of scissors in the cell, and indeed all but impossible to have smuggled them in in the first place. By the light of morning Anya's choice was clear, and she sat up in her bunk, looking around cautiously. Her cellmates were asleep, she could hear their steady breathing. Terrified she might be caught, but even more terrified by the possibility that she might be sharing a cell with a madwoman in possession of a large pair of sharp scissors, Anya sneaked over to Ira's bed. She probed the pillow, looked underneath it, and found—nothing. She lifted the blanket and gave it a tentative shake. Again, nothing. It would have been impossible to hide even a kopeck beneath the undersheet. That left the mattress. Anya got down on all fours and, contorting herself, peered under the bed. Through the mesh of the frame she could see there was nothing there either.

"What on earth are you doing?" a puzzled, sleepy voice inquired. With a gasp, Anya straightened up, banging her head on a metal cross-bar. Clutching the back of her head, she struggled out from under the bunk to see Maya had raised her head from the pillow and was staring at her agog.

"I thought I heard something rustling in there," Anya blurted.

"What?"

"Well, maybe a rat . . ."

"A ra-a-at?!"

"I only thought it might be."

"And you went in to look?"

"Well . . ." Anya said hesitantly, her explanation unraveling by the minute.

"And?"

"There doesn't seem to be one."

"This is too awful!" Maya exclaimed, sitting upright in her bunk. "We must report the matter immediately and have the thing trapped without delay. We must be provided with alternative accommodation. We must be set free! I refuse to remain on premises infested with rats!"

"Well, I didn't actually see it . . ."

"But you heard it! What else could be rustling down there? Unless it was a mouse?"

"Well, yes, maybe it was a mouse . . ."

"Well, whether it's a rat or a mouse is quite beside the point. This is wholly unacceptable! I shall lodge a complaint! I refuse to stay here a second longer!"

"What are you bawling about?" Katya snapped from her top bunk.

"Anya," Maya squealed, pointing an accusing finger, "saw a rat there!"

"For pity's sake!"

"Please calm down!" Anya implored her. "It was only an impression! I thought I heard rustling and decided to take a look, and there was nothing there!"

"What on earth were you thinking of, going under her bunk to look?" Katya demanded.

It was a good question, Anya had to admit. Luckily Maya started up again.

"But what if there was something there and it's run away? We've already found a cockroach in here, so perhaps there are rats? Or mice? Perhaps it was only a mouse?"

"Maya, do stop going on!" Katya said with a scowl. Maya fell silent and looked at her contritely. "You've been told a hundred times there was nothing there. Let me sleep, will you?"

"But what if there was?" Maya whispered in desperation.

"There wasn't, there wasn't," Anya repeated, finally getting to her feet. The back of her head was still smarting.

She returned to her bunk and could hear Maya tucking the blanket under herself for some time, making sure no rat could get in. Anya felt a vague sense of unease. She had not, of course, found the scissors, but what if Ira was carrying them around on her person? You could hide a machine gun under that denim carapace of hers. She sighed. "Don't fall victim to paranoia," she told herself. "It was only a dream." Unfortunately, these efforts to reassure herself only made the irrational fear flare more brightly.

Natasha and Ira soon came back from breakfast. Anya kept a surreptitious eye on them, but Ira continued to look exceptionally normal. They went to their bunks, Natasha continuing to curse Ira under her breath and Ira responding too quietly for Anya to hear what she was saying. Before long all was quiet again, and a few minutes later Anya could hear gentle snoring coming from Ira's direction. She could not imagine a monster snoring so innocently.

She lay in her bunk and listened to the sound of a scuffling broom outside the window. Anya again found herself reflecting that a detention center was a very strange institution. Strange and not fit for purpose. All the punishment amounted to was a strictly regulated holiday. You were allowed to sleep as much as you liked, and to idle about all day, reading and chatting. You were taken for exercise and to eat, and this package of measures was supposed, somehow, to cure you of antisocial behavior.

Time was passing and the building was slowly coming back to life: footsteps and voices were heard more frequently in the corridor, doors were slammed, and someone was dragging something along outside the windows. Now and again a guard would look into the cell through the peephole, which Anya found really annoying, as if she were a mouse being observed in a laboratory. The increasing clamor finally woke her cellmates for good. First to crawl from her bunk was Katya. Yawning and tying her hair into a ponytail as she went, she headed for the washbasin. Unlike Natasha and Ira when they went to breakfast, she had no qualms about waking other people up. She turned the faucet on as full as it would go, splashed about noisily and, when she dropped the soap, cursed roundly. Anya's other cellmates stirred in their beds and woke up.

Anya expected someone to ask why she had been screaming in the night, but no one did. Instead they discussed Ira, who had been tossing and turning and not letting Natasha, in the top bunk, get a proper night's sleep. Listening to her fellow inmates, Anya thought it would be strange for this topic to be taking priority over her own hysterics during the night, so perhaps she really had only dreamed the scream—and everything else?

When everyone was fully awake and sitting up drinking tea, the cell door was flung open and four cops—three women and a man—marched in. Anya had seen none of them before, but immediately found them far less agreeable than the people on yesterday's shift. Three were stony-faced while one, a young girl, seemed so frightened she looked more like a prisoner than a jailer.

The new arrivals formed a semicircle and one of the women took a step forward. She was plump, her tucked-in blouse emphasizing an already sizable gut, pants stretched as tight as a drum, and her hair in ringlets. To make matters worse, she had squashed, piggy features—her nose a button, her eyes slits, and her lips as thin as thread. Strangest of all, however, was her expression. She had none. She appeared lifeless. Anya suspected that, even practicing in front of a mirror, she would never be able to replicate that look.

The woman opened a register and coughed. Anya's cellmates stood up as if at her command. Only she and Maya remained seated.

"Stand up!" the woman instructed them in a voice devoid of intonation.

Maya rose very slowly to her feet and rested her arms languorously on the bunk. Anya stayed where she was, looking at the others in bewilderment.

"Stand *up*!" the woman repeated.

"What for?" Anya asked, genuinely puzzled.

"The regulations require prisoners to rise. For the third time, *stand up*!"

Anya was so taken aback she did as she was told. It was not only the words that seemed extraordinary but the tone in which they were uttered: the woman raised her voice, but with no hint of irritation or impatience. It was not as if a live human being were putting Anya in her place, simply that the volume on a radio was being turned up rather loud.

"Names," the woman demanded, looking down at the register.

"Vilkova!"

"Orlova!"

"Leonova!"

"Ivanova!"

"Andersen," Maya said wearily.

Anya said nothing, continuing to observe the procedure, speechless.

"*Names!*" the woman repeated, turning up the volume.

"Romanova, of course." Anya muttered irritably in response. "What's the problem, can't you read your own register?"

Without deigning to reply, the woman snapped the register shut and nodded to the stony-faced policewoman standing beside her. This one, embellished with heavy eyeliner, took a black item from her belt, which Anya did not immediately recognize as a metal detector. She ran it over the bunks in total silence.

The inspection lasted only a couple of minutes, but the woman scanned Anya's bunk with particular thoroughness, turning the pillow over and shaking out the blanket. Anya felt a flare of indignation at this casual invasion of her private space, but managed to keep her mouth shut.

Their inspection over, the guards exited without another word, the scared young woman trailing behind them.

"What a horrible bunch they are, that shift, and what a repulsive duty officer," Katya remarked with a shrug, plonking herself down on Diana's bunk. "The only good news is that we'll soon be out of here and rid of them."

"How many different shifts are there, then?" Anya asked.

"Oh, three, I suppose. Tomorrow a decent old grandpa type is on duty, then it's yesterday's lot, then that bitch again. She's the only one who does it all by the book."

"She doesn't give a damn about the book," Anya retorted. "She's just deliberately offensive. There's something almost undead about her."

Natasha, meanwhile, went over to the toilet cubicle and disappeared behind the door. She was her usual grumpy self, but now looking very purposeful. A moment later there was a crashing sound and she emerged, blowing a lock of hair away from her forehead. In her hands she carried a bowl and a bunch of twigs bound together as a broom, and had a mop tucked under her arm.

"Right, t-time to clean the cell!" she announced.

Anya tensed. She had little idea of the pecking order here, but did not doubt that she as the newest would be the drudge required to do the cleaning. What would be the best way to react? Should she disdainfully refuse to "pick up the rag"? Make a joke of it? Argue with them? Or pretend she really loved mopping floors and saw nothing humiliating in it?

Not waiting for her, Natasha dumped the basin down by the sink, leaned the mop against it, and vigorously got to work with the twig broom. The others paid not the least attention, only raising their legs so she could sweep under their bunks. Anya followed all this in amazement and could not believe such consideration could be without a catch. When Natasha reached her bunk she could stand it no longer and asked timidly, "Would you like me to help?"

"Nah, that's okay. I j-just like everything clean. Something I learned in prison."

Anya nodded silently. She might try kidding herself that this was just a special kind of holiday camp, but Natasha had a knack for bringing home the reality.

When she had finished sweeping up, Natasha set about washing the floor. Anya watched fascinated as she unflinchingly grasped a dirty cloth with her bare hands, gave it a rinse in murky water, and dropped it down on the mop. The others still paid no attention but Natasha's zeal was undiminished.

Her cleaning was in full swing when the radio suddenly came on, making everybody jump, except for Natasha, who continued mopping the floor with unflagging dedication, not allowing something so trivial to distract her. When she had finally finished, she declared with satisfaction, "There, now you c-can walk on it barefoot!" She promptly kicked off her flip-flops. Anya shuddered at the thought.

Time was passing, not so much slowly as quite independently of Anya. There was no clock, so she could not even tell whether it was time to be bored out of her mind or whether she should wait a little longer. The radio played an endless succession of songs, interrupted periodically by advertisements. There was no news, and never a mention of the time. She had a feeling it must be about ten o'clock, but was far from certain: without a clock she was disoriented. She suddenly remembered her old boyfriend Sasha and his superpower: he could tell her to wake him at three, but he would always wake up by himself a minute before he needed to. "How do you do that?" she asked. "When you're asleep you can't possibly know how much time has passed."

Sasha said he had been able to do this since he was little, and that in the countryside it was a knack most people had. They would decide they wanted to wake up at five in the morning and they would. "You're a townie, and townies have to rely on alarm clocks," he said disparagingly. Anya hated his village-boy inverted snobbery, but had no comeback. His ability to sense the time was undeniable, almost supernatural.

Anya shook her head, trying to dispel the memories. She had trained herself to avoid them for so many years that it was usually easy to switch away because there were lots of other things to think about. Now she looked around. Her cellmates were either reading or asleep. Diana was drawing with felt-tip pens in a notebook, and with her tongue stuck out she looked quite touching, stately, even, despite the childlike expression on her face. Anya took one of the books her friends had put in the bag for her, opened it without bothering to look at the title, and stared at the page. The letters were a blur, but she kept gazing into the open book as if it were a window through which she could see a dorm room, a two-tier bunk against a wall, and Sasha asleep. She seemed to be in two places at once, in a cell in a detention center and there in that room with Sasha. She knew he was about to wake up, to come over, bleary with sleep, and hug her. She would give him a little time, then wriggle her shoulders to be free of him, and he would instantly release her without any resentment. Over the course of several years her relationship with Sasha had swung between the frenzy of love and complete indifference, but they had never burdened themselves with unrealistic expectations.

Anya half closed her eyes, and kaleidoscopic images swirled in front of them: the chipped parquet flooring in the dormitory room; Sasha's red blanket, so shaggy her fingers sank into its deep pile; the low, rumbling sound of the kettle, always followed by the slight creaking of the closet where the crockery stayed; the pimply beige wallpaper on which Anya, having mercilessly plowed through its pimples with a ballpoint pen, wrote a rude word; the number 2 askew on the door. And Sonya: the twirl of hair on her brow and her slightly snub nose; the way she sat in the front desk with her legs tucked under her, gnawing her pen; her hazel brown eyes, and that gaze, softer than velvet, warmer than an open fire. That thought alone was enough to engulf her in a tidal wave of jealousy.

Sasha was always boasting about his birthplace. That tiny village in Novosibirsk province was the core of a mythology into which he happily initiated anyone and everyone. Anya was impressed by such unconditional love for his origins, and the fact that they were students at Moscow's elite Institute of International Relations made it all the more exceptional. Their dormitory was full of poor, bright provincial students who had won regional competitions in their subjects and aspired to merge inconspicuously with the main metropolitan contingent. Sasha alone stayed so loyal to his roots. He loved telling the tale to all these hothouse Muscovites of his harsh life in Siberia, chopping firewood, drinking improbable quantities of moonshine, driving to the disco in a neighboring village in a clapped-out Lada. To enhance the effect he would sometimes lapse into a village dialect, which Anya suspected he had cooked up himself. All in all, he was a reincarnation of Sergey Yesenin, the adulated, tow-haired peasant poet of late Tsarism, though Sasha had dark hair.

The strategy paid off: girls swarmed to this exotic man. Anya viewed Sasha's tales with an irony bordering on skepticism, but when in their fifth year he invited her to accompany him to Novosibirsk, she accepted with alacrity. It was as if she had been reading for years about a fictitious place, only now to have a magical opportunity of being transported there and able to explore it. Sonya, naturally, also agreed and so they went as a threesome.

They were officially representing their university at an academic conference, but spent no time at all in Novosibirsk itself, traveling from the airport straight to the rail station, and from there taking local trains to Sasha's village. It was not strictly a village, but an administrative district center, although in Anya's cynical view the only difference seemed to be that it had a minuscule square overgrown with weeds and boasting a statue of an impetuous Lenin on a pedestal.

In the end only Sasha made it to the conference, feeling, as the principal organizer of their trip, a certain obligation toward his university. It took up precisely one day of his time. For the rest of the week their main occupation was migrating from one house full of Sasha's relatives to the next. He was a local legend—the boy who got into the Institute of International Relations. He was recognized by every second person on the street. At the endless family banquets in honor of his return there was invariably some drunken old relative who would relate reminiscences of Sasha's childhood.

Within a few days, Anya was forced to admit that Sasha had not been exaggerating. The flowery tales that had so turned the heads of girls in Moscow were true, or at least, they periodically resurfaced in what other people said about Sasha in conversations or in toasts they gave. Anya was in no hurry to admit defeat, however, and kept her usual ironic detachment. Sonya, on the other hand, gazed at Sasha more rapturously with every passing day. She had always hung on whatever escaped his lips, and now was at last able to feast her eyes on him here, where he had the aura of a full celebrity.

That trip had been special, and Anya often returned to it in her thoughts. Every morning began in exactly the same way. She would wake up with the sunlight playing on her face. She would open her eyes and, through the thin curtain partitioning off her part of the room, see blue, blue sky in the window. Her bed was amazingly high, with an airy white feather quilt, and Anya slid off rather than got up from it. The icy coldness of the wooden floor scorched her feet. She dressed hurriedly, washed with icy water that invariably wetted her sleeves and ran down her neck, and rushed outside. It was April. Everything around seemed young and dazzlingly pure: the lofty sky, the puddles covered with brittle ice, the frost on the newly sprouting grass, the houses sparkling in the sunlight. Anya ran down the street, filling her lungs with the freshness of the air. She gazed around and could not believe how beautiful everything was. But, as if comparing herself with this amazing, full-on beauty, she felt insignificant, and devastatingly alone. She ran to the house where Sasha and Sonya had spent the night. Anya was in a different house because there seemed not to be enough room for the three of them to stay. They had breakfast together, then they went to Sasha's old school, where all the teachers competed desperately to get him to sit in on their lesson so they could show the class a living icon that proved the importance of education. They drank tea with the head teacher, paid a visit to someone or other, and then Sasha took them around his old neighborhood, which featured such local attractions as a collection of derelict garages and a rope for swinging on over the ravine by the river.

Only once did they all sleep in the same house. That day they had gone to a nearby village to visit yet another of Sasha's uncles. It was an exceptionally noisy and drunken evening. The drinking began before dark and went on all night. In the middle of the festivities Sasha suddenly decided he would like to go to the bathhouse. He announced he would heat it up himself and vanished. In the morning he was found to have staggered there and fallen blissfully asleep on the wooden bench. For as long as he was in the house Sonya had been inseparable from him. Anya stared at them until she could stand it no longer.

She went out and sat on the porch. An enormous white dog came running to her. Its name was Astra, and the first thing their hosts did was introduce guests to the dog: either so that they would not be frightened of her, or so she would not savage them by mistake. Astra nuzzled Anya's forehead, allowed herself to be hugged, and obediently stayed while Anya wept floods of jealous, angry, hurt tears. "Oh, Astra," she whimpered, burying her face in the dog's thick fur, "this is so awful. How can everything have worked out this way?"

She heard footsteps behind her and pulled away from the dog, which melted into the darkness. Sonya sat down beside her. She was only a few inches away and it seemed to Anya that they were sitting so close she might end up with scorch marks. With difficulty she suppressed an urge to move away, and instead asked, somewhat aggressively, "Where's Sasha?" Sonya shrugged. "He's gone off somewhere." She said it so gently it made Anya want to howl. Flaring up at her own weakness, she asked, "Are you really able to be without him for a whole five minutes?" "I decided it was far more important for me to be with you," Sonya replied.

Anya's resistance crumbled and she looked at her. Sonya's hair seemed gilded by the light flooding from a half-open door, and the look in her eyes was so tender that Anya felt everything inside her falling away. She looked quickly aside, sniffed loudly, and said something funny and rude. Sonya laughed out loud, and it was her best laugh, the way she had always laughed with Anya, who at that instant felt everything might not be over after all. She seized Sonya's hand and Sonya carefully intertwined her fingers with Anya's. Anya jumped up, drawing Sonya after her into the house and up the stairs. They ran into the first room they came to. It was dark and there was a sofa bed covered with a bedspread with a barely perceptible smell of dust. From downstairs came muffled laughter and shouting. Sonya did not even kiss her, only brushed her lips with her own, and in a frenzy Anya tore at her clothes and dug into her skin in a way that was painful. Anya wanted to make it even more painful, to pinch and hit and slap her face and at the same time press her to herself as tightly as she could, to nestle against her neck and never let her go.

Sonya was panting and everything inside Anya was in joyful turmoil—yet at the same time some small part of her seemed to be observing it all from a distance and not believing she could really be here: on a sofa covered with an old bedspread, in a house crowded with strangers, in the middle of the Siberian forest. It was a microscopic dot on the map, one of a countless number of places where she had ended up by chance and to which she would never return. But now, suddenly, it had turned into the epicenter of her life. She was holding in her arms the girl she loved, and for the first time in months she was happy.

The morning was overcast and, predictably, Anya had a hangover. There was no Sonya next to her, and she heard the clatter of crockery from downstairs. What was needed was to pluck up courage, go down and face other people. Even though she knew no one had suspected anything last night, the idea that she should now put on a smile and make small talk with strangers was too much. At the last moment, already on her way to the kitchen, where she could hear voices, Anya changed her mind and slipped out. She managed only a quick glance through the kitchen's open door, enough to see Sasha and his uncle back at their measures of vodka, the uncle's wife washing dishes and Sonya drying them.

Anya went through the garden gate and strode off quickly down the road, afraid someone might call after her and that she would be unable to come up with any logical reason for just wanting to get away. Happily, nobody did, and the house was finally left behind after a bend in the road. Anya slowed down.

She soon reached the end of the village, and the well-worn road was reduced to a cart track. Anya wandered on completely aimlessly, not looking around her. Images from the night before flashed through her mind, making her feel both warm and a little ashamed. The images were followed by a moment from an earlier memory, of Sonya at the table, straddling a bench and gazing rapturously at a drunken Sasha. The spasm of jealousy that this memory brought on was so painful that Anya pressed a hand to her breast as if to hold it inside her. Why did feelings always seem to arise in the rib cage, and how come they could cause such palpable physical pain?

The road led Anya to a birch grove at the top of a hill. A short distance away she could see the remnants of a fire in a circle of cracked bricks beside a fallen tree. She sat on the tree and looked down the hill. From here the village looked like a scattering of toy houses. A short distance away a rusty, opened tin can lay on the frozen grass. There was a motionless butterfly on it. Anya stared so long everything became a blur.

She thought of Sonya. She pictured her getting up this morning and leaving the room quietly so as not to wake her. She imagined her going downstairs and finding Sasha. How at ease she was with his relatives, volunteering to help in the kitchen. She probably did not even have a hangover. With a pained sigh Anya pressed her face into her knees, envying Sonya for her poise, her openness, and the unambiguousness of her desires. Here was Anya, sitting on a hill, blown by chill winds, her feelings fluctuating between jealousy, love, hope, and doubt, while Sonya was standing drying the dishes in a warm kitchen, knowing exactly why she was doing that, and what it was that she wanted in life.

Anya groaned quietly as she recalled the way she had grabbed Sonya's hand the night before and dragged her upstairs. Why had she succumbed to her friend's warmth? For a long time now she had avoided being alone with her because she was sure everything would end in a depressing deflation the following day. And now it had. Anya ground her teeth. She tried to be angry with Sonya for her heartlessness, for being unfaithful to her, but the anger did not come. She knew Sonya had been moved not by spite but by pity, and that knowledge only pained Anya all the more.

Unable to bear her own thoughts any longer, she quickly stood up, disturbing the butterfly, which fluttered up into the air before settling again on the tin can. She walked purposefully back to the village. Running away was not going to resolve anything and she needed to face the consequences of her actions without fear. As she was marching down the hill, gusts of wind pushed her in the back. She was coming back to the people she most loved, but it felt like she was going into battle.

Sitting on her bunk in the detention center, Anya could hardly believe she could remember so much detail: the butterfly, the tin can, even the gusts of wind. It was as if she had been immersed in a movie, reliving all the emotions she had felt back then. Carried away by her memories, she was paying no heed to what was happening in the cell, until she was brought down to earth by a whistle from up to her right.

Anya's mental movie show was dispelled, but at first she did not understand what was going on around her. Her cellmates, on the other hand, were immediately alert and all turned to face the window. A man outside was hanging on to the grille. He poked his nose into the cell and inquired jocularly, "Well, hello, girls! How are you doing?" Another head appeared alongside and asked, "Got anyone new?"

"Yep," Katya replied authoritatively. She put down the magazine she was reading and viewed them through half-closed eyes, feigning disinterest. Anya thought she looked like a predatory big cat waiting for its prey to lose concentration and stray nearer.

"Got any cigs?"

"Andryukha, do we?" the first boy asked someone out of view. There was a pause, followed by a low voice saying, "Nope."

"So who's new? Newbie, let's have a look at you!"

Anya's cellmates peered across at her but she pretended to be reading and brought the book closer to her face.

"She's not going to give you a look if you aren't going to give us any cigarettes," Katya pronounced and retreated behind her own magazine.

"Fair enough. Where's Maya then? Mayechka, why don't you let us see you?"

All this time Maya too had been reading, but when she heard her name she ruffled her feathers and looked inquiringly at Katya. Katya shrugged, not bothering to look up from her reading.

"Where's Maya, lads?" a third voice asked, and immediately materialized in the window. Anya thought they must all be very uncomfortable clinging to the grille like baboons.

"I am here," Maya said coyly.

This caused a commotion outside the window. "Maya, give us a look, come talk to us!"

With a show of reluctance, Maya climbed up to the empty top tier of her bunk. She tried to move as gracefully as possible, but missed a step and nearly fell. She ignored that little problem. "Come closer, come closer!" the men implored her. Natasha occupied the adjacent upper bunk and gave Maya a frown but, seeing she intended to move over, muttered disapprovingly and tucked her legs in. Maya moved into the space vacated and placed her hands primly on her knees, assuming the most modest pose imaginable.

From outside there came a roar of approval and even more people were clutching the grille. Anya feared it might come away from the wall.

"You're so beautiful, Mayechka!" said the guy first on the scene. "Is anybody there treating you badly?"

"No," Maya replied flirtatiously, flapping her eyelashes.

"And do you have a boyfriend?"

"Yes."

"Dump him and let's date!"

Maya shook her head, causing ripples to run through her long, shiny locks.

"Why are you holding out on me? When are you getting released?"

"Three days from now."

"There you are, I'm getting out the day after tomorrow. What time?"

"Why would you want to know that?"

"Why do you think, Mayechka? I'll be there to welcome you and we can hit the town. How about I give you my number?"

"A detention center is not a suitable place for introductions," Maya informed him demurely.

It seemed extraordinary that, no matter what she said, she carried on smiling sweetly. Any rational person would surely have been puzzled by such contradictory signals, Anya thought, but the lads outside the window showed no sign of puzzlement, and indeed clearly attached no importance to anything Maya actually said.

"What beautiful hair you have, Mayechka!" they chorused from the other side of the bars. "Is it really yours?"

"Yes, of course!"

"And your eyes? So beautiful. So blue! So rare!"

"Of course!"

"And those lips of yours, they are so beautiful. Are they real too?"

"Yes, of course!"

"What great people your mom and dad were to produce such a beautiful girl!"

Anya brought the book even closer to her face in order to be completely hidden. All this action was leaving her half-amused, half-bemused. Sex-starved men were beleaguering their cell, pushing their hands through the grille to entice Maya, begging her to come closer while she, unyielding, modestly lowering her eyes in a pretense of angelic innocence, kept them at a safe distance. It occurred to Anya that the scene was a literal reenactment of the rules everyone was taught as a child: boys should be forward and girls always impregnable. It also struck her that she had never before witnessed such willingness to play by the rules of such an artificial game with such authentic ardor.

There is no telling how much longer Maya's posturing might have continued, but suddenly there was a new distraction. The cell door opened and one of the morning's stony-faced women, the one who had searched Anya's bunk, inquired with an ill grace, "Telephones?"

Everyone shouted, "Yes!" and cascaded from their bunks.

* * *

The women were taken out to the corridor and lined up. First was Diana. With a stylish swing of the hips she proceeded to the reception area where, at the ready, her legs apart like a goalkeeper's, stood the robot from this morning's inspection team. "Orlova," said Diana.

The woman peered at her with gimlet eyes as if to ascertain whether she was perhaps merely impersonating Orlova, and disappeared into the reception area. She returned thirty seconds later with a striped bag identical to the one Anya's "valuables" had been placed in yesterday.

"Telephone and charger?" she checked in a surly manner.

"Yes."

The woman dipped into the bag and rummaged around, all the while keeping a close eye on Diana. Anya was half expecting her to draw out not a telephone but a bingo number. This did not happen, but before issuing her property to Diana, the woman had her sign for it.

"How long do we get for calls?" Anya whispered to Natasha, who was immediately in front of her.

"F-fifteen minutes in theory, but you might get longer if they lose track. Only this shift's not going to forget. You can g-go before me. My people are out at work, so most likely n-no one will answer."

Katya, Maya, and Ira followed Diana one by one into the tiny room where Anya had been medically examined yesterday. When it was finally her turn, every detail of the procedure was repeated: the woman stood there immobile until Anya stepped forward and gave her name, then went off to fetch her bag, came back and said, "Telephone and charger?"

"No, just telephone," Anya said.

The woman, about to dip into the bag, stopped and stared at Anya, her look not one of surprise but of dumb incomprehension. "*And charger?*"

"I don't need it at the moment."

"Are you sure you don't need it? Or are you going to come back in five minutes asking for it?"

"I already said no."

The duty officer pulled out Anya's phone and she reached for it, but the officer pulled it back.

"Sign first."

"Are you afraid I'm going to run away with it?" Anya asked defiantly, signing the book.

"Whether you are going to run away with it or not is beside the point, the regulations are there to be observed!" the woman responded, again with that unexpected increase of volume. Anya grabbed the phone from her and entered the cubbyhole.

It was impossible to make calls normally: the network signal was weak, the tiled walls reflected sounds, and everyone's simultaneous talking merged into an unintelligible babble. Anya checked out her social network accounts. There were tons of mentions on Facebook, photos of the riot police dragging her away, angry antiregime posts by friends, and on her page lots of messages urging her to stay strong, slogans like "Russia will be free!," and vows to visit terrible retribution on all involved in her arrest.

Having gone through the social networks, Anya moved on to the messaging apps. Here too she was mainly being urged to stay strong, but by real friends rather than just Facebook friends, their tone accordingly less emotional and more ironic. There were three messages from her mother, to whom Anya replied that her cellmates were fine, her conditions too, and that the food was simply wonderful. She also found a message from her father, who asked how she was bearing up and which detention center she was being held in. This was unexpected, because her father had by now been living for several years in a different country and had not previously taken any great interest in her life. Anya suppressed an urge to reply "Why would you want to know that?" and simply told him. After all, the likelihood of his turning up in Moscow was negligible, and a special detention center seemed well adapted not only to keep people in but also to keep people out. Anya had in any case long ago decided to maintain contact with her father on a superficial, courteous level. This involved replying briefly but politely to communications, sending greetings on festive occasions, asking him no questions, and never trying to get even.

She had just sent her last message when the door opened and the robot said, "Telephones back!"

There was a spate of hasty goodbyes. Natasha, who had been playing Snake, immediately handed hers in and left. Anya too had no regrets about returning hers. Fifteen minutes on the internet was so vanishingly little that there had been no time to reflect on what she was being deprived of.

"I asked for cigarettes," Katya reported when they were back in the cell. "We should get them tomorrow." Everyone dispersed to their bunks.

"I talked to my husband and just felt so homesick," Diana said dreamily, stretching out on her bed, which sagged noticeably under her weight. She let her luxuriant hair down and it spread over the pillow. "When I'm at home I feel I could kill him, but after a few days of not seeing him and being away in here, I miss him."

"See how good a stay in the slammer is for you!" Katya said with a snigger. She shifted restlessly in the top bunk, getting more comfortable.

"Don't jump around up there. There's dust flying everywhere," Diana said, frowning and flapping her hand. "Yes, you get a different perspective here. When my husband was doing time and I had to haul myself to Bryansk province to see him I never missed him at all."

"Oh, did your husband spend time in prison?" Maya asked. She tucked the pillow behind her back and drew the blanket up over her legs, her face expressing the moderate interest appropriate to polite small talk.

"Yes, Article 228. They caught him with weed. But that was my second husband. He died."

"This is some lady!" Katya exclaimed, bouncing over in her bunk to face her cellmates. Down below, Diana again flapped her hands to dispel invisible dust. "Not yet twenty-five and already on her third husband!"

"Actually, I'm going to be twenty-five next week," Diana admitted with a frown. "What about you, Natasha, do you miss your husband?"

Natasha shrugged her bony shoulders and put her crossword puzzle down in front of her on the bunk, pondering it and gnawing ruminatively on her ballpoint pen. "In here I g-get to take a break from him!" she said finally. "Although while I was in the labor camp I did miss him, yes."

Anya felt she was by now sufficiently established to ask something that was bugging her. "What were you in prison for?" she inquired cautiously.

"Article 158."

"What's that?"

"It's for theft," Katya responded on Natasha's behalf.

Anya stifled a sigh of relief.

"And what is worse, being in prison or in a detention center?" Maya continued in her tone of polite conversation.

"Well, wh-what do you think?" Natasha answered. She threw the crossword puzzle to the end of the bunk and turned over on her stomach.

Diana had for some time been intently examining Katya's mattress above her head. She now raised herself and pulled a long thread out of it. She twisted it around her finger and, without looking at the others, as if imparting a secret, said, "Actually, I had imagined everything here would be exactly like it is in a labor camp, like what my husband told me. The second one, that is. When I was being brought here from the court, I expected that when I came in someone would throw a rag down at my feet."

"Why would that matter?" Maya asked, furrowing her brow.

"It's a test in the camps, haven't you heard about it?"

Maya shook her head anxiously. Anya knew what she was feeling.

"You need to step over it or wipe your feet on it. I don't remember which," Diana confessed. "The main thing is not to pick it up, or even ask what it's doing there."

"And what if you pick it up?" Maya asked, her voice trembling.

"For heaven's sake, nobody throws rags anywhere," Natasha interrupted irritably, again breaking off doing her crossword. "Everybody's just human in there. As long you behave nothing bad is going to happen. F-first time I went into my hut the boss there was this Vasilisa. She c-calls me over straight off and explains the rules. 'I've got this phone,' she says. 'I g-give it to the girls to make calls at night, d-don't ask anything in return.' Then she asks me, 'Get it? What did I just say?' I say, 'Nothing. D-did you just say something? I didn't hear nothing.' She says, 'Good girl. You're not new to the camp, eh? Or did someone tell you what to say?' I say, 'Yeah, my b-brother.'"

"I simply don't understand," Maya whispered plaintively to Anya.

"Well, that way she was showing she wouldn't say anything to the screws if they asked about it. My husband taught me that too," Diana explained impatiently. "And this Vasilisa of yours, what was she in for?"

"She k-killed twenty people," Natasha answered matter-of-factly, entering a word in the puzzle.

"Twenty people?!" Maya gasped.

"Well, n-not on her own. You might remember, there was this high-profile case a few years ago. Skinheads killing Asians in Moscow. Even did in one of their own pals, cut his head off in a bathroom. Don't you remember? Anyway, Vasilisa was one of that g-gang. Really smart, she was, used to be a student at Moscow University."

For a time nobody said anything, reflecting on what they had just heard. Natasha, as if it was nothing, got on with her crossword puzzle. Diana removed the thread from her finger, then wound it on again.

"I've always wondered about people like that. Do they feel bad about what they've done?" she said.

"Search me!" Natasha muttered, not looking up from the crossword. "I never thought to ask."

A key again rattled in the door and Anya reflected that, for a penal institution, they seemed to have a very full cultural program.

The timid police girl was standing in the doorway. "Time for lunch," she said, barely audibly.

"Seems early today," Katya said, yawning.

Ira, who had uttered not a word during the conversation and had stayed in her usual position huddled in the corner of her bunk, came suddenly to life at the mention of lunch. "Oh, just what we need!" she exclaimed, friskily getting to her feet.

Anya was immediately on the alert at this sudden display of vigor, recalling her nightmare. Although right now Ira really bore little resemblance to a demonic murderess, Anya was alarmed by how rapidly her mood seemed to shift. She could sit motionless for hours with a witless smile on her face, and then inexplicably react violently to some random phrase.

Getting ready to go for lunch took only a moment. All they needed to do was remember to take an empty plastic bottle for hot water. As everyone headed for the door, Anya noticed Maya still sitting on her bunk. "Aren't you coming?" she asked in surprise.

"She doesn't," Diana remarked in an offhand manner.

Anya looked from her to Maya in amazement. "Why not?"

"I simply can't eat the food," she answered mournfully and, as if confirming how profound her sorrow was, pulled the blanket up to her chest.

Anya was shocked. "Is it that bad?"

"There's nothing wrong with the food," Katya, already at the door, commented dismissively. "She's making a fuss about nothing, as usual."

Anya looked back at Maya, sitting there. She looked so miserable that Anya was reluctant to leave her on her own.

"Well, why not just come along with us anyway," Anya coaxed. "It would be terrible to leave you sitting in here."

Maya thought this over, then got up from the bunk and, wobbling on her perilously high heels, followed her cellmates.

This time when they emerged they proceeded along the corridor in the opposite direction. Anya was amazed that anyone would paint walls such a depressing shade of green. In the stark light of the lamps it seemed almost eerie.

The corridor was short. They passed a couple of robust metal doors leading to other cells and stopped in front of a locked grating. Behind it was a staircase to the second floor, lit by a large window. The police girl opened the grating and Anya's cellmates went up the stairs.

If the stairwell struck Anya as uncommonly well lit, when they entered the cafeteria she was taken aback: it was dazzling, with white tiles, white walls, and two huge windows through which poplar trees and prefabricated apartment blocks could be seen in the distance. The cafeteria was not large, and the furniture was predictably minimalist. In the middle was a table consisting of several smaller tables pushed together, and along the length of it were two benches bolted to the floor. In a wall there were two square openings and the girls all headed for one of them. Anya followed.

Through the hatch they could see into the kitchen and all the hustle and bustle going on in there. Several men were dragging aluminum cans around with something painted in red on the sides; another was carrying trays of mugs. Three kettles were simultaneously boiling on the sole gas cooker, while a fourth, electric, was bubbling away on an adjacent table. There was not a single woman working in the kitchen, which struck Anya as surprisingly progressive for a detention center. She whispered as much to Diana, standing next to her.

"Oh, they're not employees, they're in jail like the rest of us," Diana whispered back. "They're just servers, and get privileges in return."

"Oh, here come the girls!" a fair-haired youth who appeared from the recesses of the kitchen welcomed them. He came to the serving hatch and leaned out holding a ladle.

"What's the soup?" Katya asked brusquely, going up to the window and standing arms akimbo.

"Borsch," the boy replied, raising the lid of the container. Steam billowed out.

He duly issued Anya's cellmates an aluminum bowl of soup and they each sat down at the table. Maya went nowhere near the hatch and sat on the bench looking devout and martyred.

When it was Anya's turn, the lad scooped up the borsch with a practiced hand and asked, without looking up, "Are you the new girl?"

"Yes," Anya said, watching him pour it into a bowl for her. "What is there besides borsch?"

"Buckwheat kasha with meat patties."

"Can I have just the kasha?"

"Of course." The boy tipped the soup back into the container and dished a portion of buckwheat porridge into the same bowl. "What are you in for?"

"A protest rally."

The boy whistled. "A protest rally? What were you protesting about?"

"Corruption."

"Are there a lot of you protesting about that?"

"Yes."

"What's it worth?"

"What do you mean?"

"Well, how much do you get paid for protesting?"

The fair-haired boy was holding the full bowl in his hands and seemed in no hurry to pass it over. He viewed Anya with smiling condescension. She felt herself beginning to bristle and answered primly, "We don't get paid."

"Oh, sure, tell me another. Why else would you have gone to a protest?"

Anya carefully took the bowl of buckwheat from him, trying not to betray her exasperation, and instead asked, "Why are you in jail?"

"I was riding a moped without a crash helmet," he said with a shrug.

"And for that you're doing time here?"

"No, the cops just wanted me to give them a bribe and I wouldn't. So then they wrote I was riding while drunk."

"And you're asking *me* why I would go to an anticorruption rally?"

He chuckled. Anya considered the conversation at an end and went to the table.

"You're not having any soup?" Ira asked greedily, having downed her own at such speed she had almost choked.

"No."

"Alyosha, give me the new girl's borsch if she's not going to take it!" Ira shouted in the direction of the kitchen.

"Are you sure there's nothing else I can do for you, your highness?" Alyosha shouted back to Ira, reappearing in the hatch.

"Why, are you keeping it for someone special?"

"Okay, bring your bowl over. And why are you sitting there like a lost soul?" he asked Maya. "Don't you want any food?"

Maya gave him her martyred look and shook her head.

"Aren't you eating anything at all?" he asked in a kind voice.

"I can't eat that kind of food."

"Oh, come on, the food is fine. The borsch, I mean, that's actually really good."

"And besides, I couldn't eat from bowls like these."

"What's wrong with them?" Katya asked sharply, putting her spoon to good use.

"Well, they're just not right. They look like dog bowls."

For a time the silence in the cafeteria was broken only by the clatter of spoons.

"Are you intending to eat nothing for a full five days?" Anya asked, glancing sideways at Maya. She found it embarrassing that everybody else should be eating so noisily in her presence.

Maya nodded. "My sister has promised to bring apples."

"So what do you usually eat, in the outside world?" Diana inquired with her mouth full. "Do you cook for yourself?"

Maya was aghast at the suggestion. She raised her hand to her bosom in perplexity and said, "Goodness me, no. I order everything in. Although once I did cook pappardelle, but I ordered that from the Food Party. You know, that's where they send you all the ingredients along with instructions on how to mix everything properly."

"Pappardelle is what the rest of us would call pasta, right?" Katya asked scornfully, getting up from the table to go for the buckwheat and patty.

"Well, pappardelle is . . . just pappardelle. But I expect it can be called pasta as well. What else do I eat? . . . Well, I like oysters, for instance, and lobster. In fact I very much like seafood in general."

"Hmm, you're not going to find it easy in here," Diana concluded after a short pause.

An elderly man in a flannel shirt shuffled out of the kitchen carrying a tray of mugs and a teapot.

"Tea, girls. Take it while it's hot."

"B-best to give the tea a miss," Natasha whispered to Anya. "They make it from grass, not tea."

Katya held out a plastic bottle to him and said, "We'd sooner just have the hot water, Viktor Ivanovich."

"Boiling water? Of course, of course, no problem," Viktor Ivanovich said politely, and shuffled off back to the kitchen. "Andrey, pour the girls some boiling water!"

A minute later another prisoner appeared in the hatch. He was wearing a bright yellow hoodie with a zip and his face was so young and innocent he seemed little more than a child. He placed a misted bottle distorted by the hot water on the ledge.

"Good heavens, how old can he be?" Anya exclaimed, leaning toward Natasha, who shrugged.

"M-must be at least eighteen, I suppose."

"But what's he in here for?"

"Oy," Natasha shouted hoarsely to the boy. "What you here for?"

"They caught me without a license," he replied. Anya had the impression he was trying to turn up the bass in his voice.

The frightened police girl, who had been sitting in the corner all this time, stood up and asked if everyone had finished. Anya had forgotten she was there.

"I need to visit the first-aid post!" Ira announced.

"Uh-oh, here we go," Diana said with a smirk, licking her spoon.

"Why do you need that? Are you feeling unwell?"

"I have to get pills there."

The police girl looked around helplessly.

"We'll stay here," Katya assured her magnanimously. "We won't run off. The first-aid post is just over there and you'll be able to keep an eye on us from inside."

Anya looked in the direction Katya was indicating and there, sure enough, was a white door with a red cross directly in front of them, by the cafeteria entrance.

"What pills are you supposed to get?" the police girl asked.

"Lyrica."

"If the doctor really has prescribed them for you, I'll bring them to the cell. Back you come now."

"But I need them straight away! I always get them after lunch!"

"I'll check, and I'll bring you them, if you really have the prescription."

Ira was not mollified, but the others were clearly disinclined to cause a scene over her pills and they all headed downstairs.

Anya pricked up her ears when she found out Ira was taking a mystery drug with a strange name, and also that the police girl doubted it had really been prescribed. She was too embarrassed to ask directly, but Maya didn't have the same a problem.

"What do you take the medicine for?" she asked as soon as the cell door closed behind them.

"Well, you know . . . I have fits," Ira muttered after a moment's hesitation.

Not a trace remained of the vibrant energy that had startled Anya before lunch. Now Ira was looking morose, gloomy, and lethargic. She shuffled over to her bed, making a point of being hardly able to lift her feet from the floor, and collapsed on her bunk, crossing her arms on her chest.

"Oh, you poor thing!" Maya exclaimed.

Natasha, however, hearing Ira's explanation, snorted contemptuously but made no further comment. Climbing up to her bunk above Ira's, she very purposefully straightened the blanket, arranged herself comfortably, and only then said with grim satisfaction, "What a lie! It's just dope."

"Shhh!" Ira hissed, mortified, leaning out of her bunk and looking up at Natasha.

Anya looked in amazement from Ira to Natasha. "What dope?!" she finally squeaked, surprised at how high her voice sounded.

"The usual sort of d-dope," Natasha replied, clearly pleased, despite her ostentatious cool, by the effect she had produced. "You c-can buy it over the counter in the pharmacy. It's perfectly legal."

"It genuinely is an antiepileptic, but you can get high on it," Katya broke in, lighting a cigarette. She climbed up to the windowsill and blew the smoke through the grille out into the yard. "Junkies and alkies get doped up on it, right, Ira?"

"No, it's just a medicine," Ira insisted stubbornly. She didn't look at anyone and just sat staring at her sheet with her arms crossed.

"But you do also get high when you take it?"

Ira was silent. "Yes," she admitted reluctantly.

"She's already been bragging to us about how she pulled a fast one," Diana sneaked, also lighting up a cigarette, going to stand next to Katya and blowing smoke out the window. "Some alky pal brought it here for her. She's supposed to have been in a car accident years ago and to have been taking Lyrica ever since to prevent fits."

"What does it feel like?" Maya asked curiously, settling down on her bed and not taking her eyes off Ira.

Now all the others were looking at her too. Ira, conscious of this universal attention, absentmindedly ran a finger over the sheet.

"Well, you know . . . fun," she said finally, sounding far from certain.

"You n-never know what to expect from this one," Natasha muttered, swathing herself in blanket. "One moment you can't shut her up, the next she's moping about with h-her tail between her legs. Anya saw that when we were being used as witnesses as they booked her in. H-hardly said a word did our Ira."

Anya mused that all she had needed yesterday to complete her sense of information overload was to discover that her witness last night had been as high as a kite.

"Do you use it in your everyday life?" Maya continued her interrogation, eyeing Ira with the curiosity of an investigating officer.

"Well, yes, when I've got the money, but usually I just drink."

Katya and Diana guffawed.

"But what makes you drink?" Maya persisted.

Ira seemed to think very seriously about that question. She looked up and gazed for a while at Maya, her lips moving soundlessly.

"Having nothing else to do, probably," she said eventually. Anya was taken by the unexpected common sense of this, but Maya was less easily impressed.

"Then why don't you find something to do?"

"Like what?"

"Well, I, for instance, wouldn't know how to just sit around doing nothing. I'm constantly on the go: having manicures, massages, going to the gym. Do you really not have anything like that?"

"What am I going to find to do?!" Ira asked with a faint smile. It struck Anya that, compared with the rest of her cellmates, Ira was by far the most innocent. Her smile was silly but sincere, and when she frowned she looked genuinely dismayed.

"I've tried to find a job, but I can't. That's why I don't pay to support my daughter. I don't have a job—that's all there is to it."

"So who does your daughter live with? Her father?"

"Her father? You must be joking!" Ira giggled. "She lives with my mother. My mother is, like, her guardian."

"And how long have you not been paying to support her?" Maya continued the inquisition.

"Well, let me see now . . . how long has she been with my mother? Four years, I suppose. To begin with I was paying because I had a job, but for the last couple of years I haven't paid. Or three. Three years, probably. But it doesn't matter, because in a month from now she'll be eighteen and then I won't need to pay anything anymore."

"Is that why you've been sent here?" Anya asked. This artlessness made her feel sorry for Ira. "Did your mother complain you weren't paying?"

"No, of course not," Ira pooh-poohed. "She didn't complain, it was the state who made a complaint. They are supposed to take the money from me and give it to my daughter, only I have nothing for the state to take. My mother says it's a good thing I've been sent to prison—at least that's two weeks when I won't be getting drunk."

"So you're in jail here, then you're released and they leave you in peace?" Katya asked, blowing smoke rings. "After all, like you said, you don't have any money for them to take away from you."

"They could still sentence me to hard labor," Ira volunteered. "For six months. My mother said that would be even better because then I would be off the bottle for half a year."

They were all silent.

"Actually, maybe that would be good for you," Katya remarked wryly.

Ira pondered that.

"I don't really want to go to a labor camp," she finally admitted. "And I don't really want to work either because I always get fired for being drunk."

"But you must have something you're living on," Maya insisted. "How do you pay for the booze?"

"Well, most of the time my friends give me some. For instance, I have a friend who sells stuff from a booth in the courtyard. Arsen he's called. He gives me beer sometimes, and vodka."

60

"Just for doing nothing?" Diana prompted. She and Katya were obviously enjoying Ira's unexpected talkativeness and trying to provoke her into telling them something so hilarious they could laugh their heads off.

Anya felt that Diana and Katya were like two mean schoolgirls hounding a vulnerable classmate. She looked across at Maya, and thought that she was no better, indeed she was more hypocritical. As she listened to Ira, Maya was exuding polite attentiveness, which only seemed like a different kind of outright bullying. Natasha on her upper bunk sat silently, staring daggers. She was taking no further part in the conversation, only grimacing at particular remarks of Ira's, but it was impossible to tell whether she was more annoyed by her simpleminded answers or just the fact of her existence.

It was becoming more painful by the moment to watch Ira. She was so enjoying being the center of attention that Anya wanted to rescue her from herself. She was clearly taking her cellmates' interest at face value.

"Well, no, of course, not just for nothing," she said. "He gives me beer, for instance, if I suck him off."

There was dead silence in the cell. Katya, who at that moment was stubbing out her cigarette in a plastic cup, turned to stone.

"What?" she asked, astounded, after a few seconds.

"I said he gives me beer, for instance, if I suck him off," Ira repeated more loudly.

Everyone was again silent.

"And what about vodka?" Diana asked after a pause.

"Vodka if we have full sex."

"You sleep with him for a bottle of vodka?" Maya asked, bizarrely keeping up her tone of polite interest.

"One time he gave me five-hundred rubles, but for that I had to do some other stuff."

"Spare us the details!" Diana yelled. She fell back on her bunk, which creaked loudly, hugging the pillow in an apparent effort to hide herself.

"And to think I'm sharing a bunk with this person!" Natasha snarled.

Katya leaned against the window and said, with profound disdain tinged with admiration, "Ira, you are a completely shameless slut!"

Ira giggled and Anya found her attention again drawn to that toothless mouth.

"Sometimes I get paid even more. One time three of us drove out to the countryside. I earned two thousand that night!"

"Rubles?" Maya checked briskly.

"Well, yes."

"Obviously not d-dollars!" retorted Natasha. "You've seen her yourself. Who in their right mind would want to screw her?"

"I want to hear no more," Katya said, jumping down from the windowsill. "When we go out for exercise we'll get a breath of fresh air . . . Do you really see nothing wrong with that?"

"Wrong with what?"

"Fucking for a bottle of beer!"

"I like it better when I'm given money," Ira said defensively.

Continuing their expressions of moral outrage, the others got busy discussing Ira's immorality and gradually lost interest in Ira herself. She several times tried to regain their attention by offering new biographical details, but the other women were now far too interested in honing their collective disapproval. She soon gave up and Anya, who had not been joining in on the entertainment, buried her nose in her book, finally noticing that it was by Dostoevsky.

Now time really did drag. Nothing was happening and their conversation gradually fizzled out. At first Anya was pleased she would be able to concentrate on her book, but soon discovered a new problem:

it was impossible to read with the radio blaring away. She found she could just about ignore foreign songs, but any songs in Russian wormed their way into her brain, displacing all thought. On her bunk she tossed this way and that in a hopeless attempt to find a position that would provide the necessary tranquility but, predictably, failed. There would be footsteps passing the door, other cell doors clanging. She could hear voices outside the room but she and her cellmates appeared to have been completely forgotten.

A contingent of prisoners were admitted to the indoor courtyard and Anya's cellmates at first livened up, but soon lost interest when nobody offered them cigarettes, and they had no wish to listen to more praise of Maya. Even Maya herself was deaf to such appeals and declined to appear before her admirers. She had found a much-thumbed crime novel by Jo Nesbø in the locker, left behind by a previous inmate, and was now lying on the bed, her brow furrowed, occasionally turning the pages. Anya was surreptitiously observing her and trying to decide whether she found Maya attractive. She was eye-catching, certainly, although it was difficult to say whether this was mainly because her features were so conventionally beautiful or because they were so brazenly unnatural and doll-like.

Out of all the things in the cell, Anya hated the radio most. The pillow followed second, along with her mattress, and the lack of rational thought behind the design of the bedstead. It was absolutely impossible to get comfortable in her bunk. She had only to feel for a second that she had finally found a comfortable position for a problem to show itself. The pillow would slither through the bars at the end of the bunk and the metal rods would start digging into her back. Or she would get pins and needles in her side and her neck became numb. The upper bunk obstructed the light. When finally the stony-faced policewoman with the eyeliner came into the cell and told them to come for the exercise period, Anya was surprised by a surge of passionate love for her.

The exercise yard failed so completely to live up to Anya's expectations, however, that no amount of such feeling could redeem the impression it made.

To call it a yard was straining credibility: the place she and her cellmates found themselves in was closer to a room, just with a transparent ceiling. One side was the wall of the detention center, onto which three other walls had been built to form a long, narrow rectangle in which the prisoners were expected to perambulate. Underfoot there was asphalt, overhead a grating, above which was a transparent plastic roof. There was a small gap between the walls and the roof through which fresh air could enter this peculiar kind of outdoor room. The design was fairly dysfunctional, however, because, even now with the sun gradually declining in the sky, the "yard" was as humid as a greenhouse. Anya shuddered to think what it must be like to exercise here at midday.

A solitary bench had been placed beneath the window of their cell—Anya realized this was where the boys stood to get the height to latch onto the grille. The windows of several other cells faced onto the courtyard. Anya looked around and everywhere the cream-colored paint was pristine. Only under their windows was the wall covered in black marks left by shoe soles.

Natasha marched purposefully to the bench, lifted it, and carried it single-handedly into the shade of the opposite wall. The others trailed after her, only Katya standing where she was, tossing an odd-looking plastic bag up and down in her hands. It seemed to be stuffed with something and to have its handles tied together. She had brought it out from under her bunk in the cell the minute they were called for exercise.

She caught Anya's eye and said, "This is our ball. Want to play?"

"Yes, sure . . ."

"Diana, come and join us. Hot Potato. Ira, coming?"

Ira jumped up eagerly.

"You can be piggy in the middle," Katya said, bringing her down to earth.

"Why do I have to be piggy again?" Ira whined. "You always throw it too high so I can never catch it."

Katya ignored her and flung the "ball" to Diana, who tossed it to Anya. Ira, standing in the triangle between them, tried listlessly to intercept it. Anya threw the bag to Katya, beginning to wonder why she had agreed to join in on the game. The ball moved in a slow, heavy way. Katya directed it back to Diana, and Diana said, "I'm tired of Hot Potato. Let's play Bruiser instead." She promptly flung the bag straight at Ira, who squealed when the bag hit her sideways but immediately burst out laughing. Katya, giving her no time to recover, grabbed the bag from the ground and also threw it at her. "I'm out," Anya said and retired to the bench. She sat there and watched Diana and Katya continue bombarding Ira with the dusty "ball," and Ira yelping before laughing wildly.

"Oh, look, the girls have come out to play!" someone said from a window opposite.

Anya could barely make out the faces in the cell behind the bars, but judging by the commotion the audience there was growing.

Maya, sitting next to her, instantly straightened her posture and gracefully half turned her head, pretending to watch the game.

"Hey, Mayechka, my lovely girl, I see you're there too," somebody cooed.

"They've started!" Natasha muttered grumpily.

Sitting next to Maya felt like being on display in a shop window. The lust emanating from the cells was palpable. Anya had soon had more than enough and moved to the opposite wall, where she was out of sight. Maya, however, was reveling in it, while pretending not to notice she was driving her audience crazy. Someone asked her to turn around and she stood up and rotated slowly about her axis, as demurely yet seductively as possible. All the while she maintained an expression of innocent bewilderment, as if unable to imagine why anyone would want to look at her from different angles.

After twenty minutes of this, Anya could not wait to get back to her cell with its incessant radio and its iron maiden of a bunk. Luckily, she was not the only one. Katya finally got tired of playing Bruiser, went to the grating separating the exercise yard from the bowels of the detention center, and began shouting for them to be taken back in.

"I've not been given my medicine," Ira whimpered when they had been taken back to the cell.

"What medicine?" the stony-faced policeman who had been there during the morning inspection demanded.

"Lyrica. I need it for my fits."

"Have you had it prescribed?"

"They give me it every day. The girl who took us to lunch promised to bring it."

"I'll check it out," the man remarked without any hint of enthusiasm.

In the soft evening light, the cell looked almost cozy, or was Anya just beginning to get used to the surroundings? Lounging on her bunk, she reflected that her stay here could be seen as a quirky kind of downshifting.

Maya, meanwhile, took off her high heels, positioned herself in the center of the cell, took a deep breath, stepped forward confidently and, raising her arms high above her head, stood immobile in that position.

"What are you d-doing?" Natasha, back in her usual place on the top bunk, asked, startled. She had a particularly good observation point for viewing Maya.

"Yoga," Maya replied, motionless.

They all turned to stare at her, and even Katya, who had just settled herself, sat up again for a better view.

Maya stood immobile for a few seconds before changing position, placing her hands and feet squarely on the ground and lifting her butt as high as she could. She held that posture before going down on all fours, sitting back on her heels, and resting her forehead on the floor.

"Are you praying there, or what?" Katya asked, never taking her eyes off her.

"This is the child's pose," came Maya's muffled voice. "It helps you relax."

"What a lot of crap," Natasha pronounced. Maya straightened up and blew the hair away from her brow.

"Well, no, actually it's really cool. Especially on a beach. Waves, sunset, no people . . . I'm about to go off to Bali. They have marvelous detox programs there."

"What kind of p-programs?"

"It's when you eliminate all the toxins from your body. There are special juices you drink to cleanse yourself, and of course you also go to the spa. I stay for a few days every year. You lose weight right away, and you can really rest and restore yourself."

"If you carry on refusing the food here you'll lose weight faster than you ever would in Bali," Katya said with a snigger, moving to be flat on her back.

"They never brought me my pills," Ira whined again. Nobody paid any attention.

The day was drawing to a close. Anya was finally able to immerse herself in her book, and was quite upset when they were taken to dinner. This time it was pilaf, which, to Anya's amazement, was delicious, if very salty. She had imagined the food in such establishments would be a cross between a kindergarten lunch and the gruel dished out in *One Day in the Life of Ivan Denisovich*, so for a second time she was pleasantly surprised to find it entirely palatable. Maya again accompanied her cellmates, and stoically watched them putting away their meal. Viktor Ivanovich tried to coax her into at least drinking some tea, but she was implacable.

"I can't drink from mugs like these," she protested. "The handles are hot."

"Well, wait for it to cool down. If you won't eat anything you'll end up totally scrawny!" Viktor Ivanovich said in a worried voice. Maya pursed her lips, registering something between a well-bred smile and condescension towards his crassness.

"Why haven't they given me my pills?" Ira began moaning again. "They usually give them out in the morning, but I haven't had any at all today."

At that very moment the door with the red cross opened and an old woman in a white coat emerged. Anya had to admit that if the doctor who examined her yesterday had seemed the height of unfriendliness, it was only because she had yet to encounter this one. She was small, stooped, very, very old, and with close-cropped, flaming-red hair. She shuffled slowly toward the girls, fixing them with a look of such ferocity that they stopped eating and anxiously watched her approach.

"Who was asking for Lyrica?" the old woman demanded, looking around at all of them, including the policeman, with a baleful gaze.

"I was," Ira said, a spoonful of pilaf halted halfway to her mouth.

The woman stared at her for a while without saying a word, and Ira slowly lowered the spoon back to the bowl.

"Let's go then. Does anybody have any other complaints?" she rasped. As one, they shook their heads.

She moved slowly back toward the door with the red cross. Ira looked helplessly at her cellmates, then at the policeman, but saw no sign of anyone coming to her rescue. She stood up from the table and walked behind the doctor, trying to keep a safe distance. "Shut the door!" the old woman ordered when Ira entered the first-aid post behind her. Ira cast one last plaintive glance at her fellow inmates and closed it.

"There's someone I really would not want to be dependent on if I got ill," Diana muttered.

"Yes, she might drop dead in the middle of treating you," Katya agreed. She and Diana tittered.

By the time Ira came back, everyone had finished the meal and was waiting for their hot water. She was still looking rather scared, but also pleased.

"Got your fix?" Natasha asked and, without waiting for an answer, shoved a bottle into her hands. "Hold this yourself, then."

Anya glanced now and again at Ira, scanning her face for signs of incipient insanity but finding none. She looked no weirder than usual.

Back in the cell, Diana suggested playing Associations. This was an intriguing game where everybody in turn had to name an object and the next person had to say what they associated with it. If you hesitated for more than three seconds you were disqualified. Katya enforced this rule, officiously intoning "one . . . two-oo . . ." but before she got to "three" everybody, even Ira, managed to come up with something. Only Natasha immediately refused to take part, saying a stutter made it impossible to get the word out quickly enough.

"Ceiling!" said Diana.

"White," Katya answered and continued: "Painting!"

Ira was silent.

"One . . . two-oo . . . two and a half . . ."

"Oh, er, what's it called . . . museum."

"Well?"

"What?"

"Go on!"

"Oh, is it still me?"

"Yes!" they shouted in unison, and Ira said uncertainly, "Locker."

"Wooden. Um, pillow," Anya said.

"Soft! Sky."

"Overcast. House!"

"Brick! Dacha!"

"Scissors," said Ira.

Anya shuddered and stared at her. The cell immediately faded to a blur and the only thing still highlighted in it was Ira, who was smiling as if butter would not melt in her mouth.

Somewhere in the darkened periphery the others were shouting, "Come on, it's your next word!" but Anya could not even see them.

"Why did you say 'scissors'?" Anya asked.

Ira turned around and looked at her.

"Oh, come on, why bother to ask? She's not right in the head," she heard Katya say.

"Why did you say 'scissors' after 'dacha'?" Anya persisted.

All the emotion in Ira's face, which a second ago had been radiating joy, seemed to drain away. Her lips were still stretched in a smile, but it was mechanical, an expression with no life in it.

"I told him straight out, I wouldn't do what he wanted me to," she whispered.

"Who?" Anya asked, also in a whisper.

"He told me that if I went with him to see his friends at their dacha he would pay me ten thousand rubles. But when we got there he began making me do things I didn't want to."

"What's she talking about?" Katya asked in perplexity.

No one replied.

"Then he said that if I didn't want to do it nicely he would do it anyway, nastily. He tied my hands to the bed and went downstairs."

Ira faltered now and again, but there was absolute silence in the cell. Nobody was making associations anymore. Anya heard a car honking far away in the world outside.

"I thought he was going to come back with his friends and I wouldn't be able to run away," Ira said, her face ashen. "I started gnawing at the rope. He didn't come back up for a long time, but I could hear him downstairs. I was really drunk at first, but when he tied me up I was suddenly sober."

"Anyway," Ira went on, "while he was away I managed to get myself untied. I wanted to jump out the window but I was scared because it was on the second floor. There were all these cupboards and nightstands in the room. I opened them and found a pair of scissors and thread in one. Then I heard someone coming up the stairs, just one person it sounded like. I was so scared. I ran out to face him. I was drunk, right? I thought I would scare him with the scissors and be able to run past him." Ira fell silent again.

"Did you manage to run past him?" Diana asked levelly. Anya could feel the tension in the cell.

"No," Ira said. "He saw me and tripped. It was so unexpected, I suppose. He fell. All the way down the stairs."

"What?" Katya asked, taken aback.

"He fell. His friends rushed to help him, all yelling, but I could see a pool of blood oozing out from under his head. He must've cracked it on one of the steps. Well, I decided not to stick around. I rushed back into the room and jumped out the window. By that time I was past caring. But everything was fine, I didn't even get any bruises. I walked all the way back to Moscow. It was getting light already."

"And what happened to the scissors?" Anya queried for some reason.

"Oh, I threw them away as I was running over to the window," Ira replied without hesitation. As she finished her story she suddenly beamed that placid, witless smile again.

Maya, saucer-eyed, looked at Ira as if seeing her for the first time.

"And was the guy dead?" she finally asked.

Ira shrugged vacantly.

Katya looked at her sternly. "You've made the whole thing up. Admit it," she demanded. Ira shook her head.

"It's a load of baloney from start to finish: the dacha, the men, getting tied to a bed and nearly gang-raped, and then one of them accidentally gets killed. Things like that just don't happen!"

"My word of honor!" Ira said, getting really upset. "It did all happen!"

"Come on, what man would even want you?"

"Arsen!" Diana replied, gloatingly. "For a beer!" Once again she and Katya split their sides laughing.

"Y-yes, she's got stoned on Lyrica and is making it all up!" Natasha said. "Yuck!"

"I'm not making it up!"

"Yes, sure. Tell us another one!"

While the others were falling over themselves to make fun of Ira, Maya suddenly leaned over to Anya and whispered, "So, why did you ask her about scissors?"

Anya was longing to share her experiences with someone, and had opened her mouth before suddenly realizing she could hardly just put them into words. ("I had a nightmare about Ira and a pair of scissors, and when she said 'scissors' I felt there might be a sinister link." That didn't sound good.)

"I was just puzzled by her odd association," Anya muttered in reply.

The conversation changed tack only when Katya and Diana ran out of cruel jokes and had so offended Ira that she stopped answering. Anya glanced across at her periodically, perhaps in the hope of detecting something out of the ordinary, but found nothing. She was not sure herself if she believed Ira's story, but an unrelenting anxiety was gnawing at her. The coincidence of the scissors seemed just too great. She was well aware that anybody she told about the previous night would think she was a kopeck short of a ruble, but she could not shake off a general sense of unease.

When the lights were turned out in the cell, Anya did not close her eyes for a long time, keeping her guard up. Her cellmates lay in their bunks, breathing evenly. As for Ira, she started snoring the moment her head touched the pillow. Anya peered intently into the darkness, making sure she would not be caught out if yesterday's devilish doings resumed. All around, however, silence reigned, disturbed only by the occasional dripping of the tap or water flushing in other cells. Without noticing, she fell asleep.

DAY THREE

Through the drowsiness Anya could feel someone's eyes on her. They were staring so obtrusively that it cut through even the dense layer of dream fantasies. She tried to wake up but could not. Sleep had her manacled and she lay there impotent, unable to move. She felt like she was being dragged deeper and deeper, down to the seabed, and the power of that other gaze was forcing her down, not letting her rise. Concentrating all her willpower, she rushed forward and, quite unexpectedly, opened her eyes wide. She was breathing as hard as if she actually had just burst up to the surface.

There was no one nearby and no one was looking at her. All Anya's cellmates were still asleep, except Maya, who was reading yesterday's Jo Nesbø novel. Her doll-like face was as still as a pool of water on a windless day, reflecting not a ripple of emotion. She sat in her bunk, holding back a page and twisting a lock of hair around her finger. Anya was so pleased to have broken free of her disconcerting dream that she had no intention, despite the early hour, of sleeping more. Instead, she too sat up in her bunk and quietly, in order not to wake the others, asked Maya, "Is it good?"

Maya grimaced. "Well, not especially. I thought it would be like the film of *The Snowman*. Have you seen that? There was so much action, but I'm forty pages in already and nothing is happening."

"Perhaps it'll get better."

"Perhaps . . . But why are you awake so early? What woke you?"

Anya shrugged. "I couldn't sleep."

"I can't sleep here either! The bed is awful, so hard. I have a firm orthopedic mattress at home but it's not this hard! And the pillow is as flat as a pancake. And the blankets! Dirty, stinking, all of them! How could anyone curl up in—"

Maya was becoming more and more agitated, but suddenly broke off in midsentence. It looked as if she had unexpectedly remembered something and was now anxiously pondering it. Looking at her concentrated expression, Anya held her breath, feeling that Maya might be about to do something extraordinary. She did. Taking a deep breath she instantly began to sob, without warning, as if someone had flicked a switch.

Anya stared at her in astonishment. By now she was used to Maya's phenomenal changes of mood, but had not anticipated anything so abrupt. In floods of tears, sniffling and on the verge of howling, Maya wailed, "And as if that wasn't enough, I'm pregnant!"

"Pregnant?" Anya asked in shock, not knowing whether to rush to console or congratulate her.

"Ye-es . . . I-I-I think so . . ."

"Why do you think so?"

"I don't kno-o-ow! . . . I just feel I am!"

Anya's sense of shock diminished somewhat.

"Do you have any particular reason to think that?"

"I don't know," Maya sniffled, "I just have a feeling. I was driving to see the doctor when I was stopped by the officer."

"Never mind, you'll be out in a couple of days and be able to find out then," Anya said to cheer her up.

"But what if I really am pregnant?"

"Don't you want to be?"

"Of course not! You can see what I look like now. Where would that leave me? I had my boobs done just recently. It will completely ruin my figure." Maya relapsed into her sobbing.

"I'm sure it will all be fine. If you don't have any solid reason to think—"

"I even agreed on everything with my sister!" Maya interrupted her, sniffling. "When I decide to have children, she will be my surrogate."

"Oh, you've really thought about this . . ." Anya murmured, somewhat distracted.

"Why not? She loves children and doesn't take much care of herself. But I can't afford that luxury. I've invested so much . . . I just cannot afford to get pregnant. In any case, before you start having children you need to get married, and I'm not ready to get married yet, it's too soon."

As she discussed her life plans, Maya's tears began to dry and her tone became more businesslike.

"In general, children are a good thing, of course, and we need them. I am planning to have two, a boy and a girl. I've decided on their names. The boy I'm going to call Max. I want him to have that sort of international name. He's going to be a footballer."

"And the girl?" Anya inquired, not knowing what else to say.

"The girl will be called Nicole," Maya announced solemnly. "And I'm not going to have her doing anything beyond just enjoying life. I consider that a woman's only duty."

"That's very modern of you."

"Well, why not? My mother slaved away at three jobs all her life. My sister too, even when she was still living in Izhevsk. She once said to me, "I'm not going to turn out like you, I am too good for that." And what do you know—I bring her to Moscow, she sees the life I'm living, and now she's asking me to find her someone!"

"And how exactly do you make a living?" Anya asked cautiously, but then the peephole in the cell door opened and yesterday's policeman said morosely, "Breakfast."

Anya's other cellmates started wheezing and stirred into life. Natasha seemed only to have been waiting for the word, jumping down from her upper bunk. Ira sat up in bed and rubbed her eyes. Diana sighed and turned to face the wall.

"Oh-ho, our p-princess is awake early this morning. Perhaps you'll even join us for breakfast," Natasha said to Maya.

Looking like an actress, Maya lowered her head and declined the invitation, saying, "No, I don't eat porridge."

"Yes, we know, you only eat lobsters!" Natasha gave her a smile that was quite without malice and went to the washbasin.

"It's not true," Maya whispered to Anya earnestly. "I don't only eat lobster."

"Wa-ter!" Natasha yelled suddenly.

Anya was so startled she almost fell off her bunk. Diana and Katya, who had been asleep, sat up in theirs with a crazed look in their eyes.

"What is it? A fire?!" Katya shouted hoarsely, looking around wildly.

"No, it's water! They've turned on the hot water!"

Only then did Anya notice that the tap was snorting and spitting, and a stream of rust-colored water was gushing from it and splashing in all directions.

"Hurrah!" Diana exclaimed, leaping out of bed and rushing to the washbasin as if it were a sacred spring. "That means showers today! Finally!"

"What is it with you people?" Katya grumbled, straightening her blanket and pillow and collapsing back on the bed. "Big fucking deal. They've turned on the hot water. What's that to shout about?"

"Oh, you just look for excuses to moan! As if you're not pleased yourself," Diana retorted. She waited for the water to run clean and put her hands under the tap in true delight.

Katya pulled the blanket right up over her head and mumbled from beneath it, "It's not like being at home."

"Of course it isn't," Diana conceded, "but I'm grateful for small mercies."

Above the washbasin, in place of a mirror, someone had glued a little square of foil in which, with a slight effort, it was possible to discern one's reflection. Diana looked into it and smoothed her curls.

"Personally, I'm only going to be happy when I'm back in my own bathroom," Katya said. This time her voice was more clearly audible: she had made an opening in the blanket and was speaking into it.

"And I probably won't come out of mine for three hours," Diana chimed in, still twirling in front of the makeshift mirror.

"Literally just before I was arrested I bought myself this really cool shampoo and hadn't yet even washed my hair with it," Katya carried on, not listening. "They wouldn't have let me bring it in here, of course, because it's nontransparent. In any case, I wouldn't want to use it here, better to wash at home where you can feel like a human being. I've been walking around for a week now, dreaming of nothing more than being able to cut my fingernails. What a life!"

Diana's mood had darkened.

"Yes, here, of course, it's not a real shower, just something they call a shower. No razor, no half-decent soap. Hell, Katya, you've completely depressed me!"

Katya gave an evil laugh.

"Oh, girls, I just can't wait to be back home!" Maya said, sounding close to tears. At first she had been taking a great interest in the conversation, but now her mood had changed again and she was deeply upset. "I have such a beautiful bathroom at home. Pink! I bought an apartment recently and the makeover has just been finished. I haven't even had time to get used to it. When I get out I'll spend all day in the bathroom!"

"You probably won't feel much at home in this shower," Diana observed, eyeing her dubiously. She finally relinquished the washbasin, ceding it to Natasha, who was muttering grumpily. "Do you at least have some shampoo of your own?"

Maya dismissed that possibility. "Oh, come now, I'm not going into the shower here. I'll wait till I get back home."

"We've got hot water today. What more do you want?" Natasha, her face already washed, asked indignantly. "Someone can share their shampoo with you!"

"Oh, I wouldn't be able to use it. I mean, I don't want to offend, but my hair needs special shampoo. And I must have conditioner and a decent comb. And a hair dryer. And tongs."

"Does your hair tangle then?" Anya asked sympathetically.

"No, it's just to make it lie properly."

"God Almighty!" Natasha finally exploded. Maya's refined expectations were driving her crazy. She turned away from the washbasin and stared irately at the younger woman. "Get a grip! You haven't been sent to some f-five-star hotel! It's grim here. Prisons are supposed to be grim!"

"Oh, I quite understand," Maya replied demurely. "But without my creature comforts I couldn't dream of even combing my hair."

"Do you wash your hair often?" Katya asked politely. Finally giving up on trying to sleep, she sat up in her bunk and lit a cigarette.

"Every day."

"How long does it take you to get it how you want it?"

"Oh, forty minutes at least."

"Forty minutes every day!" Diana said with a respectful whistle. She went back to her bunk and took the cigarette out of Katya's hand. "I could never be bothered like that."

"What on earth's the point?" Katya demanded contemptuously. "I tie my hair up in a ponytail and I'm off. I couldn't spend half the day on it."

There was a clattering and the door swung open.

"Breakfast," an unsmiling cop informed them.

Ira scampered over to the door, buttoning her denim shirt as she went. She could get up a bit of speed when it was time to eat. The policeman let her out to the corridor. Natasha went next, muttering something under her breath and clutching a water bottle under her arm.

"Perhaps we should go too," Katya said, taking the cigarette back from Diana, her voice meditative. "I can't usually be bothered to get up, but today Natasha has woken everyone anyway."

"I've decided to go on my last day," Diana replied. "As a kind of celebration."

"What are you going to do the minute you get out?"

"My husband's collecting me, so the first thing I'll do is give him a cuddle. Then, when we get home, I'll give Tiger a cuddle. I've missed him so much. Then I'll have meat patties or pancakes—I haven't decided yet. My husband's a good cook, so I'll give him the order before I get out. Then I'll take a shower, and immediately celebrate my birthday. After ten days on the wagon I'll probably have got so out of the way of drinking I'll be completely blitzed within half an hour."

"Is it your birthday?" Anya asked.

"Yes, the day before release. Can you imagine, I'm going to have my twenty-fifth birthday in a detention center! When the judge sentenced me to ten days I realized I'd be in prison for my big day. I almost had hysterics there in the courtroom. I'm over it now, though. It will be something to remember!"

"I'll get drunk too," Katya said dreamily, stretching on her bunk and looking up at the ceiling. "But my first port of call has to be McDonald's. Double cheeseburger, mmm . . . potato wedges . . . with cheese sauce! God, I'm just dying to pig out on Mickey D's. Then, home and straight to Olga."

"Oh, who's Olga?" Maya joined the conversation.

"Olga is my girlfriend."

"Oh . . . Are you dating a girl?"

"Yes. What about it? You have a problem with that?" Katya raised herself on an elbow and, narrowing her piercing blue eyes, looked squarely at Maya.

"No, I was just asking. I've always wondered how that works for . . . er . . ." Maya faltered.

"For lesbians? Just say it. What's up with you? But actually I'm not really a lesbian. I only ever went out with men before. But now there's Olga."

"So how did that happen? I'm just curious. I'm not . . . what's it called?" Maya wrinkled her brow. "Well, not against gays. I'm not homophobic. I just don't understand how you . . . All my life I've only liked men."

"Well, this is how it is," Katya said lazily, lying back down on her bunk. "It's not a matter of guys or girls, it's about people. Presumably you don't like every person you meet? You meet someone and imme-diately know they're more right for you than anyone else. When I met Olga I just knew straight away, that's for me. She's so calm, so serene. When I'm with her it's like being on holiday."

"And you fell in love with her at first sight?" Maya asked with wonder in her voice, like a child listening to a fairy tale.

Katya grunted. "Well, very soon after that we started dating. I don't believe in wasting time."

"And how do people react to you in the street?" Diana now asked as she lay back down in her bunk. Her eyes were fixed on the underside of Katya's mattress, which made it appear that was what she was talking to.

"They live with it."

"You don't come across dickheads who shout about how you're promoting homosexuality?"

"As if!" Katya said disdainfully. "Anyone who tried that on with me would be lucky if they could walk away afterwards."

"We had a boy living in the same courtyard as us in Izhevsk who everyone thought was gay. Anyway, one day the local boys ambushed him and beat him up so badly he had to go to the hospital," Maya said. "I really could never understand that. You can't go beating people up, not even gays! In any case he hadn't done anything terrible, only dyed his hair blond."

An image from the past surfaced in Anya's mind. She was on the bus with her mother on their way to the cemetery to visit her grandmother. There was nothing special about the trip besides Anya's mood. She had lately been feeling she was no longer the self she had always known and loved, but a stranger, someone she was ashamed to be. The sense of shame had been tormenting her for several weeks past, but now, as they approached the cemetery, it became intolerable. She felt like a character in a sci-fi film who suddenly finds she has been taken over by an evil alien. The girl she used to be no longer exists, the good person has been replaced by someone new and unpleasant whom she is doomed to drag around with her and conceal for the rest of her life. If she hid under the blanket in bed she could just about get by, but traveling like this to the cemetery, with its atmosphere of grim solemnity and even holiness, was unbearable.

To keep her mother from noticing anything, Anya sat with her face turned to the window. When the scenery distracted her, the shame shrank into a small, disturbing lump that she could ignore, but as Anya was revisiting her thoughts she had only to bump into the shame for it to flood all through her body. She tried to imagine what would happen when she arrived. She knew, of course, the earth would not open up to swallow her, and that she would not be struck by a thunderbolt, although either might have been preferable to the constant, secret mental flagellation to which she was subjecting herself.

Anya could not even tell when the alien had taken possession of her. That instant should have stood out from all others, but instead she felt she had slid imperceptibly into this new reality, and by the time she realized what was happening, the alien had long since taken up residence.

She had met Zhenya at English classes several months previously, and at first had not even liked her. Zhenya was too in-your-face. In the very first lesson she had unceremoniously glanced in Anya's exercise book and jabbed a pen down on a mistake without so much as a by-your-leave. Zhenya was altogether too much, constantly interrupting everybody, laughing too loudly, and smoking during the break. At first Anya kept a safe distance away from her, and even moved to a different desk in the next lesson, but that day Zhenya had forgotten her textbook so she was obliged to share with her. Zhenya seemed impervious to Anya's disapproval and went out of her way to talk to her, asking what movies she liked, and when it turned out that they lived quite near each other, offering to drive her home after the class. Anya was seventeen. Zhenya was twenty-one, liked rock music (the Night Snipers in particular), and had pierced eyebrows.

One week she did not turn up for the class, and Anya was shocked by how much that upset her. She had no idea she had become so attached. Zhenya missed the next class too. In the past when Anya entered the classroom looking forward to seeing her it had seemed somehow lit up, but now it was empty and soulless and without any trace of its former magic.

By the third week she had almost given up hope, and again Zhenya did not show. Anya looked at her empty place and thought in a detached way that she would soon get used to it. She did not even have Zhenya's phone number to text and ask what had happened. Anya could have asked the teacher for it but felt a vague reluctance to do that. For some reason she did not want anyone else guessing her interest. Outside the window the sun was setting and the wall opposite the door to their class was flooded with bright yellow light. It had a calming effect on Anya. She pictured it as a portal.

And then it opened. The flawless yellow background was suddenly bisected by a black silhouette that grew as someone approached. Anya watched, mesmerized. She knew whom she was about to see, but did not want to rush the moment. The delight of their meeting became a certainty and she could afford to savor the anticipation, to relish the yellow wall and the growing silhouette against it. Zhenya came in and Anya was instantly filled with joy. She felt blissfully warm. Half closing her eyes she watched Zhenya approaching, claiming her orphaned seat, opening the textbook. Perhaps this was the moment Anya realized she had been possessed by an alien, although the idea did not alarm her. Instead she just gloried in the bliss of the moment.

From that evening on, however, Anya was adrift. On the one hand, she was in love and happy. She looked forward eagerly to each class, ran out with Zhenya during the break to smoke, downloaded all the Night Snipers' songs she could, talked to Zhenya on the phone for hours, and started to look down on the rest of humanity. It seemed an unimaginable stroke of luck, a win in life's lottery, that Zhenya had singled her out from all the rest.

On the other hand, Anya was at a loss. It seemed that someone else had replaced her, someone of whom those around her, and indeed she herself, could not approve. The feeling of being in love with a woman was shaming, and it was terrifying that someone might find out. When she was with Zhenya happiness seemed logical and right, yet as soon as she was on her own, it felt bizarre and unnatural. Anya was tortured by the contradiction—and then there was the cemetery. In the bus that day she felt particularly corrupt and offensive to the rest of humankind.

"Olga and I went to a local bar one time," Katya was meanwhile telling her cellmates, "and this wasted dude starts pestering us. Like, 'Oh, girlies, can I watch, and how about we have a threesome.' In short, a complete perv."

"What did you do?" Diana asked.

"I beat the shit out of him," Katya said with a shrug, proudly adding, "Then I told the manager to ban him. The manager's a pal of mine and he says, 'Katya, leave it to me. If he shows up here again he'll have to collect his teeth in a matchbox afterwards.'"

"I met up with a mark one time," Maya said, choosing her words with care. "He started trying to get me to agree to a threesome. I dropped him instantly. I really don't see the point. If you already have a woman, why would you need another one? And if you do want another one, it means you can't be much taken with the first one."

"I would totally say yes to a threesome," Diana proclaimed, and sat up in her bunk. "I think it's hot. It's not about being unfaithful, it's about having a new experience."

"What do you mean 'I would totally say yes'?" Katya asked incredulously. She hung down from her bunk and looked at Diana. "You'd allow your husband to fuck on the side in front of your eyes?"

"What makes you think it would be my husband doing the fucking?" Diana asked with a frown. "It would be an experiment between three consenting adults."

"Well, in my opinion that would still be cheating. I feel very strongly about it," Maya said. "If I found out my man was being unfaithful I would leave him immediately. I even had an experience of that sort one time. I was dating this mark. Actually, I first became acquainted with his father and thought of hooking up with him but somehow it didn't work out. I immediately found a common language with his son, though. He was handsome and sporty, just my type. We embarked on such a passionate relationship that after three weeks he suggested I move in with him. I did wonder at first whether that was a bit fast, but I really liked him. He was such a sweetie. He would bring me a bouquet of roses every time we met."

"Don't tell me: you moved in and he cheated on you?" Katya anticipated scornfully. She propped her head on her hand and looked at Maya.

"Well, actually, yes. I moved in with him and things started going wrong. He squandered all his money on alcohol and weed. Almost every evening his friends would come to visit and get stoned out of their minds. I really don't care for that sort of thing, I try to lead a healthy lifestyle. I didn't say anything in front of them, and the next morning he always apologized and vowed to change, saying it was just difficult to alter his lifestyle overnight."

"And you believed him?" Diana asked in a tone of exasperation.

"Well, he said that he'd always lived on his own and it was what he was used to, but I had changed his life and he would try really hard to live up to my expectations." Maya gave a sigh. "It was just so sweet the way he said that. Even now while I'm telling you this I miss him a bit, although he did, of course, turn out to be a complete asshole."

"Well, what happened next?"

"Oh, we lived like that for a couple of weeks, and then one time I was trying to find something. I went into the bathroom and looked in one of the drawers. I hadn't pulled it right out before, and this was completely by chance. Anyway, I found a toothbrush, a hairband, and a pack of sanitary napkins. Imagine! He was at work. I was completely distraught all day, and when he came home in the evening I said, 'What's this? You told me I was the first girl you'd ever lived with.' So then he starts making excuses, 'Oh, that was nothing, just a girl spent the night here a couple of times but it's all been over for ages.' I said, 'If it's all over why is all this stuff still here?' 'Oh,' he says, 'I didn't even know it was there.'"

"Typical male cover-up!" Katya exclaimed, her eyes glinting. "When they've got their backs to the wall they start coming out with all this 'I didn't know,' 'I hadn't noticed.' I'm so glad I'm through with men for good!"

"Really I should have seen what was going on straight away, but I decided to give him the benefit of the doubt. The more so because after that incident he didn't smoke for several days, and I thought he'd actually given it up. Anyway, another day he was out at work and I got just so bored I thought I could at least post a photo. I took a snap of myself in the mirror and uploaded it to Instagram. I geotagged it 'White Swan Residence.' That was where he lived. So then I thought, while I'm at it I'll take a look at what other snaps have been posted from here. I turn on geotagging and see the last photo is some tart snapping herself in the mirror. I take a closer look and see—imagine it!—this is the same mirror as in his apartment! The sofa's in the reflection, the walls are the same. And the photo was taken two days earlier! I hadn't spent that night there, I'd gone to see my mother."

"He really is an asshole," Diana agreed.

"So what did you do?" Katya asked.

Maya tossed her hair back, looked around solemnly at everyone, and announced proudly, "I just decided I would text this bimbo. 'Blah, blah,' I say, 'actually I'm dating this guy and we're even living together. What's going on, what were you doing in his apartment?' And what do you think—it turns out she thought she was the only woman in his life. She was seeing him regularly and he hadn't said a word to her about me. In short, he had treated us like a pair of total idiots."

"What happened then?"

"What happened then was that we discussed it all on Insta and agreed to teach him a lesson. She came to the apartment and together we trashed it. We didn't do anything too violent because he's got connections and we didn't want to end up with a ton of bad problems, but we made a real mess! We took his clothes out of the closets and spread them all over the place. When he came home from work we welcomed him together. You should have seen his face! I still enjoy that memory. I even spat at him for good measure. 'That's for all the lies and cheating,' I said."

"Wow," Diana exclaimed, with new respect.

"That's why I've had it with men," Katya reminded them. "It's all you can expect from them."

"They're not all like that."

"As near all of them as makes no difference. When did you last meet even one decent man?"

Maya and Diana tried to recall such an occasion, while Anya observed them with anthropological interest. At this point, however, Natasha and Ira returned from breakfast.

"Ira ate three bowls of porridge," Natasha told everyone as she put her bottle of hot water on the locker. "I warned her she won't be able to squeeze through the door when she's finally released."

"Not three, only two!" Ira mumbled, and added guiltily, "Usually I don't eat all that much. When you're drinking you don't feel hungry but I've been on the wagon in here for almost two weeks and it's given me the munchies."

"Hey, Ira, your mother might be right. If you sat it out in the camps for six months you'd fatten up nicely and stop being an alky," Katya said with a snigger.

"But I don't want to be sent to the camps," Ira protested.

Everybody laughed.

The morning passed uneventfully: first they drank some tea, and even persuaded Maya to eat a chocolate, a whole packet of which Diana found in the locker, a present from a prisoner released before Anya's arrival. Next Ira started doing a pencil drawing on a sheet of paper Diana tore out of a notebook for her. Natasha again set about cleaning the cell. Anya tried to read but kept being distracted by snatches of conversation. For example, Diana said her favorite singer was Philipp Kirkorov, who represented Russia in the Euro-vision Song Contest back in 1995. This announcement shocked them to the core.

"Are you out of your mind?" Katya asked in amazement. "He's an old man! He must be sixty! Even my mom has stopped liking him!"

"What of it," Diana persisted. "He has beautiful eyes! And he looks like a real man."

"Well he d-dresses like a w-woman!" Natasha yelled. Overcome by indignation, she stopped swabbing the floor and stood with one arm raised toward heaven and the other grasping the mop, looking for all the world like the statue of Peter the Great at the helm of Russia.

"That's just show business, they all dress like that!" Diana replied, unabashed. "And Philipp is moving with the times. Have you seen the video of 'A Mood Colored Blue'?"

"You and your Philipp," Katya laughed. "I can't believe it!"

"Oh, and Olga Buzova is in that video too. Now Buzova I do like!" Maya said happily.

Anya listened goggle-eyed to most of what they had to say but then pulled herself together and put a pleasant smile on her face. She did not want the rest of them thinking she was stuck-up, and would even have tried to join in their extraordinary conversations, only she had never seen the video of "A Mood Colored Blue," and the last time she had seen Kirkorov was at home on their big old television on New Year's Eve 2004.

The peephole in the door slid open and somebody called in cheerfully, "Wake up for inspection!" Doors could be heard banging in the corridor, where someone was engaging in loud conversation.

"Today is the nice shift," Natasha remarked with satisfaction, tidying away the mop and bowl. "All done, you can walk on it barefoot!"

Four people came into the cell: a young, moon-faced cop, an older cop with bushy black eyebrows, a tall red-haired woman who looked like a vixen, and a little old man.

"Hello-o there, girls," said the old man. He had an unexpectedly low, booming voice and sounded like Santa Claus at a children's matinee. "How is everything?"

"Fine, fine!" they all replied, smiling. Ira giggled coquettishly.

"Do we have any complaints? Any suggestions?"

"No, no!"

"Can we go to the shower today?" Diana piped up.

"The shower?" the old man repeated in amazement, looking first at the vixen and then at the men. "Your shower is scheduled for tomorrow, girls."

"But the water, there's hot water today," everyone babbled.

"Ah, well, if there's hot water . . ." the duty officer said understandingly. "But only after lunch, girls, and you'll have to be very quick."

"Hurrah, hurrah!"

"Let's have the roll call now. Don't want to find someone's run away or, come to think of it, forced their way in."

They all laughed and Anya, to her surprise, found that she too was half smiling. The old man seemed so sweet and humane by comparison with the previous cops, you wanted to smile back out of sheer gratitude.

"Vilkova!"

"Present!"

"Orlova!"

"Present!"

"Leonova!"

"Present!"

"Ivanova!"

"Present!"

"Andersen!"

"Present," Maya said, fluttering her eyelashes.

"And Romanova?"

"Present," Anya said. The old man closed the register, but Anya went on, "And I would like to submit an application to appeal. Can I do that through you?"

Everyone turned and stood staring at her. Ira, not taking her eyes off Anya, scratched an itchy knee with her pencil.

"You want to appeal against your arrest?" the old officer checked cautiously.

"Well, yes."

"What were you sentenced for?"

"Attending a rally."

"Ah, are you a political?" The old man instantly relaxed a bit. "Then write a statement to the court where you were tried and we'll forward it."

"When?"

"Today, of course, no point in delaying. We don't want to keep you here for no reason," he said with a laugh.

"Can you give me some paper?" Anya asked. "I only have a notebook."

"Certainly we can, why would we not? Nastya, could you bring some paper for the young lady?"

The vixen next to the duty officer nodded.

"Right then, if there are no more questions, have a relaxing morning," the old man said and made for the door. Reacting to a barely noticeable nod, the rest of the officers followed him.

When the door closed behind them, Katya folded her arms, gave Anya one of her predatory looks and asked, "So what's this appeal you're planning to submit?"

"Against being subjected to unlawful arrest," Anya replied.

Ira laughed: "'Unlawful,' ha-ha-ha!"

"Idiot, maybe she really was unlawfully arrested!" Katya said, raising her voice.

Ira stopped laughing and, her face expressionless, began tracing the pencil over her jeans again.

"They gave her more Lyrica at breakfast," Natasha explained, with an unfriendly glance at Ira.

Anya felt the mood in the room had subtly changed. Her cellmates were initially at a loss to know how to react to the news of her appeal, and had been waiting for Katya to give them a signal. As soon as she chastised Ira they all relaxed. Submitting an appeal was deemed acceptable, and Anya was seen to be acting within her rights.

"Well, yes, why are people being arrested at all for attending rallies?" Diana asked in a philosophical tone of voice, plonking herself on her bunk, which creaked.

"Nowadays you can be jailed for absolutely anything," Anya said with a shrug. "This was supposedly an 'unsanctioned' protest rally . . ."

Katya, still standing in the center of the room, turned and looked at her in astonishment.

"What, you mean protest rallies need to be sanctioned?"

"Well, actually, they do."

Katya frowned: "And what were you protesting against?"

"Corruption. The government."

"And where do you have to get it sanctioned?"

"City hall."

"In other words, you need to ask the government for permission to hold a demonstration to protest against the government?" Katya spelled it out, her hands on her hips. "No, did you hear that? Well, I'll be fucked . . . And do they ever actually sanction any rallies?"

Katya's indignation was so genuine that Anya involuntarily smiled.

"Recently, no, which is why people just go out and demonstrate anyway."

"Hmm, it's hardly surprising that they've put you in jail. After all, they're not going to be happy about people criticizing them," Diana remarked. She got up, took some biscuits from the locker, and munched noisily. Even while chewing, she managed to register concern.

"A friend of mine went to a rally and invited me along. I nearly agreed. Are you going to have any more? I might turn up next time. I ought to at least see what's going on."

"So then what? They'll b-bust you too!" Natasha croaked from her perch by the ceiling. She had climbed up there and now looked down sourly at the girls.

"They've already busted me, I'm not scared of it anymore!" Diana said, laughing.

"I c-can't understand you," Natasha continued, disgruntled, looking at her cellmates in turn. "Who n-needs these rallies anyway? Have you achieved anything?" She glared at Anya. "All you want is to organize revolutions. You should l-learn to live in peace!"

"I don't want to organize revolutions," Anya parried. "I want to live a decent life."

Natasha threw up her hands.

"What's wrong with the life you're living now?" She was so indignant, she had lost her stutter. "People in Russia have never lived as well as they do now. Look at our parents, look how it was in the 1990s under Yeltsin! It's the difference between heaven and hell. We ought to be saying thank you!"

"Well, I don't like our government," Katya said forthrightly, again folding her arms. Although she was looking up at Natasha, she was now the one who appeared dominant. "I didn't vote in the last election and I talked my mother out of voting too. It doesn't change anything, so why bother turning out? My mother worked as a schoolteacher for the whole of her life and her pension is pennies, while that lot are busy stuffing their pockets."

"Stuffing their pockets!" Ira giggled without looking up.

She carried on drawing things on her jeans. Anya doubted Ira was following the conversation; she seemed to be just repeating words she liked the sound of.

"You keep your mouth shut!" Natasha yelled at her, jumping on the bed with the intention, apparently, of intimidating her down below. Ira didn't even look up.

"Well, I like Putin," Maya said dreamily, twisting a lock of hair around her finger. "He's such a strong leader. Everyone respects us now . . . You know, girls, sometimes I think maybe I should go into politics?"

Katya snorted, "You?"

"Well, why not? There's some lady deputy, I can't remember her name, but she acts in movies *and* she works in the Duma. I could do that. Then I could track down the judge who put me away and get her sent to jail as well!"

The hatch in the door opened and conversation instantly ceased.

"Who was asking for paper? Here you are." It was the vixen.

Anya took the sheets and strolled back to her bunk. She had no idea how to write an appeal, but everyone was looking at her with so much respect there was no way she could admit this fact.

"I would write an appeal too," Maya said with a sigh, "but it wouldn't reach the right person in time. Anyway, I'm being released the day after tomorrow."

Under a barrage of curious stares Anya arranged herself on her bunk, taking time to ready herself for the task.

She settled comfortably, aligned the sheet with the edge of her book to write on, and wrote in the upper right corner, "To the Tverskoy District Court of Moscow, from Anna Grigorievna Romanova." Then, centered, she wrote, "Appeal."

Katya's curiosity got the better of her. "What do you think, will they really let you go?" She was observing Anya from under the window and had been about to light up only to find there were no cigarettes left.

"I don't expect so, but at least I can try."

"Hey, Diana, how about you and me write one of these too?"

"Why, were you driving and you had a license?"

"No. I didn't have a license."

"Same here. So what is there to appeal about?"

Anya rummaged through her plastic bag and found the court order she had been given after the hearing. She thought for a moment and then copied out the ruling. She added, "I consider my arrest to have been unlawful and demand that the verdict be reconsidered." She dated the letter and signed it.

The radio cleared its throat and started up.

"That's really getting on my tits," Diana said irritably. "I usually love listening to music on the car radio, but this I absolutely hate."

"There, there, perhaps 'A Mood Colored Blue' will come on," Katya consoled her sarcastically.

Natasha stretched out on her bed and recalled, "I heard in the camps about a time when people who had done something really bad had the song from *Pinocchio* played to them all day long."

"Hell, that would drive you crazy. I'm already being driven crazy just by the radio here." Katya paced around the cell, stretching her legs. "Perhaps we should play a game."

"I can't be bothered," Diana answered lethargically.

They all eventually found something to do. Ira helped herself to Anya's leftover paper and drew all over it. Natasha decrypted her crossword, Diana read, and Katya climbed onto her bunk and lay down facing the wall. Maya returned with a sigh to her assault on Jo Nesbø.

Anya went over to the cell door and knocked politely. The peephole slid open immediately, as if the policeman outside was just waiting to be summoned.

"I've written an appeal. May I give it to you?"

The young moon-faced cop opened the hatch and said something. Anya noticed with some annoyance it was so low that a person of average height would have to bow low if they wanted to hear a word of what was said.

"Will you send it off straight away?" she asked into the hatch.

"I'll pass it to my superiors. They'll send it when they have time."

Anya returned to her bunk and opened her book. She had read only a line of it when the songs the radio had been quietly playing seemed suddenly to be invading her consciousness. With a pang of nostalgia she recalled a discovery made in her student dorm days. People fall into two camps: those undisturbed by light and those undisturbed by noise. At this moment it was unfortunate for her that she had never been one of the latter.

After some more time had passed they were taken to make their phone calls. On this occasion the ritual of issuing the phones was curtailed to a short procedure of handing everyone their phones at the same time and letting them into the tiny room. Anya called her mother, assiduously pretended not to have a care in the world, and assured her that life in the detention center was just great. Her mom asked anxiously if anyone was being mean to her, and Anya assured her that no one was. All around, her cellmates were jostling her and shouting into their phones, so that even if Anya was being kicked about, she would have had no opportunity to convey the information.

When they left, the register they had to sign when returning their phones was waiting, as was, unexpectedly for Anya, another scrap of paper.

"What's this for?" she asked Katya in a whisper.

"We have to sign for the food we're eating. It's supposed to happen every day. I imagine they just forgot yesterday."

The old man on duty passed Anya the sheet to sign, and she looked at it in more detail: against all the prisoners' names was a number: 136.95.

"So, what does this mean?" Anya asked, pointing the pen at the number.

"It means that yesterday you ate food to the value of 136 rubles," the old man willingly explained.

Anya raised her eyes and looked at him shocked: "For the whole day?!"

"Oh, it's always the same amount," Diana said with a dismissive gesture. She took the sheet from the bewildered Anya and signed against her surname. "Here every day you eat precisely 136 rubles and 95 kopecks' worth of food. We already don't give it a moment's thought."

Anya looked from her cellmates to the duty officer and back again.

"And you were asking why I don't eat the food here!" Maya remarked reproachfully.

For lunch there was pea soup. Burdened with her new knowledge, Anya scooped it up with a degree of curiosity. In fact it again tasted fine, only very salty. At the bottom of the bowl she found a lone piece of "textured soy protein" masquerading as meat.

"Are you still not eating?" Alyosha, the fair-haired server, asked Maya. She shook her head. "Why? Are you minding your figure?"

"Oh, I don't need to worry about my figure," Maya instantly responded with a coy smile. "I've been lucky with my genes. It's just that I'm used to different food."

"I can believe that," he remarked with a chuckle.

No sooner were they back in the cell than Diana, who throughout lunch had been casting suspicious looks in Maya's direction, said, "It's not true, is it?"

Maya flapped her eyelids. "What?"

"That you've got your figure because of your genes?"

"A-ah! I see what you mean. No, of course not. I had my bosom enhanced and my butt too. I've had a lot done, but a man shouldn't know about these things, not even one like that boy in the cafeteria."

"I knew straight off," Diana said smugly. "It struck me the moment I saw you, she's had that ass pumped up. They don't just grow like that."

Crossing to the window, she peeked into the cigarette pack before irritably crumpling it up and throwing it on the sill.

"Of course they don't, but I'm not going to point out to some fellow what I've had work done on," Maya responded reasonably enough. "I once met a guy who thought my eyes were actually blue."

"What, you mean they aren't?" Katya asked, puzzled, sitting down on Diana's bunk.

"No, of course not. It's lenses! I tried ever so hard to keep him from finding out. When we spent the night together I waited for him to fall asleep before I took them out. In the morning I woke up early, washed, cleaned my teeth, did my hair, put the lenses back in, and lay down again in an attractive posture. He would wake up and say, 'Oh, Maya! You even sleep like an angel!'"

"Well, I'll be fucked!" Diana exclaimed in amazement. "Why would you do all that?"

"Because for a man I should always be at my best, and he should think that is the real me!"

"Hell, in the mornings I can hardly get my head off the p-pillow, but she's already given herself a complete makeover!" Natasha muttered disapprovingly. She too did not bother to climb up to the top bunk but perched on Ira's. She sat there, hunched over, and Anya again felt she looked like some bird of ill omen.

"I've never been able to understand why anyone would prettify themselves for someone else," Katya declared in a bored way, straightening her ponytail. "All I do is get my hair together and I'm off. A fat lot of time I'm going to spend for someone else's benefit!"

"Well, don't you just sometimes feel like putting on makeup, or a pretty dress?" Maya asked romantically.

"Me? A dress? Give me a break! Makeup? Well, sometimes, but just for fun."

Maya was confused. "Well, I do it for fun too, but I also want other people only to see me looking my best."

"Okay, so what else have you had done?" Diana asked inquisitively. She was sitting cross-legged next to Katya, hugging her pillow like a child.

"What do you mean?"

"You said you haven't just done your boobs and your butt. So what else?"

"Oh, right. Well, first I had my nose done. Your nose is your most prominent facial feature. I keep telling my sister that. She has such a schnozzle! I had one just the same. I spent almost a year saving up for a rhinoplasty."

"A what?" Natasha inquired disparagingly.

"It's to correct the shape of your nose. I'm planning to have a second one done. Then there's your cheekbones. I had the buccal fat pads removed from my cheeks."

"God Almighty!" Katya yelped, screwing up her face. "I don't know what that is, but if you're taking bits out of your cheeks that sounds disgusting!"

Diana's eyes, however, were sparkling.

"I've heard about that!" she said excitedly. Your cheeks look just like Angelina Jolie's now."

"I know," Maya replied graciously. "Then there's all sorts of little things: eyelashes, lips, hair transplants . . ."

"You have hair transplants?" Anya asked unnecessarily.

She was sitting in her bunk and viewing Maya from behind. Her hair was very beautiful, and Maya herself now and then touched it, tossed it from shoulder to shoulder, or twisted it around her fingers so that it gleamed.

Maya laughed.

"Of course. Did you think my own hair is like this? I have a graft every two months. What else now? Oh yes, I've had Botox injected into my armpits."

"Wha-at?" Katya asked in disbelief.

"It's to stop you from sweating. Why are you all looking at me like that? It's a perfectly ordinary procedure. It stops the muscle from contracting so no sweat is released. I don't really know how it works."

"But whatever for?"

"Well, it's just convenient. And you don't need to go on buying deodorants. I may have broken even on that. Although, of course, it's hardly likely . . . Well, that's it, apart from the breasts and butt. At first I just wanted a boob lift. As nature made me I only took a size D. But then the surgeon and I decided it would be nice if we also put in small implants. Actually, I'm fed up with them now. I'd like to remove them but it turns out my skin is prone to scarring. It's already left some scars and I don't want more surgery."

"How can you tell guys everything is your own if you have scars from the operations?" Diana queried.

"At first I hid the scars with foundation, but it soon wears off. Now I just tell them I've had a lift. If it's not an augmentation that's considered okay."

"Considered by whom?" Anya asked. She had a persistent sense that Maya inhabited a parallel world, but kept forgetting to tell them.

Maya turned to face her and paused. "Well, marks," she said meaningfully, as if that magic word explained everything about her life.

"And what kind of 'marks' come your way?" Katya asked with a show of disinterest.

"Oh, various kinds. Mostly all sorts of businessmen. I did have one politician."

"How do you meet them?"

Maya gave a sigh and smiled, obviously amused by her cellmates' lack of sophistication in needing everything explained to them, but at the same time greatly enjoying her sense of being the most knowledgeable person in the room in these matters.

"I don't allow just any old contact, in a restaurant, say, let alone in the street. Or on Instagram. My directory is swamped with messages like, 'Mayechka, come on vacation with me to Thailand, I'll pay for everything,' but I don't even read them. Usually a guy will see me on a snap or live somewhere. Then he checks me out through friends and asks them to recommend him. Without a recommendation it's no deal. Well, then sometimes a friend will text and say so-and-so would like to meet you, he's a good guy, line of business is such-and-such."

"But, just casually, you absolutely never hook up with someone?" Diana asked, plainly interested. Unlike the others she was taking this conversation seriously.

"I did one time, in Dubai," Maya admitted with a sigh. "There's this huge shopping mall and I was in there choosing a handbag. I was standing in the Gucci store and this guy spotted me. He offered to pay for the handbag. I agreed, and he said, "Well, you'll probably need a pair of shoes to go with the bag." He ended up buying me a whole bunch of stuff, and then invited me to join him for dinner. Well, I agreed. He did, unfortunately, have to fly out the same night, so we parted immediately. It was really quite sad. I liked him."

Katya raised an ironical eyebrow.

"Do random guys in stores often pay for things for you?"

"Oh, no. Someone I haven't met before? That was just the once," Maya said, dismissing the suggestion. "In restaurants people often order things for the waiters to bring us, if I'm there with a girlfriend, for example. But I've already said that's not the way I meet people. Who knows how that kind of thing might end! I prefer respectable people that I know something about."

"It all sounds a bit . . . commercial," Anya remarked cautiously.

Maya shrugged.

"Well, I don't force them to buy me anything, it's just I often get given presents. I like it when a guy isn't stingy. And anyway, how else could they court you and show they like you if they couldn't give presents?"

"Are you seeing somebody at the moment?"

"I don't have a steady boyfriend. It's all a bit of this and a bit of that, nothing serious. I go out on a date now and again. I guess I've got four guys I'm dating right now. I see three more or less regularly, and the other one I've only been out with once so far."

"Do they all know you're seeing other men?" Katya asked.

Maya giggled.

"Well, I don't shout about it, but they all realize that, until we've agreed on something definite, I'm dating. I didn't understand that to begin with. I thought if I went on a date I was immediately under an obligation. When I first moved to Moscow I met a fellow and he invited me to dinner. He was very heavily built and I was really scared. I thought he'd force me to do something, but he turned out to be a complete sweetie. After the restaurant he drove me home, said good-bye and left. I didn't look in my bag until I was back in my apartment, and found a wad of money. He had put fifty thousand rubles in it when I went to the bathroom! I was almost in tears!"

"From sh-shame?" Natasha asked icily.

"No, of course not. From joy! At the time I thought that was an unbelievable amount of money when all I'd done was go out to dinner with him!"

Katya narrowed her eyes and looked at Maya with disdain.

"It's okay by you for a man to slip you cash?" she asked. "Personally, I would find that insulting."

"Well, being given money so discreetly, no, that has never happened again," Maya cheerfully reported. "But that man just felt sorry for me, I think. I was such a wuss back then. It was too awful!"

She laughed but no one laughed with her. She continued, "I went on seeing him for a couple of months, and each time he would give me some little present, an iPhone one time, or earrings. Well, it was just little things for him, I see that now, but at the time I thought they were unbelievably expensive gifts!"

"And was that all just for going out to dinner with him?" Katya, after a moment of silence, prompted her skeptically. Everyone looked expectantly at Maya.

"Oh, no. I slept with him on the second date, of course," she answered unselfconsciously. "Well, what did you think? I was grateful to him!"

A longer, more loaded silence ensued.

"And d-do you sleep with all of them?" Natasha finally asked, scowling.

"No, of course not. I sleep with them if I fancy them. If I don't like a guy, or if I've got something more ambitious in mind for him, then I don't. Nobody forces me to do anything, everything is what I choose."

"So what do you live on?"

Maya drew herself up proudly.

"*This* is what I live on. But I'm very economical and always put something aside. I got enough together over a few years to buy myself an apartment, and a car, and, well, the surgery costs money too."

"How much?" Diana asked, instantly pricking up her ears.

"Oh, well, it's a while since I had some things done, the prices have gone up. But probably a million and a half."

"A million and a half?" Katya squawked. She swung her feet down off the bed and leaned forward, as if seeing Maya for the first time and wanting to get a better look at her. "A million and a half?! How many years did it take you to save that much, if you weren't even working!"

"Well, if every stud who fucked her tossed her a ruble a day, it would soon mount up!" Natasha grunted. She was, however, visibly impressed.

"Oh, but presents are just the icing on the cake," Maya assured them. "My real earnings come from being kept."

Katya looked critically at her a while longer, but then leaned back against the wall as if giving in and asked on behalf of them all, "So what does that consist of?"

"If some mark has really taken a shine to you, and you also like him, you can agree to be kept. That means you'll date him exclusively."

"And what about him?"

"Oh, he just provides for you. He's your sole source of income."

Diana gave a nervous laugh before inquiring, "How much do you ask per month for being kept?"

"Oh, I can't divulge something so personal!" Maya answered with a knowing smile.

"But how much do you think it would be usual to take, so as not to sell yourself cheaply but also not to be brazen?"

"How much would be usual? A million rubles a month. That would be about right."

"How much?" Katya gasped.

"A million a month. Why are you looking at me like that again? Work it out for yourself: a half-decent handbag is a hundred grand, shoes—another hundred grand. And on top of that you need to put something away. You won't be able to find marks to keep you forever. You need to think about the future."

"A million rubles a month . . . Girls, did you hear that? I earn twenty-five thousand!"

Katya was so taken aback she even got out of bed. She looked stunned.

"It can be less," Maya said, trying to calm her down. "Depends on how good you look and how much your mark is in love with you. Oh, and how much he's worth, of course, but I don't waste my time on cheapskates."

The effect was the opposite of what was intended. Katya began nervily pacing around the cell.

"I can't get my head around this. Where do all these people live who are happy, just like that, to shell out a million a month on some floozy?"

Maya took umbrage.

"It's not that simple. And anyway, what's so amazing? It seems perfectly normal to me: you meet a guy, he pays for you. Isn't that what you do yourself? When you go to a restaurant the woman is hardly going to pay, is she! Well, this is just the same thing. The man has to look after you. In any case, investing in a woman is good for their business."

"How so?"

"It's like having an expensive car," Maya said, doing her best to explain. "Or a watch. A guy needs his status to be instantly visible, and nothing shouts it out better than a sumptuous woman by his side. So a real man needs constantly to invest in his girlfriend if she isn't to make him look small!"

Katya stopped pacing and just stared at Maya, speechless. Diana, clasping her pillow, said in an awed tone, "Invest?"

Anya was not sure what had most confounded Diana: the meaning of what Maya had said or the financially savvy way she had said it, but at just this moment the young moon-faced policeman arrived again and the conversation ended.

"Which of you is Andersen?" he asked.

"I am!" Maya said, a note of joy in her voice.

"Your sister's here. Follow me."

Maya squealed with delight and teetered out of the cell.

"Well, how d'you like that . . . ?" Katya said, staring at the closed door. "A million rubles a month! I feel like at some point in my life I must have taken a wrong turn."

"What really pisses me off is that she believes a woman is just a sex object!" Diana weighed in.

"H-handbags, sh-shoes, rh-rhinoplasty . . . pah!" Natasha growled, climbing up from Ira's bottom bunk to her own. "Enough of you and your conversations, I'm going to sleep."

"I need a drink," Katya said. "Pity we only have tea. Anyone else want some?"

Anya came over and held out her glass.

"Hey, what are those marks on your arms?" Katya asked, looking at her wrists in surprise.

Anya felt a familiar urge to pull down nonexistent sleeves.

"Nothing. I'm just prone to scarring too," she joked, hastily putting the glass down on the locker so she could hide her arms behind her back. Katya went on peering at her suspiciously.

"What, have you attempted suicide? What a lot of fucked-up people we've got in this cell!"

"I'm not suicidal," Anya snapped back. Diana looked up from her bunk.

"What's up with her arms?" she asked inquisitively.

"She's got scars! Show us them!"

"Back off, will you! There's nothing to see. I was in a road accident and got cut by the windshield glass."

Katya, still studying her dubiously, poured the hot water into her cup.

"What a cell we've got here," she said to no one in particular. "Everyone is so . . . special!"

She and Diana hooted with laughter.

"Let me s-sleep, will you!" Natasha shouted at them from under her pillow.

Everybody gradually calmed down and stopped talking—one person asleep, someone else reading. Anya pulled the blanket over her head, letting just a chink of light get in, and pretended to be dozing. In fact, lying under the heavy cover in semidarkness, she was running her fingers down her arms from elbow to wrist and back. They glided smoothly over the clear skin but snagged on the scars. Those scars dated back more than ten years and Anya knew them by heart, but they still freaked her out with a mixture of fear, self-pity, and revulsion.

* * *

She had planned the slitting of her veins in detail, thinking it over for weeks and meticulously choosing the instrument. It was fairly obviously she would be needing a blade, but where you got one she had no clue. Would you take one out of a safety razor? Use the blade of a box cutter? That struck her as disproportionate in terms of the wound it might inflict. An ordinary knife hardly seemed suitable either. She carefully inspected all the kitchen knives in the house, but they did not seem sharp enough to make a thin, deep cut in her skin. Actually, there was one she could have used, but it was so large Anya was afraid she might end up amputating her hand. Having considered the available options, she became irritable. Cutting her veins had seemed so elementary she had given no thought to the technicalities, but now the whole thing seemed much less straightforward than she had expected.

Anya had gone back home on her first university vacation. It was February and her hometown in the south of Russia was cheerless and slushy. The apartment that she had grown up in seemed impossibly small, almost toylike. As a child she had supposed she was living in an enormous space with impossibly high ceilings, looming bookshelves, and pictures hung well out of reach. When she entered it for the first time since leaving for Moscow, it was as if she had stepped into a doll's house. As she wandered through the rooms she felt like Gulliver. The doorframes seemed so low she felt she should lower her head to walk through them. All shelves were now within easy reach and the pictures were hung at eye level.

Actually, it was not only the apartment, but the town itself seemed to have shrunk. When she was little Anya had felt that all the distances between places were enormous, but now everything was within a stone's throw. The streets were deserted, the buildings few and far between. Hanging out in the town was boring because she no longer had any friends there, so for days on end she did little more than sit at home and read, only occasionally going into town with her mother for one thing or another. Loneliness had a cleansing effect. Her head gradually cleared itself of all the extraneous noise and the associations with everyone she had left behind in Moscow. As her other preoccupations receded, however, one became dominant: where to obtain the blade.

The answer presented itself to her. One evening she and her mother were returning from shopping and stopped at a kiosk in an underground passageway to buy batteries. There were all sorts of things for sale and Anya suddenly spotted a small box of razor blades in the window. It was so neat and miniature and black that she felt her blood run cold. It was what she was looking for.

She could hardly buy the blades with her mother standing beside her, and for the next two days her thoughts were constantly returning to that kiosk. The place seemed highlighted in her mind, with the rest of the town grayed out. There was a problem, in that throughout the vacation Anya had been greatly averse to leaving the house at all. She had no one to hang out with, the weather was dismal, and she had no reason to go out. It was not easy to come up with a plausible reason for wanting to go into town on her own. At the same time, Anya's heart yearned to take possession of that little black box. There were obviously other underground passageways with similar kiosks and identical boxes closer to home, but for some reason Anya only hankered after that one.

She finally made her mind up, literally begging her mother to give her an errand to run in the town, and set off to bring home the blades. The kiosk was open, the box was in the window. Her face red, not looking the vendor in the eye, she poked a finger at it. When the box was finally in her hand, Anya was so pleased she could not wait to get back home. She felt her intentions must be written all over her face. She put the box in her pocket and did not touch it either on the bus or for the rest of the day at home. The moment she would first open the box seemed so personal that it was impossible to risk anyone else witnessing it. Only late at night, when her mother had gone to bed, did Anya bring it out. It contained five very thin, silvery blades, each wrapped in translucent paper. A single glance was enough for her to see how sharp they were. Holding her breath, Anya unwrapped them one by one, like presents, examined them and put them back. This was not yet their time. She hid them in her backpack and fell asleep with a sense of excited anticipation.

Quite when the idea of slashing her wrists first entered Anya's head she could not remember, but she did know exactly where it had come from. Almost a year ago, before she went to university and was still living at home and attending the English course, Zhenya was driving her home as usual. She was talking about an earlier unrequited love—Anya was tremulously hanging on every word, comparing it with the love she herself felt for Zhenya. No matter what she was talking about, whether it was something monstrous, comical, or deeply felt, Zhenya's tone was unemotional. On that occasion she had said, "I realized I was so fixated on this other person that I needed something bad to happen to me. For instance, to fall really ill. Then I would be able to start thinking about myself again."

Anya was baffled. She had no experience of being fixated on another person and could not imagine how anyone might wish to harm themselves. She simply could not see how it might be possible to be so crushed by an emotion that you would want to terminate it at any cost. Her own emotional burden was no longer grinding her down. That trip to the cemetery had altered something in her. Having endured the feeling of intense self-loathing, Anya had developed an immunity to it. She felt she had accomplished an agonizing hike up a huge mountain and was now speeding downhill, footloose, carefree. From that moment on, everything was as it should be: she herself was normal, if a bit unusual; her love for Zhenya was natural, if unrequited.

It was the first time in her life Anya had felt she was walking on air and she could not imagine how anyone could choose to reject that feeling voluntarily.

Zhenya, though, was unfathomable and Anya had long ago given up any attempt to think critically about things she said. She decided to regard them as incontrovertible truths she did not need to comprehend, only to memorize.

Within a few months she left for Moscow, happy and full of hope. She had a life of her own to look forward to, and pictured it as an endless celebration and adventure. Her feelings for Zhenya had in the meantime somehow leveled out or, more exactly, become internalized and devoid of the features characteristic of love. Anya was not feeling jealousy, yearning, mood swings, or indeed any obligation to be faithful. She felt a constant, unrebellious warmth welling within her and it seemed that this love was now her best quality, an indestructible moral core around which her personality was being built.

In Moscow Anya instantly found herself in a new reality that had nothing in common with the measured life she had been accustomed to in her hometown. It was not that everything immediately went pear-shaped, but the speed with which she was bombarded by new experiences gave her no time to catch her breath.

She found she was ill-adapted to living a life of her own. It was not that she did not know how to do everyday things, but rather that life as an adult consisted of a million overlapping and contradictory relations which she simply did not know how to manage. Back home Anya had always been on her own. Her mother was never far away, and there were a couple of girls she was friendly with, and classmates she saw for several hours every day. But there she was not truly close with anyone.

In order to defend herself from this reality Anya began to think that everything she had left behind at home was good and proper, including her, while everything that comprised her life in Moscow seemed stressful, confused, and unmanageable. To top it all, Zhenya wrote to say she would shortly be getting married.

For Anya this was a bombshell. The jealousy she had all but forgotten flared up again. It was all the more agonizing because she thought she had left Zhenya behind, having fallen for a boy in her year. All these contradictory feelings seemed to be pulling in different directions and her sense of identity was becoming blurred. She needed urgently to concentrate and get herself back in focus.

Anya recalled what Zhenya had said and seemed to have found the solution: she needed a personal mishap in order to restore a sense of her own significance. She was reluctant to leave it passively to fate to come up with the goods because, in the first place, fate might dither, and in the second, it might overdo the mishap. What Anya needed was a proportionate, controlled misfortune. Upon reflection, she decided that slitting her wrists would be the most satisfactory option. It would hurt, it would be scary, and there would be blood—but that would make it an ideal springboard to break free from her surfeit of worries and finally give her the presence to focus on herself. She had not the least intention of actually committing suicide, and even checked on the internet that the least dangerous cuts would be from left to right rather than down her arm. Anya wanted to harm herself tangibly, but not irreparably.

The idea finally took shape just before she was due to go home for the vacation, so its execution had to be postponed. Presenting herself to her mother with bandaged wrists would be far more self-destructive than merely slitting her veins.

Now in possession of the blades, Anya began counting the days to her journey. She would periodically inspect the backpack to be sure the precious box was still there. Thinking about what she was planning both scared and energized her, meaning that beneficial effects were soon apparent. Before long all her attention was focused on what she was sensing and experiencing.

After saying goodbye to her mother and boarding the train, Anya felt she could wait no longer. She would arrive in Moscow only at noon the following day, which seemed infinitely far in the future. There was another consideration: she felt that if she arrived at the dormitory, locked herself in her room, and started hacking at her wrists it would seem too obviously attention-seeking. It would look as if she wanted to be seen doing it and rescued. The reality was that Anya felt no need at all for an audience. Slitting her wrists was a procedure she had to undergo, one that would best be done in private.

The train started moving. There was the usual commotion in the reserved-seat car, with people shoving bags under beds, changing their clothes, pulling down mattresses. All this business was so much at odds with Anya's own meditative serenity that she imagined she must be all but invisible to others. The conductress passed through, checking tickets and issuing bed linens. Anya made up her bed, anticipating that later she wouldn't be up to it. She waited for the hubbub to subside and then, clutching the box of blades, slipped along to the toilet.

The train creaked and swayed, occasionally clattering over joints in the rails. Anya had always believed the swaying was more pronounced in the toilet than elsewhere in the car. The toilet pedal was broken, the drain hole did not close properly, and an icy draft was coming up from it. She rolled up her left sleeve. The train clattered and jerked and she fell back against the door. She stayed like that, her back pressed against it for balance. The train rattled on, speeding through the darkness. Without waiting any longer, Anya drew the blade across her wrist. Nothing. It had passed a millimeter above the skin. She tried again: still nothing. Instinct was preventing her from hurting herself. The anticipation of pain rose to new heights. In a rage she slashed at her wrist with the blade as hard as she could. Her arm was instantly burning. She watched in slow motion as the skin parted, layering back, the cut filling with blood. It was in reality a very minor injury but it goaded Anya on and she stabbed at her wrist several times more, forcing the blade in deeper and deeper.

The train jerked again and Anya dropped the blade. She felt suddenly feverish, her cheeks and brow flushed. Blood was dripping onto the floor, her arm was on fire with pain, and she suddenly felt very sorry for herself. Holding her wounded wrist in midair, with the other hand she picked the blade up and rinsed it, staggering either because of the motion of the train or from a sudden tiredness. Anya tore off some toilet paper and blotted the blood. The bleeding did not stop. She tore off more paper and soaked it with water. Gritting her teeth, she wiped the wound. Blood instantly refilled the cuts and flowed over her wrist.

She was suddenly very frightened. Had she overdone it? What if she could not stop the bleeding? The thought that she might need medical help, might have to tell someone what she had done, horrified her. She frantically ripped off more toilet paper and pressed it to her arm, hoping to staunch the bleeding, and at that moment someone rapped on the door. She again felt hot, her rushing only making the panic worse. She had used up almost the entire drum of toilet paper and could see no improvement. Someone was now banging on the door. She gave up, wound paper around and around her arm and pulled the sleeve of her sweater down as far as she could. Staggering, Anya opened the door. "About time too!" a man yelled. He all but pushed her aside and rushed into the toilet.

Holding the wounded arm out in front of her, Anya reached her berth and lay down, enveloping herself in the sheet. Her arm was burning all the way from her elbow to her hand. She peeped furtively into her sleeve and was relieved to see no blood showing through the paper yet, which might mean the bleeding was stopping. Rolling up into a ball, cradling her hurt arm, Anya felt she must be the loneliest, unhappiest person on earth.

In the morning she realized she would have to remove her improvised bandage, and that getting it off was going to hurt. Still, that seemed a minor problem compared with yesterday's terrors. She was alive and feeling okay. Indeed, in the light of day her course of action seemed embarrassing and ridiculous.

Anya went back to the toilet and began unwinding the paper. Her arm, which had stopped hurting during the night, was immediately on fire again. She was bathed in sweat as she pulled away the last layers, but managed to finish the job. Her arm didn't look good. The cuts began bleeding and the skin around them was red and swollen. She felt tearful and full of self-pity but resolved to steel herself, pulled down her sleeve (the sweater felt like sandpaper on her skin), and went to get a glass of tea.

The morning was so clean and fresh that Anya gradually relaxed. Through the window frost-covered trees and houses scattered over the hillside flashed by, the snow glistened in the sun, and in a nearby berth a sweet child was playing with a toy car. A teaspoon tinkled merrily in the tea glass holder. Anya felt a rising sense of anticipation about her arrival in Moscow. She was constantly checking how she felt against what she had planned: had she succeeded in moving her attention away from burdensome preoccupations to focus on herself? Was Zhenya's prescription working? She could not be sure, but her sense of elation bathed reality in a radiant light. Everything in the future promised to be pure and wonderful. In a more ordinary moment, Anya would doubtless have detected something unnatural in such an exalted mood, but for the present she did not doubt she was benefiting from the violent therapy.

Within the first few hours of her return to the dormitory she was caught by the janitor smoking in a prohibited place, quarreled with the classmate she was in love with, learned to her displeasure that Sonya would be returning from home several days late, and got drunk in the company of some older students she barely knew and did not much care for. Anya's resolution to get a grip on her life soon foundered in the chaos and disorder.

Fleeing from the older students, Anya sat alone in the smoking area gloomily swigging wine from a bottle. There was no prospect that the future could be pure and wonderful because she herself was worthless and corrupt. With exquisite cruelty she formulated charges against herself. The next time she reached for the cigarette lighter, she felt the box of razor blades still in her pocket. Without more ado, Anya quickly took one out and slashed her good wrist again and again. This time she had no complicated justifications in her head, she just wanted to cause herself pain, to hurt herself till she saw stars in her eyes, to drive a tank through the wall of loathing she felt for herself. Blood dripped on the tiled floor but Anya did nothing about it. She sat there on the sill, slumped against the side of the window with her hand hanging down. This time she really did want someone to find her in this state, preferably someone she knew, ideally the classmate she fancied.

Needless to say, nobody did. Her back went numb, the bleeding stopped, Anya got off the windowsill and staggered back to her room.

The next day, she woke up with a hangover but a very sober mind. Both arms were aching terribly, but Anya was suddenly tired of feeling sorry for herself. She went to the pharmacy, bought some hydrogen peroxide, and disinfected the cuts. She threw the razor blades in a trash can on the street, tidied up the room, put on all her warm clothes and aired it for an hour to clear the smell of tobacco. To smoke, she went outside rather than to the illicit smoking area on the stairs.

As she stood out on the porch taking a drag on her cigarette, Anya reflected that she would inevitably be left with scars. Even ordinary bruises took an age to disappear on her, and cuts like these had no chance. She did not feel guilty or sentimental about that. The past night had unexpectedly put an end to the sense of portentousness Anya had been trying to instill into what had happened. Her cuts were just cuts and Anya knew she would attach no importance to them once they stopped smarting.

The years that followed were to show she was being overly optimistic about that. She did worry what people might think when they saw her scars, and very soon learned to conceal them. This was not too difficult, given that many people were so unobservant and self-obsessed that they quite failed to notice such matters. Even so, there were awkward moments. For example, in the subway in summer holding the handrail in a crowded car it was impossible to hide your arm, or at a medical appointment. A couple of times there had been incidents, like today. Sometimes other people saw things.

The cell door rattled and opened and Maya came in. No one paid her any attention at first, but then she sniffled loudly.

"Are you crying?" Diana asked, putting down her magazine.

Anya extricated herself from beneath the blanket and took a closer look at Maya, who was red and tear-stained. Instead of answering, she sobbed.

"What's up?" Katya asked, seating herself on the bunk.

"I want to go ho-ome!" Maya wailed in floods of tears. She stood in that state in the middle of the cell, clutching a white plastic bag.

"Where were you taken? What's happened?"

"My sister came to see me-e," she whimpered, sobbing even more.

Natasha growled, turned over in her bunk, and pulled the pillow back over her head.

"We know—and you'll be home the day after tomorrow," Katya said, bewildered. "What did your sister tell you? Didn't she just come to see how you were?"

"Ye-es . . ." Maya, gulped, wiping her eyes with her fist. "She brought me some apples . . ."

"Oh, apples!" Ira reacted, beaming and instantly forgetting her drawing.

"And she also brought cigarettes for you . . . I asked her to."

This news stirred everyone into life. Even Natasha emerged from her pillow and gave Maya a grumpy but warmer look.

Maya gave Anya an apple, washed one for herself, and bit sadly into it. The rest lit up cigarettes.

"Smile!" Ira said to Maya, demonstrating how it was done. Maya took a long look at her toothless grin and burst into tears again.

"Well, what is your p-problem?" Natasha demanded indignantly.

"I'm pregnant!"

Anya rolled her eyes.

"What? What?" everyone was asking at once.

In response Maya only wept the more bitterly.

"You silly fuck! Do you at least know who the father is?" Katya inquired.

"Yes . . ."

Diana elegantly sent out a stream of smoke and remarked, "It's against the law for them to send you here if you're pregnant."

This news amazed Maya, who perked up immediately and stared around at her cellmates. Her tears were dry in an instant and she looked as if she'd just had a great idea. "What, seriously?"

"But to prove it, you need to have a certificate, and you don't have one," Anya pointed out. Maya wilted.

"Of course, I may not be pregnant," she said pensively. "It's just that I have a really good feel for that sort of thing. Back when we were still living in Izhevsk my sister so wanted to get pregnant by this guy. She hoped then he would marry her. Every month she was sure that this time she'd managed it, but I kept telling her no, no, it's too early to say. And every time it turned out I was right. She even took offense and said I had jinxed her. So then I took offense. I pulled out one of her hairs, tied a knot in it, and said, 'Look, now I'll jinx you the other way and you'll get pregnant!' And what do you think? She did get pregnant almost immediately."

"And then what? Did they get married?" Diana asked skeptically, while at the same time contriving to blow her cigarette smoke downwards.

"No, of course not. They split up when she was in the sixth month of pregnancy. He supported her for a while but then dumped her."

"I told you—all men are animals!" Katya said gleefully, her point made.

They were taken for exercise an hour later. Finding herself once more in the grim, claustrophobic courtyard, Anya inspected it more closely for recreational potential, but found nothing new. Her fellow inmates were squeezed together on the bench and again, as one, had lit up cigarettes. The availability of cigarettes seemed to confer immunity to boredom and Anya regretted having quit smoking long ago. To suffer without tobacco in a special detention center would, of course, be unbearable, but to be reunited with it once more would be a joy beyond compare.

Having stood around for a while, Anya considered the possibility of doing some exercise. To be stuck in the same place for three days was proving more of an imposition than she had imagined. The hot, sultry courtyard was the least inviting imaginable venue for sporting activity, but it was more or less categorized as outdoors, so exercising there should not be regarded as abnormal. Anya had only to imagine, however, how many male spectators she would attract for her positive thinking to evaporate.

To get a modicum of exercise, she decided she would at least walk from one end of the courtyard to the other (length being the place's only merit), but quickly discovered that even something as unprovocative as walking excited the interest of the male prisoners. She eventually concluded that taking exercise was even worse than being locked in the cell. The only unembarrassing thing for the women to do in the yard was to stand beneath their own windows and, to the best of their ability, not move.

They were finally rescued from the exercise period by the vixen. Letting them back into the detention center, she asked, "Anyone want a shower?" They all yelled affirmatively, and she added, "Only you'll have to take it in turn. One cubicle isn't working."

As soon as they got back to the cell everybody fussed about, tucking towels, shampoo, and a change of clothing under their arms. Anya reflected that at any other time the tiny waffle-weave square she had been issued along with her bed linen, the spare shirt smelling of cigarette smoke, and the piece of soap would have seemed a dubious blessing, but by this time she had been thoroughly cured of snobbery. Of all her cellmates, only Maya was determined not to settle for half measures and wait, as she had said she would, until she got back home. She sat down in her bunk, adopted her martyred expression, and opened her book.

When they had collected their stuff, the girls crowded around the locked door and Katya knocked on it loudly. The vixen opened it instantly and, looking them over, ordered, "Four of you go first."

"Me, me, me," Anya's cellmates yelled, rushing out into the corridor while she dithered in the cell.

"Your turn when they're done," the policewoman announced and shut the door.

Anya sighed and returned to her bunk. Her shower might have been delayed but that had the advantage that she would go in alone. She stretched out on her bunk, waiting for her cellmates to come back. She listened for sounds in the corridor but the women did not return. Time, which had not exactly been flying by, was now creeping at a snail's pace. Tired of lying on her bed, she got up and went to the sink to wash. Wonderfully warm water gushed from the tap and Anya stood there for a while, wriggling her fingers under the jet and thinking that she would soon at last be in the shower. She scooped up some water, washed her face, and looked blinking into the reflective foil above the sink.

Maya was standing about a meter behind her. At first Anya could see only her face, unnaturally white, the eyes closed. She stared at it and didn't feel any fear at first. She looked at Maya, waiting for her to open her eyes and say something but the seconds passed and nothing changed. Anya's gaze slipped down from Maya's face and in the mirror she could see her whole body. She felt a chill run down her spine.

Maya was standing upright, as still as a statue. Her arms were bent at the elbow, her hands turned upwards, but her fingers were moving. She seemed to be groping for something invisible, but for all the smoothness of the movements there was nothing graceful about them. She appeared to be measuring something, rummaging in a void, her fingers flexing in an uncanny, unhuman manner. Black hair was flowing down over Maya's shoulders and breasts and being braided by her unseeing, fumbling fingers as it slipped through them. The way her hands moved was both repellent and hypnotic. Anya shuddered, revolted but continuing to watch, unable to blink or look away.

But then, overcoming huge resistance, she did tear her eyes away and saw that Maya's hair was literally flowing. It was enveloping Maya's body in an impenetrable black cocoon, leaving only the snow-white triangle of her face. It was streaming down to the floor and spreading like a lake beneath her feet. Slow and viscous it was seeping out in all directions. Anya could not breathe from the horror. Everything comprising Maya seemed to have a separate existence: her face was placid and smooth, like a mask. At the same time her fingers kept on moving, while her hair flowed down and spread across the floor. Anya realized that at any moment this heavy blackness would reach her feet. That anticipation was so intolerable that everything went dark in her eyes. She spun around, almost blinded by fear and longing for this all to be over, no matter how.

There was no one behind her. Maya was sitting in her bunk, engrossed in her book. Sunlight was streaming into the cell and everything was as calm and peaceful as the morning after a storm.

Anya clutched the edge of the washbasin in order not to fall. She thought she was going to faint. Maya looked up and Anya watched in a detached way as the horror in her own face communicated itself to Maya.

"What is it, Anya? Are you feeling unwell? Can I help you?"

Maya rushed across and helped her back to her bunk.

"I am losing my mind," Anya thought looking down at Maya's hand in hers. The fingers were just fingers.

"Did you come up and stand behind me just now?" she asked, surprised at how far away her voice sounded.

"What? When?"

"Right now, while I was standing at the washbasin. Did you come up to me?"

Maya looked at her, worried.

"What are you talking about, Anya? I was sitting here on my bunk. You were standing at the sink for just a couple of seconds and suddenly almost collapsed. Did something happen?"

"I felt dizzy."

"And why are you asking if I came up to you? Did you imagine something?"

Anya shook her head.

"Perhaps we should call the doctor?" Maya suggested. She was still holding Anya's hand and looked frightened.

"No, no, I'm feeling better already. I just had a bad turn. I'll sit down for a moment and it will be fine."

"Would you like some tea, perhaps? Or water?"

"Everything is fine. I just need to sit for a moment."

Not wholly convinced, Maya moved back to her bunk, but Anya was aware that she was still worried as she kept glancing up at her from her book.

Something's happened to me, Anya thought. Two nightmarish visions in two days, one of which she had seen while fully awake, was not a coincidence. She never experienced this sort of thing, she was a down-to-earth person—no hallucinations, no mystical epiphanies or ghostly sightings of the kind children love to hear about at bedtime. The idea that someone might not be able to tell the difference between dreaming and waking life was something she had only ever read about, and had never believed was really true. The fact that in two days she appeared to have seen so much that was strange was more alarming than what she had seen, because it seemed to indicate that she was no longer in her right mind.

Anya cast a furtive glance at Maya. As with Ira, there was not the least suggestion of the supernatural about her. Indeed everything around her seemed almost unbelievably ordinary: the bed frames gleaming in the sun, the crumpled packet of candies on the locker, the felt-tip pens scattered over Diana's bed. Anya could only wonder how this gray soulless place, which seemed designed to preclude any sort of mystery, could be causing her to see visions.

Her heart gradually stopped pounding and she took a deep breath. Almost immediately she felt a sense of shame. She pictured herself going off to take her shower and Maya telling her cellmates how she had almost fainted. That, however, was not her worst fear: the main thing was that no one should know what had been going on at that moment in her head.

Her cellmates returned from their showers, refreshed and jubilant. Even Natasha was smiling and seemed to have made peace with life.

"You next?" the vixen asked Anya.

"Absolutely!" she said, getting up. She wanted as quickly as possible to wash away whatever had happened.

"And you?"

Maya, looking put out, shook her head.

The shower was immediately opposite their door. Entry was impeded by a grating not unusual in this place, beyond which a small anteroom could be seen. A more substantial door led on to a larger changing room. After letting Anya in, the vixen closed the grating and said through it, "Call me when you're finished and I'll let you out."

Anya closed the heavier door behind her and gave a deep sigh. It struck her that for the first time in two days she was entirely alone. She sat down on a bench and buried her head in her knees. It was curious that she had really not found it any great hardship to be sharing a room with her cellmates, yet only now, sitting silently and in solitude behind multiple doors, did she for the first time feel able to relax.

The shower room was badly lit and cold, but improbably clean. The wall tiles had a bluish tinge, and newly installed taps gleamed chillingly. Through a small, half-open window Anya could hear sounds from the street. She peeped out. This side of the building was not visible either from her cell or from the canteen. The perimeter fence was just a few meters away and the entire space between it and the wall of the detention center was overgrown with tall weeds. Immediately beyond the fence were tracks along which the clattering trams ran. She could see only their antennae sticking up above the fence. Outside, the sun was blazing, the birds were singing, children were shouting, and it seemed extraordinary that such a wholehearted, dazzling Moscow summer should be in full swing outside, while she was cooped up in this tiled container.

The hot water, however, soon raised her despondent spirits. Anya wanted to wash herself clean enough for the effect to last through the week ahead. The shower was like a magical blessing. Suddenly her anxieties did seem insubstantial. She felt she was now so clean and recharged that none of that schizophrenic lunacy would be able to trouble her again.

Right through until evening Anya was feeling contented. For the first time, the food for dinner seemed only averagely salty, the songs on the radio almost worth listening to, and the cigarette smoke no longer so annoying. Katya, as promised yesterday, was passed another two packs of cigarettes, so now everyone was more or less chain-smoking and Anya found she could put up with that. Her cellmates, their hair disheveled after the shower, looked almost comical and the atmosphere in the cell was so friendly it was as if they were all there at a slumber party of their own free will.

After dinner Anya readily drank a glass of tea and ate a chocolate candy, laughed loudly, and even played Crocodile with the rest of them. All the bad things she had imagined were behind her, back in a time when she had been too highly strung and emotionally exhausted. Anya felt an extraordinary surge of strength and her stay in the special detention center began to seem more like an adventure. She pictured herself emerging, being met by her friends outside. They would drink wine and she would tell them all about these ten days, while her friends gasped with admiration.

Just before going to bed Anya recalled her home in detail and imagined what she would do first when she was back there, where she would go then, and whom she would text. It was so exciting and delightful that she fell asleep feeling tranquil and, despite everything, perfectly happy.

DAY FOUR

Anya slept a deep, even sleep all night. Nothing disturbed her. Her cellmates did not make a lot of noise, by now she was used to the bunk, and she had no more nightmares. Towards daybreak it suddenly got colder and, half-asleep, she snuggled deeper into the blanket. She even dreamed she got out of bed, took a second blanket off the upper bunk, and covered herself with it. In reality, though, she just lay in bed, feeling cold.

When Anya woke up, the day had already begun. She did not hear the call for breakfast, nor Natasha and Ira leaving and coming back. Poking her nose out from under the covers, she found everyone except Diana was already up. Cold, damp air was coming in through the open window.

"Good morning," Anya said in a hoarse, sleepy voice, and sat up in her bunk. The blanket slipped off her shoulders and she quickly drew it back up. "Can we close the window?"

"I'll finish my smoke and then we can shut it," Katya said. She was sitting cross-legged on her bunk wearing a warm top buttoned up to the neck, smoking, and dropping the ash into a plastic cup with water in the bottom of it.

"Some summer we're having this year," said Maya. Like Anya she was swaddled in a blanket, with only her head and a hand holding an open book poking out.

Ira and Natasha, on the other hand, seemed not to be bothered by the cold. They were both sitting on the lower bunk. Ira, as usual, was firmly packaged in denim, and was drawing on what remained of Anya's paper. Natasha, her bare, bony shoulders gleaming, seemed to be weaving something. Anya could see what looked like white tape in her hands.

"Aren't you cold?" Anya asked tentatively, shivering at the very sight of her.

"Yup," Natasha replied, concentrating on what she was doing. "But if we c-close the windows completely w-we'll suffocate in the smoke. It's better this way."

"What are you doing?" Anya asked again, watching her hands moving.

"B-braiding string."

"What for?"

"That f-fool wrecked our b-bottle," Natasha said, nodding in the direction of Ira.

"You're the fool," Ira snapped, getting on with her drawing.

Anya concluded she had not yet been given her Lyrica today.

"Your bottle was crap anyway," Katya observed lazily, dropping a cigarette stub into the cup.

Putting her ashtray on the windowsill, she pulled the window so it was only open a crack. Anya noted sadly that the cell got no warmer.

"If she'd carried it properly the handle wouldn't have broken off," Natasha continued.

"What are you making the string from?" Anya recalled the prohibition on bringing into the cell anything bearing the least resemblance to a rope.

"From the bed linen they gave us."

"It's from our ball. You know, the bag we use to play Bruiser with. We stuffed it with bedclothes from here, these rags," Katya explained. "And now our Natasha is braiding string out of it. People come out of prison a bit cuckoo. You learned this in the camps, right?"

"Yes, but there it's for the prison post," Natasha explained. "String always comes in handy."

"What's it made from there, if you're not allowed to bring anything in?"

"You unpick clothes. S-socks, for instance."

"Whatever for?" Maya asked in amazement. She welcomed any conversation that could distract her from her book.

"It's how you p-pass stuff. Through a h-hole in the wall, say. Or through the shithouse."

"Through the what?"

"The shithouse. In one hut they throw whatever is needed into the hole and flush it on its way, and another hut f-fishes it out."

Maya's eyes were as round as saucers. Anya felt an urge to give her a reassuring pat on the shoulder.

"There, it's done!" Natasha said, satisfied, holding her handiwork up for all to admire.

They saw she had been weaving a kind of string bag out of her braids and placed the plastic bottle inside.

"Totally amazing!" Katya said with a snigger.

"At least now it will be easier to c-carry," Natasha replied benignly, not reacting to the sarcasm. With great care, she placed the bottle on the floor by her bunk. There came a pattering from outside, like gravel being scattered. Everybody turned to look at the window. Heavy raindrops were falling on the plastic roof of the inner courtyard. Maya, still looking dumbfounded, pulled the blanket around herself more tightly.

Natasha lit a cigarette, casually leaning her elbows on the headboard—Anya shivered at the thought of her bare skin touching the metal bars—and said, "In our camp, if you were sent to the p-punishment cell where it was cold, some of them warmed themselves with newspapers."

"They what?" Katya asked, puzzled, and also lit up. To Anya's great regret, she threw the window wide open again. "How do you mean?"

"They covered themselves with newspapers. Heats you up straight away. I d-don't know how."

"But why didn't you cover yourself with a blanket?" Maya asked, her voice a mixture of sympathy and wariness. By now she no longer expected to learn anything comforting from Natasha's tales.

"Because there are none. It's a punishment cell. There's nothing there at all. They even fasten the b-bunk to the wall early in the morning so you can't lie down during the day. They only bring newspapers. If you order them."

"How frightful! And were you sent to a cell like that?"

"I wasn't, but people who were told me. It's just a god-awful place to be—cold in the winter, and so hot in summer you would want to hang yourself."

For a moment there was silence. Maya's expression suddenly changed, as it tended to when a thought occurred to her, and she blurted out, "Is there a punishment cell here too?"

"Of course there is," Katya said solemnly. "You get put in there if you ask stupid questions."

"Is that really true? But there are no newspapers here!"

"Never mind, it's not winter," Anya reassured her.

"There is no p-punishment cell here, for heaven's sake," Natasha responded, dropping a stub into a plastic cup beside her. "That's the last thing we need."

Maya put her book aside, drew the blanket around herself even more tightly and complained, "We are talking about such strange things. If someone had told me a week ago I would be talking about things like this I would never have believed them!"

Katya laughed unkindly.

"What of it? When you get out of here you'll know something new. You'll be able to brag to your gentlemen friends about the five days you spent in the slammer!"

"What are you thinking! I shall never tell anyone I was here! When I get out I'll forget it like a dreadful dream."

"What about you, Natasha? Will you tell anyone?" Katya inquired.

Natasha shrugged her bony shoulders and answered reluctantly, "Wh-why would I?"

"Well, what does it matter to you? You've already been in a prison camp!"

"So? It's nobody's business where I've been locked up."

"What about you, Ira, will you tell people about it?"

"Nobody's going to ask me," she muttered.

"And what about you?" Katya asked, fixing her scornful gaze on Anya.

"Oh yes!" Anya said. "I shall be telling everyone!"

They all turned to stare at her.

"Whatever for?!" Maya asked in amazement. "I can't imagine why you would want to talk about it."

"Because I didn't do anything wrong. Quite the contrary. I went to a protest demonstration, and for that they sent me to a detention center. In my opinion that is exactly what we need to be talking about openly, so everybody knows what the situation is."

"Oh yes, you're our political prisoner," Katya grunted and stretched herself like a cat. "Special, not like the rest of us."

Anya did not yet sense a threat in her tone of voice, only the promise of one, but she braced herself.

"And are you yourself going to be talking about it?" she asked.

"Me? No, of course not. Do you take me for a fool?"

"What will you tell them where you work?" Maya inquired.

"I'll say I was out sick."

"It's lucky I don't have to work," Maya said with a sigh. "I'll just tell everyone I flew off for a holiday and turned my phone off so as not to be disturbed."

There was a pause. Katya had lost interest in this conversation and was looking around the room in search of some new distraction. Unable to think of anything better, she hung down, looked at the sleeping Diana, and gave the bed a shake.

"How much longer are you going to be sleeping in, madam?"

"Leave me alone," Diana murmured grumpily, without opening her eyes.

"Everyone is up already. They'll be around for the inspection soon. Oh, sounds like they're here already!"

The door opened and several people came into the cell. It was the same shift that had admitted Anya to the detention center. She immediately recognized the self-important, fat-cheeked duty cop who had listed her valuables. He was accompanied by the blonde who had taken her fingerprints, and another woman Anya had not seen before but who certainly set her imagination racing.

In their cell, which had until that moment seemed even more gloomy than usual because of the overcast sky outside the window, this woman was dazzling. She was wearing a yellow blouse, a tight-fitting black skirt, and violet slingbacks with stiletto heels. Blonde hair cascaded to her shoulders in gentle waves and she exuded a heavenly fragrance of flowers and purity. She was clearly a creature from a different world, where people could take a shower whenever they felt like it, where people used washing machines, put on makeup, and did not smoke.

While the fat-cheeked policeman was taking the roll call, the woman examined the prisoners with discreet benevolence. She was clearly unfazed by her environment, although Anya felt that ladies of such quality should faint at the very mention of prison. With the roll call completed, the woman looked at them all warmly and asked, "Do you have any complaints about your conditions?"

Everybody grimly shook their heads, and Anya realized to her surprise that her cellmates had no interest at all in their exquisite, scented guest.

Suddenly Maya spoke up.

"I have a complaint."

The woman gave her an encouraging smile: "You have my full attention."

"I want to complain that I am being detained here illegally," Maya said, her voice serious.

The woman seemed a little surprised. Barely perceptibly she raised a graceful eyebrow and sought clarification: "Illegally in what sense? Do you find yourself here without an order of the court?"

"There was a trial but I should never have been arrested in the first place."

"And what were you arrested for?"

"For driving without a license. But I had a license."

The fat-faced cop took a step forward, clearly eager to intervene, but the woman made a slight movement with her head towards him. This seemed to deflate the man, who stepped back. She paused, and then asked, "Did you show it to the police officers when they detained you?"

"Yes I did!"

"Then on what grounds were you detained?"

"Illegally! They said my license had been canceled."

"But if your license had been canceled that would mean you did not have one."

"I did! And what's more it was canceled illegally."

"Why?"

"It was an insurance scam crash!" Maya pronounced. "Eight months ago. I saw what it was straight away so I didn't even stop. I drove on."

"That is, you failed to stop after an accident?"

"But that's what I'm saying. It was a fake accident, and they canceled my license because of it. Of course I carried on driving using it, and when I was stopped I showed them it straight away."

"Wait—I'm sorry, what's your name?"

"Maya."

"Maya, the fact that you had a canceled driver's license on your person didn't mean you could drive on it."

"But I'd been driving on it just fine up till then!"

The woman appeared slightly thrown by this.

"And nobody stopped you?"

"Well, yes, but not very often. I'm a good driver. I don't go through red lights."

"But you must understand it is illegal to drive without a valid license."

"What's illegal is canceling my license because of a fake car crash! And the main thing is that I did have a license on me, and they said in court I didn't."

Katya and Diana giggled. The woman rubbed her brow.

"The reason your license was canceled is not what matters. What matters is that you were not allowed to drive on it. If, apart from this, there are no other complaints . . ."

"And also I'm being held here for a day too many," Maya announced.

Barely perceptibly, the woman sighed.

"How is it a day too many?"

"I was given five days, but they didn't count the day I spent at the police station."

"That is unfortunate, but regrettably I cannot help you there. I am authorized to deal only with complaints relating to the conditions in which you are being held here."

"Well what do you think I ought to do?"

"You can appeal against the length of your sentence."

"But I'm being released tomorrow. Now I don't have enough time to appeal," Maya said, dejected.

The woman again looked around the cell.

"Well, if there are no further complaints . . ."

"And anyway, they had no right to lock me up in a special detention center."

The woman closed her eyes for a moment, opened them again, and looked at Maya. Maya had not disappeared.

"Why did they have no right to detain you here?"

"Because I'm pregnant."

Katya grunted.

"Are you really pregnant?" the woman asked in perplexity.

"Yup."

"Did you provide the court with a doctor's note?"

"Nope."

"Why not?"

"Because I don't have one."

"But you do have a note somewhere, right? Otherwise, how do you know you are pregnant?"

"She has a feeling," Natasha said sarcastically.

The woman looked from her to Maya.

"You . . . have a feeling?"

"Yes, but I'm never wrong about that sort of thing." The woman stood silent for a few seconds before, swaying on her stiletto heels, she headed for the door.

"Well, can I get seen by a doctor here? To get a note?" Without looking around the woman walked swiftly out of the cell. The police marched after her and slammed the door behind them.

"Well, no harm in trying," Maya remarked philosophically.

"Who was that?" Anya asked.

Katya waved her hand languidly.

"Oh, she's the prosecutor. Comes around regularly to ask whether there are any complaints. As if she would do anything if there were."

Anya reflected that just a few days ago she had felt that all this was incredibly remote from her—the police, prosecutors, courts, and prisons—but now she too knew that, of course, the prosecutor did not give a fuck about anyone's complaints, and it was even pointless and risky to complain: if they didn't get back at you for it, they certainly were not going to help. Where had this intuitive knowledge come from? Anya turned against herself. She was not going to give in to this sense of impotence. Ten days was a piddling little sentence, and she firmly intended to treat it as a comical misunderstanding for the rest of her life. She did not belong in this detention center and had nothing in common with the other detainees.

She suddenly felt awkward about her smugness. Was she saying she was too good for this place, unlike the other five women? She had to admit that, in her opinion, the others were not all that great. Even if they had ended up here for the most harmless reasons, Anya was secretly thinking that they were, after all, the sort of people you might expect to land in a detention center. It really was only by a fluke that she, a girl from a good family, with a good education and a strong résumé, found herself here. Accordingly, she had no reason to be ashamed of her time behind bars. Anyone could see that in her case it was simply a ridiculous mishap, and totally unjustified.

Anya glanced at her cellmates. The sad truth was that all of them, even the most likable, struck her as worse people than herself. She blushed slightly at this brazen, improper thought. Luckily no one could guess what she was thinking, and Anya had no intention of telling them. She already felt like a fish out of water, which was why she was trying to remain as inconspicuous as possible, at least outwardly. Inwardly, the main thing was to stay herself, to stay different.

The radio speaker above the door came to life but, instead of the usual music, what came out was a woman's voice. The whole cell froze and everyone looked at the source of the sound.

"What's this?" Diana asked in surprise. She was pulling on a sweater and paused, not slipping her arm into the sleeve.

"Sounds like it's the news," Anya said hesitantly.

"Vladimir Putin has arrived at the summit in South Africa," the voice announced.

"News?" Katya said slowly, looking at the radio, aghast. "Are they joking?!"

She jumped down from her bunk and rushed to the door, as if pursued by ravening wolves.

"Are you dudes out there completely crazy?" Katya bawled, drumming on the metal. "Turn on the normal radio!"

The peephole in the door opened, and a male voice asked irascibly, "What are you yelling about?"

"Turn off the news, will you! Bring back the music!"

"Everyone gets the same radio station. You may not like it, but other people do!" the policeman barked in response and dropped the cover back. It swung from side to side. The sound of retreating footsteps was heard.

"Fuck . . ." Katya said indignantly.

"'You may not like it, but other people do!'" Diana repeated, looking scandalized. "Who could possibly like that bullshit?"

Anya actually really liked listening to the news, but thought better than admit something that would clearly not win her any friends.

Her cellmates sprawled on their bunks, grumbling among themselves. Anya lay back too, closed her eyes and listened. The remote voice of the newscaster, the familiar news clichés, the lists of exchange rates seemed irrefutable evidence that outside the walls of the detention center normal life was continuing, and that she had not forfeited it forever. The news gave hope in the same way the prosecutor's perfume had.

In the courtyard a door clanged as cell number 1 was taken for exercise. Lying there with her eyes closed, Anya carried on listening to sounds. Men's voices immediately filled the courtyard. A bench beneath the window creaked, the grille rang, and peering into their cell a playful voice said, "Well hello, girls! How's life treating you?"

"That fucking radio," Katya replied angrily.

"I know," the guy agreed. "We banged on the door to get it changed but some dickhead said, 'Other people like it.'"

"We b-banged on the door too and he told us the same thing," Natasha added.

There was a silence, during which the voice of the newscaster was especially audible. Anya opened her eyes.

"Is the weather bad out there?" Diana asked from her bunk.

Because the window was now again wide open, the cell had instantly become cold.

"Pretty shitty. Only four of us have come out to exercise. You probably wouldn't like it."

"Why?" Diana asked, puzzled.

"Well, because of who you are," the guy explained in some confusion. He made a vague gesture. "It must be warm where you come from."

Diana narrowed her eyes. "I was born in Moscow, you idiot. It's just my grandfather was from Cuba."

"Erm . . ." the guy mumbled and quickly changed the subject. "Where is the lovely Maya?"

"Keeping warm."

"Anybody new in there?"

"No."

"They've brought us a new guy. An Uzbek. He drove someone else's car into a tree."

"Why? Had he stolen it?"

"No, course not. It was some sort of love triangle. He fancied a girl. Cozied up, wanted to help her. She was down to her last kopeck. He got her a job at the car repair center where he works. She's hitting the bottle but he won't touch a drop. He's a Muslim, right? Anyway, she gets it on with a mechanic, they buy a bottle of vodka and drive off together. This Uzbek is so upset he gets drunk for the first time in his life, piles into someone else's wheels that he's repairing, steps on the gas, and drives straight into the first tree he comes to."

Katya snorted: "Lucky he hit the first or it might've been car theft. As it is, he may get away with it."

"He might or he might not," the guy answered philosophically. "Got any smokes?"

"Sure, help yourself, here's the packet." The guy jumped down to the ground and Anya heard the window slam. Relieved, she emerged from under the blanket but her joy was short-lived: Katya lit a cigarette and immediately reopened the window.

"It's true, we haven't had anyone new for a long time," Diana commented, also lighting up.

"Well I'm leaving tomorrow!" Ira announced unexpectedly, looking out for a moment from behind an upturned denim collar.

"The sooner the better," Natasha muttered and, taking advantage of the open window, she too lit a cigarette. "Wh-what time do you get out?"

"At ten minutes past two!"

"I'm getting out tomorrow as well, but only at five in the evening," Maya said with a sigh. She was sitting on her bunk with a blanket wrapped up to her neck and plaiting her hair into a braid.

"It's not good to be released in the evening," Katya observed, tapping off the ash. "It's supposed to be over, but you feel you've been kept hanging around here for an extra day. I'll be out of here at 9:15 a.m. sharp."

"I don't get out till evening either. Just my luck," Natasha said grimly, scratching her shoulder. She cast a hostile glance at the radio and added, "That news is really getting on my nerves."

She moved purposefully towards the door and kicked it several times with her pink slipper.

"Turn the radio off!" Natasha yelled.

Nobody replied.

"Have you tried breaking it?" Anya asked. The news wasn't bothering her, but the thought of a possible future of endless songs encouraged thoughts of violent solutions.

"There's a camera up there," Katya pointed out, nodding at a black hemisphere in the corner of the ceiling. "You'll get 'damaging state property' added to your charge. And how could you break it anyway? The speaker is screwed to the wall."

"Do you think they're watching us through the camera?" Maya wondered, suddenly anxious.

"You can bet on it."

"What, even when we're . . . well . . . in the toilet?"

Everyone went silent.

"No, of course not," Diana said, though her voice was uncertain. "My husband told me that the cameras are positioned so that they don't cover that area."

"But do they have them in the shower?"

Everyone fell silent again.

"I'm extra glad I didn't take a shower," Maya concluded, looking at the women's expressions.

"I don't know what you'd be worrying about," Natasha said. She came away from the door and plonked herself back down on Ira's bunk, looking like a thundercloud. "You've had all those nose jobs and fuck men for money."

"I don't f— I mean, I don't sleep with them for money!" Maya exclaimed.

"Well, what you were telling us yesterday really did sound like escorting," Diana remarked, abandoning her cigarette.

Maya pursed her lips and shook her head. She looked weary, presumably at the irredeemable stupidity of human beings.

"There is a very big difference between me and those who work on websites like leisure.ru."

"What do you mean, 'work'?" Anya asked.

"On Leisure. It's a site where you can rent a prostitute."

"Oh . . ."

"Those women are *obliged* to sleep with their men. In other words, some dude rents a woman and that's it. She doesn't get to vote on the matter. With me it is quite different. I date whomever I choose and decide for myself whether or not I'll sleep with them. I'm under no obligation. They can take me to a restaurant and after that I might just say goodbye."

"And do you often just say goodbye after being taken to a restaurant?" Katya asked skeptically.

"Not very often," Maya admitted. "But all the same, I can if I want! It's entirely my choice."

"It's entirely their own choice for the g-girls on your Leisure website," Natasha snorted. "It's up to them whether they post their photos there."

Maya was about to respond but at that moment the radio went silent. Once again they all turned to look at it. Spluttering sounds came from the speaker above the door, followed by deafening music. The volume was quickly reduced.

"At long last!" Natasha exclaimed. Even in moments of joy her eyebrows remained paradoxically knitted.

The peephole in the door was suddenly opened.

"Romanova!" the fat-faced duty cop shouted through.

"What?" Anya asked, amazed.

"Get yourself ready. You're being taken to the court."

"What court, for heaven's sake?"

"You filed a complaint? Well, get yourself ready. The guards are here to take you."

The peephole slammed shut.

"Wow, that was fast! You only wrote up the complaint yesterday and you're off to court already," Katya said with some admiration, as if the rapid turnaround was based on Anya's personal merit.

"I should have filed a complaint yesterday too!" Maya lamented. "Then I might have been released today. Only a day early, but at least it would be something!"

"They never let you out early," Natasha said, grim as ever. "We had a woman in the camp and she was forever appealing about everything. Got her nowhere. She only made things worse for herself."

Anya, meanwhile, had changed into jeans and pulled on a sweatshirt. She glanced into the reflective foil over the sink and saw a puffy face with disheveled hair. Anya imagined the court must be a very grand place and that she would need to look smart, so she tidied herself up as best she could. She smoothed her hair and gathered it in a ponytail. But as she pulled on her sneakers, it occurred to her that if a court has illegally imprisoned you in a special detention center, you are probably within your rights in not making too much of an effort to dress up.

"Might they give you a longer sentence, though?" Maya asked as she watched Anya getting ready.

"I don't think so," Anya replied, though she sounded less than confident. Ira giggled. Everyone turned to look at her, but she was just completely carried away shading her drawing with a pencil, paying no attention to what was going on around her.

"If they let you out today I will never forgive you!" Katya said in a menacing voice, but then she laughed. "Only joking!"

The door opened and the fat-faced duty officer appeared.

"Ready? Let's go."

Anya obediently went out of the cell.

"If you're not back in time for dinner, we'll keep it for you," the cop informed her in a businesslike manner as he locked the cell. "We won't keep lunch, though, if that's all right."

"Fine," Anya said with a shrug.

She followed the cop to the end of the corridor. A few seconds later it hit her that those in the detention center plainly did not believe her appeal was going to be successful. Anya smiled to herself, but said nothing. She herself doubted she would be released today—that would be an extraordinary turn of events—but even so she could not completely extinguish the hope. She periodically dared to picture herself being set free in the courtroom, a line of discredited police dejectedly stepping back to allow her to pass.

In reality there were only two cops, and they were standing motionless at the detention center entrance. One was young, with ginger hair and eyebrows that were almost invisible on his sunburned face; the other was considerably older, with a gray mustache that made him look like a walrus. Both their faces registered total indifference. The young one was chewing gum.

"Did you get the documentation?" the duty officer asked them.

The guards nodded, giving Anya a neutral glance and, without saying a word, went outside.

Anya looked at the duty cop. He had also adopted an expression of extreme indifference. She felt like an inanimate object, a parcel being delivered. She strolled outside. It was cold, damp and chilly. Squalls flung raindrops in her face. Despite her sweatshirt, Anya instantly started shivering. Her escorts proceeded swiftly to the car, their faces retaining an expression of unswerving seriousness. Anya hurried after them. The young redhead sat in the driver's seat, and the older man with the mustache next to him. Anya climbed in the back, her teeth chattering.

"What foul weather," grumbled the older cop, lighting a cigarette and, against all logic, opening the window. Anya watched in dismay as the glass slid down. "I'm going to smoke. Is that okay?"

"Yes, of course," Anya said, surprised that her opinion should matter at all.

"Do you smoke yourself?"

"No."

"Quite right. It ruins your health. I've been doing it for so many years it makes no sense to quit now, but you shouldn't start."

The young guard, meanwhile, turned the car around in the courtyard and drove out through the open gate. Anya pressed her nose to the window as if she had totally forgotten everything about the outside world during the three days of her incarceration. She wanted to take in everything at once: the buildings, the people, the cars. She felt that, however the appeal turned out, the journey to the court had already made it worthwhile.

Outside, everything looked dreary and desolate. The police car drove on down quiet green streets. Shop signs and occasional pedestrians wrapped in raincoats flashed by. Anya kept expecting to feel a kind of euphoria at the sight of this precious everyday world, as she had hearing the news on the radio or smelling the prosecutor's perfume, but for some reason no such feeling came. The scene outside the window seemed cheerless, ordinary. When they drove out onto the highway and slipped into the stream of cars, she gave up peering out the window. Viewing the city from the back of a police car was far less exciting than she had expected. She had no illusion of being free. The city outside seemed no more than a stage set.

For all that, a car ride was, of course, an improvement on sitting in a cell. Anya had always adored being driven, whether by car or in a bus. There was a sense of being part of the space surrounding you: it was immense and stretched in all directions, and you were so small and rushing through the very heart of it. This was not so noticeable in trains, which crawled over the land without the same feeling of movement, and running on rails left no hope of a surprise. Airplanes were even worse, just a room hanging in the air with a view of blue and white nothingness. For Anya, the real buzz came only from being on wheels.

She had hit on the idea of hitchhiking in her first year at college. She thought it seemed very romantic and exciting, something that she absolutely had to try. Embarking on independent living in Moscow, Anya set about deliberately trying anything that sensible people would consider too risky.

For her first trip she hitchhiked with friends to Tula but the trip was not a great success. First, they got a lift for ten kilometers in a heavy truck, then a depressed-looking woman in sunglasses gave them a lift in her SUV. She said not a word all the way, and Anya and her friends didn't like to speak in front of her, so they finished the trip in deathly silence. The promised excitement of hitchhiking was nowhere in evidence, but Anya decided the problem was the short distance and they just needed to choose a city farther away.

Of course, the next time they went to St. Petersburg. Those words—"hitchhiking" and "Petersburg"—pretty much evoked romance and freedom for Anya back then. The trip to St. Petersburg was a lot more like an adventure. Swaying on the seat of a tractor-trailer truck, Anya watched as indistinct masses of forest swept past in the darkness of the night. A speaker just above Anya's shoulder belted out ballads throughout the journey. At first she found it intriguing from an ethnographic point of view, but after several hours could only imagine ripping the speaker out of its casing, stamping it underfoot, and hurling its remains out the window. It was early morning when they arrived in St. Petersburg. The driver dropped them on the ring road and trundled off to his depot.

Their taxi to the city center cost half the train fare from Moscow to St. Petersburg. Anya thought that an amusing touch that in no way detracted from the adventure. She had not the slightest interest in what most people considered the point of hitchhiking, namely that it was free. For her the main thing was that sense of independence, of not needing to fit in with a timetable or a predetermined route. You had only to leave home and your journey had begun. It was not the fastest way to get somewhere, but certainly the most interesting. Watching the meadows spreading out beyond the windows of an eighteen-wheeler, Anya would feel just how accessible the world could be. When as a child she had read *The Lord of the Rings*, what had most impressed her was the ease with which the characters left their familiar haunts and set out on their travels. At the time, Anya had a mother and a school to attend, so she could not set out on travels, but now, standing at the side of some road filled with potholes, a wall of forest behind her and the flatness of the fields in front of her, she felt like one of those heroes.

She soon developed all manner of hitchhiking rules and rituals. For example, she always set out at night. It seemed to be an efficient use of time: the less precious hours of night were spent on the road, and daylight hours were saved for impressions that really mattered. The paradox was that for Anya traveling the road was the most important part of the trip, but she clung to her tradition. There was something rebellious about nighttime trips: instead of being tucked up in bed like decent folks, she was hurtling across wide open spaces in a huge truck.

There were, of course, some minuses in all this—or more just additional sources of jitteriness. For example, Anya read somewhere that hitchhikers are traditionally anxious about the hours from two to six a.m., when drivers are said to be reluctant to stop and you can end up standing on the highway for many hours. After that, Anya started being anxious at those hours too, although she always got picked up, even in the early morning. All the same, any time she was given a lift she felt a sense of relief when she saw dawn breaking.

She did, of course, have less exotic fears. At night everything seemed riskier than during the day. At the start of every trip Anya had a presentiment that something bad was going to happen. Nothing ever did, and her fears always melted away after the first car picked her up. Nevertheless, there were certain precautions she invariably observed: never get into a car where there is more than one person, and never split up on the road when you are traveling with a companion.

She quite soon learned to avoid sedan cars. If trucks were unproblematic—it was clear where they were going and why and what you could expect—with sedans there was a critically high level of unpredictability. On one occasion she met a young fellow from whom anyone could see it would be a fatal mistake to accept a lift. He was physically huge, pumped up, his head close-shaven, his arms completely covered in tattoos, and with rings on his fingers. The whole trip he sang along with rock group Splean, fed Anya apples, and engaged her in philosophical conversation. Another time she encountered an exhausted-looking middle-aged driver, but no sooner had Anya opened the door than he wearily announced he would give her a lift only in return for a blow job. From that day on Anya's heart missed a beat when a private car stopped for her.

A truck was a different matter, and Anya always hoped she would hook one of those. Anya greatly liked the inside of trucks. Some had curtains and a carpet, while others had cans full of cigarette butts and a garland of faded miniature flags, depicting naked women, swaying on the windshield. Anya was fascinated by how the former resembled a real home, although life in the latter was much more relaxed and democratic.

The drivers also divided into two groups: those keen to chat and those as mute as fish. All long-distance truckers were interested in the following topics: what was Anya's occupation; where was she heading; did she have a boyfriend and, if so, was he happy for her to hitchhike like this; and was she not afraid she might fall victim to a maniac along the way. "I'm a regular guy," every driver would quickly add, "but it's dangerous nowadays!"

Anya had her own list of prepared questions. Where are you going? Where is your usual route? Where is the farthest you have gone? There was also one question not to ask: What is your cargo? Even though asking that might seem like the most innocent way to keep the conversation going, Anya very soon realized that drivers thought otherwise. They were all desperately anxious about the possibility of robbery, and a traveling companion with an interest in what they were carrying immediately rang alarm bells. Highway robbery sounded to Anya like something out of the Middle Ages, but all the evidence suggested the world changed far more slowly than she had believed.

Anya's main insurance in case of trouble was never to hitch alone. The main reason she did this was to placate fate, but it was also true that hitching alone was boring. She wanted to have someone to share all her experiences with.

Most often her companion was Sonya. She missed out on that first trip to Tula and very much regretted it. Like Anya, she considered hitchhiking wonderfully romantic. She did not want to miss out again. Initially, it was just this fact that attracted Anya—that Sonya seemed as avid for adventure as she was.

Anya saw her on the very first day at university—they were studying in the same group. Sonya was sitting at the desk in front of hers, with her feet tucked under her and gnawing a pencil. She had auburn hair, braided in a short plait, and when she turned Anya could see in profile that she was slightly snub-nosed. Anya sat examining her throughout the entire double period. Sonya was wearing a full skirt with tiny flowers on it and a black top. Something about the skirt and her posture and the eager way she bit the pencil was so captivatingly spontaneous that Anya could not take her eyes off her. Sonya turned around at one point and glanced at her too, before looking away. Anya just had time to notice that her eyes were dark and seemed very friendly.

For several days they met regularly at lectures without speaking, but when they unexpectedly ran into each other in the dorm they realized they both lived there. Sonya was walking along the corridor with a bowl of grapes. When she spotted Anya, she was so delighted. She greeted Anya as if they were old friends, and Anya was slightly taken aback by the warmth of her welcome.

They ate the grapes together. Sonya chattered on endlessly, bombarding Anya with questions. She wanted to know everything: what Anya's favorite films were, what she was making of their first days at college, where she came from, what she liked reading, and why she had chosen this faculty. She talked about herself a little too, but Anya barely noticed those details under the flurry of questions she had to answer. By the time they parted she was reeling from Sonya's curiosity. It was what drew her back to her. Sonya seemed more vivacious and restless than any of the others, but Anya's main impression as they talked was that all of Sonya's attention was focused on her. Sonya engaged with her so actively and completely that she took the place of everyone else. Anya felt she was on stage and Sonya was the audience, and she could not imagine a more appreciative spectator.

Within a few days they had become inseparable and were chattering away without pausing for breath. Anya felt like she was talking properly to someone for the first time in her eighteen years on the planet. She had never before felt such instant trust in anyone. With Sonya she felt she wanted to be frank to the point of sharing her most intimate thoughts. It was wonderful to meet a person who understood her so well. Whatever Anya suggested—skipping a class, or climbing up on the dormitory roof, or going hitchhiking—Sonya agreed instantly. She was like an antenna tuned to Anya, tuned in to her every word.

Anya was so dazzled by their unexpected similarities that it did not immediately occur to her that Sonya's responsiveness was down not to innate adventurousness but to the fact that Sonya found Anya attractive. This discovery came like a bolt from the blue, and at first seemed to Anya terribly burdensome. It seemed that all this time she had been exploiting the attraction of another person, obliging them to do things they perhaps were not enjoying at all. Anya felt guilty and embarrassed, because it was impossible for her to reciprocate. At that particular moment she herself was far more interested in a boy in their year, to say nothing of Zhenya, for whom her great platonic love kept returning in waves of phantom pain.

Sonya, however, was not asking for anything from Anya, she just carried on following her around, and occasionally Anya would catch an adoring gaze, nothing more. Her sense of guilt began to melt away. After all, she reasoned, Sonya was an independent adult who could make her own decisions. She seemed to be perfectly satisfied with their friendship. As their relationship showed no sign of ending, it began to seem quite natural to Anya that Sonya should look up to her, and that she in return looked at her warmly and (perhaps just a little) condescendingly.

Anya did not notice she was becoming dependent on Sonya's attention. The more Sonya admired her, the more Anya wanted to look good in her eyes. She began to fret if she spent a single evening apart from her. She felt she had thoughts crowding her head that were left hanging in midair, uselessly taking up space until they could be uttered in Sonya's presence. Anya needed her to participate in everything she did. Hitchhiking with her became Anya's favorite thing to do. It was nowhere near as interesting or as much fun with anyone other than Sonya, and without Sonya beside her she felt nowhere near as safe.

"So, then, organizing protest demonstrations is what you do, is it?" the older cop suddenly asked, looking at Anya in his rearview mirror.

The question took her aback. She was so lost in thought she had forgotten where she was and needed a few moments to come back to reality.

"And I suppose breaking them up is what you do?" she retorted.

The cop chuckled. "Me? Never in my life. I've not been put on demonstrations and hope I never am."

"Why so?"

"It's too boring. You stand in a police line while idiots all run around yelling." He gave her another sly glance to check her reaction to this.

"Is it more fun carting people who've been arrested to court, then?"

"I've only recently started escort duties. So far I don't find it too boring."

"I'd have thought it might be more fun catching criminals," Anya said, "and that breaking up demonstrations and driving protesters to court was a bit humdrum."

"It's a job. I don't choose who I drive. I do as I'm told. Tomorrow it might be a criminal, as you say, today it's you."

"So you do at least agree that I'm not a criminal?"

"You?" The cop gave her a cheery glance as he lit another cigarette. "From the court's point of view you're an offender, but from my point of view you're a silly girl who's been fed a lot of nonsense. They didn't spank you when you were little and now here you are running riot in the city's squares."

Anya sighed, calling on her reserves of composure.

"Who's been feeding me a lot of nonsense?" she asked.

"That internet of yours, of course. They write all sorts of drivel on it, and you fall for it."

"And do you think I should be put in jail for ten days for that?"

"The law is the law. In Russia it's for the court to decide. Personally, I'd have let you go. You're obviously not up to anything and have just gotten tied up in this by accident. But the person who thought it up wouldn't get away with just ten days' detention if I had anything to do with it."

"The person who thought what up?" Anya demanded. "Attending demonstrations?"

"Going to demonstrations. Trying to arrange coups. Feeding people a lot of nonsense. It's obvious why you're running around the streets with your placards: you're bored with regular amusements and are looking for something new."

"In other words, in your opinion people are protesting because their life is too cushy?"

"People like you—definitely." The cop flicked his cigarette butt out and rolled up the window. "You're all young, healthy, living well—and long may that continue—so you think you'll play the hero. The real question is, what's it all for? Who's stirring it up and drawing in idiots like you?"

"Well, who is it?"

"Work it out for yourself. Russia has always had a lot of enemies trying to destroy her that way. You might remember the Germans sent us a certain Comrade Lenin in a sealed railway car all those years ago."

Anya was silent, taking that in.

"Are you a monarchist then?" she asked hesitantly.

"Me? I'm for Putin," the cop said, offended.

"We've arrived," said the young policeman and turned off the engine.

They all got out of the car, and Anya was again chilled by the bitter wind. The bulk of the gray courthouse outlined against the gray sky looked particularly grandiose and ominous. Inside, however, everything was bathed in electric brilliance. The lights were reflected by the marble pillars, in the polished floors and a huge mirror on the wall. The mirror attracted Anya like a magnet. Luckily, she and her police escort had to walk past it, and she peered with keen interest at her reflection. This mirror bore no comparison with the vaguely reflective foil over the washbasin in her cell. It was amazing to see herself in such detail without having to make the slightest effort. Amazing, but a little sad, because the mirror in the cell made Anya look much better than this one. She discovered that her face looked tired, and there were bags under her eyes.

The cops led Anya along deserted corridors that spiraled around like intestines. Each change of direction was marked by a plant in a container on the floor. One side of the corridor was a row of identical doors with numbers, while the other had a row of identical benches.

They did occasionally encounter people who were sitting silently on the benches. Their eyes followed Anya as she passed. In the stillness, the footsteps of the police sounded inappropriately loud.

They stopped at a door with the number 265 and tried the handle. There was an electronic display on the wall to one side. It was glowing blue but showing no other signs of life. The door was locked. With a sigh, the older policeman who resembled a walrus sat down on the bench opposite. The young one remained standing.

"Well, we'll have to wait," the older policeman announced, stating the obvious.

"What's the time?" Anya asked. She missed having a watch almost as much as she missed a decent mirror.

"Just after twelve," said the young cop.

"And what time is the sitting?"

"One o'clock."

Anya sighed and joined the older policeman on the bench. Her excursion to the court looked like it would be immensely boring. In the cell you could at least read or talk to the others, but here, in a nearly empty corridor in the custody of two policemen, there seemed absolutely no way to pass the time.

"Can you at least explain what it is you were protesting about?" the older policeman asked. He looked at Anya, putting on a show of disinterest, but she could see that he too was bored. She stifled another sigh.

"I was arrested at an anticorruption demonstration."

"What's that supposed to mean?" the policeman responded argumentatively. "You were planning to overthrow the government?"

"It means that we are against government officials thieving all the time."

The policeman thought about this for a moment before grunting, "Is that all you can find to protest about?"

"It seems to me that you don't, as a matter of principle, like the idea of demonstrations," Anya commented politely. "But I don't think you would deny that thieving is a bad thing."

"Of course it is, but what's the use of demonstrating against it?"

"What would you suggest doing?"

"Nothing, of course."

"That sounds pretty weak, especially coming from a policeman."

"Okay, personally I am against thieving of any kind," the walrus said ponderously and folded his arms on his belly. "In my entire life I have never stolen a kopeck, but that is the way our people are: they help themselves to anything that is not nailed down. I had a friend who worked in the 1990s at a factory and at night he made off with canisters of diesel fuel. They weren't the slightest use to him! I asked him, 'Why are you doing this? They're just piling up in your garage.' He wasn't even selling them. He said, 'Oh, you never know, they might come in handy sometime.'"

"So what's your conclusion about Russia then?" Anya asked wearily.

"My conclusion is that this is in our blood. I don't like saying that, but it happens to be true. Everybody is on the take. Officials too, of course. The main thing is for them to do less stealing than they do good. Right now, for instance, we are living well enough, and for that I am very grateful to our government. If someone pinches something for themselves here and there—well, what can you do? Who's to say what I would do in their place? You know what they say, 'Judge not if you don't want to be judged.'"

"Right now I'm all in favor of that," Anya muttered. The walrus looked at her blankly. "But you just said yourself you've never stolen anything. What makes you think that would change in different circumstances?"

"Because I've never been in a position to thieve," the policeman said with a grin. "Given the chance, I might not be able to resist."

"I think you're being hard on yourself," Anya replied.

The walrus looked more serious. "I'm telling it how it is. Everyone thinks they're a saint till it comes to the crunch. That's why your meetings are a waste of time, if not worse. You're squeaky clean now, but what if you had to try ruling a country, especially one like ours!"

"The way you talk you seem to think we haven't had a single person in power who wasn't a thief!" the young policeman suddenly exclaimed.

The older cop and Anya turned in equal astonishment to look at him. He frowned, moved his weight from his heels to his toes, and looked down at his boots.

"Uh-oh, looks like we've smoked out an oppositionist!" said the walrus, taking his time and scrutinizing his partner as if seeing him for the first time. "Perhaps next time you'll be going along too to their *anticorruption* rally."

The young policeman again swayed backwards and forwards, his gaze fixed firmly on his boots.

They sat in silence, Anya occasionally glancing over at the young cop, wondering whether he might expand on his seemingly subversive thought, but he said not another word. Looking at his round, naive face and cropped head of ginger hair, she would never have imagined he was capable of such an act of, by police standards, insubordination. Appearances could evidently be deceptive.

Anya felt a hunger pang. Back at the detention center they must be having lunch now. She thought almost nostalgically about her cell. In this empty, echoing court building she felt isolated and ill at ease.

Soon, she heard footsteps from around the bend and a mustached man in judge's robes appeared in the corridor. He had a ramrod-straight back and an unassailable expression. As he walked, his robe swirled around his feet. He looked like a wizard.

"Are you for one o'clock?" he asked in a muted voice and looked sternly at the policemen. They separately nodded. "The clerk will be here shortly and admit you to the courtroom. You will have to wait a little."

With these words, he turned on his heel (the robe swirled around his legs), looked intently at Anya, and disappeared through an adjacent door.

"Smart aleck!" the old cop said grumpily when he'd gone.

The clerk, a short young girl wearing a tight dress, really did come five minutes or so later. She unlocked the door to the courtroom and muttered over her shoulder "Go through" in an unfriendly tone.

This courtroom was quite different from the one in which Anya had been sentenced a few days earlier. That one had most resembled a schoolroom, with lettuce green walls and flimsy desks. This one was somber and ceremonious. A huge Moscow coat of arms, mounted on red velvet, hung on the wall. The tables were massive and the chairs high-backed. Three such chairs, really more like thrones, were elevated on a special platform. These were evidently for judges. Was her small complaint really going to be ruled on by three judges? Instead of feeling intimidated, she suddenly felt a pang of disappointment. If she and her idiotic complaint were going to be reviewed in such an imposing manner, she had no prospect of success. They would reject it if only to remind her of her place.

Anya sat at one of the tables. One opposite was reserved for the prosecutor who, she remembered from the initial trial, would not be present during a case of this nature. The cops, after a moment's hesitation, sat in the public area. The clerk shuffled her papers and paid no attention to anyone else. They sat in silence. At Anya's first court appearance her friends had been around, and the court had seemed more lively. Now she was increasingly succumbing to a feeling that just lodging her appeal had set in motion a juggernaut of a process. She had inconvenienced a whole team of people, obliged the court building to open and turn on all its lights, the judge to don his wizard's robe, the clerk her tight-fitting dress, and now all of them were obediently awaiting an invisible cue to stage a performance in her honor.

An inner door next to the thrones suddenly opened and the mustachioed judge entered the court. He had evidently been waiting all this time in the next room. No one else emerged and Anya was relieved he was going to be on his own.

The judge proceeded to the throne in the middle, adjusted his robe, and sat down. Then he produced thin, gold half-moon spectacles and perched them on his nose. Anya scrutinized him. His resemblance to a wizard was off the scale. Taking in the courtroom, his gaze rested for a particularly long time on Anya. His expression was completely inscrutable.

"Let us begin by verifying your identity," the judge said finally.

The clerk instantly jumped up and placed an open file before him.

"What is your name?"

"Romanova, Anna Grigorievna."

"Anna Grigorievna, you are required to rise when answering," the judge gently advised her.

Anya hastily stood up. She really had no wish to get on the wrong side of this judge.

"Where are you registered for residence?"

Anya told him.

"What is your address?"

Anya told him.

"Your education?"

"Moscow State Institute of International Relations," Anya said, unsure if she was answering correctly.

"That is, you have higher education," the judge patiently corrected her, making a note in his papers. Anya felt embarrassed, as if she had gotten something wrong in an exam.

"Your marital status?"

"Unmarried."

"Then be seated. Do you have any requests at this stage?"

Anya anxiously shook her head.

"According to the file on this case . . ."

For the next twenty minutes the judge was reading aloud. Anya listened attentively. In his words her case sounded very important but, more to the point, totally absurd. It would have been obvious to a babe in arms that there were no grounds whatsoever for arresting Anya for what she had done. The judge seemed to be fully aware of that, because he took his time and read thoughtfully, particularly emphasizing the words "court of first instance" in a way that made clear his contempt for that court. Anya also felt only the utmost contempt for it.

When he concluded his reading, the judge looked at her over the top of his gold-rimmed half-moon spectacles and asked, "Anna Grigorievna, do you confirm that you were present at the rally?"

"I do." Anya saw no reason to dispute that.

The judge barely perceptibly inclined his head and Anya, immediately remembering herself, stood up.

"And did you take part in organizing it?"

"No. This is something the *court of first instance* concluded purely because I posted about the rally on my social media page. A single time."

"And when you wrote about it, were you aware that it was an unsanctioned demonstration?"

"No. I wrote about it like a hundred years ago, when I first read that it was being planned. I reposted it and tagged it 'important.' I have no idea whether the rally had been sanctioned or not at that time."

"But then you did not later delete the post?"

"No," said Anya, becoming flustered. "But hang on, the point is not whether I had a post on my page or not, but that I have absolutely nothing to do with organizing rallies. I haven't the faintest idea how you would go about that."

The judge nodded pensively but it was unclear whether he was agreeing with Anya or dismayed by her criminal wickedness. When he spoke, it was so wearily that Anya again felt ashamed for exhausting the poor man.

"Is there anything you wish to add?"

"No. Or rather, I just want to say again that from start to finish this is something the police made up and which that first court decided to take seriously. After they took us to the station I think they just did not know what to do with me. In the end all the others were released, but they decided to say I had organized the rally by reposting about it on VKontakte. They evidently just needed to arrest someone to show how terrifically effective they were, although why they picked on me I have no idea. I mean, it is ridiculous to claim I organized a meeting by reposting. I only got about twenty views on that post—that should be visible on the screenshot in the file. You can see that the rally was not my idea, although I certainly support it. But they could equally well blame anyone who was there. So I hope you will listen to what I have said and release me."

"Well then," the judge said, standing up. "The court will retire to the deliberation room."

With a flurry of his robe, he disappeared behind the inner door. It slammed shut and silence again descended.

Anya looked around her. The clerk was sorting through papers on her table.

"Does this part take long, do you know?" Anya asked. In response the clerk shrugged, not deigning to look at her.

"Is the court actually in full session today? You seem rather on your own here." Anya was somehow really keen to piss her off.

"It is," the clerk muttered.

"I don't suppose you know . . ."

The clerk scooped up her papers and, visibly annoyed, clacking her heels, left the court. Anya leaned back in her chair. The urge to be irritating overwhelmed her.

"When you are escorting a prisoner do you always spend this much time just hanging around?" she asked the cops. They did not reply. "This strikes me as even more boring than standing around in a police line at rallies."

The door burst open so abruptly it might have been kicked open, and the judge hastily returned. The cops jumped up like twin puppets. For a moment Anya thought he must have forgotten something.

"Stand up," the elderly cop whispered.

"What?"

"Stand up, I said!"

Anya stood up, shifting her puzzled gaze from the policemen to the judge, who was saying something while looking into the file. Anya could not immediately make out what he was saying.

"The Moscow Municipal Court . . . in the person of Judge Kryuchkov . . . the court of first instance ruled . . ."

"Is he reading his verdict already?" Anya whispered in a daze, turning back to the policemen.

"Shh!"

She turned back to the judge, who was continuing to rattle away without looking up, and only occasionally pausing briefly to take a breath. What he was actually saying was barely audible. Not a trace of his decorous restraint remained. Now, in his robe and half-moon glasses, he looked less like an imposing wizard and more like a crow from a children's cartoon.

"Taking account of all the above enumerated facts, the court rules not to uphold the complaint and to confirm the first court's verdict," the judge announced, and loudly slammed the file shut. "Do you understand the verdict?"

"Who, me?" Anya asked, still stunned by what was taking place.

"Yes, you."

"No."

"What is it that you do not understand?"

"How you managed to write the decision so quickly!"

"Do you have any substantive questions?"

"You weren't even five minutes back there!"

"If you understand everything . . ."

"You might at least have sat out there for half an hour if only for appearances' sake!" Anya exclaimed, incensed to the depths of her soul. "What's the point of having a court if you don't even observe the formalities?"

"You will be given a copy of the verdict in the registry on the first floor," the judge said coldly and, without looking at her, left the court.

"Have you ever seen anything so ridiculous?" Anya asked the cops, in shock.

They said nothing, though the younger one might, barely noticeably, have let out a sigh. Their faces, however, showed no sign either of sympathy or of ill will.

"We need to go to the first floor," the older policeman said tersely.

The office on the first floor was of course shut, so Anya and her guards once more sat down on the benches by the door. This time the waiting seemed even more infuriating. Anya again found herself thinking longingly about dinner at the detention center and, five minutes after that, about her bunk. The benches in the courthouse were so uncomfortable they seemed to have been specifically designed to intensify the tedium.

"Where's the toilet?" Anya asked.

"You take her," the elderly cop said lethargically. "I'll wait here in case someone shows up."

Compared with the facilities at the police station and the detention center, the toilets here struck Anya as palatial. She was embarrassed to be so pleased, but in her present situation the gleaming white washbasin, paper towels, and a soap dispenser that was actually full of soap were a luxury. When she went into the toilet, Anya immediately rushed to the mirror and began closely examining her reflection, centimeter by centimeter. Left on her own—the cop was standing around outside—Anya again, as yesterday in the shower, was surprised by how tiring it was to have other people constantly watching her.

When finally she peeled herself away from the mirror and went reluctantly back out into the corridor, the cop said, "As we're so near the exit, let's go out and I'll have a quick smoke."

Anya was not keen to go out into the cold, but sitting outside the door of the court office was even worse. She obediently followed the young policeman. They emerged from the courthouse and turned the corner. He walked along for a bit, and halted precisely opposite a sign depicting a crossed-out cigarette. He lit up.

"Aren't you worried you'll get fined for smoking in the wrong place?" Anya inquired, for the sake of something to say. She had not fully gotten over the urge to be troublesome. The policeman pulled a face and shrugged. "That camera hasn't been working for the past six months." Anya looked up at the spying eye mounted on the wall.

"In fact, there's hell all works here," the policeman suddenly went on. "Look at how they handled your appeal. Why do you think that was?"

"Why?"

"Because the ruling had already been written. They just write in the name and stamp a copy." Anya glanced uncertainly at him. He took a quick, deep drag on the cigarette and looked unhappy.

"We brought someone else yesterday. They were from the demonstration too, and what do you know—it was exactly the same. Five minutes' deliberation and it's off to your cell. It takes longer than that to drive here and back. As if there's not enough actual evil stuff going on to keep us busy."

"Well, why are you doing this work, then?" Anya asked cautiously, still suspecting this might be a trap.

"I'll tell you why," the cop replied, and spat on the ground. "I'm twenty-six. When I joined up the organization had just changed its name from *militsiya* to *politsiya*. The police, not the militia. They were promising the earth. Reorganization! Benefits! Even an apartment eventually. And? Sweet F.A. No benefits. An apartment? Don't make me laugh! Still, never mind, I thought, at least it'll keep me from getting called up into the army for national service. But guess what . . ."

The absence of his senior partner had evidently loosened his tongue. Anya could see this policeman needed no answers from her, and confined herself to looking interested.

"Zilch! Not even that. Eight years in the police force doesn't count for anything with the army. So now I'm waiting to be twenty-seven, and I won't stay on a day after that."

"What will you do instead?" Anya asked, feeling something bordering on sympathy.

The cop did not shrug, but shuddered, which apparently indicated he saw that as a foolish question. "I don't know," he said. "To tell the truth, I could do with getting an education. Otherwise what do I amount to? I came here straight from school. Or maybe I'll join your lot."

"What do you mean?" Anya prompted.

The policeman threw his cigarette butt on the ground (where there were a lot of others; evidently the camera really had been out of action for a long time), pulled out another cigarette, and for the first time looked directly at Anya.

"The opposition," he said seriously. "When I first came, and we'd been renamed 'the police,' I thought we were going to see real change. I voted for Putin, I voted for United Russia. I expected them to get to work on reforms. In the end, though, all that changed was the name. You are all dead right at those demonstrations of yours. I don't go to them, of course, but perhaps I might soon. They're thieves and liars. We need to put the country to rights."

Anya realized she was staring at him slack-jawed. He took another long drag on his cigarette—its fiery edge jumped a good centimeter closer to his fingers—and said, "There's only ever been one ruler worth his salt in Russia. Under him there was order, and no thieving. Guess who!"

"Tell me."

"Stalin."

Anya opened her mouth to respond, but closed it again.

"We won the war, got our industry off the ground," the policeman continued as if stating the obvious. "If we had someone like him now, he would chase those rats out of the Kremlin in no time and get down to business."

Finishing his cigarette, he threw down the butt and summarized: "So, maybe I'll quit and come over and join you. You might say we're close in spirit. It's time we took power into our own hands."

They returned to the courthouse in silence.

The office was finally open and the elderly cop was waiting for them with the ruling in his hand. The three of them began walking toward the exit again. A double door at the far end of the marble vestibule opened, and from it came noise and the smell of food. There was evidently a cafeteria there. Anya's stomach rumbled, and she imagined brewing instant noodles in her cell and tea steaming in a plastic cup. She hoped that the hot water from dinnertime would not have gotten cold.

In the car nobody spoke, and Anya cast furtive glances at the driver's close-cropped hair. In her eyes he had been transfigured so rapidly from a standard cop, first into a uniquely honest policeman, and then immediately into a bloodthirsty Stalinist, that she still could not get her head around it. Adoration of Stalin seemed to her one of the most irrational things on earth, especially if it was being expressed by someone of her own generation. Anya tried to imagine what could have led him to this conclusion, but knew there were no logical reasons: only an interaction of self-contradictory, pathological, almost superstitious beliefs that had welded entire generations to this absurd love.

Then Anya began wondering where her own convictions, which ultimately landed her in a special detention center, had come from and, much to her surprise, realized she could not remember. She had supposed she had always been like this but now saw that was not true. She and her mother had once even quarreled because Anya would take no interest in politics.

Her mother felt that everybody had an obligation to take an interest in what was happening in their country. She liked to tell the tale of how, a few hours before Anya was born, she had been listening on the radio in the maternity hospital to a speech by Andrey Sakharov. She was so agitated, because people were shouting in the hall and making it difficult for him to continue, that she refused to go to give birth until she knew how it was all going to end. After that, it seemed to her mother that Anya, born under the sign of such a powerful expression of parental opposition, should surely have absorbed a passion for politics from birth. She was dismayed when her daughter showed no evidence of such passion.

Anya stayed apolitical until her last year at university. She began working at that point in the Ministry of Foreign Affairs because, like all graduating students, she needed to complete an internship. She really liked the Foreign Ministry. She liked its grandeur and air of mystery, its high ceilings, creaking stairs, and heavy doors. She liked drinking tea with the typists in their office. She liked looking down from the top floor at Moscow's Garden Ring Road, terminally clogged with cars. She liked wandering through the Ministry late in the evening when the offices were deserted and the corridors dark. After she graduated Anya was hoping to work there. Well, not exactly there. She was hoping to be posted far, far away to an embassy in some African country. By this time everything was beginning to get her down: the university, the dormitory, Sonya, Sasha . . . She could not bear to watch the two of them falling in love. Anya herself could not understand what connection she had with them now, when Sonya had finally made her choice but seemed incapable of just dumping her. A decisive gesture was required. Anya concluded that hightailing it to another continent would strike just the right note.

At the beginning of winter, elections to the Duma were to be held, and in early spring, there would be the presidential election. These were not the first elections in Anya's adult life. Despite being of voting age, she had ignored the ones four years earlier. At that time politics had existed for her not just on the sidelines but in a parallel universe. But in her last fall at university, Anya discovered that parallel universe seemed to have expanded and was now encroaching on her own.

Everyone in the Foreign Ministry was planning to vote and the election was a frequent topic of conversation in the dorm. On VKontakte she noticed political clips starting to appear among the usual funny ones.

Anya had no understanding of what was happening, but was caught up in the general excitement. It seemed as if something important was brewing. She remembered going with her parents to the polls when she was little. She recalled the booth, the curtain, the ballpoint pen on a string, the surrounding sense of solemnity and her own envy that her parents were so grown up and important that they were being given special slips of paper she wasn't allowed to have. Now, though, she was at last a grown-up and deserved to be given her own slip of paper. She found that a pleasing thought.

Anya had no hesitation over whom to vote for: anyone at all as long as they were not standing for the ruling party. She did not have any particular grudges about it, but decided that if something was wrong in the country, that party must be most to blame. There was a further factor. She still half suspected the election was a waste of time, and she was not going to make them even more pointless by voting in favor of the government. Why would you bother to turn out to vote if there was nothing you wanted changed?

On a Sunday morning in December, she went with Sonya and Sasha to look for their polling station. It was in a neglected pink school set among bare black trees. Anya's name was found in the register and she was given her long-anticipated ballot paper as an indisputable confirmation of adulthood. Anya carefully reread it several times to make sure she would not put her check mark in the wrong place, though that was all but impossible. As she dropped the slip into the slot on the urn, she felt a mixture of pride and disappointment. At that instant she was transfigured into a responsible citizen, but it was so fleeting she had no time to enjoy it properly.

Her sole news source had always been the home page of the Yandex news portal. The top five most popular headlines had seemed to her an exhaustive roundup of everything that was happening in the world. That evening Anya, effectively for the first time in her life, consciously searched the internet for news. She felt involved in important events.

At first she thought nothing out of the ordinary had happened: the ruling party had won. Anya felt that was a shame, because she had after all personally sought its downfall, but it was entirely to be expected. As days went by, however, public unrest, of which she had previously had only a vague sense, was clearly growing. Anya knew that from those same Yandex headlines where the topic of the election obstinately remained, from jokes on the internet about the magical counting of votes, and from the contempt for the result, which was being expressed by everyone from her mother to the staff in the Ministry of Foreign Affairs. The dissatisfaction took different forms, but Anya felt it everywhere and was constantly on edge and irritable. It was as if a window had been left open in the room, which she wanted to close but could not because, for the first time in ages, what was happening externally was affecting her. And then she read on Yandex that a rally was being held to protest the rigging of the election. At that, finally, she too became really indignant. Anya was not sure herself how that came about. The announcement of the rally seemed to augment the inadequate resentment she had felt earlier when she was reluctantly following the news, and she could not make up her mind just to ignore it as she had in the past. Passively being dismayed at the dishonesty of the regime was uninteresting, but as soon as the opportunity to take action appeared, Anya's anger was kindled.

Her friends did not share her sudden enthusiasm. Sasha, speaking with the authority of someone who in the past had taken at least a slight interest in politics, said he already had other plans and would not be going to the rally. Sonya, who turned like a weathercock to support anything Sasha said, announced that she too already had plans, although the rally certainly did sound like a great idea. Anya supposed Sonya must find herself in a very difficult situation, obliged as she was to fight a constant, exhausting battle to find compromises between her and Sasha. Actually, it had only the semblance of a compromise because Sonya invariably tilted in one direction, but did at the same time try with all her might not to offend Anya or disappoint her too much. The end result was that Anya went to the rally on her own.

She recalled that, when she got onto the right metro line, she was amazed how packed it was with people. She could not believe they were all going to the rally, and on the way racked her brains as to why that should be. Perhaps today was a holiday? Was it the school holidays? Was this a large tourist group? When the train stopped at Tretyakovskaya station, most of them got out together with Anya. The vestibule was crammed. There was a policeman standing by every pillar. Everywhere Anya looked there were people with placards. There was a lot of noise. A girl beside her recognized someone in the crowd and rushed towards them with a shriek of delight. Anya went up the escalator, looking all around her in a daze. There was a family immediately in front of her—a mother and a father carrying their little daughter, who was wearing a hat with two pompoms. She had a ribbon attached to a blue balloon tied around her wrist and it was floating up and bobbing about in the air currents. The little girl looked down towards Anya and gave her a big smile. It all felt like New Year celebrations.

Outside, Anya was preparing to use her cell phone's navigation app, but immediately realized she was not going to need it. The crowd emerged from the metro and everybody headed in the same direction. She followed them. Occasional tiny snowflakes were falling.

She came out onto the river embankment and into a squally wind blowing from the right. Anya could see the island she was making for ahead, across the river. First, she saw bare, skeletal trees, and then a colorful sea beneath them. For a moment she could not tell what it was, but then realized it was people, a lot of people with placards and flags in their hands. Anya was almost upset there were so many. She had somehow imagined she was the only person who knew about the protest, that it was her personal secret and special adventure. Now she saw in front of her a living, restive crowd and felt simultaneously annoyed that they had gotten here before her, pleased that she was not on her own, and generally amazed, proud, and jealous. Losing no more time, Anya hurried over the bridge.

There was a stage set up on the island from which music was coming. She began making her way closer. She said "Excuse me" to everyone, and everyone replied "Of course, of course." The whole time Anya was advancing through the crowd, she did not come across a single miserable-looking person. All around was a holiday atmosphere and a feeling of buoyant, almost effervescent joy.

She could hardly hear anything of what was being said from the stage. She was much more interested in the people standing beside her. In any case, she knew almost none of the speakers: Anya recognized only a television presenter and Yury Shevchuk from the rock group DDT. She could hear that a letter of some kind was being read. The people around her were excited about that, but Anya had no idea why. She made out only a few words. The political part of the proceedings really did not make that much of an impression on her. She experienced much the same feelings when she was little and had, during family celebrations, to listen for ages to the adults talking at table.

Nevertheless, the emotion that came from being so close to such good, friendly people meant that it had been worth coming. Anya was intoxicated by the sense of unity. At first, when people began chanting some slogan in the distance, she just felt embarrassed. Were these lovely people really going to start all shouting some sort of slogan? Anya stood and heard the chanting growing stronger, spreading out over the island and pausing in front of her like a wave about to break, and when the woman next to her also began chanting, and then the people behind her, Anya found herself caught up by the wave. The next time she found she liked it: the inexorable way these unfamiliar words came rushing towards her, growing in strength and becoming clearer, was overwhelming and at the same time wonderful.

That day made such an impression on Anya that she didn't hesitate to go to the next rally, eager again to enjoy an unscheduled holiday-like celebration. With time, the euphoria passed, but Anya continued attending the rallies on principle. After several such protests, she felt like a seasoned revolutionary and would have been ashamed now to desert the banner of opposition. Over time, that sense of principle changed into a sense of duty, and when protest rallies went out of fashion, Anya discovered she had developed an unflinching determination to attend them, even if nobody else did. It was a particular kind of heroism, based on nothing more elevated than Anya's stubbornness. It was only a few years later that for the first time Anya went to a rally not mostly for the sake of it but primarily because she was outraged by injustice. By then, however, politics had long meant something more to her than just manning the barricades.

* * *

Anya's gaze returned to the hedgehog haircut of the young policeman, and she tried to imagine where she would be if she had not gone to that wintertime rally. Although, perhaps what had mattered was not the rally, and she should really be asking what would have happened if she had not gone to vote. Or if she had not done her internship at the Foreign Ministry, where political life did to some extent seep in, in marked contrast to the circle of friends she had in the dorm. Each new question gave rise to a further one, and perhaps, giving scope to her imagination, she might even have traced the political predetermination of her destiny to her mother and Sakharov. Anya did not actually believe in fatalism, however, so she confined herself to the supposition that there had been no single turning point in her life, but that each successive step had brought her closer to making the right choice.

When they arrived at the detention center, the weather turned really foul. There was something demonic about the howling of the wind and the lilac clouds racing across the sky. Anya leaped out of the car and ran ahead of the police back to the building. To an outsider it might have seemed like she could not wait to get back behind bars.

"It's so cold," she explained to the astonished blonde policewoman who met her at the entrance.

The cops came in behind her. The ritual of Anya's return was soon over: the walrus handed the court documents to the blonde and, without a word, headed together with his partner for the exit. At the last moment, the young policeman turned around and curtly nodded goodbye to Anya.

Back in the cell, she was immediately bombarded with questions.

"Well? Did they take anything off your sentence?" Katya shouted from her upper bunk.

She was sitting in the same position as that morning, cross-legged, with a lit cigarette in one hand and her plastic-cup ashtray in the other.

Anya shook her head. "Oh dear. And we were thinking you might not even come back," Maya said. She too was sitting on her bunk and, when Anya came in, leaned forward, clutching the bars of her headboard. Everyone was looking at Anya, even Ira, who now seemed a good deal more cheerful and friendly than she had in the morning (doubtlessly thanks to the Lyrica).

"They left it unchanged. Is there any hot water?" Anya asked hopefully.

Natasha got up without a word, took her bottle in its net holder out of its blanket cocoon, and went over to the locker with the tea. Anya watched her movement impatiently, slightly disappointed she was not being allowed to do everything herself and at the same time to hold the warm bottle in her hands. Natasha dropped a tea bag into a cup and poured the hot water over it. She put the bottle down on the floor, but immediately picked it up again and began examining it closely.

"Hell, the string is tearing already," she said anxiously.

Anya, unable to wait any longer, went firmly over to the locker and took the tea.

The cup was warm but, alas, not really hot.

"Make yourself a s-sandwich. You must be hungry," Natasha said absently, continuing to inspect her bottle.

Anya did not wait to be asked twice.

"It'll soon be time for dinner," Diana said encouragingly, observing how enthusiastically Anya was munching. Maya gave a wistful sigh, discreetly reminding everyone of her continuing fast.

A gust of wind suddenly blew open the half-closed window. The frame hit the wall and rebounded, the glass rattling but not breaking. It made everyone jump.

"Oh, fuck!" Katya exclaimed indignantly, threw a cigarette butt into a cup and slammed the window. "If it really does break, we'll freeze to death."

"It is so, so cold!" Ira confirmed cheerfully. Sitting there in her denim spacesuit, however, she didn't look too cold at all.

"If the window broke I assume we would be moved out of here," Maya speculated optimistically.

"Moved? Where to? To the men's cells?"

"But how are we going to smoke?" Diana inquired lazily from her lower bunk, watching Katya firmly pull down the handle on the window.

"We'll just have to not smoke. Adopt a healthy lifestyle, ever heard of that?"

Diana grunted and turned to the wall. Her bunk squealed in protest beneath her.

The wind periodically blew in great gusts on the courtyard's plastic roof. Every blast shook it strongly and made the windowpanes rattle. Anya slid down under the blanket with her book, but occasionally looked outside and could see how violently the storm was shaking the poplar trees. The sky became as dark as if night had fallen, and by contrast the light in the cell seemed particularly yellow.

"There's going to be a thunderstorm," Katya remarked.

Maya darted a glance at her and whimpered, "I'm so afraid of thunderstorms!"

"How can you possibly be afraid of thunderstorms? You aren't ten years old," Diana said and turned back to face the others.

"I was left alone at home when I was little and there was a thunderstorm," Maya explained, her voice shaky. "I looked out the window and saw a tree struck by lightning. I've been afraid of lightning ever since."

—— "How do you think you're going to be struck by lightning if you're indoors?" Katya asked caustically.

A gust of wind hit the courtyard roof with such force that it cracked. Maya squealed and crawled under her blanket.

"Shall we play Crocodile? Or Towns?" Diana asked after a silence.

They chose Crocodile. Anya again declined to play, but looked up from her book at times to watch the game. She was feeling at peace with the world. The weather raging outside made their cell seem cozy and almost like home. It was remarkable the way the sandwich she had eaten could reconcile her to life.

Rain again began drumming on the roof in the courtyard, and almost immediately there was a flash of lightning. Maya glanced fearfully at the window, but only Anya noticed. The rain beat down more and more loudly and then there was a crash as something fell on the roof. This time everyone turned to look out the window.

"Must've been a branch," Diana said with a shrug.

"That's nothing short of a hurricane out there," Katya murmured, peering into the darkness.

Outside everything was cracking and moaning and clattering, but, inside, the detention center seemed to be holding its breath. When a key was turned in the lock, its rasping seemed so deafening it made everybody jump. "Are you coming for dinner?" the young police boy asked sternly, examining them from the doorway and trying hard to look grown-up.

The stairs to the canteen were not lit, and the large window in the stairwell shone dark blue. The black silhouette of a tree growing outside fell on the glass and the wind was shaking it from side to side. It beat against the window, its branches spread-eagled against the panes. There was another flash of lightning that, for an instant, bleached the treads of the stairs and the heads of Anya's fellow inmates. There was a crash of thunder.

"I'm frightened," Maya whimpered, clinging to Anya.

"Well, you should have stayed behind in the cell."

"What do you mean? It would be even worse in the cell on my own!"

In the canteen Anya went to the window, and from there she could finally see what was going on outside. A hurricane was raging. Trees were bending down to the ground, leaves were flying. Black puddles glinting in the light of streetlamps were furrowed by the gusts of wind. There was yet another lightning flash and the thunderclap seemed directly above the detention center roof.

"Perhaps we'll all be drowned," Katya said jokingly, straddling the bench and banging her bowl down on the table.

Dinner was a meat patty with mashed potatoes. Anya was reminded of how hungry she had been feeling all day and hastened to the serving hatch.

The food was being dispensed by Andrey, a server who looked like a baby chick in his yellow sweatshirt.

"Did you have any luck with your appeal?" he asked, generously scooping the mash out of a huge container.

"No joy. How did you know about it?"

"The other girls told me. I'm studying law, so I was just interested."

Anya forced herself to stop staring at that large, hypnotic ladle and looked up at Andrey.

"Where are you studying?"

"Moscow University," he said with a sigh and placed her full bowl on the tiled ledge.

"Are you here for driving without your license?" said Anya, trying to remember.

"Yep. I was with friends in the dorm and drove to the next block to get some booze. They got me on the way back. I was ten meters from the entrance!"

"Well, never mind," Anya said, wanting to console him. His baby face made him look so vulnerable she felt an urge to take care of him. "Regard it as an adventure! It's summer anyway, so they won't hear about it at university."

Andrey was about to say something more, but evidently decided he had done enough complaining already, and only nodded, looking dejected.

Anya went to the table, sat down, and stuck a spoon into the patty, feeling good. Warm steam rose out of it. Feeling pleased for the first time that day, she helped herself to a big spoonful, but before she could bring it to her lips several things all happened at once.

Andrey said, "Here's your hot water," and took hold of the bottle by the string handle Natasha had woven. He was intending to make a grand gesture of placing the bottle on the ledge, but the string suddenly broke, the bottle hit the wall and bounced back, drenching him in scalding water. He gave a heartrending shriek, which was shortly followed by a clap of thunder. The lamp in the ceiling fizzled and went out, plunging the canteen into darkness.

For a moment Anya froze, still absurdly clutching the spoon she had brought to her mouth. She could see nothing in the new darkness, but continued staring, stupefied, at the place where Andrey had been. His silhouette suddenly emerged from the shadows. He was standing perfectly straight and looking undistressed. Anya could see his face clearly. It was expressionless and seemed as still as a graveyard. She could not understand how he could be so tranquil when he had only now been screaming in pain. She was about to call out to him, but then saw there was someone else standing in the darkness behind Andrey. She stared. Two more silhouettes appeared beside the boy. For a moment Anya thought these were other kitchen workers, but as her eyes adjusted to the darkness, she could see more clearly that they were not people she recognized. One was a gray-haired man and the other a young girl of Asian appearance. They stood there, also motionless, looking at Anya blankly.

She lowered her spoon slowly, and just at that moment another flash of lightning lit up the canteen for an instant. It was teeming with people. They were crowding around her table on all sides, leaning over her. Behind every row of heads she saw another row, a whole army of people, looking at her without emotion. There were faces of children, disfigured faces, old faces, faces both beautiful and ugly, hostile and kind—a whole kaleidoscope of deathly pale cheeks and brows. Anya fell backwards on the bench, incapable of uttering a sound, and with her shoulders felt someone immediately behind her. Looking straight ahead at all the people standing there in silence, she was determined on no account to look around, but her head slowly turned beyond her control. Anya held her breath. The silence around her was compounded by a silence within her, and her heart stood still.

At just that moment, there came another clap of thunder outside the window, the ceiling light again poured forth electric brightness, and Anya heard Andrey howling over in the kitchen section. Her cellmates were sitting at the table, looking around in total confusion, and the young policeman was standing with his arms comically stretched out in front of him as if trying to catch someone invisible. He was staring in amazement at the electric light with no clue as to what he ought to do. Anya had no idea either, but something forced her off the bench and she rushed through to the kitchen.

By now Andrey was whimpering, staring at his legs with his trousers down. Great blotches were reddening on his thighs. Anya ran to him and immediately looked around helplessly for a refrigerator, but in the kitchen of the detention center none was to be found.

"Do you have ice?" she shouted in the direction of the canteen, where the police boy was still standing. But at that moment he himself ran into the kitchen.

"Come out of there!" he yelled in alarm at Anya.

"Have you got ice, I said. He needs something cold!"

"Come out, you don't have permission to be in here!"

Andrey was whimpering more quietly. Anya saw her cellmates staring goggle-eyed at them from behind the police boy. "Andrey, we need to apply something cold to your skin here," Anya said, as gently as she could. "Where is there cold water?"

Andrey sobbed and jabbed a finger in the direction of a door leading to another section of the kitchen which was not visible from the canteen.

"Let's go back there," Anya said, carefully taking him by the hand and moving towards the door. The police boy strode forward to bar them, but Anya gave him a wholly unimpressed look and, fully confident that he would do as he was told, said curtly, "Get the doctor."

In the next room there was only a table and, running the length of the wall, a long, low sink with several taps in a row. Anya turned on the cold water.

"We need to pour water on the burn," she told Andrey. He was almost in tears but, looking at her now, he nodded. Cupping his hand, he splashed water on the skin of his leg and immediately yelled again.

"It's freezing!" he hissed between gritted teeth and splashed some more. The water ran down his legs, straight into his pants.

The doctor came shuffling into the kitchen at great speed in her slippers. She was the woman who had examined Anya when she was being admitted to the detention center. The police boy trotted after her.

"What happened?" she gasped.

"He's been scalded," Anya replied curtly.

Andrey continued frenziedly pouring water over his legs.

"Ice, on the double!" the doctor ordered God knows whom, and promptly rushed back out of the kitchen. Anya heard her unlocking her room next to the kitchen and hastily opening and shutting cabinet doors in there. Half a minute later she was back with an ice pack.

"There is only one, so apply it alternately to both legs!" she instructed Andrey, who did as he was told. "Now come with me to my office."

Andrey took a few small steps after her, unable to go faster with his pants down. Anya felt laughter tickling her nose. She had long been aware of having this reaction to any strong emotion—while others sobbed, she would burst out laughing. It was no easy matter to explain such abnormal behavior to other people and, in order to contain herself, she swiftly averted her gaze.

"Take your pants off, for heaven's sake!" the doctor exclaimed, immediately leaning forward to help pull on a trouser leg. Andrey managed eventually to get his trousers off and took exaggeratedly long strides toward the doctor's office. He seemed to have stopped crying.

When the door closed everyone continued looking at it for a while. Eventually, the young policeman regained his presence of mind and, turning his gaze from Anya to her cellmates crowding in the doorway, masterfully ordered, "You all, back to your cell!"

"But what about our dinner?" Ira asked, crestfallen. No unexplained happening could distract her from that.

"It's over."

"Well, what about the hot water?" Natasha asked sullenly.

There was a silence. Diana glanced over her shoulder to where their bottle was lying on the floor.

"The hot water will be brought to you later," the police boy said with a scowl. "Out you go!"

After a moment of reluctance, everyone moved toward the exit, only Ira sighing and casting sorrowful glances at the table they were leaving.

On the stairs they met Lyokha and Viktor Ivanovich coming up carrying a huge aluminum can. The expression on the faces of Anya's cellmates caused them to stop, and Lyokha asked uncertainly, "What's happened?"

"Where do you think you're going?" the police boy demanded. He was evidently seeking to restore his authority by this show of aggression. "We've left one of your bunch up there, a fool who can't even hold a bottle properly!"

"We were told to bring the food up. Dinner hasn't even started yet. They just let the girls in ahead of the men."

"Move along there," the police boy muttered to Anya's cellmates, who were clustered on the stairs.

They filed silently past the servers, who looked after them, puzzled. Anya was the last to leave.

The tree was silhouetted in the window on the stairs. It was motionless except for the leaves shuddering under raindrops. The storm seemed to have calmed and there was now only the sound of rain outside. The prisoners entered their cell in total silence. When the door closed behind them, Anya felt such emptiness she could hardly stand on her feet.

"Did you *see* it?" she asked.

"Well done, Anya! You really kept your head," Katya said with grudging approval and made for the locker. "Damn! I'm hungry."

"No, when the electricity went off, did you see . . . *that*?"

"See what?"

"Those people."

"I was so-o scared when the lights went out!" Maya cried, and crossed her arms on her bosom like a pious old woman. "I'm always afraid of the dark, and then there was that thunderstorm. What happened?"

"Oh, some power outage, I expect," Diana said, flicking her lighter. "But it sure was spooky the way there was this thunder and the guy instantly screaming. Like something in the movies, forces coming together. Are you making a sandwich? One for me too, please!"

"Did you see those people when the lights went out?" Anya snapped, finally losing patience.

"What people?" asked Katya, with a frown. She took some bread out of a bag, put a piece of cheese on it, and handed it to Diana.

"Personally I couldn't see anything at all," Maya said. "I was so frightened I immediately shut my eyes tight. What sort of people were there?"

Anya looked at them all, disheartened.

Diana responded, "I don't know who you saw there. I wouldn't think you could see anything at all when it was so dark. Anyway, how long did it last—a couple of seconds?" She munched her bread and cheese and sat down on her bunk, which sagged.

"Damn, now we don't even have tea to drink," Katya grumbled. "And all because of your handiwork, Natasha! They don't seem to have taught you too well in the camps."

"I made it fine. The man was all thumbs," Natasha retorted. She had climbed up to her top bunk and was now under the blanket, about to start her crossword puzzle. "He took hold of it wrong, that's why it t-tore."

All Anya's cellmates settled down in their bunks. She thought about making herself a sandwich, but then just lay down. She had completely lost her appetite, which was disturbing, considering how eagerly she had been looking forward to dinner.

Lying on her bunk, Anya listened to the sound of rain dripping on the courtyard roof. It was no longer drumming, only tapping gently. Her cellmates were joking about something, collapsing with laughter at moments, then they lit cigarettes and threw the window wide open.

It was impossible to deny that every day since she had ended up here, inexplicable things had been happening. Anya would have been fine to admit she had gone a little crazy. That would at least have provided a rational explanation of sorts. Otherwise, the devil only knows what she might be forced into believing. The problem was that Anya felt totally healthy: clearheaded and with an unshakable belief that all the things she had seen had actually happened. It had not been a dream, a figment of her imagination, or a play of the shadows. But in that case, what was the explanation?

Anya could not help remembering being surrounded by that wall of motionless, spectral people and, at the mere thought of it, felt her hair stand on end. Who were they all? Why had they appeared to her? Except for Andrey, she had never seen any of them in her life before.

Anya shifted onto her other side and secretly inspected her cellmates. Ira was all innocence, drawing again. Anya stared at her with great intensity, trying but failing to detect features of demonic possession. It was impossible to imagine anyone looking less evil. Maya was just the same. She was sitting reading her crime novel and, as usual, twirling a lock of hair around her finger. Not a hint of menace emanated from her.

Anya sighed and rolled onto her back, staring at the flowery mattress above. She had always considered herself sensible. Nothing remotely mystical had happened to her in her entire life. She was not superstitious, did not believe in astrology, fate, or parallel worlds. She did not believe in God either. To renounce these certainties seemed to Anya such a betrayal of herself that she would, indeed, prefer to think she had gone crazy. The symptoms did point in that direction, after all. From stress or exhaustion she had begun to see hallucinations nobody else could see. The fact that to herself she seemed perfectly compos mentis proved nothing.

This was not a comforting thought, but Anya suddenly felt so weary after the day she had lived through that she could not find the strength even to worry. Perhaps all she needed was a really good night's sleep. Maybe she just needed to get out of this place and go back to her ordinary life for everything to return to normal. And as she was thinking that, she was already sinking into a deep slumber.

DAY FIVE

The first thing that came to mind when Anya woke was an onion. A crunchy, purple, succulent onion with a thin, brittle skin. How she would love to eat one now! She would take a bite of it as if it were an apple. Anya imagined the crunch, the smell, the sweet-savory flavor, and her mouth watered instantly. It was amazing what five days in prison could do to a person. When she was allowed access to her phone she would text her friends and ask them to bring an onion for her. It was bound to be permitted. Surely they could not deny someone such a modest wish.

Anya leaned on her arm and looked around the cell. Everyone was still asleep. To keep the cold out, her cellmates had closed the windows the evening before and, with no ventilation, the air had become stale during the night. Anya's blanket smelled of cigarette smoke. She quickly got out of bed and opened the small top window. Returning to the bunk, she reluctantly climbed under the cover, making sure the blanket was enclosed in the sheet and could not touch her skin. Water dripped steadily from the faucet.

Anya suddenly felt a burning anger, generated by the smell from the blanket, the dripping faucet, the dirty floor she had just had to walk on barefoot. What on earth was the point of holding her here under arrest like a criminal? She felt truly sorry for herself. While everyone else was out enjoying life, she, because of some fluke, was stuck in a prison cell where she could hope for nothing more sublime than an onion. She felt rage and a desire to burst into tears.

The irritating water continued to drip. Losing patience, Anya got up again and put half the soap dish under the tap. For a time, the dripping was muted, but it soon restarted, only at a new pitch. Anya shoved her head under the pillow.

She tried imagining what she would do when she got out. Every previous day in the detention center this had been a great distraction, but the trick did not work today. She was too resentful that she, a completely innocent person, had been reduced to imagining the joy she would take in things she should be able to take for granted.

In the neighboring cell a toilet flushed and the pipes gurgled. A couple of minutes later, the door to the exercise yard clanged open. Listening to the sounds outside, Anya for some reason wondered what it must be like to exercise there in the winter, when the snow settled on the plastic roof and shut off the sky—it would be a freezing dark room. All the same, it must be better to be imprisoned in a detention center in the winter than in the summer—you'd have less of a gnawing sense of wasting your life.

While Anya was a student and living in the dormitory, she tried to spend every summer in Moscow. The others went home as soon as the exams were over and stayed away until September. Anya, however, found it unthinkable to be stuck in her hometown for so long. In order not to upset her mother, she did, of course, always come home for a week or two, but she found even those few days excruciatingly boring.

After the first winter holidays, in dank, slushy February, when she was unable to think of an excuse to go out into the city, Anya decided to set herself a rule to force herself to leave home each day. The summer holidays were better, but still not ideal—during the day the sun was so fiery it hurt your eyes and the asphalt became as soft as modeling clay. There was usually not another soul in the streets, but Anya would intrepidly leave the house every day. These excursions were, in part, an opportunity to smoke without her mother knowing. In order to bring some variety into her day, Anya would go to the market, go shopping, visit the doctor—and even went so far as to visit her father regularly.

Her father lived with his new family on the other side of the city, and for many years communication with Anya was minimal, a Skype call once every two months. Their conversation centered mainly on his new children. Her father inundated Anya with photographs of them and details of their achievements. She was less than thrilled, but the infrequency of their conversations made their dullness bearable. She was a well brought up young woman, and took care not to offend her father by showing a lack of interest. If asked straight out if she loved him, she would unhesitatingly have said yes. But she never missed him, not in the slightest.

Her parents had divorced when Anya was nine. The event had had surprisingly little effect on her. Her father was constantly away at work, so Anya had in any case never spent a great deal of time with him. His eventual complete absence had so little impact that a couple of weeks later she had no recollection that she and her mother had ever lived any differently.

Despite this, Anya spent the next few years mythologizing her father. Her mother loomed so large in Anya's life that she more than adequately fulfilled the role of both parents. As a result, Anya wanted to reimagine her father—who was in some sense an ancillary parent— as someone exceptional. On the basis of various small impressions, she meticulously, year by year, built up a collage in her mind of an extraordinary father. This was not actually too difficult. If you did not look closely, her father fit the bill well: he was handsome, rich, educated, liked jazz and scuba diving, explained to Anya how spaceships and diving gear worked, discussed literature and politics with her, and taught her how to draw and to catch fish. He saw Anya regularly, but not very often, so their meetings were always special for her.

Because of the infrequency and preciousness of these meetings, Anya was very forgiving towards her father. You could hardly expect such an elusive, special individual to perform the general duties of fatherhood. He could be forgiven for forgetting her birthday and then, a month later, giving her an electric toothbrush (at the age of twelve) or a doll (at the age of fifteen). He never asked how she was doing. If Anya was telling him something about school, he would nod while obviously not listening. All this she noticed and deliberately ignored, not wanting to let anything spoil the image of her ideal father.

Then he acquired another family and other children, and his absentmindedness toward Anya became more pronounced. They began to see each other even less frequently, and in a sense that was a relief, because now her father no longer had opportunities to inadvertently mar his image. Over the years it finally took shape in her imagination: she thought warmly of her dad and was proud of him, but did not seek out his company. When she moved to Moscow, their relationship became all the more distant. On her annual visits Anya would watch his homemade videos about diving in Indonesia. She would be appropriately admiring of her younger brother, and hardly talk about herself. It seemed to her a fair price for continuing to enjoy such a good relationship with her exceptional dad. Just occasionally a feeling of resentment would begin to gnaw at her, but she ignored it. If her father was the perfect dad, then she must be the perfect daughter: never quarrel, never take offense, never be demanding, be genuinely pleased for her younger brother, and to the question "How are you?" always reply "I'm fine."

From immediately beneath the window of their cell came the scratching sound of a broom that brought Anya back to reality. The detention center gates opened with a screech, and a large vehicle, probably a garbage truck, came wheezing in. She wondered why her father had asked which detention center she was being held in.

"Time for breakfast!" the blonde policewoman who had taken Anya's fingerprints told them through the peephole.

Natasha and Ira's bunk came to life. Anya heard Natasha twisting and turning in the top bunk, sniffing and muttering. Ira jumped up like a runner hearing the starting pistol.

"Hurrah!" she exclaimed in a loud whisper, giving her toothless grin. "I'm going home today!"

"Well, some good news at last," Natasha muttered from above, though she didn't sound happy. Then again, everything under the sun incurred Natasha's displeasure.

Ira was fluttering around the cell from the washbasin to the bed and putting her clothes on along the way. Noticing that Anya was awake, she immediately rushed over to her.

"Come to breakfast with us!"

"I don't want to."

"But it's delicious, honestly!"

"I really just don't want to."

"Why doesn't anybody ever come for breakfast?"

"Why are you p-pestering her? She told you, she doesn't want to," Natasha hissed at her.

Ira was immediately silent, but the blissful smile never left her face. She was usually like this only under the influence of Lyrica.

Natasha and Ira went off and the cell lapsed into silence. Anya did not notice herself dozing off.

She woke again when her cellmates returned. Natasha's face lacked its usual expression of antipathy, which given her emotional range could be taken for an expression of unbounded joy. She was triumphantly bearing a new bottle of hot water.

"The s-servers gave it to us," she explained, looking at Anya, although she had not asked.

"So how is Andrey?"

"Who?" Natasha stopped beside Anya's bunk and frowned as she tried to recall.

"The server who got scalded with boiling water yesterday," Anya said, an image of the dark canteen full of specters flashing into her mind before she shook it off.

"Oh, him . . . We d-didn't see him. I don't know."

Natasha went over to the locker as if it was a matter of no consequence and started making tea. Anya gave her a dark look. She found Natasha's indifference objectionable. After all, it was she who had tied her stupid string holder around the bottle and caused Andrey to be injured, and now she didn't even know who Anya was talking about.

The morning was little different from other mornings. People woke up and immediately started smoking. Natasha, slurping her tea, was languidly swearing at Ira for some reason, not even because she was angry but just out of habit. In response Ira only laughed, today even more blissful than usual, annoying everybody with her unclouded joy. Maya asked Diana to lend her a comb and, tossing her mane of hair to one side, sat like Rapunzel stroking it with the comb. For someone who had spent five days in a cell without taking a shower, she looked unforgivably glamorous.

Today's shift was the really unpleasant one: the rotund female robot and her fat-faced colleagues. When they came into the cell and everyone stood up, Anya did so with ostentatious reluctance. She did not at all like standing in front of this woman, but even less did she want to get into a war of words with her. Her very appearance aroused such animosity in Anya that the prospect of coming into conflict with her again was just too repulsive.

Having read out their names in her lifeless voice, the duty officer nodded to her stony-faced subordinate with the eye makeup, who immediately started searching around the beds with a metal detector. Anya felt the blood rush to her head, even though she personally had nothing to fear. Just the fact of being subjected to it once more seemed so invasive that she felt an urge to make a scene. Nevertheless, she gritted her teeth, said nothing, and concentrated on focusing all her contempt in her look.

When the police had gone back out and the stony-faced woman with the metal detector was about to close the door, Anya asked, "Is it permissible to bring an onion into a special detention center?"

"What?" the woman asked in astonishment, her stony face registering disbelief.

"I said, is it allowed to bring an onion to a detention center for a prisoner?"

"An ordinary onion?"

"Yes, of course."

"Well, what are you going to eat with it?"

"Just tell me, is it allowed? Yes or no?" Anya said sharply. She was still angry about the search.

The woman shrugged in an offhand manner and said, "Of course."

"But really, what do you want an onion for?" Katya inquired after the door had closed.

"I just do."

"Well, I would like tvorog," Diana said. She plonked herself down on her bunk, making her monumental breasts wobble under her dress, and added with a pout, "Who would have thought they could bring me to the point of dreaming about plain old cottage cheese?"

They all started talking about their food cravings. Anya's stomach rumbled. Shielding herself behind her book, she tried not to listen, but fragments of words reached her all the same. Within five minutes she was picturing potato pancakes, butter, prawns washed down with beer, stuffed peppers, black cherries, goby fish in tomato sauce, milk, boiled corn, Napoleon gateau, and chicken Kiev. Any one of her cellmates had only to remember some food item for all the others to sigh, "Oh, *yes*."

"Will I really be back home today?" Maya all but moaned ecstatically. All this time she was combing her hair, which now gleamed with a dazzling sheen.

"Me too! Me too!" Ira squealed jubilantly. "My people told me on the phone yesterday they'll be here to meet me."

"What do you mean, your 'people'?" Natasha asked, slurping her tea and looking down at Ira with boundless contempt.

"Well, my friends . . . Oh dear. I've put on so much weight in here, I can't think what they'll say."

Ira jumped out of bed and skipped over to the washstand. She examined herself in the mirror, twirling first to one side, then to the other, and tut-tutting in dismay.

"What will they say? 'Some bimbo we've got here!'" Katya sneered. In contrast to Natasha's sullen contempt, Katya's scorn was bright and spiteful. Perched on her top bunk, she followed Ira's every move with her big, predatory blue eyes. "What could your alky pals have to say anyway?"

"I expect I've gotten fat because I haven't been drinking," Ira concluded. Standing side-on, she sucked in her stomach, assessed the result, and relaxed it again. "I don't usually, like, eat anything. I just drink."

Diana, lying on her side, stretched gracefully. She resembled Rembrandt's Danaë and watched Ira through half-closed eyes.

"It is curious, of course," Diana finally observed, and fell silent. Everybody turned to her, expecting her to continue, but she was in no hurry. She slowly adjusted the pillow and propped her head on her hand.

"What's curious?" Katya asked, losing patience and leaning down from her top bunk with her ponytail dangling in midair.

"Well, you see, Ira—only don't be offended—Ira is a drunk, but she still worries about what her fellow alkies might say about her being overweight. Women will always be women."

"Oh, and I suppose you are some kind of special woman, right?!" Katya snorted. "You never worry about your weight!"

"I don't!" Diana threw haughtily back at her. "I like myself just the way I am."

Katya cackled.

"Everyone's favorite excuse! How much do you weigh anyhow? A hundred kilos?"

Diana kicked the mattress. Katya shrieked, but without ceasing to cackle.

"You're just jealous," Diana advised her good-naturedly. "Look at you, all skin and bones. You've got no tits on you. Not like me!"

She patted her bosom proudly. Katya again chuckled derisively, but did not argue.

While they were joking, the others were silent. Anya was again reminded of school, where there are always two friends who are the most popular girls and the center of attention, and the rest of the girls are split into those who also want to be their friends and suck up to them, and those who are afraid of becoming the butt of their jokes. Anya invariably belonged to the second group.

"Actually, plus-sized models are in fashion right now," Diana informed her. "Especially black women."

The peephole in the door opened.

"Anyone want to make phone calls?" the policeman asked in an unfriendly tone of voice.

For some reason, the line for phones was especially slow this time, or was it just that Anya was so impatient to call? Every time the duty officer waddled off like a goose to her office to collect another prisoner's bag, Anya rolled her eyes.

"Perhaps you should just give their phones out to everyone at once and we could sign for them afterwards," she suggested to the stony-faced cop standing alongside her.

"Against regulations," he muttered, without even looking at her.

Taking her phone, she asked the duty officer, "Am I right in thinking people I know can come here to see me? To check how I am?"

"While serving their sentence a prisoner may receive one visitor for a period of one hour," she rapped out robotically.

"And bring a parcel?"

"Not exceeding thirty kilograms."

"That will be more than enough," Anya assured her.

The duty officer fixed her unblinking, expressionless gaze on Anya, evidently waiting for her to join her cellmates. With a sigh, Anya went to the phone room.

Turning on her phone, she immediately began typing a message for her friends. Inflamed by all the recent discussion of food, Anya gave free rein to her imagination. In addition to the onion, she asked for chips, crackers, cookies, bars of chocolate, nuts, and salty cheese. This was only a small part of all the things Anya wanted, but she was already sufficiently familiar with the ways of a special detention center to know that a Napoleon gateau would not be allowed entry. She again felt a surge of self-pity. How many ordinary, simple things she was deprived of here! And how humiliating it was that even some of these simple treats would be forbidden. Outside this prison she had never craved chips or crackers, but here such things were her only joy. Trying to feel less sorry for herself, Anya magnanimously added a couple of packs of cigarettes as a treat for her cellmates.

When they returned to the cell, the radio was on, and voices could be heard through the open window. They went to their bunks, and Katya promptly climbed onto the windowsill and lit a cigarette. She looked from behind the bars out over the exercise yard with an independent air that suggested it was her personal domain. Ira, meanwhile, folded her bed linen and sat down on the bare mattress. For want of anything better to do, she began pulling threads out of it. She twisted one around the index fingers of both hands and then broke it. Her expression as she did so was blissful, but vacuous, as if in her mind she was being carried off to somewhere very far away. She must be imagining being released, Anya supposed.

"Hey, girls, look at this," Katya said suddenly in amazement. "There's a dude out there wearing a suit!"

Natasha sat up on her upper bunk and looked out the window.

"It's true," she confirmed, not seeming surprised, and sat back down. "He's w-wearing a jacket of some kind."

Ira also tried to look out the window, but was pushed aside by Diana.

"Stylish guy," she observed, nudging Katya with her elbow. "Gimme a puff."

Katya handed her a cigarette and shouted out the window, "Dude, why so trendy? Are you getting married?"

"No, I'm the best man," came from outside.

"What? The best man?" Maya pricked up her ears and climbed onto Natasha's top bunk. She tried to move gracefully and, climbing up, remembered to point her toes.

Natasha was, as usual, displeased, this time about having an uninvited guest. Muttering under her breath, she yanked her blanket out from under Maya, but did not shoo her away.

"What, have you really ended up here after a wedding?" Katya asked in amazement.

"Yep." The voice approached and was now immediately under their window. "I went at night to buy booze and they got me. Here it seems to be the same story for just about everyone."

"Were you plastered?" Katya asked in an understanding voice. "And don't stand down there, you should climb up on the bench."

The bench creaked and a dazzling ginger head of hair appeared at the window.

"I was totally out of it," the head confirmed. "I tried to shake the cops off by driving around in courtyards for ten minutes. Hello, ladies!"

Anya's cellmates reciprocated in a ragged chorus.

"So what's your name?" Katya asked, taking the cigarette from Diana and taking a drag.

"Kirill."

"And what did they do, bring you straight here?" Diana asked. She laid her arms flat on the windowsill, her chin resting on her hands. Her face was very close to Kirill's. She fluttered her eyelashes.

"No, they took me to the police department first," Kirill said, not noticing Diana's interest. "I slept it off there. Then there was a court hearing, then I was brought here. I suppose I was lucky, the cops were fairly decent guys. As we were driving here I asked them to go to the bank."

"What bank?" Maya asked, puzzled.

"I work in a bank. I wanted to fill out an application for leave. I'll be stuck here for ten days now. How am I going to explain that at work? Then we drove to a store, and then here."

"You seem to have been really lucky with your cops," Katya remarked, half closing her eyes incredulously and blowing smoke toward the ceiling.

"Oh, I just bought vodka for them. By the way, would you like some?"

"Some what?"

"Vodka!" Kirill raised his hand to show Anya's cellmates a bottle of Shishkin Woods mineral water.

"What, is that—vodka?" Diana whispered, her eyes wide with amazement.

Ira, who all this time had been unsuccessfully trying to gain a better position by the window, rushed forwards like a scalded cat.

"Have you really got *vodka*?" she exclaimed.

"Shh, you!" Diana hissed, deftly brushing her aside.

"How about it?" Kirill asked, waggling his Shishkin Woods.

Anya's cellmates fell silent as they contemplated the bottle.

"Nah," Katya finally said in a regretful voice, speaking for everyone. "It won't fit through the bars anyway. "How did you smuggle it in, though?"

"Oh, they didn't give a fuck. I poured it into this bottle while I was in the car with the cops. Here nobody even sniffed it. Well, if you don't want to, fine."

Kirill unscrewed the lid and took several gulps. The women watched in fascination. Taking his lips from the bottle, he wiped his mouth with the back of his hand without so much as wincing and, as if it had been nothing, asked, "Don't suppose you've got any cigarettes?"

Katya silently held out the pack.

"Oh, there are only two left. Well, never mind. Someone's bringing me cigarettes tomorrow. I'll be able to repay you."

Kirill put his hand between the bars and took the lighter from the windowsill. He took a drag, closed his eyes, and slowly exhaled.

Such pleasure was written on his face that even nonsmoking Anya felt jealous.

"Well, fine," Kirill said at last. "Thanks for that. I'll bring you something tomorrow in return."

After that, he jumped down from the bench.

"What's he going to bring us tomorrow?" Ira asked. "Some vodka perhaps?"

"What difference will it make for you, half-wit?" Natasha snarled. "You're getting out today,"

"Oh, of course, that's true," Ira said, blossoming. Natasha's observation seemed to bring her back to reality. "I'd better get ready."

Skipping away from the window, she dragged a battered plastic bag out from under her bunk and started rummaging through it enthusiastically. The others slunk back to their bunks. "Vodka. Just great!" Diana muttered under her breath.

Ira dug a pair of misshapen yellowish sneakers out of her bag, switching them for her flip-flops. She went to the washbasin, let her hair down, and immediately started gathering it up more neatly. Turning her head from side to side in front of the mirror and evidently satisfied with the result, she flitted back to the bag and extracted a bra from it. Under her breath she was quietly keeping up a running commentary on her actions. She referred to her bra as "the flak." It took Anya a moment to understand she meant it like "flak jacket." Taking off her denim, she put the bra on and got dressed again. She ran back to the mirror to restore her hairdo, which had come adrift.

At lunch the only servers were Viktor Ivanovich and another mousy lad. When Anya asked where Andrey was, Viktor Ivanovich's face fell and he said, "He's lying in the cell. An ambulance was called for him yesterday, they took him away then brought him back. He's alive, but the scalding was very bad."

At just that moment, the new lad plonked a full kettle down on the stove, water spilled out and landed on the burner with a loud hiss.

"Watch what you're doing! Don't be so clumsy!" Victor Ivanovich reproached the young server, forgetting all about Anya and clearly relishing being in charge of the kitchen.

Anya sat down at the table and fished through her bowl. Grated carrot topped gluey pasta. After carefully inspected this offering, she sighed and waited with redoubled anticipation for her friends to arrive with their parcel.

She did not have long to wait. No sooner had they returned from lunch than the stony-faced woman with painted eyes came into the cell.

"A visitor for you," she said to Anya.

Anya jumped up and slipped her feet, although not at the first attempt, into flats and pattered across to the door. The woman watched her icily. They went along the corridor toward the phone call room. There was no one at the duty desk and the grating in front of the room was unlocked. The woman let Anya through. She was almost dancing with impatience down the short corridor. The grating slammed shut behind her.

At a wooden table, his hands resting on it, sat Anya's father. This was so completely unexpected that at first she didn't recognize him.

In a sad voice, her dad said, "Hello, daughter." He got up from the table and came and hugged her. He kissed her on the cheek.

Anya hesitantly raised her arms, and awkwardly poked her father's neck with her lips. They registered a barely perceptible salty taste. Her father smelled nice, of eau de cologne and laundry detergent.

"Well, how come you are in here?" he asked with a mixture of sympathy and irritation.

It was not clear what was irritating him, Anya's being in a special detention center, or the government for putting her in one.

"You've lost weight," he said.

"It's just you haven't seen me for a long time," Anya finally responded and cautiously sat down in an adjacent chair. Her father sat back down on the other side of the table and continued to look at her with concern. "Personally, I'm fine," she said, "but how come you are here?"

"I could hardly just leave you in a situation like this!"

"I mean, what are you doing in Moscow at all? I thought you were now . . ." Anya faltered, "living outside Russia."

Her father had for years been spending his summers abroad, before finally moving to Italy. Anya had learned that only several months later, despite their having exchanged emails in the interim. All this time her father had, as usual, preferred to talk about his younger children, omitting to mention the move. Later, he did, of course, send her photographs of the new house, described the eccentricities of the Italian way of life, and invited her to visit, but she could not rid herself of the impression that the move was something he had wanted to keep secret from her. Anya felt it really was better just not to ask questions. There was no knowing how far her feelings corresponded to reality, but not wanting, as usual, to inconvenience her father, and accustomed to the fact that the link between them did not extend beyond conversation on safe subjects, she persuaded herself it was probably better that way. Since then she had not only asked no questions about Italy, she had not even mentioned the name of his new country of residence, confining herself to the vague "outside Russia."

"I'm here on business, and see how good the timing is," her father sighed. "There's an exhibition on now in Moscow. We have a whole stand at it, so I came to network with everyone and sign a contract with a new supplier. I've brought you our brochure. Otherwise I imagine you probably have nothing at all to read here!"

Her father laughed heartily, as if that were a clever joke. Anya smiled mechanically and said, "I have things to read."

Her father abruptly stopped laughing and, again assuming an expression of great concern, repeated: "How are you doing here?"

"Fine."

"Fine . . . And are you alone in your cell?"

"No, I have five other people with me."

"And what are they like?"

"They're all fine too."

"I'm very worried about you, daughter," her father said, leaning forward. For a moment Anya thought with horror that he was about to take her hand, but he did not. Anya mentally counted to two, so that the movement would not seem too impolite, and removed her hand from the tabletop, squeezing it between her knees for good measure.

"Everything is perfectly fine," she repeated. "You don't need to worry about me."

"Well, but you're in prison. That is beyond a joke."

"This is not a prison," Anya corrected him.

Her dad dismissed that.

"It doesn't matter what it's called. The main thing is it's now not just a matter of you attending rallies. You are going to be under scrutiny, and that is a serious matter."

So many words flared up at once in Anya's head: she wanted to feel indignant, to say she had never had any intention of limiting herself to actions that were not serious, that half measures were of no interest to her, that if you have decided to take up the struggle you should not be daunted by the difficulties, and many more high-minded ideas. But in the end she kept her mouth shut. Given that she had kept her father at arm's length for so many years, it would be odd now to demand that he should fully understand her decisions.

"You think a special detention center is something terrible," Anya reassured him. "But in fact it's just a place where you sleep and read. So don't worry about me. I'm only in for ten days."

"And what if next time you are jailed for longer?" her father expostulated.

Anya almost frowned, but showed her typical restraint.

"Well, then I'll be in jail for a bit longer," she replied with a gentle smile.

Her father again leaned back in his chair and looked Anya over, as if seeing her for the first time.

"It's your mother who stuffed your head with all this nonsense," he said bitterly.

Anya was freaked out by this abrupt change of tone.

"What did my mother stuff into my head?"

"It's just part of her personality. She's so uncompromising, so argumentative. Always at loggerheads with everyone. I remember I helped her get a job after we had separated. I asked a friend to take her on. She arrived, worked for a month, and then quit. She told me my friend had insulted her. It would have been beneath her dignity to put up with such a thing. I asked him later what had happened, and he . . . Well, there's really no point going into it now. She got something into her head and ended up her own worst enemy."

Anya was wide-eyed with surprise. She stared at her father, quite forgetting her practiced impartiality. His tirade was so far outside the carefully defined limits of permissible topics that Anya was not immediately aware of what he was talking about.

"What has all this got to do with my mother?" she asked foolishly.

"Forgive me," her father said with a sigh, a guilty expression on his face. "But you need to understand that in this world it is those who are flexible who win. Those who can adapt to circumstances. Your mother is not like that, and I can see how much of her there is in you. It is probably my fault too. If I had been at home too, I could have tried to put things right, to explain to you that sometimes it is best to compromise, to sit it out rather than immediately get into a fight. But you see, I couldn't be there for you, because one fine day your mother decided to throw me out of her life too."

Perhaps if they had been sitting at home this kind of conversation would never have happened. But that boxy little tiled room with its scratched table and bars on the window was not conducive to good manners. Anya had been in a foul mood all day, and her father turning up there with his attacks and his questionable lessons on how to live her life completely took the feet from her.

"She didn't just 'throw you out of her life' for no reason," Anya pointed out wryly. "You cheated on her."

Her father sighed again.

"That behavior did me no credit and I am not at all proud of it. But living with your mother was very difficult. It's her personality . . . She is so full of herself, she always knows better than anyone else. It is very difficult to live in harmony with someone like that."

"So in the end was the reason you weren't at home because she threw you out of her life, or because you couldn't live in harmony with her?" Anya tried to keep her tone icy, but she could feel the heat building up inside her at his unfairness, the injustice of it, and her shock. What was happening now should not happen, but she knew it was already too late to prevent it.

"My dear daughter, I want you to have a happy life. Circumstances can be good or bad but the important thing is to try to turn them to advantage, or at least not to let them harm you. You know I'm no fan of our government and can see all the problems myself. I have even emigrated because I understand that the situation in Russia is far from ideal. Perhaps you should get out too? Find a university abroad where you could study?"

"I don't want to study abroad," Anya said, as crisply as she could. "You have emigrated but I intend to stay."

Her dad shook his head. His grave expression turned to one of concern. Anya reflected unemotionally that she did not for a moment believe he was being sincere. It had always seemed to her that, just as she kept him at a distance with her reticence, her father kept her at a distance with feigned emotions. Neither of them ever revealed their true emotions to each other.

"I worry about you," her father said again. "It is very dangerous to go to protest rallies these days. You can see what is going on. And if you do get thrown in a real jail, God forbid, who is going to get you out? Who is going to help you then? Your friends? Your mother? No. It will be me!"

Her dad was saying this almost in a rage, and for a moment it seemed to Anya that his mask had slipped, but then he assumed an expression of great sorrow and concern.

"I shall never abandon you. But it is up to you to use your head. If anything happens to you, there will be no one else to help. You will come to me and say 'Daddy, Daddy, help! Daddy, you were right!'"

Anya was furious.

"I will never come to you and will never say that to you," she said harshly.

"Who always helps you? Who always comes to your aid?" her father persisted. "I do! Remember when you ran away from home and I found you? And what did you say to me then? 'Don't give me back to Mother!' And I didn't. I arranged for you to stay with Irina Sergeyevna. I funded you!"

Anya felt a fire spreading through her whole body. Her eyes even seemed to be misting over and she blinked twice. She was fizzing with rage.

"You can rest assured I will never ask for your help," she repeated, enunciating each word. Her father was brought up short, as if hearing her for the first time. He looked at Anya in surprise.

"It's good you've recalled that. When I ran away from home, you didn't take me in, you foisted me on some woman I didn't know and paid her just to be rid of me. That was all the help I got from you."

Her father was silent for a few moments, staring at Anya in shock.

"How can you say such things?" he finally managed. "Why, if it hadn't been for me . . ."

"I've never been good enough for you," Anya interrupted. The flames were so raging inside her that the words felt like sparks. "You never gave a damn. Do you actually know anything about me? You keep telling me about your children, and you don't even try to find out how I'm doing. And now that I'm locked up here, you come and start lecturing me. Where were you up till now? Where was your anxiety and concern? You remember my existence once a year and think you can come and teach me how to live my life."

Her father continued to look at Anya with wide eyes, but the stunned expression disappeared from his face, giving way to a hint of a smile—as if he had decoded the meaning hidden behind her words and was feeling pleased with himself. When she stopped talking for a moment to catch her breath, he said, "It's simple jealousy."

Anya was about to carry on but was stopped midsentence.

"What is jealousy?" she said, so surprised it came out almost calmly.

"You're jealous of my other children," her father explained. "Older children are always jealous of the younger ones. You are envious of their successes and offended that I seem to pay you less attention."

Anya blinked several times. The fury came over her in an instant, everything went dark in her eyes, and in another instant it drained away without trace. Anya felt her shoulders relax and sag. She had not been aware of the tension.

"Is that all you understood from what I have said?" she asked wearily.

"What I have understood, daughter, is that you do not know how to be grateful, and that hurts me a lot." Her father pronounced this with such theatrical bitterness and shook his head so dramatically that Anya realized the window had been slammed shut. He had come back to himself. It suddenly dawned that her dad had never managed to be a real father. He had faked the feelings that, in his blurred imagination, fathers were expected to experience in particular situations, and had no inkling that they were perceived as completely false.

Anya looked instead at the window. There, behind the grille, the branches of a cherry tree were swaying with tiny fruits. They hung close, but Anya knew that her hand could never reach them through the grille. In a place where you were deprived of so many simple things, you should surely at least have the luxury of terminating a disagreeable conversation when you felt like it, Anya thought, standing up.

"Goodbye, Dad."

"Wait, daughter . . ."

Anya went to the grating and shook it.

"Hey, open up. I'm finished," she said loudly.

The bulbous duty officer looked out of her room and stared blankly at Anya.

"Finished?" she asked flatly.

"Yes, finished."

The duty officer looked behind Anya's back. Her father had evidently come up behind her.

"We're not done yet. My daughter is evidently just impatient to get back to her cell," he said with a forced laugh. He was trying to behave as if nothing had happened.

The officer now subjected him to the same expressionless stare. *Is she even human?* Anya thought irritably.

"No, we're done," she repeated.

The officer looked at her again but made no move. She looked like a hen that had just now been wandering around the yard and suddenly froze in one place. What thoughts might be racing through her tiny head, if indeed there were any, was far from clear.

"Anya, come back, please. Let's talk this through," her father said gravely.

"We've already done that. Are you going to let me out of here or not?" The luxury of terminating a conversation had proved illusory and existed only as far as the nearest grating. It was intolerable to have to stand in front of that blank stare of the duty officer with her father burbling embarrassing stuff. Anya felt she was again beginning to seethe with anger because of her sense of powerlessness.

"Are you going to let me out or not?" she rasped, pushing angrily at the grating.

The officer moved a few steps nearer.

"Anya, don't be silly," her father said, taking her by the hand.

Anya was so surprised she jerked to one side suddenly and her shoulder hit the grating. The officer froze half a meter away from them.

"So are you still talking?" she asked, looking first at Anya, then at her father, the perfect vacuum of her gaze filling with something akin to annoyance.

"No!" Anya exclaimed, feeling that she was on the verge of disgracefully bursting into tears from the shame of it all: herself, her father, and this imbecile lack of freedom.

The duty officer finally inserted the key in the lock and made a great show of turning it very, very slowly.

"Anya," her dad said again, but Anya shot out of the room like a bullet and rushed to the corridor leading to her cell. Her flight did not last long, however, because another grating blocked the corridor. Detention centers were clearly not designed for dramatic exits.

Very slowly the officer came waddling up and fiddled with the key in the lock, all the time looking sideways at Anya with those inscrutable hen's eyes. Anya could not read what she was thinking, and that unnerved her all the more. At last the door was open.

"Take her to her cell," the duty officer called to the stony-faced policewoman who was lurking in the corridor.

"Goodbye, Dad," Anya said again and, without turning around, walked quickly off down the corridor.

She could feel her father staring after her, and cringed inwardly for fear he would call to her again, but this time he was silent. With a great rattling of keys, the policewoman opened the door for her and Anya darted into the cell.

"What happened?" Maya asked, staring at her in alarm.

Anya shook her head. Without a word, she made straight for her bunk, lay down, and pulled the blanket over her head.

At first she just lay there, unaware of anything—not the smell of cigarette smoke, nor the sound of water from the leaking tap, nor the talk of her cellmates. Waves of adrenaline swept through her, and somewhere deep inside there was absolute emptiness, the absence of thought. It was so pleasant just to lie there and not think. Unfortunately, to remain in that blessed state of tranquility for long called for too much acrobatic skill. Unable to keep her balance, Anya began to turn things over in her mind.

She remembered herself well from the age of fourteen. Before that time there seemed to have been no Anya. Instead of her, there had existed an elusive, changeable substance. After it, that substance gradually assumed form, set, and Anya seemed to become fully aware of herself.

From that moment on she could conduct a dialogue with herself, compare impressions, and register changes. The process of solidifying, when personality was coming together from a bunch of disparate impulses, was not quick and was accompanied by real storms. Other people usually refer to this condescendingly as a "transitional age," and are no doubt partly right. Only for Anya the transition was not from childhood to youth, but from nonbeing to being.

It was a very bumpy transition. The way ordinary children grow up is by experimenting with naughtiness from birth. By the fourteenth year of this systematic experimentation, they have usually reached the point at which they try smoking for the first time, are rude to their parents, and slam their bedroom doors. In Anya's case, however, the chronology was completely upturned. She was the most accommodating child in the world. Not because that was her personality, but because she did not have a stable personality. She felt no need to defend her opinions or probe the boundaries of freedom, because no event in the outside world came into conflict with her. There was nothing there to be in conflict with. She was good at her lessons because she found learning easy. She read a lot because reading was not boring. She did not stay out late because she was not much interested in boys her own age. She did not lie to her parents, was not scared of the dentist, wore a warm hat in winter like a good girl, and went to bed at the right time. To an outsider, Anya must have seemed like a perfect little girl.

But then one fine day, she suddenly began to develop, like the outline of a figure in a Polaroid photograph. It happened so rapidly that in an instant the perfect little girl was gone. It transpired that she did not actually like almost anything in her daily routine. Her schoolwork she promptly abandoned. Books too. Anya began actively exploring the world and people around her. All her classmates were interested in boys, and Anya too took an enthusiastic interest in them. She soon discovered, however, that she was no less interested in girls. Especially her classmate Masha.

Masha had gleaming golden hair and blue eyes. She sometimes colored her eyelashes, and invariably smeared her golden bangs with black mascara. Anya thought she was perfection—beautiful, grown-up (six months older than her), and daring. Masha sometimes bought cigarettes and Anya smoked them together with her—she sucked the smoke into her mouth and let it out again. They skipped classes together. Once they bought a Screwdriver in a store—vodka and Fanta—and drank it together. Masha boasted that she had already tried alcohol several times before, but for Anya it was an epoch-making moment, a true initiation, as it seemed to her, into grown-upness. She was so desperate to be drunk she could almost make herself imagine she was.

Relations with her mother, needless to say, went rapidly downhill. She had no idea that her adult daughter was coming into being right now and decided to nip rebellion in the bud. She might as well have tried dousing a fire with gasoline.

The first time, Anya ran away from home for just one day. How it happened was: in the morning she went to school as usual, but decided not to return home. Masha's mother was a nurse and that night happened to be staying at the hospital. They could not have hoped for a better set of circumstances. After school Anya went home with Masha. There they ransacked the kitchen cabinets, found rubbing alcohol, diluted it with water and drank—Masha for no particular reason, Anya for Dutch courage. After that, she called her mother and announced she would not be coming home that night. Her mum shrieked, "Anya! Anya!" into the phone, but by sheer force of will, she hung up on her. Putting on the very shortest skirts they could find in Masha's house, they went out on the town.

Oddly enough, nothing bad resulted from this rebellion—neither during their partying nor the following day, when Anya finally returned home. Her mum was so alarmed by her escapade and so happy to see her back alive and well that she did not make a fuss. Anya decided she was now ready for adulthood.

Three weeks later she ran away from home again. This time for real. She even left her mother a farewell letter. According to plan, she met up with Masha in the city center and for a start went to where Masha's boyfriend worked. The boyfriend was four years older than them and worked in an amusement park. His highly exotic job was to run, wearing a protective suit, between two human-sized cardboard cacti while customers of the sideshow attempted to shoot him with paintball guns.

Masha informed him that she and Anya were leaving for St. Petersburg. The boyfriend showed his serious reservations about the plan by screwing a finger at his temple, but new customers arrived and the conversation had to be put on hold. Anya and Masha spent the next few hours continuing it when they could. They thought the best idea was for the boyfriend to help them get to Petersburg, but he clearly did not share their enthusiasm.

It eventually got dark, and Anya and Masha began wondering where they could spend the night, given that they had not yet departed for Petersburg. At just that moment Anya noticed some visitors to the park who were heading directly to their sideshow, and recognized her parents. It was so unimaginable that her mum and dad might be together, no more than half a meter from each other, that Anya froze, and even gasped in amazement. Her goggle-eyed parents all but ran toward the sideshow, and it finally occurred to Anya that they were here because they were searching for her and by some fluke had found her. Without stopping to think, she started running away but tired quickly. Her dad caught up and took her to the car. Anya found out later it was Masha's mother who helped her parents track her down by remembering Masha had a friend of some description who worked at the park.

From that day on Anya was under house arrest. Her mother confiscated her cell phone and, when she left for work, took the landline phone out of the apartment and locked it away in the outside storage area. It was the beginning of summer, school was over, and Anya slunk around the house alone for days on end, contemplating a plan of escape. She tried to access the internet but did not know how to send a message to Masha, who did not have an email address. Anya's apartment was on the seventh floor, so jumping out the window was not an option. She tried poking at the door lock, but soon realized she was flogging a dead horse. Only in books do characters manage to pick locks with hairpins.

When her mother returned in the evenings the situation got worse. Not only did she not talk to Anya, she seemed quite unaware of her existence. If Anya caught her mother looking at her, the gaze was so icy that she found it unendurable. Most of the time, Anya sat in her room, wondering how and when this would all end. A couple of times she mounted covert raids on her mother's handbag in an attempt to find her cell, but was always detected and failed.

Finally it was the weekend, but that was even more terrible, because her mother was at home all the time. Determined at all costs to punish Anya, she succeeded also in punishing herself. She did not retrieve the landline from storage, and kept the front door locked and the key hidden. Lying facedown on her bed, Anya was listening to her mother hanging the washing on the balcony.

Just at that moment, the doorbell rang. Anya did not know for sure who it was, but instantly an idea came to her. She leaped out of bed and yelled, "I'll get it!" The corridor to the door was the road to freedom.

"I'll open it myself," her mother replied. Without looking at Anya, who was shifting from one foot to the other at the door, she peered through the peephole before slowly taking the key out of her bag, inserting it in the lock, and turning it. Anya followed her movements intently. Giving the door a shove, her mother stepped back to let the visitor come in. It was a neighbor from upstairs. Without a second's delay, Anya hurtled forward like a bowling ball, sweeping her mother and the neighbor out of the way, and jumping down the stairs five at a time.

She heard her mother shouting and calling her back, she heard the echo of her feet slapping on the stairs in the cathedral silence of the stairwell, the elevator coming to life with a howl as it rocketed towards the seventh floor, but by now there was no catching Anya. She rushed outside and headed for the nearby woods. If she could only run into them and hide between the trees, she would never be found. Anya had no plan. She had left her phone, money, ID—everything—at home, but she was carried forth on a wave of exhilaration.

After she had run a couple of hundred meters into the woods, she slowed down to a walking pace. She had left her home far behind, fully confident her mother would not catch up. She felt so angry with her, and was so exhausted by the last few days, that just walking past trees was a delight. The path, which was soft underfoot after recent rain, changed to gravel, and it was only then that Anya realized she had fled the house in slippers. Not only did that not faze her, she found it rather amusing. In fact, right now she was finding everything amusing.

The far end of the woods opened on to a road with a bus stop, from which she could travel to the city center. Anya decided she would go there and take a bus to Masha's house. The plan ended at the moment when she met up with Masha, but Anya had no doubt that together they would come up with something. Admittedly, she felt a slight gnawing anxiety that Masha might not be home, and a somewhat greater anxiety that Masha might have forgotten all about her because they had not been in touch for so many days, but she brushed those unworthy thoughts aside.

She left the wood and walked along the road. A hundred meters from the bus stop she noticed a dark green car. It suddenly did a U-turn and moved swiftly towards her. On the snow-white license plate, radiant in the rays of the sun, was written "011." Anya watched as the car approached, unable to take her eyes off it. It was just as bewitching and impossible as a scene in a movie. By an effort of will, she took her eyes off the license plate and looked at the driver, although she already knew who he was. The person looking straight at her through the windshield was her father.

Her mind instantly empty, Anya started running. What was happening was so strange that logic was powerless. Her dad lived on the far side of the city. He had no reason to be here, yet here they were: Anya running along the road verge, with her father running after her. She could hear him gaining and panicked, realizing that in a few instants more he would catch her. The inevitability was so dreadful that she was powerless to resist. She halted in her tracks. Taken by surprise, her father ran straight into her and either hugged or grabbed her. Burrowing into his chest, she wailed desperately, "Just don't give me back to Mother! Don't give me back to Mother!"

And he didn't. Instead he took Anya to his own home, then called her mother and told her Anya was all right, but would be staying with him for now.

Her father was the epitome of calm. He did not scold Anya. She heard not a word of reproach. Instead, he gave her lunch and even poured her half a glass of wine. Anya felt such an overwhelming sense of gratitude that at times she was speechless. All her life she had dreamed that her father would be her knight in shining armor and now, he was. Finally she could relax and stop agonizing over what to do. Anya gazed lovingly at her father's refrigerator magnets, at the meat patty on her plate, at her father's wife, who kept shooting her quick glances, at her little brother who had been wakened in the middle of his afternoon sleep and was now screaming the house down. Anya felt a keen affection for everything, and a complete sense of peace.

The following day, her dad said they would go for a picnic. He was cheerful and relaxed and Anya daydreamed how they would live together, how she would move to another school and make new friends. The previous day he had lent her his phone so she could call Masha. She had answered, but had been less than delighted to hear of Anya's escapade. Anya felt hurt and relieved at the same time. She no longer had any close friendships and could plunge wholeheartedly into her new life.

It turned out at the picnic that they were not alone. They were unexpectedly joined by a woman Anya did not know, and her daughter. Anya's father said this woman was the former nanny of Anya's little half brother. Her daughter was two years older than Anya. Anya did not want strangers invading her new life with her dad on this very first day, but braced herself to be tolerant. In any case, the new girl did not seem utterly ghastly. She was tall and thin, wore enormous hoop earrings, and looked down on her mother so much that Anya could not help being rather taken by her. Her name was Dasha.

By evening, Anya was completely bewitched by Dasha, mainly because Dasha knew absolutely nothing about her. Anya felt this was just what was needed for her new beginning: people who had not already made up their minds about her. She could be anything she liked with them, and since Anya was only just beginning to know herself, there was scope for experimentation. She was saying goodbye to Dasha almost with regret, when her father suddenly said that if Anya liked, she could spend the night at Dasha's, because she and her mother had no objection to that at all.

That was how Anya ended up in a modest old apartment on the very outskirts of the city. Although the district was officially considered part of the city, to Anya it looked more like a village. The houses were low, clotheslines with washing hung between trees in the yards, cigarettes were sold individually in tiny basement shops, everybody knew everybody else and, when they met in the street, they talked for a long time. Here Dasha lived with her mother and stepfather, a strange, quiet man who scuttled about the apartment as if apologizing for his presence. Nobody paid any attention to him and neither, of course, did Anya—until that first weekend when she, together with Dasha and her girlfriends, went to a lake to swim. Anya got sunburned, and in the evening Dasha's mother told her to rub kefir over herself. Standing in the kitchen in a short skirt and bra, Anya gasped as the cold kefir dripped over her burned shoulders. Suddenly, she saw Dasha's stepfather standing around the corner in the corridor, reflected in a mirror. In that same mirror he was leering at Anya with a disgusting, sleazy look in his eyes. Realizing Anya had spotted him, he immediately looked away and disappeared into the room. After that, Anya did her best to avoid him.

Apart from that unpleasantness, at first she liked living with Dasha, and when a few days later her dad suggested she might move there for a longer period, Anya agreed without any fuss. Dasha introduced her to her friends, who were all a few years older than Anya and treated her rather patronizingly, but this did not offend her. She liked to feel accepted by older friends.

This was probably the first summer in Anya's life she was able to do as she pleased. Nobody checked how many times she ate, what she got up to, or what time she came back home. She and Dasha never woke up earlier than eleven, went through to the kitchen and ate whatever she wanted straight out of the refrigerator. Then she and Dasha got dressed and went outside. Anya felt there was nothing to stop you from going out even in pajamas. That was how ephemeral the boundary was between home and the outside world. They mostly just hung out around the district, but sometimes they would go off into the countryside. It was fifteen minutes by bus to the lake. If they were hungry they could buy an ice cream. Toward evening they returned home and put on their makeup—an obligatory ritual—and went out again, now looking more sedate. Their evening outings consisted of Dasha and her girlfriends meeting up with boys they knew, and then just driving around the area in their cars at night listening to deafeningly loud music. The first time, Anya kept expecting they were going to actually arrive somewhere, but it turned out that riding around itself was the entertainment. Initially she was bewildered, but gradually became accustomed and even began to enjoy it. She usually rode in the back seat (Dasha, being more popular, sat in the passenger seat), half closing her eyes and feeling the warm breeze in her face, smoking, and thinking contentedly that this was all very exciting and romantic.

Anya saw nothing of her mother. Naturally, she knew where her daughter was—her father had told her—but Anya did not really want to know what she felt about the situation. Although she did call her mother several times, she took great care to keep all details of her new lifestyle from her, as if afraid she might come barging in to destroy it. Her mother, of course, had no intention of barging in anywhere: on the contrary, she talked to her so calmly and gently that Anya began to feel guilty—but when she felt that coming on she tried to terminate the conversation as quickly as possible.

In all the summer her dad never once visited her.

Anya began gradually to notice little things that had not bothered her initially. The main problem was Dasha's mother. In the first place, she made a great show of being religious. In the evenings she would pray, kneeling in the hallway. The entire house was littered with images of Christ and handwritten prayers. There was even one on the toilet door. In the second place, not detecting any contradiction, Dasha's mother was absurdly superstitious. She demanded, for instance, that the lid of the toilet should be kept closed so that "money should not leave the house" by way of it. These traits became a serious problem only when Dasha's mother took Anya's religious education upon herself. For example, she first forbade Anya to read a fantasy novel about the adventures of a young witch, because witches were devilry and an abomination to the Lord. Anya listened politely to her sermonizing and proceeded to ignore it. A couple of days later, she found Anya reading the same book and threw it out, accompanied by much shrieking.

Quite soon, to this were added quasi-biblical homilies and efforts to teach Anya prayers. This was all the more bizarre because Dasha's mother ultimately turned out to be far removed from any semblance of meek, Christian charity. From the first week, she gave Dasha and Anya what, to be fair, was quite generous pocket money. Anya was touched and surprised by her kindness, until Dasha let drop that the money was part of what her father was providing each week for Anya's upkeep. Anya gave the matter no more thought, and remembered it only when the pocket money was suddenly reduced. Indeed, now they had to coax the money out of her, or Dasha did. This meager pocket money was the only luxury now in Anya's life. From the first day her meals had been simple: an open sandwich for breakfast and pasta or potatoes for dinner. Where the money her father was sending for her upkeep went, she had no idea.

Even though the way Anya spent her days was of no interest to Dasha's mother, she did for some reason like revealing certain longer-term plans she had: that Anya was to go to study at night school with Dasha and be able to earn extra money during the day. After all, such a grown-up girl had no business taking money from adults. Dasha's mother declared that all three of them would be going on vacation in a month's time to a health resort near Moscow. She had been talking about this spa ever since Anya arrived. Dasha's mother obviously thought it was marvelous and enthusiastically described the mud baths, mineral waters, and other delights it boasted. Anya did not really fancy going to a health spa, which seemed like a place for old people, but she did not sense any danger in the plan. It was all so vague that she mostly just ignored it.

But the resort proved to be the last straw.

Her father must surely have guessed that Anya's vacation this year was hardly ideal, and may even have felt some pangs of conscience that he was paying so little attention to his daughter. In one of their conversations on the phone he mentioned he could send Anya to summer camp. This was very much his style: to formally honor his parental obligations by shipping Anya off even farther away, but at the time she was very pleased. She had been living with Dasha for two months by now and was beginning to tire somewhat of the disorderliness of life, the monotonous entertainments, and the eccentricities of Dasha's mother. Anya was reluctant to admit it to herself, but she did sometimes feel abandoned and unwanted. The constant mess in Dasha's room, which at first had aroused her respect as an obvious signal of opposition, started to annoy her. The dusty, creaking furniture, the peeling paint, and the broken door on the shoe cabinet, which she had not noticed previously, also suddenly seemed to matter. Talk of going to evening school seemed to rule out all the earlier dreams she had shared with her mother of attending Moscow University. Dasha, meanwhile, was to finish her evening classes and then go to college and study to be a cook. If at first Anya felt a great sense of relief that a burden of ambition was being lifted from her shoulders, she soon found that, without it, she felt lightweight and uneasy. She was upset that in her new environment no one was predicting a bright future for her, and that when she herself hinted she wanted to study at Moscow University, Dasha's mother shooed the idea aside like a fly and said there would never be enough money for that.

Anya cheered up a lot when she thought about the prospect of summer camp, but when she told Dasha and her mother that she would be going away for a few weeks all hell broke loose.

Dasha's mother started shrieking. Anya had never seen anyone become so infuriated in such a short time. "What about the resort?" she screamed. "What sort of ungrateful little brat are you? How dare you make secret plans to go on holiday on your own after all Dasha and I have done for you?" Not satisfied with her ranting, she called Anya's father. "Do you know your daughter is a cheat? She agreed with us we would all go on holiday together and now she is making a fool of us!"

Dasha did not shout, and smirked at her mother's yelling and Anya's excuses. Only late that night, when she and Anya were alone together, she said, "I always knew you were a traitor. That's why you don't have any friends."

That left Anya completely at sea. She sobbed her heart out until late into the night, seething with resentment, feeling that she was being taken advantage of, overwhelmed by a sense of isolation and shame. Never in all her fourteen years had she felt so engulfed by an abyss of despair. Early the next day, she packed her bags and went back to her father.

Everything in his clean, cool house was the same. The same magnets were on the refrigerator, her half brother crawled on the carpet in front of the television, and his wife cast furtive glances at Anya. Anya was waiting for the old magic to return, for her again to see her dad as a hero, and for the wonderful, amazing life that had been promised to return. For some reason, though, being at home with her father only increased her sense of being lonely and abandoned. Her dad was here, but to Anya it seemed he was avoiding her. His jokes were awkward, he did not answer her questions, and would not look her in the eye. At first she thought he was angry with her, then that he was feeling guilty, and eventually that, quite simply, he did not know what to do with her.

So she went to the summer camp, and on her return went to live with her mother.

Lying under the blanket in the detention center, Anya peered dry-eyed into the darkness. Images appeared before her. She remembered the crazing on the blue mug from which she drank boiled water at Dasha's house; the golden Buddha her dad had brought back from Bali; Dasha with a round mirror on her knees, squeezing a pimple on her chin. And her dad's handsome, elongated face, his tall masculine form. How on earth had she managed to kid herself for so many years that he wanted anything to do with her?

Someone touched Anya's shoulder and she extricated herself from the blanket.

"Are you all right?" Maya asked. "You're lying there, not moving. Who came to visit you?"

Anya sat up in her bunk, reluctant to answer, and gestured vaguely. "Oh, just someone."

While she had been away, Katya and Diana had unearthed a checkerboard and were now aggressively playing Chapayev. Diana was trying to knock her opponent's checkers off the board with a flick of the finger, while Katya was targeting Diana herself. Natasha was sitting with her customary frown on Ira's bed, busy with a crossword puzzle.

"Where's Ira?" Anya asked in surprise.

"Sh-she was released while you were away," Natasha replied, not looking up from her crossword. "Practically drove me crazy with her whining. 'I've p-put on so much weight, oh, so much weight! Whatever will p-people say?'"

"I, on the other hand, am worried that this hunger strike of mine will mean I'll lose all the pumped-up fat from my butt," Maya said, suddenly contemplative. Everyone turned to look at her. "And it's barely six months since I had my ass done. Take a look."

She got up on all fours on her bunk and pulled off her pants, revealing, in a G-string, her exquisitely rounded butt.

"See," Maya said matter-of-factly, arching her back and pointing to a small red mark on her thigh—she had one of those on both sides— "That's where they injected the fat. You can't get yourself a nice ass just by going to the gym. Well, actually, you can, but not in all the right places. If you haven't got enough on your butt, you can only correct it by surgery."

"Where do they get the fat from?" Katya asked, inspecting Maya's loins from a distance and with an expression of distaste that was wholly undeserved.

"They take it from the person themself. But I had so little fat on me they had a lot of trouble getting enough. They even sucked it out of my knees!" Maya said proudly, pulling her pants back up with the greatest elegance imaginable.

Katya violently flicked a checker.

"Were you ugly before?"

"Why would you say that? I have always been beautiful. Well, likable for sure."

"Then, why are you doing all this to yourself? If I had a daughter, I would kill her for that. Everybody who gets themselves these identical huge boobs and big ass looks like they've come off a factory line. My dad always told me: a woman should have something special about her. A big nose, say, or a gap between her teeth."

"Ira certainly had a great deal special about her," Diana laughed, and with a deft flick knocked one of Katya's checkers off the board.

"I'm being serious, dumbfuck!" Katya said with a laugh. "You said yourself today that you just are a big woman, and you have African roots. That is what is special about you. But what about her?" Katya demanded, gesturing in the direction of Maya. "She looks like a Barbie doll. They all look the same."

"Well, that's what I always wanted to look like," Maya retorted, pursing her lips. She adopted her favorite pose, with her hands primly in her lap. "I really like it. It's what my type likes. The truth is, all types divide into two groups, some who like a fixed-up model, and others who prefer something au naturel."

"They prefer what?" Anya asked, puzzled. She was quite relieved this idiotic discussion had sprung up to distract her from thinking about her father.

"I'm fixed-up, when everything has been improved. But there are also girls who are au naturel. That is when everything is, like, real. They usually have small breasts and a childlike face. Au naturel is more in fashion just now. It appeals to Arab sheikhs. But I never kidded myself it was for me. From the very beginning I wanted everything about me to be perfect. That's why I've invested so much in myself."

There was a silence.

"Imagine investing a small fortune just to get f-fucked," Natasha drawled, putting her crossword puzzle to one side. Her voice was a mixture of amazement and indignation. She seemed outraged that people could squander their money in such a manner.

"Well, Maya has already told us that for a man, in her opinion, a woman is just a plaything," Diana said contemptuously, again taking careful aim and firing one of her checkers. Three of Katya's pieces were instantly dispatched. Katya tut-tutted. "Like a new car or a watch. No mystery."

"You don't begin to understand," Maya said stubbornly, pouting her lips. "I'm not doing all this for my marks. I'm doing it because I like it. I'm telling you, if I were just following fashion, I would look completely different. And anyway, I've earned enough to pay for my own car, and for my own apartment."

"By sleeping with m-men!"

"Well, it's not my fault if they give me presents! But I'm good with money. I'm economical! And actually quite smart! I just don't show it to my marks."

"Why not?" Katya asked, staring intently at the checkerboard.

"Because it's just what they don't need. Here's an example. Someone promised to introduce me to a particular guy. 'He's smart,' they said. 'The real deal! A complete genius. He's worked his way to the top from nothing.' Well, I thought, I'd better be up to scratch. I read the newspapers for three days, learned the news by heart so we would have something to talk about. In the end, we had a date and everything was very nice. Whatever he started talking about, I was able to pick up the thread and show I could keep the conversation going. I was on my best form all evening. I was so nervous I even lost weight later from the stress. And what do you think? He never called back. And all because that kind of thing is not what men need. I was young and inexperienced and I got it wrong. What men really need is, well, supportiveness. They need you to understand their everyday lives. And all that economics and politics—leave them to talk it out among themselves."

Anya's cellmates turned as one to stare at Maya. Katya and Diana even stopped playing for a moment. They all seemed to be thinking. Anya looked from them to Maya, who was a little flushed by the argument and was looking back at her cellmates with her brow furrowed. This touching seriousness suited her.

"Well, I'm not sure about that," Diana finally said, leaning back against her pillow. She seemed to have tired of the game. "We need to support men. I wouldn't argue with that. And it's true they don't like it if they see a woman understands something better than they do. But to go out of your way to conceal your own intelligence . . . personally I've never done that."

"Oh, I'm not saying you need to actually conceal anything!" Maya said hastily. "Only that it's best not to go out of your way to show how smart you are. That only freaks them out. A woman's main weapon is guile."

Maya had raised her index finger and looked naively pleased with herself, proud of the wisdom she had just imparted.

"Whatever works for you," Katya said with self-assurance, "but personally my main weapon is a quick right hook." She interlocked her fingers and pointedly crunched them in front of her.

Diana laughed.

"Oooh, aren't we dangerous! Do you often have to deploy your main weapon?"

Katya tried to thump her but Diana, with a laugh, shielded herself behind the blanket. Katya blew the hair away from her face.

"Well, I did beat a cop up on one occasion," she announced, and looked around at everyone in turn to check the impression she had made.

Natasha immediately came to life. There was even the suggestion of a smile on her face.

"How d-did that happen?"

Katya shrugged, and even gave a slight yawn, as if it was all just slightly boring.

"Well, my uncle's a cop," she said. "In charge of a police department. He effectively gave me permission to beat up the cop."

"How come?"

"It was a long time ago, must be ten years now. I was walking home with friends, three guys and me. They were all eighteen or nineteen and I was fifteen. We were going along the road in the evening, laughing our heads off, minding our own business. We weren't even particularly drunk. This police car stops beside us and two dudes get out. They start questioning us, making out that we're drunk or on something else. We'd all had no more than a couple of cans of beer, nothing out of the ordinary. Well, my pals got pissed off. What were they playing at? We were just walking down the road. Anyway, someone gave someone a shove and it all kicked off. They really beat the shit out of us, stuffed us into the car, took us to the police station, locked us in some room, and gave us a bit more.

"How awful!" Maya exclaimed. She was so flustered she took a deep breath, and her perfectly tuned-up breasts rose very high.

"To make a long story short, those cops didn't know who they'd arrested, and my uncle just happened to be in charge of their police department. We didn't say anything, though. The cops put us in cells—or rather, they put me in a cell on my own, and the boys in a monkey cage. And there we sat until morning. I just thought over what I was going to do to that cop who beat the crap out of me. He was young, not Russian, but wearing an Orthodox cross. His cross came out from under his uniform in the process. I sat thinking how I would strangle him with it, the shitty hypocrite. Anyway, in the morning my uncle arrived at work and found us there. He went apeshit, of course. I had quite a bruise covering half my cheek. Anyway, he let us out, told us to wait, then came back and said, "The guys who beat you last night are in this room. I've turned the cameras off. Go in, you have fifteen minutes." He gave us police batons.

"What, did he actually say that?! And gave you batons?" Diana asked incredulously. She emerged from under the blanket and listened to Katya with growing skepticism. "I'm never going to believe that."

"Fine, don't believe it! I'm telling it like it was. I can stop right now."

"No, no. Go on, please!" they all shouted, staring at Katya.

She paused sternly to teach them a lesson, and then, relenting, continued: "Well, we went into the room where those two cops were sitting. One immediately started whining, saying they had no idea . . . The other one, the would-be Christian, sat there looking down on us and saying nothing. That pissed me off so much I really went for him with that baton. It was great."

Everyone was silent.

"You d-didn't strangle him with his cross?" Natasha asked.

"No. I just tore it off. Not even on purpose. It just came out from under his shirt again, so I yanked it. Served him right. Orthodox, my ass!"

"So what happened in the end?" Anya inquired.

Katya shrugged.

"Nothing really. Only that so-called Christian died a week later."

"Because of how you beat him up?"

Katya scowled.

"Nah. You stupid or what? He got run over, nothing out of the ordinary. It was just a coincidence. My uncle told me. As if I cared!"

"Quite r-right," Natasha said, grim again but with a hint of approval in her voice. "Death to the police! Have we got any cigarettes left?"

Diana peered into the crumpled pack and shook her head.

"For some reason, people around you are constantly dying," Anya remarked grouchily.

Katya suddenly swiveled around and stared her straight in the eye. Anya felt transfixed.

"You mean around you they aren't?"

"No," Anya said, distraught. "Everybody around me stays alive." Katya instantly turned away, but for a while afterwards Anya continued to feel the impress of that gaze on her. She was unsettled.

The rest of them were meanwhile discussing how to get hold of cigarettes. The idea of sending a courier to the other cell—that is, the cop in the corridor—was immediately dismissed. The present shift was clearly not disposed to succor them in their hour of need. Natasha suggested smoking tea or twigs from the makeshift broom, but that did not find favor with the others. In the end Katya gave up and started poking around in the ashtray. She found a reasonably substantial cigarette butt, lit it, and, rather squeamishly, took a puff. Natasha looked revolted—smoking other people's cigarette butts was clearly in breach of the prison standards she observed.

Towards evening everyone was taken for exercise, but Anya did not go. She wanted to be on her own, although she was aware that, being in the sights of the CCTV, her solitude would be illusory. This proved not to be the only problem: as soon as her cellmates left and their voices had died away in the corridor, the sound from the radio occupied the space they had left. Until then the radio had been at least partly neutralized by their conversations, but now Anya was left to cope with it unadulterated. The noise was so unrelenting that she was soon forced to move to the windowsill and start listening to her cellmates. They had just secured a single cigarette and were taking turns to smoke it, blissfully discussing some nonsense.

Anya's friends from outside still had not shown up. Several times someone rang at the gate and Anya inwardly readied herself, but no one came to fetch her. Her cellmates had returned from their exercise when the lock rattled and the duty robot appeared in the doorway. Anya prepared herself.

"Andersen to the exit," the duty officer said.

Maya jumped up from her bunk, forgetting, apparently for the first time, to remain graceful. She grabbed her plastic bag, then dropped it and started pulling on a sweatshirt. She grabbed the bag again, rushed to the mirror, and then to the duty officer. She was already at the door when she suddenly gasped, turned around, and came back to say goodbye to all of them. Having kissed everyone, radiant with happiness, she rushed back to the duty officer, her doe-like legs tottering comically in her high platform shoes. She was terribly flustered, as if afraid the policewoman would change her mind and leave her in the cell. She gave one final parting wave to her cellmates and disappeared behind the door.

"How I envy her," Diana said wistfully. "I still have tonight and tomorrow night to go."

"I need to g-get them to let me take a shower today," Natasha said grimly. "At least wash my hair before I get out. Or my husband will see me tomorrow and won't recognize me."

A key again turned in the lock and everyone looked at the door in amazement. Anya for a moment thought Maya must have forgotten something and come back for it. But no, the stony-faced cop appeared in the doorway holding a large white plastic bag. He took a step into the cell and placed the bag on the floor. Behind him came the duty officer with a form in her hands.

"Who is Romanova?" she asked, looking displeased. This was perhaps the first time any emotion at all had registered in her face.

"Me," Anya said, baffled.

"Parcel for you. Signature!"

Anya took the slip of paper and on the line for "sender" saw the name of one of her friends.

"But what about the visit?" Anya asked.

"You already had a visitor," the duty officer snapped.

"But, but . . ." Anya spluttered in bewilderment, not at first understanding what the woman meant. "I didn't want to see my father. I didn't invite him."

The officer shrugged.

"How am I supposed to know what you want and what you don't want? He filled in the application form for a visit from a relative. By the way, you'll also need to sign for his visit."

Anya continued to stand there, looking aghast at the form.

"Are you going to sign or not?" the officer shouted. Her voice, as it had before, for a moment came out full blast and then immediately tailed away, as if the volume had accidentally been turned up for an instant.

Anya raged. Not only had her father unwittingly deprived her of her visitor, the duty officer was now pretending that everything was fine, when her only, long-anticipated joy had just vanished.

"Don't poke me!" Anya snapped.

The officer, without another word, looked at her with empty eyes. Her small mouth remained tight shut.

Anya signed the sheet with a flourish and shoved it back at the policewoman, who carefully took it, folded it in half, and meticulously ran her fingers along the fold. Her lips remained closed. Having finished her business with the form, without saying another word, she left the cell. The stony-faced cop followed her out.

"Hmm . . . What's that they've brought you?" Katya asked inquisitively.

Anya gestured wearily, indicating that she was welcome to take a look. Katya did not have to be asked twice. Springing up from Diana's bunk, in two bounds she was at the bag and enthusiastically rummaging through its contents. It again occurred to Anya that there was something predatory in all of Katya's movements and manners. "Oh, chips!" Katya was meanwhile rejoicing as she removed the pack from the bag, admired it, and dropped it back in. "And Snickers! Cigarettes!"

At the mention of cigarettes, the rest of Anya's cellmates also came to life.

"But you don't smoke," Diana remarked, deftly opening a pack Katya had thrown her.

"They're for you," Anya replied gloomily, feeling like nothing could make her feel happy today.

Gradually, however, her good humor began to return. First Natasha managed to negotiate that they would all be taken for a shower. Then they brewed some tea and had a real feast, greedily guzzling the crackers and bars of chocolate. At the bottom of the bag the purple onion was discovered, for which Anya took a lot of ribbing from her cellmates. She informed them that tomorrow she would be taking it with her to lunch and they could all watch on with envy as she ate it.

Natasha, who had mellowed as a result of the food, announced she would now teach them all how to drink chifir. She eviscerated several tea bags, emptied their contents into a glass, and poured boiling water over it. This, she explained, was not, of course, real chifir. Real chifir needed to be boiled over a flame, but in their current circumstances this would have to do. Chifir could only be drunk in a circle and from a single glass. You had to take a couple of sips and pass it on. Anya skeptically slurped from the glass. The tea was hot and so bitter that it was astringent in her mouth. Everyone drank in turn and grimaced in succession. Natasha was very pleased with the effect.

In the shower, the drain in one of the cubicles was blocked, so only three were operational. The cellmates had again to take turns. This time, Anya happily stood back. She quite liked the fact that each time she had the shower for her exclusive use. Left alone in the cell, she experienced an unexpected sense of tranquility. Actually, she thought, lying in her bunk, the fifth day was already coming to an end and, counting her overnight stay in the police department, it was the sixth. It was really not so long before she would be released, and when you had delicious things to eat and could enjoy a shower, surviving in a special detention center did not seem that great an ordeal.

The girls were soon back, showered and jolly. Anya jumped up from her bunk.

"Where do you think you are going?" the stony-faced woman with painted eyes demanded.

"What do you mean? I'm going to take a shower," Anya said warily.

"It's too late to go to the shower. You should have gone earlier, or at the same time as them."

"You only have three cubicles working. How could I go with them?"

"Nothing to do with me," the woman snapped and nodded at Natasha. "The duty officer told me only to take her to the shower because she is leaving tomorrow. She didn't say anything about the whole cell going. Anyway, it will soon be lights-out."

Without a glance at Anya's long face, she went out and locked the door.

"What a bitch," Diana said, patting Anya's shoulder sympathetically. Her shampoo left Diana smelling outrageously fragrant.

"It's all the doing of that duty officer," Anya said. "She did that on purpose."

"C-could be," Natasha agreed. Standing in front of the mirror, she twisted her thin hair into a tight, scrawny bun. "I d-don't think she likes you much."

Anya plonked herself down on the bed, looking miserable.

"Don't let it get to you," Diana said. She went to her bunk and started toweling her head. Her hair swirled in gleaming black curls. "Tomorrow it's a decent shift. You'll be able to go tomorrow."

Anya nodded dismally.

Lights-out came only much later, further proof, if any were needed, of the lying nature of cops. Anya was beginning to drop off. Her body clock seemed finally to have adjusted to the rhythms of the detention center. The frightened young policewoman came in on her rounds. Anya had not seen her earlier in the day. Stammering, she asked if everything was in order and was answered with a ragged chorus of yeses. She darted back out of the cell and the light immediately went out. Only above the door was a dim, pinkish light. A few minutes later the radio was turned off. Sinking into sleep, Anya heard the click of a cigarette lighter, and Katya and Diana whispering together.

Anya dreamed she was walking over a vast snow-covered plain. The night was dark, with no light from the moon or stars, but the snow was so pure it seemed itself to be aglow. Here and there, blocks of ice jutted out of its smooth, pristine surface like broken teeth. It seemed to Anya at first that there was nothing here besides snow and ice, but then she noticed the orange dot of a campfire far ahead of her. She moved towards it.

Almost immediately, she made out a dark figure by the fire. From such a distance it was impossible to tell what kind of creature it was, but it did not look like a human being. Anya could swear she could make out horns above its head.

Only when she had come very close could she see that it was, after all, a human clad in armor and with a horned helmet resting on its bowed head. The metal was of such mirror-like clarity that the fire was reflected in it like the glow of a sunrise. The being seemed unaware of Anya's presence.

She sat down on a rock on the opposite side of the fire and bent low to see the warrior's face.

It was Katya, or rather, an impossible, beautiful version of her. Every feature of her face seemed to have been perfected to a sublime, transcendental harmony. Her snow-white skin was like porcelain, her cheekbones, nose, and brow were molded faultlessly, her eyes unimaginably blue. She was gazing into the fire, a strange look on her face. Anya sat, barely able to breathe, afraid to move, unable to look away. It seemed to her she was like a mendicant wandering in the desert who had finally stumbled upon an oasis and could not tear herself away. Katya's beauty was exquisite. You would never tire of it. The icy realm surrounding them, silent and desolate, was a perfect setting for her.

They sat for a long time in complete silence, until Anya ventured to look away from Katya's face for a moment, to see what she was doing.

A fine silvery chain, which Anya had not at first noticed, ran from Katya's hands to the ground. Holding it with her fingertips, Katya pulled the end and, after measuring a short length, effortlessly broke it off. The chain was so long that the end was lost in the snow. It was hung with what Anya thought at first were tiny bells. They quivered and twinkled in the firelight, but when Anya looked at them more closely she realized they were not bells but tiny crosses.

"What are you doing?" she asked in astonishment, and was shocked by how harsh her voice sounded in the surrounding stillness.

Very, very slowly, as if overcoming an impossible resistance, Katya raised her eyes and looked at her.

Anya felt like a mountain had been laid on her shoulders. An unbelievable weight forced her to the ground. Katya's gaze was almost tangible, and it pressed Anya down, crushing her, smearing her over the snow. She wanted to ask Katya to stop looking at her but could not open her mouth. Her jaws were so tightly clenched it seemed that her teeth would shatter. Anya slid from her rock into the snow, unable to move so much as a finger. She tried to breathe but could not. Her chest was being crushed. She could see she was about to die, but for some reason the thought did not alarm her. Katya's beauty so overpowered everything else that even the fear of her receded. Anya gazed and gazed at her until her eyes closed.

But then, the next moment, Anya opened them again, as if she had burst to the surface. She was lying in her bunk in the detention center, it was night, and she was freezing cold. The window had been left open again, and even her blanket was no help. No wonder she had been dreaming about a snowbound wilderness. After lying rolled up in a ball for a few minutes in the hope of getting warm, Anya gave in. She threw back the blanket and ran quickly across the icy floor to the window. Outside, the moon was shining brightly. Anya slammed the top window and turned to whizz back to bed.

Katya was standing not twenty centimeters away.

Anya did not at first even realize it was her. She recoiled from the dark figure, and banged her head on the windowsill. The pain blocked the urge to panic and, stifling a gasp, she rubbed the bump, forgetting all about Katya for a time. She, however, was still standing nearby in silence, and Anya finally had to look at her.

For a moment she thought she was still in her dream and that at any moment she would witness something impossible, but no. An entirely ordinary person was standing next to her. Anya could feel the heat coming from Katya and saw the tiny scar above her lip. She must have been cold too, and had also gotten up to close the window.

"You scared me," Anya whispered. The next instant, Katya's face suddenly became distorted out of all recognition. Her eyes narrowed, her nose became pointed, like the snout of a predatory animal, and with a low, feral growl she pounced on Anya.

Anya's shoulder blades hit the wall behind her. She tried to break free, but Katya was clutching her shoulders with a viselike grip. They both crashed to the floor. Anya kicked and twisted, but Katya fell on her and pressed her down. Anya thought the sensation was very reminiscent of her dream. They struggled on the floor without a sound. Anya could not understand what Katya was trying to do: she seemed only to be pressing her down to the ground. With all her might, Anya rolled to one side, but Katya was still clutching her shoulders. Anya tried to grab her hands and tear them away, but Katya's grip was just too strong.

Then suddenly, very distinctly, Katya hissed right in her ear: "Give it to me. It belongs to me."

This was so unexpected, and Anya was so frightened, that she froze and, no less unexpectedly, Katya froze too. The pause lasted only a moment, but it was enough for Anya to refocus. She gathered what remained of her strength and flung her cellmate aside, immediately feeling a heavy blow to her head in the same place where she had just hit it on the windowsill.

She found herself lying on the floor by the side of her bunk. The sun was shining outside the window. Anya could hear the sparrows twittering and clattering their little claws on the plastic roof of the yard. There was no one beside her.

Very slowly Anya sat up. She could feel she had banged her head, as well as her shoulder and hip, having evidently managed to fall out of bed. This was so ridiculous and embarrassing it was laughable. What a relief that this had only been another of her stupid nightmares. A dream within a dream. It was not that unusual. Smiling now that it was all over, Anya raised her hand to feel the bump on the back of her head.

Wrapped around her index finger was a thin silver chain.

DAY SIX

Anya tore the chain from her finger as if it were poisoned, and jumped up from the floor. There was complete silence in the cell, only broken by the measured breathing of her cellmates. All three were peacefully asleep in their bunks. Katya was lying on her back with her head turned to one side and her mouth gaping like a clown. There was nothing remotely menacing about her face, and right now she looked even more youthful than usual. Outside the window the morning was sunny and settled.

Anya went to the washbasin and turned on the water. She did not look in the mirror, afraid she might again see something that was not there. As she washed her hands she noticed something moving out of the corner of her eye and recoiled in fright, before realizing it was just her own reflection in the white tiling of the washbasin surround.

Anya looked around the cell again. The sun was blazing down outside, but had not yet lit up the cell, which was still semidark and cool. Against the wall the windows were dazzlingly bright, like paintings illuminated in a museum. The sky was improbably blue, and the leaves on the trees a venomous green. Anya half closed her eyes, well remembering how spacious the cell had seemed to her on that first day. Now it seemed like a box. Her imprisonment itself suddenly had a different feel. Before, the succession of activities—eating, exercising, phone calls, conversation—had made the fact of her detention fairly imperceptible. Apart from the fact that you were unable to leave this particular location, there was nothing all that burdensome about it. Now, for the first time, Anya felt truly imprisoned, not just in the detention center but in her own head. In the world outside she would have been able to go for a walk to clear her mind, to keep herself busy, but here she was doomed to think endlessly about her condition.

Feeling profoundly tired, she shuffled back to her bunk and sat down. She wanted to sleep, but knew that sleep would not help. On the contrary, when she was asleep her visions were all the more real. She gazed aimlessly at the floor in front of her. The chain caught her eye. It was sparkling in a square of sunlight falling through the window. Anya looked at it for a long time, then picked it up and twisted it between her fingers. How could it even have gotten here? Perhaps one of her cellmates had dropped it accidentally, or maybe it belonged to someone who had been in this cell before she got here? Perhaps Anya had stumbled across it during the night in a fit of sleepwalking? She scoffed at that explanation. No matter how desperate she might be, she could not bring herself to believe that. Unfortunately, no less absurd explanation suggested itself.

Anya decided that she should just ask Katya outright. It did not matter how crazy it sounded or what the others might think. Her cellmates would, after all, soon be leaving and then Anya would never see them again. And if she did not ask, she might never be free of her demons. Only, how should she phrase it? "Did you attack me last night?" . . . No, that was too full-on. "Has anything strange happened to you lately?" That was too mealymouthed. "Ever since I ended up here I have had constant nightmares. You were in one I had last night, and you seemed to be demanding this chain back. I need to understand what is going on." Also terrible, but at least it was true.

Anya got out of her bunk and headed over to Katya's. Katya was still asleep and, looking at her, Anya was in a quandary. In sleep she looked so vulnerable it was impossible to imagine she could ever attack anyone. Anya hesitated—surely she should at least wait for Katya to wake up before asking such an embarrassing question.

"What you up to?" a voice whispered behind her.

Anya jumped and turned around to find Natasha, in the adjacent upper bunk, looking at her sleepily and suspiciously. The bun on the top of her head was ludicrously lopsided.

"Nothing," Anya said. "I was just going to open the window."

As proof, she went over and flung the window open.

Natasha continued watching her dubiously, and Anya had no option but to retreat to her bunk. After a couple of steps, however, remembering how weary and fearful she had felt sitting on it just two minutes before, she stopped, unable to condemn herself to a repetition. She half closed her eyes and blurted out, "Have you experienced any strange happenings lately?"

Natasha frowned.

"Like what?"

"Well, something you can't explain?"

"I d-don't understand."

"Hallucinations. Strange dreams."

"Come again?"

"Oh, forget it," Anya said, her voice faltering. What good had she ever imagined might come of asking about it explicitly? She dragged herself back to her bunk.

"Why, has s-something happened to you?" Natasha asked, frowning. She sat up in her bunk and looked at Anya intently; even, perhaps, with concern. "It's not the first time I've heard you talking about this sort of stuff."

Anya paused. Natasha's sympathy was so unexpected that she felt a wave of self-pity, which she had been holding back, suddenly engulf her. Tears welled up in her eyes.

"You see, I keep imagining things," Anya murmured, almost sobbing. "Visions, nightmares."

Natasha continued to stare at her, and Anya began speaking more rapidly.

"For instance, last night I dreamed that Katya attacked me, and when I woke up I found this." Anya opened her hand, in which lay the chain.

Natasha took one look at it, another at Anya, and exclaimed, "Well, you're a right screwball!"

Anya felt a thousand tiny needles pricking her face. The humiliation dried her tears in an instant. Hiding her hand behind her back and without another word, she walked firmly back to her bunk.

"P-perhaps you should go to see the doctor here," Natasha continued.

Anya collapsed on the bed and got comfortable under the blanket, making a show of shaking it out.

Having lost sight of her, Natasha lay back in her bunk and hung down.

"That chain you've got—I nicked it from the d-duty officer," she said.

Anya froze with the blanket raised in midair.

"What, yesterday's one?"

"You bet."

"How come? What for?"

"Just because. Can't stand the woman. But I liked her chain. At first, anyway, I did, but then when I took a closer look at it I decided it was crap. T-too thin. I chucked it somewhere. Forgot all about it."

Anya thought this over.

"How on earth did you manage to steal it?" she asked at last.

Natasha gave her such a stern look that even her wonky bun stopped seeming absurd for a second.

"Know too much and you'll grow old early. Have you forgotten what I was in the camps for?"

Natasha's head disappeared from Anya's field of view.

Lost in thought, she twisted the chain around her finger. Anya's fear began to subside, either because she was beginning to forget the nightmare or because at least a small part of it had been cleared up, if not in a wholly comprehensible way. She was grateful for the breathing space. Stretching out in her bunk, she closed her eyes.

"Breakfast!" a cop barked through the peephole.

Natasha, as usual, jumped down nimbly from her bunk and went to the washstand. First there was the sound of the tap running, then something fell into the washbasin. Anya continued to lie in bed with her eyes closed, listening to Natasha cursing through her teeth. Katya stirred in her bunk.

"Diana!" she called quietly. Diana did not respond. "Diana! Diana!!"

"Oh, what is it?" Diana mumbled sleepily.

"Happy birthday, honey!" Katya yelled cheerily and jumped to the floor. Anya opened her eyes.

"Come here, I want to give you a hug!"

For a moment Diana stared at her vacantly, but then her expression changed abruptly and she yelled, "Hip hip hooray! It's my birthday today!"

She hugged Katya in a warm embrace, then leaped out of her bunk and started dancing around the room.

"Not right in the head!" Natasha commented grimly, observing Diana in the makeshift mirror and unplaiting the bun on her head. "Happy birthday!"

"Many happy returns," Anya contributed politely.

"Thank you! Thank you!" Diana exclaimed, continuing to dance around the cell. "This is going to be my oddest birthday ever. Hey, let's all go to breakfast! What do they usually serve?"

"Porridge," Natasha grunted. She had finally unbraided her hair and gave it a good shake. Her bangs hung over her forehead, while the rest of her hair curled chaotically. Natasha appeared pleased with the result.

"Let's celebrate it with porridge!"

"Ugh, what a disgusting idea," Katya declared, pulling a face.

"Please, in honor of me!"

It was impossible to hold out against Diana's love of life and accordingly, grumbling a little more for appearances' sake, Katya fell into line. So did Anya, not at all keen to be left behind alone in the cell. As the nightmare faded in her memory, she felt less afraid of her cellmates and more afraid of herself. She sensed that, as soon as she was on her own, her mind would start playing tricks on her again and she had no desire to give it that opportunity.

Breakfast was a blot of oatmeal with a piece of white bread on top. Anya scooped out this delicacy and put it in her mouth. Oddly enough, the porridge tasted a lot better than it looked.

"What a lot of you there are today!" Viktor Ivanovich said, looking out approvingly from the kitchen at the detainees. "A veritable flower garden!"

"Today is our Diana's birthday," Katya announced proudly.

"And how old is the birthday girl?"

"Twenty-five!" Diana declared resoundingly. She was so radiantly happy that Anya could not help feeling a twinge of jealousy. Her own birthday never bestowed such cloudless joy on her.

Back in the cell, however, Diana's mood darkened.

"It's my birthday and I can't even celebrate it!" she complained. "I would like everyone to be wishing me happy birthday and giving me presents and saying nice things! Lucky you, Natasha! You're getting out today."

Natasha shrugged her shoulders, as if she saw no cause for celebration in that.

"I hope we go out to exercise soon," Diana continued. "I need to do the rounds of all the cells and get their phone numbers."

"Whatever for?" Anya asked in surprise.

"Well, a lot of people here want to get to know me. I promised that on my last day I would take their phone numbers."

"But I thought you were married."

Diana looked Anya up and down with a condescending look that suggested she clearly knew nothing about life.

"In the first place, asking for someone's phone number does not oblige you in any way. And in the second place, I'm already on my third husband. I met him at the funeral of my second. If I didn't take the opportunity to get acquainted with everyone I meet, I would probably be an old maid by now."

"Did your husbands know each other, or what?" Katya pried.

She lit a cigarette and leaned back on the far end of Diana's bunk. Diana took the proffered pack and, leaning on the headboard, she too lit up.

"They were doing time in the same camp. Only the one who is my present husband had been released before the second one died. He came to the funeral and that's how we met."

"But what did your husband die of?" Anya asked cautiously. She imagined that people in the camps never died of natural causes, and prepared to hear some bloodcurdling tale.

"He was sick—for a long time," Diana said with a shrug. "He would get a bit better, then a bit worse. Towards the end I was just wishing he would make his mind up one way or the other, because both of us were completely worn out."

At the morning inspection—today it was the shift with the friendly old geezer who sounded like Santa Claus—Katya told the cops it was Diana's birthday, and Diana immediately took the opportunity to successfully scrounge a shower for them all in the evening. This cheered her up for a while and, after the cops had gone, she suggested playing Crocodile. Anya, as usual, declined.

The game did not go well. With only three players it was less interesting. Anya's cellmates were just wondering what to do next when Kirill's ginger head appeared at the window.

"Hey, girlies," he said. "You let me have a cigarette yesterday, so today I'm repaying you. Someone brought me a parcel."

He put his hand through the bars and placed a cigarette on the windowsill.

"Well, what a remarkably well-mannered young gentleman," Natasha muttered suspiciously. "I suppose you'll be wanting something in return."

"I don't want anything," Kirill said, miffed. "I was just being friendly. Well, so long, girls."

"Hang on!" Katya shouted, rushing over to the window. "Listen, do you remember yesterday you offered us some vodka?"

"I do, only I don't have it anymore. We knocked it back."

"Oh dear," Katya drawled disconsolately. "I was just thinking . . . It's Diana's birthday, we'd been hoping to celebrate."

"Diana? Is that you?" Kirill asked.

Diana nodded languidly. As soon as Kirill appeared at the window she had seemed to change in some elusive way. She became more fluid and relaxed, and was now standing, leaning on the bunk, displaying the seductive curve of her hip, and waiting for him to finally notice her.

Kirill hesitated, as if considering something.

"How old are you today?"

"Twenty-five," Diana said in an uncharacteristically low, gravelly voice that really didn't sound much like her usual one.

Kirill thought some more.

"Actually," he said at last, "I do have a little something. Celebrating your birthday here sucks, so, what the hell, I'll share it with you."

He reached into his pocket, pulled something out, and placed it on the windowsill. Anya craned her neck to see what it was. On the windowsill lay a small piece of paper.

"I'm guessing you all know what to do with it," Kirill said with a laugh, looking alternately at Diana and Katya.

Katya walked assertively over to the window and unwrapped the paper. Her expression changed instantly and she stared wide-eyed at Kirill.

"How did you smuggle that in here?" she hissed.

Diana peered over her shoulder, and also stared in amazement.

"Curiosity killed the cat," Kirill teased. Natasha observed what was happening in silence, clearly of the view that showing curiosity was only for losers, but then even she could not hold back. Raising herself in her bunk and seeing what was in Katya's hand, she turned to Kirill and said with a note of menace, "You wouldn't by any chance be a c-cop, would you?"

"Do I look like one?" Kirill replied, offended.

"You don't," Natasha admitted after a moment's deliberation. "But there's something very suspicious about the way you b-behave. You bring us cigarettes, now this. As if you're worming your way into our circle. Or maybe you want to set us up."

"Oh, sure, I really need to win your confidence, don't I," Kirill replied rattily. "And set you up too. If you don't want it, give it back!"

Katya took a brisk step back from the window, just in case, and Diana asked, in her normal voice because she was so amazed, "No, but really, how did you not get busted with this?"

"You're like little kids! It's as easy as pie. You put it in the bottom of a jar of coffee, and that's all. The way you're going on, it's like you want to land me in hot water."

"We won't," Katya said. Clenching her fist, she quickly put it behind her back. "Thank you, Kirill. We won't tell anyone."

Kirill gave her an annoyed look, then said, "Enough. So long. Happy birthday!" and jumped down from the bench.

When his footsteps had died away, Katya and Diana exchanged glances.

"You wanted to celebrate your birthday? Let's do it," Katya said with a giggle. Diana looked at her and also began to giggle.

"Well, doing it like this is a first," she said, excited.

"Are you seriously going to do it?" Natasha said disapprovingly. "What if you get c-caught?"

Anya had been sitting on her bunk all this time, but now went over to her cellmates. She was also interested in what was happening. Katya looked at her for a couple of moments, as if wondering whether she could be trusted, then she brought her hand out from behind her back and opened it.

Anya carefully took the piece of paper and unfolded it. Inside lay a piece of hash the size of a pea.

"Wow," was all she said.

"Want to join us?" Diana asked. "I'm not sure," Anya replied, looking sideways at the camera in the corner. The others looked at it too.

"We'll soon fix that," Katya said confidently. "We'll hang blankets over Ira's bunk and then there will be nothing to see."

"That prick is a cop for sure," Natasha announced categorically. As usual when she was agitated, there was no hint of her stutter. "The moment you start smoking other cops will come running. He gave you it on purpose to trap you."

Diana dithered, looking at Natasha, then at Katya. She obviously wanted Natasha to be wrong, but she was worried.

"You said yourself he doesn't look like a cop!" Katya reminded Natasha.

"He doesn't," Natasha agreed grimly. "But I don't trust him. This is not going to end well."

"That's garbage!" Katya said. "Why would he want to trap us, for heaven's sake? If we smoke it quickly no one will know. I thought you wanted to celebrate your birthday!"

Diana shifted uneasily.

"And what if someone comes in while you're puffing away?" Natasha asked. "The smell will hang around."

For a moment that seemed to shake even Katya, but she immediately pulled herself together.

"The longer we put off smoking it, the greater the risk they'll find it here and that will be even worse. Come on, Diana, make your mind up. Either we smoke it or we throw it out."

Diana looked unhappily at her, then back at Natasha, then at Anya. Katya's expression was defiant, Natasha's uncompromising, while Anya just shrugged.

"Okay, let's smoke," Diana decided finally.

"Don't say I didn't warn you," Natasha croaked from above.

"Stop trying to make trouble," Katya said amiably.

She went over to the locker by which they kept their empty plastic bottles and selected the least crumpled one. Diana, meanwhile, hung up two blankets as a kind of curtain around what had been Ira's bunk. She tucked the blankets in under Natasha's mattress on the top bunk. Natasha observed Diana darkly but said no more.

Waving the bottle around with theatrical nonchalance, Katya went over to the bed and sat inside the blanket shelter. Puffing at the cigarette, she applied its burning end to the bottle and burned a hole in it. Diana sat down next to her, with Anya on the neighboring bunk.

Chipping off a tiny piece of hash, Katya flattened it in her fingers and carefully placed it on the burning cigarette. Inserting it into the hole in the bottle, she plugged the hole with her finger. Anya watched in fascination as thick milky smoke filled the bottle.

"Right, you first," Katya said ceremoniously and handed Diana the bottle, keeping her finger over the hole.

Diana balked for a moment, but then, without further hesitation, unscrewed the lid and inhaled deeply. The heavy whiteness immediately faded to translucency. Diana tore herself away from the neck of the bottle, keeping her lips firmly closed and for, some reason, with her eyes bulging. Katya immediately breathed in all the remaining smoke, as if she were drinking it. Not speaking, not breathing, she and Diana sat for a few moments before loudly exhaling almost at the same time. There was a smell of hash.

"Wow, that's strong," Diana said hoarsely, and immediately started coughing.

Katya giggled, at the same time nipping off a new piece of hash and putting it on her cigarette. The bottle again filled with smoke, and now Katya handed it to Anya.

"Me?" Anya asked uncertainly.

"Quick. Make a decision."

Anya looked at the murk inside the bottle and thought—what will be will be. Without giving herself time to think better of it, she leaned over and inhaled deeply.

Her lungs felt raked through, her eyes stung, and her arms and legs felt numb. Anya held her breath for a few moments, and was glad to be sitting down. She exhaled. She felt she wanted to spread out over the bed, although she sensed that even if she did, that would not be relaxing enough. Everything inside soon became so weightless that just the presence of her body seemed a burden too heavy to bear. She leaned back on the pillow and contemplated her cellmates.

They were sitting decoratively in front of her on both tiers of the bunk: Katya and Diana were the base of a triangle, and Natasha, dark as a thundercloud, loomed above them. Every now and then Katya would burst out laughing and excitedly say something to Diana. Anya ignored the words, which were a mere continuum of sound, like the sound of a river. Diana was already looking dopey, and nodding occasionally.

Anya closed her eyes blissfully. It was out of the question to think of moving. All manifestations of the world around her—voices, the roughness of the sheet beneath her hands, the ray of sunlight warming her knee—seemed to be coming to her from some distance away.

She opened her eyes.

Those sitting in front of her were not her cellmates. As soon as she looked at them, they fell silent and looked at her.

The fact that they were not her cellmates was something she felt rather than saw. For some reason, she just could not see them in their entirety. They broke down into parts, as if she could not take in their whole appearance at once. Anya noticed Katya's hair shimmering with a dazzling, metallic sheen in the sun, while Diana's eyes were as dark as tunnels. Natasha's collarbones protruded under her skin so sharply they seemed about to rip it. Anya tried to unfocus her eyes so that the three figures in front of her would fit into her gaze, but continued to pick out only separate features: pointed yellow teeth, long eyelashes, the smooth slope of a shoulder blade that shone like wax. She knew the creatures sitting in front of her were not human, and was simultaneously afraid of seeing them and unable to stop looking. Her eyes continued wandering over them, stumbling on new details, until she realized that this fractured kaleidoscope was her salvation, a defense mechanism of her brain. If she had been able to comprehend these beings in a single glance, she would not have been able to bear the sight.

She closed her eyes tight and feelings flooded over her. She heard Katya saying, "Well, what is the strangest present you've ever been given on your birthday?" She realized that her neck had become numb from its awkward position on the pillow, and that the cell was now filled with smoke.

Anya opened her eyes: her perfectly ordinary cellmates were sitting in front of her—Diana and Katya below, and Natasha on the top bunk.

"I'm going out of my mind," she thought matter-of-factly. She didn't have the strength to be scared again after what she had been through that morning, and in any case the hash made her indifferent to everything. She looked at her fellow prisoners with curiosity: it was unbelievable how strangely her brain worked. A moment ago they had seemed like visitors from outer space, and now here they were sitting in front of her, perfectly ordinary.

"Two years ago, a girlfriend gave me a course in oral sex for my birthday," Diana was saying.

"What?" Katya laughed.

"A blow job course. We went on it together."

"Is there anything people won't come up with?" Natasha exclaimed in disgust.

"So what did you practice on?" Katya continued hilariously.

Diana took another toke and said lethargically, "Oh, it was all just bullshit. We practiced on rubber penises. We sat at desks, each with a dick stuck on top. The course was all being taught by an old bat who, to all appearances, last had sex twenty years ago. She walked up and down the rows saying, this is what you need to do. Lick here like this, but make sure you lick here like this."

"Fuck!" Katya yelled and fell about laughing again. "Did you actually learn anything?"

"I told her straight away I didn't need any lessons from her," Diana said haughtily. She slowly reclined in the bunk and sighed blissfully. "I could give anyone you like a master class myself. And I proved it."

"How?" Anya asked. She was still feeling very relaxed. Her fear and confusion at everything happening to her seemed now to exist in a parallel universe, while in this one there was nothing to worry about. In addition, just looking at Diana had a soothing effect on her. The smooth way she moved, the unhurried way she spoke seemed so right that she felt she could watch and listen to her forever.

"Anyway, this woman said that at the end of the course we would try deep throating, and that if anybody could do it and show it to the rest they would be awarded the title of Queen of the Blow Job. All you had to do was swallow the rubber dick right down to the base."

"And did you?" Katya asked bewitched and, seemingly for the first time, stopped giggling.

Diana spread her arms wide and tilted her head slightly, like an actress on stage. Katya hooted with laughter again.

"They're not normal!" Natasha grumbled from above. "A fine topic you've f-found to discuss. And the smell of your hash is all over the place."

Katya looked up from under the top tier to see Natasha.

"Now you tell us a story about sex," she said. "Something shocking."

"I don't have stories like that," Natasha retorted.

"No, tell us! Tell us!" Katya pestered her. The weed had made her as playful as a kitten. For now Anya had no sense of threat coming from her. "You must have had something happen in prison! Is it true everyone gets raped there?"

"Are you a complete fool?" Natasha rounded on her.

Katya giggled again, but did not let up.

"Well, I've heard it said a hundred times that women live in the camps as couples."

Natasha nodded with obvious reluctance.

"A lot d-do. If you're in prison for a long time, you find someone to cling to. I wasn't in the camps long myself. And I have a husband!"

"Prison wouldn't be a problem for you, Katya," Diana remarked in a blasé tone of voice. "You're already dating a girl."

Katya plonked herself back in place.

"Only a little left," she announced, unfolding the paper. "We need to finish it. How about you, more?"

Anya shook her head.

"Well then, you tell us something. Have you got any naughty stories?"

"I was once almost kicked out of university over some nude photographs," Anya said, smiling blissfully.

"You're perverts! The whole lot of you!" Natasha exclaimed, falling back on her pillow and pointedly turning her back to her cellmates.

"Tell us!" Katya said, delighted. With the precision of a jeweler, she dropped a tiny piece of hash on her lit cigarette and inserted it into the bottle.

Anya always believed that the evening had taken a wrong turn when they got out the radiogramophone. Another person might have said it was when they opened the third bottle of tequila, and they would have been right too, but not entirely. It was the tequila that provoked the madness, but the radiola that set the tone. In their dorm room it looked so wild and completely out of place that it imparted a kind of depraved chic to everything around it.

The radiola was with them only quite briefly. Anya had bought it as a gift and had not yet gotten around to giving it. It was accompanied by a single record, which so far they only boasted about to guests. They always had a lot of guests. Their room was popular because it was known that you could do anything there.

The three of them lived in it together—Anya, Sonya, and Sasha. Unofficially, of course. Officially persons of different sexes were not supposed to live together in the dorm rooms, but Sasha visited so often, stayed so long, and so rapidly accumulated belongings that in the end it made no sense for him not to stay. At first, they had a communal life, and after that, entirely naturally, communal sex.

It was Anya who had introduced Sonya and Sasha to each other. That had been in the first year, but initially they were not a threesome. Rather, there were two pairs, with Anya the unchallenged focus of both. She was friends with Sasha and occasionally slipped into having sex with him. This was always pleasant and not burdensome. She was also friends with Sonya and, when she fell in love, started spending all her free time with her. When Sonya and Sasha became closer to each other, Anya was initially pleased. It was fun how the three of them could all spend more time together. She completely missed the moment when Sonya and Sasha became so close that she was the odd one out.

This discovery was unbelievable and very painful, and Anya was in no hurry to reconcile herself to it. Actually, the realization took a long time to dawn on all involved. The configuration of their relationships changed periodically, and these upheavals were accompanied by mutual hurts, squabbles, and fits of jealousy. In the fifth year there came an unexpected lull. They began to live together as a threesome, and at first it seemed to Anya that they had found the optimal arrangement. Needless to say, there was nothing stable about it. On the contrary, the jealousy became more palpable the minute they moved in together. As in any standard love triangle, love was not equally reciprocated. Anya longed desperately for Sonya, Sonya longed desperately for Sasha, and Sasha was just too much of a butterfly to be desperately in love with anyone. This only added to the drama. Tensions grew.

Their room was more like a den. It was full of all manner of rubbish: a plaster head of Lenin so enormous it was used as a stool; full bottles, empty bottles; tumblers for tea; lamps and candlesticks; bicycle bells; history books; a hookah with its accompanying paraphernalia; cushions; blankets; and of course, the radiola. Anya, Sonya, and Sasha dismantled one of the two-tier bunks and laid the mattresses on the floor, creating a love nest for three. Their room was perpetually full of people smoking, drinking, singing, and playing the guitar.

When Anya thought back to that time, she remembered interminable darkness. There was the darkness of their habitation, the darkness of their relationship, and the darkness that was all Anya could see when she looked inside herself. And in that darkness there was only one point of light—Sonya. Like a beacon guiding her in the darkness: Sonya sat down, Sonya stood up, Sonya laughed, and Anya registered her every move. She knew, however, that approaching too close to the lighthouse was no longer possible. Sonya was distancing herself, and this infuriated Anya. She wanted revenge. And that was simplicity itself: she had only to switch Sasha's attention to herself. Anya availed herself of this weapon frequently, and each time experienced a paradoxical mix of emotions. Seeing the suffering in Sonya's face, she felt triumph and repentance, vindictiveness, and shame, and tenderness. Over time, these feelings became permanent. Sonya's very existence became a gaping wound for Anya.

And then, one evening a friend in the dormitory called Anya to say a journalist had arrived who was doing a report on the life of Moscow students ". . . and I thought who better for her to talk to than you."

A minute before this call, Anya had knocked back a first shot of tequila (alcohol was the main bonding agent of the union between her, Sasha, and Sonya) and had no objection to guests. Five minutes later, the journalist was at their door.

She was skinny and had a huge mop of curls. She was ugly. Anya felt regret that such luxuriant hair was not being put to better use. She seemed pushy but at the same time wary, as if feeling out of her element and trying not to let it show. She appeared somewhat intimidated by her mission and this, along with a second glass of tequila, bolstered Anya's confidence. It was not often they had a visit from a journalist so, of course, they wanted to make an impression.

They each tried to do so in their own way. No sooner had the journalist entered their room than Sasha swung into action to seduce her. Anya was always amazed how omnivorous he was, and observed him with mild irony. Sonya for her part fussed about, offering the guest a glass of tea and trying to be hospitable in every imaginable way.

The journalist introduced herself with the suitably bohemian name of Ida, and announced that she was compiling a photo report for the style and entertainment magazine *Afisha* about the life of Moscow students. "A photo report . . ." Anya repeated in some disappointment. She had supposed they would entertain their journalist with stories of dormitory life. It was hard to see what she might find interesting about their humdrum existence.

Ida took a chair and set a camera down next to her.

"Do you take the photos on actual film?" Sonya immediately asked, considering it her duty as a responsible hostess to entertain guests with polite conversation.

"Yes," Ida replied, looking around their room with an ambiguous expression on her face.

"What photos have you taken already?"

"In the afternoon I shot a birthday party, on this floor, actually, directly opposite you. There are three girls living there. Do you know them? First-year students, I think. They ate a cake their mother had baked for them. After that I photographed another girl in the shower."

"In the shower?" Anya asked incredulously.

"Well, yes. I was photographing in the corridor, the kitchen, on the stairs. I met a girl there who did not mind being photographed as she was washing."

"You mean nude photos of her in the shower will be published in *Afisha*?" Sonya asked in astonishment.

"That's for the editor to decide."

Everyone fell silent. After a pause, Sasha gallantly asked, "Would you like a tequila?"

Ida looked around at all of them and in turn asked, "Do the three of you live here?"

"Yes."

"A tequila would be nice."

Between the four of them the first bottle of tequila disappeared before anyone noticed. Sasha ran off to get a second. Ida was soon drunk and started walking around the room unsteadily, peeping into corners and examining the posters on the walls. The camera shutter clicked several times. Anya and Sonya were eager to pose but she would not let them. They politely discussed what it was like studying at the Institute of International Relations, and what it was like working at *Afisha*. With the second bottle finished, Sasha went out for a third. Ida continued to circle around the room looking worried, as if she just could not find what she was looking for. From time to time she would stop and take another photo, but the look of dissatisfaction refused to leave her face.

"Oh, what's this you've got?" Ida asked suddenly, pointing a finger into the profound darkness under the table.

"A radiola," Anya replied casually. "We sometimes listen to jazz. If you like, we can turn it on."

The radiola was dragged out into the light. It was beautiful in all its anachronism: a stout brown body with spindly legs, plastic yellow buttons, and a lacquered lid. They put on their only record and carried on drinking. Duke Ellington struck up. It would be difficult to imagine a scene of greater decadence—a scratchy jazz record, a slovenly student room, and people drowsy from overindulgence in alcohol.

While Ida was photographing the radiola, Sasha persisted in his efforts to seduce her. Sonya pretended not to notice. Anya felt a desire both to teach her a lesson for being so submissive and at the same time to protect her from Sasha's heartless insensitivity. She deliberately squeezed between Ida and Sasha and opened a window.

"Are you together?" Ida suddenly asked.

Anya turned to see whom she was addressing. Ida looked from her to Sasha and back.

As usual, there were two sides to this blow: on the one hand Anya was glad that Sonya had been left out of the picture, but on the other she was indignant about it.

"We are *all* together here," Anya said.

She turned to Sonya, who was smiling so sweetly Anya could have hit her. How could she be taking everything so calmly? Instead, she approached Sonya slowly and slid her arm around her waist. She wanted to shield her from the world, to protect her, to safeguard her from this fidgety journalist with her objectionable assumptions, from Sasha's indifference, from her own jealousy.

"What's wrong?" Sonya whispered gently in her ear. "Is something upsetting you?"

Anya shook her head, glad that in the darkness no one could see how tearful she was.

"Let's dance," she said.

The jazz record was accompanied by the clicking of a shutter, but Anya was no longer paying attention. She was completely uninterested in how she would look in these photographs or how interesting her life might seem in them. The world around her was floating and out of focus, with only Sonya's face completely clear. Anya kissed her. The clicking of the shutter became more frequent. They drank more tequila. The room was in darkness with light coming only from a table lamp with a flexible neck, which was turned towards the ceiling. As a result people and objects cast long, soft shadows on the walls. Anya felt hot, her cheeks were burning. She went to the open window and lit a cigarette. Out of the corner of her eye she could see Sasha still hovering around Ida, who seemed to be taking little interest in him. She was focused on photographing Sonya. Anya blew smoke from her cigarette out the window but it blew straight back into the room. Sonya came to her and took the cigarette out of her fingers. Anya saw a curl of hair on her brow ruffle in the breeze. Sonya kissed her. She so rarely did that first that Anya melted instantly. All her anger and resentment evaporated.

She felt Ida scuttle over to them, but the world around her had lost all significance. Anya drew Sonya down to the floor. The floorboards were smooth and Sonya's hair was as soft to her touch as foam. Anya began undressing her. She felt as if she was in a trance from the music, from the warmth flooding through her body, from the soft semi-darkness and a sense of dizziness she felt. She was overflowing with a feeling of being blessed. Anya closed her eyes, she ran her fingers over Sonya's shoulders, her breasts, and then lower, and thought she would never be happier.

"I'm going to be sick," Sonya said, sitting up abruptly, and flying out of the room like a bullet.

In the outside world someone turned on the light.

She found that Ida was hanging over her with her camera, and the room was cold because of the open window. Anya sat up on the unexpectedly hard floor and looked around, coming to her senses.

Sasha, as if there was no problem, poured her a tequila. They were by now on a fourth bottle. A repulsive sobriety returned to Anya, so clearly did she suddenly see everything around her. She downed the tequila in a gulp and immediately gestured for a refill.

"May I stay the night?" Ida asked, looking at Anya with interest. Overnight guests were forbidden in the dorms, but there were ways around that. You could climb in a window and sneak past the warden. Sasha went to see off Ida and help her come back in. Anya found herself alone in the room.

She closed the window to stop the draft and lit a cigarette. The smoke hung in a broken line in the air and she had to throw the window open again. It became cold and she felt sick at heart.

The door opened and Anya looked up immediately, hoping Sonya was back. She longed to be alone with her if only for a moment. Seeing Sonya in the doorway, Anya lurched towards her, but before she could take a step, Sonya gave a gasp and rushed out of the room again.

Ida and Sasha finally arrived back. Ida was completely drunk and as a result almost attractive. She kept laughing, throwing her head back, her curls shimmering in the light of the lamp. She was unsteady and was leaning on Sasha's shoulder, while he had a smug smile on his face as he supported her with an arm around her waist. Anya observed them with disgust and poured herself another tequila. Ida suddenly broke away from Sasha, lurched over and hugged Anya. She was so thin and scrawny that her bones could be felt through her clothes.

"Give us a drag?" she asked. Anya held out her lit cigarette, Ida took a puff, her lips brushing Anya's fingers. She felt a wicked, fatal arousal building inside her.

Soon it was night, Ida was moaning drunkenly, Sasha was puffing and panting somewhere to one side of her. Anya rammed almost her whole hand up between Ida's legs and felt such frenzy she would probably not have stopped no matter how the woman shrieked. But

Ida only moaned more rapturously. Several times Sonya flitted past them like a shadow, but was no sooner back from the toilet than she was rushing out to it again. Anya forbade herself to think about her, hoping that Ida's moaning would push all thought out of her head. She felt everything good and bright had been sucked out of her, but wanted paradoxically only to deepen this new darkness even more, to push it to the limit until nothing was left but primal instinct—no doubts, and certainly no love.

Anya woke up on the top tier of the bunk, although she had no recollection at all of how she had gotten there. She was alone. Her head was splitting so badly that the pain seemed to extend to her fingertips. She half opened her eyes and looked around the room through her eyelashes. Sonya was asleep down below, her face turned to the wall. Ida was sitting not far away from her, her face crumpled, her hair still rampant. There was no sign of Sasha, but Anya could hear the kettle boiling and spoons clinking behind the cupboard where they had their makeshift kitchen. Sasha soon appeared in her field of vision holding two cups. One he handed to Ida, and with the second he proceeded to the table and sat down. Ida said something in a low voice and Sasha answered her. Anya's head was aching unbearably, but that was probably a good thing, her physical torment blotting out everything else. One glance at Ida was enough for last night's events to loom up before her like a brick wall. Anya held back a cry and buried her face in the pillow. To get up and confront what had happened face-to-face was unbearable so, burrowing down as far as she could into the blanket, like a coward, she went back to sleep again.

When she woke for a second time, the others were already up. Still half-asleep, Anya immediately heard Sonya's voice. She would have been able to pick it out from among a thousand others. It sounded amazingly cheerful and lighthearted. Unable to hide any longer, Anya threw back the covers.

"Good morning!" Sonya said. "How are you feeling?"

"Oh, just about bearable," Anya replied. Her headache had modulated, after a further hour's sleep, into a different key, but it was still merciless. "How about the rest of you?"

"I'm good," Sasha said.

"My head is splitting," Ida complained.

"Would you like some tea?" Sonya inquired.

God Almighty, Anya thought. *How can you take all this so calmly?* She nodded. Sonya instantly leaped from her chair and went to the cupboard where the cups lived. Anya's eye followed her.

"And how about you?" she asked.

"Who, me? Fine. Everything that could come out of me came out yesterday," said Sonya with a laugh. Her spontaneity seemed so sincere that Anya found it impossible to tell whether she was deliberately ignoring the real meaning of her question.

Was there nothing behind it? Did she or did she not remember what happened yesterday?

"Did you manage to photograph everything you needed?" Sasha was meanwhile asking Ida. Anya decided it really was only she who was imagining a subtext in everything anybody said.

"Yes, absolutely. I'll send the film in to the editors and let them choose."

"What, you mean you are going to send the film in its entirety?" Anya asked, not immediately cottoning on. "With absolutely all the photographs?"

"Oh, yes. But don't worry, they won't print anything without your consent. If one of you can give me your email, I will pass it on and they'll be in touch before publication."

Everyone behaved as if nothing had happened, which made Anya feel unsettled, as if she must just have dreamed everything.

Ida finally left. Under Sasha's guidance, she slipped past the guard and was off. While Sasha was away, Anya asked Sonya, "Are you sure you're okay?"

"Yes, yes," Sonya replied, seeming even a little surprised. "God, we drank a lot yesterday!"

"That's not what I had in mind. You're not angry?"

"About what?"

"Well, about . . ." Anya faltered, panicking for a moment that if by some miracle Sonya did not remember the night's events, it might be better not to mention them.

"That you and Ida had sex?" Sonya clarified, lowering her voice on the words "had sex."

"No, of course not! I'm only sorry I felt ill and couldn't join you."

So saying, Sonya left the room with a pile of dirty dishes to wash, and Anya was left with an inner sense of impotence and something damaged beyond repair.

From that day there was a further subtle change in their relationship. Sonya seemed to start avoiding her. At first glance everything was as it had been, but Anya detected invisible signs. If the three of them were watching a movie, Sonya would sit on the far side of Sasha. When she was talking to him her face became more beautiful, but with Anya it remained the same. Sonya was still affectionate and responsive, laughed at Anya's jokes, went out to smoke and have lunch with her between classes, but Anya felt it was all only from force of habit, because she did not want to provoke a quarrel. Sonya's heart belonged to Sasha. It was as if a light bulb turned on in her the moment she saw him. Anya was overwhelmed by a feeling of possessiveness and jealousy, and demanded Sonya's attention more insistently. She tried to kid herself that she was only imagining all this, but nothing helped. It felt as if Sasha and Sonya were an axis she was spinning around and being pulled away from by centrifugal force. Anya sulked. If this was punishment for that night of drunkenness, then Sasha should be suffering it no less, if not more. However, the fact of the matter was that Sonya continued to move farther away from Anya and closer to Sasha, and there was nothing she could do about it.

Two weeks passed and, of course, no one wrote to them from *Afisha*. They didn't really expect them to. Who, after all, seriously expects to see their photos featured in an actual magazine? Then they went off to Novosibirsk for the conference and spent a week there, traveling around visiting Sasha's relatives.

One day while they were in Novosibirsk, Anya received an email.

When it arrived, she and Sonya were on the swings in the playground of Sasha's old school. He himself was inside, where several teachers had asked him to give a lesson to the ninth graders. Anya opened the email and could not believe her eyes. The photo editor from *Afisha* had indeed emailed to ask permission to use their photos. The photographs were attached, and Anya was saucer-eyed as she looked at them. All of the photos were of her and Sonya, fully dressed and kissing, undressed and on the floor, all in theatrical black and white.

Anya's vanity was instantly piqued. She was all for giving permission there and then for them all to be published just as they were, to flaunt these photos. How daring that would be! On the other hand, in two months' time when the university year ended, she was scheduled to do an internship at the Ministry of Foreign Affairs. That was a sobering thought. "What should we do, what should we do?" Anya intoned while Sonya was looking at the photographs. "Let's crop them," Sonya advised after thinking the matter over.

Half an hour later, opening the photos in Microsoft Paint on an antediluvian school computer, they looked for a compromise between frivolity and caution, expanding and narrowing the area of the rectangle selected. "No, keep more, keep more," Anya grumbled as Sonya hesitantly moved the mouse. Caution nevertheless prevailed. They cropped a photo where their faces were clearly visible down from the shoulders, deleting the provocative lower part. On another, where their faces were not visible, they cropped the top, cutting off part of Sasha's head for extra anonymity. Another photo with them kissing they rejected completely. They did not like that one much anyway. Having completed these adjustments, they gave permission to the *Afisha* photo editor to use the photos in this form. Satisfied with their efforts, they readied themselves to wake up famous in the near future.

They had no idea how widespread their celebrity was about to be.

Returning to Moscow a week later, Anya and Sonya rushed straight from the airport to the university to take their final oral exam in English. Having passed it not too indifferently, they came out to the porch, and Sonya asked someone for a cigarette. There were many other groups of smokers standing around, and a boy suddenly came out from one and made straight for Sonya. Anya recognized him as someone they knew from a junior year.

"Hi," he said. "Please can I have your autograph?"

"Where?" Sonya asked in surprise.

Their acquaintance deftly opened the magazine in his hand at a page where he had his finger and handed it to them.

There they were in the centerfold, on the floor, in each other's arms, in theatrical black and white, and in all their glory, with much more than just their shoulders included in the frame. Deprived of the power of speech, Anya's eyes moved slowly across the page, taking in her hair spread out on the floor, the cracks in the wooden boards, Sonya's exposed breasts. A white text box had been applied to her own breasts (without, alas, covering anything up). Discomfited, Anya ran her eyes over the text, which proclaimed, on behalf of a certain Natalya, that their dorm was the most drink-sodden and raunchy in the Institute of International Relations.

Sonya took the magazine and leafed through it. In all the photos shy-looking boys and girls at various universities and colleges peered out at them, with saucepans in kitchens, with guitars on stairs, hugging toys and books. Very sweet, and very boring. The Institute of International Relations section also began sweetly, with a girl in a pink bathrobe, a homemade cake studded with candles. Bright pictures on snow-white paper. They had only to turn the page, however, to fall into a realm of darkness: photographs in which you could make out only naked female bodies, Anya's hand on Sonya's belly, overturned bottles of tequila and, to crown it all, that centerfold. Only one out of all the pictures had been cropped. The editors of *Afisha* had kindheartedly allowed half of Sasha's head to be cut off. Everything else, however, the really compromising stuff, was there in full view.

"So, can I have your autograph?" their new acquaintance asked, smiling.

Sonya abruptly closed the magazine and shoved it back at him. Anya took her by the wrist—after these photographs, taking Sonya by the hand in front of everyone seemed just too brazen—and dragged her off, away from the university. Anya felt they were being stared at by everyone. At first they walked quickly and in silence, but having moved away to a safe distance where they could not be overheard, Anya said, "I don't think anyone will find out. After all, how many people read *Afisha*?"

By the next day, everybody had.

In the store nearest the dormitory, in the newspaper and magazine section, the copies of *Afisha* were sold out. Anya saw two students on the porch, busily studying the magazine. Someone had cut out the centerfold pages and taped them up on the staircase that served as a clandestine smoking area. Scans of the photographs were posted in the institute's group on VKontakte. In the comments, the discussion was mainly about how the girls in the photos should be punished.

Among the options were proposals to burn them at the stake or stab them. The most lenient recommended mere expulsion. Some of the comments considered the publication of the photographs itself an outright perversion, some accepted that women have a right to have breasts, but not naked breasts. With the imminence of the law on "promoting homosexuality," many wondered if this was a political protest. For some reason this was not imagined to be on the part of the heroines, but of the editors of *Afisha*. The expressions "liberal hipsters" and "militant homogays" came up several times, and one contributor opined that "the pseudo-freedom of the internet has eroded the notion of civilized behavior."

Neither was Sasha's involvement overlooked by the commenters. This was especially unfair, because his guilt was to be present, fully dressed, and half-headless, in the corner of one photo. Nevertheless, matters reached such a pitch that another student in the dorm, defending the impugned honor of the institute, challenged Sasha to a full-blown duel, and they punched the living daylights out of each other for twenty minutes in the backyard.

In those days, Anya listened to Boris Grebenshchikov's song "500" on repeat. There was a line in it, "Falling in an elevator, folks feel lighter every second." She would very much like to have felt lighter, even if only by feeling powerless, but it did not happen. Anya seemed physically to register the waves of revulsion she stirred in every person who happened to set eyes on her, everyone who found themselves obliged to speak to her. She was consumed by an unbearable sense of shame. The photographs themselves still seemed to her a prank, but every time she read a new comment in the VKontakte group, she gasped for breath and felt empty inside, almost as if she were about to jump from a great height. These people saw her, good, smart Anya, in a completely different light, and that spread like a dark cloud over the photographs, over her relationship with Sonya, over everything in her life. What she loved was now poisoned by the bad feeling and, succumbing to it, she began to despise herself.

A day after the magazine came out, Sasha, Anya, and Sonya were summoned by the dean of students. This was rather unexpected, and it was some time before they realized what was going on. The dean of students was responsible for good order in the dorms, and those in charge of the Institute of International Relations evidently saw the insalubrious climate there as to blame for the evil. Their conversation with the dean was long and unconstructive. They kept quiet while he expounded on the irreparable damage they had done to the university's reputation. What he found most outrageous was not the bare breasts, but the phrase in the textbox on the breasts about the dorms being drink-sodden and raunchy. That, of course, riled them all the more because none of them had said anything of the sort, although Anya had to admit to herself that the description was entirely accurate.

The following day they were summoned back to the dean's office and informed that they would be expelled. Anya had only a faint recollection of that day, of a feeling that the ground was about to open up under her when she tried to imagine calling her mother to say, "I've been kicked out of university a month before graduation because of nude photographs of me kissing a girl." She was unsure precisely which part of that sentence would be the cause of her mother's demise.

A day after that, they were told in confidence that the senior officers had thought better of expelling them. Although that removed any immediate need to call her mother, Anya was still worried, and rightly so. They were again summoned by the dean and informed this time that it had been decided to evict them from the dormitory for "not meeting the standards expected of residents." Anya and Sonya were already packing their bags when the dorm warden came in and told them they could stay, providing they atoned for their sins without delay by repainting the building's railings.

Slapping a brush over the metal rods, Anya felt like a dissolute Tom Sawyer.

Somehow, May passed peacefully. The public indignation gradually subsided, teachers benevolently pretended not to know anything, and Anya and Sonya got on with writing their graduation essays. In addition to her exams at the institute, Anya was taking the entrance exams for the Ministry of Foreign Affairs. Everything was going well, and it only remained for her to bring a certificate from her place of study. This should be provided by the dean of academic affairs, a fat, cheerful man, by no means old, whom the students loved for his easygoing nature. Confident that the certificate was a formality, Anya went to the dean's office, only to be told that she would be getting nothing. The dean of academic affairs had categorically refused.

At first she could not believe it. During the *Afisha* scandal the dean seemed to have been the only person not to express an opinion. Meeting with Anya in the corridor, he greeted her as affably as before. If Anya had not been certain that absolutely everybody knew all about it, she might have supposed the whole affair had passed him by. Now, however, it seemed clear that, not only had he known everything, he had in fact resolved to punish her. Anya waylaid him outside his office and asked if she could speak to him.

"I am not free," he said curtly, and for the first time a doubt crept into her mind that perhaps his greetings to her had not really been warm all this time.

"I'll take up only a very little of your time, whenever it's convenient for you," Anya said meekly.

"Well, talk to my secretary . . . I have no idea of when my schedule would allow that!"

Anya immediately went to the secretary, only to learn that the dean's schedule was at this exact moment extraordinarily full. There was nothing to do but lurk around the dean's office in the hope of bumping into him again.

Seeing her once more at his door, the dean took an involuntary step backwards, but then frowned and said, "Come back tomorrow at noon."

At twelve the next day, Anya timidly scratched at the door of the office. "Igor Yevgenievich is busy!" his secretary announced, plainly surprised by her boldness. Anya obediently sat down on a bench in the corridor to wait.

In films, waiting is usually conveyed by showing hands speeding round on the dial of a clock, but for Anya the reality was that she looked at the clock so frequently its hands appeared not to be moving at all. After an hour and a half, she made a further attempt to affirm her presence, but the secretary replied, "You will be called." Another hour and a half passed, then another. The corridor emptied, but still the dean did not emerge from his besieged office.

Finally Anya was called in.

She had never been in the dean's office before. Everything was massive and mahogany-colored: the huge leather sofa, a round, varnished table in front of it, the bookcase laden with books, the dean's armchair by the window. Anya perched on the very edge of the sofa. The air conditioner was on and the office was as cold as a freezer. Even the sofa was cold.

"Well, what was it you want to talk about?" the dean asked, turning away from his computer and folding his arms over his stomach. His voice was as icy as everything else in the room.

"I would like to be issued a certificate from my place of study. For the Ministry of Foreign Affairs."

"The university's officers have decided against giving you one."

"But they're issued to everyone. It's not a reference, just a confirmation that I have studied here," Anya pointed out, seeking simple justice.

The dean sighed, stood up and rolled his chair over to the table. Now he and Anya were sitting on opposite sides of it.

"We could never allow you to work at the Foreign Ministry," the dean said. It sounded heartfelt.

"Why not?" Anya asked. She was taken aback at being treated so rudely.

"Do you really not know?"

"But those were just some photographs! There's nothing that special about them! There's not even any mention of my name!"

"A diplomat is a person with the highest moral principles," the dean said severely. "Do you consider yourself to be such a person?"

"Of course I do! And those photographs don't prove anything different."

The dean leaned back in his chair and began to look more closely at Anya. She thought she detected some hesitation on his part, and she went on fervently, "I particularly want to go to Africa. I'd love to go to any country, no matter how disadvantaged. It's what I've always wanted to do, that's why I decided to work in the Ministry of Foreign Affairs."

"Why would a young girl want to go to Africa? It is a dangerous place."

"I really, really do. And I'm not afraid of anything, not diseases, or coups, I'm actually quite bold . . ."

"You've already made that clear."

Anya blushed.

"I mean I'll do a good job there," she muttered. "And I'm not afraid of the things people are usually worried about when they think about expeditions to Africa."

"That is very commendable, but I have to say to you again: we cannot allow you to join the diplomatic service."

"Why ever not?!" Anya exclaimed in despair.

Up till this moment she had not believed in her heart that she would be refused. She had imagined it would be like the plot in a movie: she would come in, impress the dean with her fearlessness and will to work hard, he would have faith in her and give her the certificate. But now she could see the way he was looking at her—without a great deal of interest, and with a certain amount of malicious satisfaction—and she sensed this was not going to work out like in the movies.

"Who knows what else you might get up to?" the dean said with a shrug. "Dance naked on a table in the embassy?"

Anya again felt her face flushing. Again she felt the person sitting opposite was not seeing her as she knew herself to be, but a different person, someone depraved and unworthy. Swallowing her pride, she explained, "I think that after this scandal you can be very certain I won't do anything of this sort again. I now know better than anyone else the damage it can do."

"Nevertheless," the dean said, slapping his knee, "we need to protect our reputation. And you with your antics are not a suitable person to represent our country."

He stood up and gave Anya a hard look. Mechanically, she got up too, and was about to say something but, looking once more at his expression, left without another word.

By the time Anya got back to the dorm, she had already gotten a grip on herself. She was good at leaving failures behind, and now redoubled her efforts to find a way out. Perhaps it was not working out the way it does in the movies, but all was not lost. Perhaps there could still be a happy ending if she made one final effort. For a start, Anya went back to the Foreign Ministry and asked whether they could, as an exception, accept her application without a certificate of study.

"No," the woman in the personnel office told her regretfully. "We have a standard set of documents required for acceptance. But don't worry, everybody gets that certificate!" Anya went home, considering her other options. There were none, other than to go back to the dean. This time, he simply could not be allowed to refuse her. She had to break down that wall.

"Igor Yevgenievich is not in," the secretary snapped, the moment she saw her in the doorway.

Anya went back to the corridor and sat down on the same bench. It was the break, students were rushing past, the sun was blazing through the huge windows, and almost immediately Anya saw the dean coming down the corridor. He was parting the crowd of students like a huge, potbellied battleship. She jumped up and ran towards him.

"Igor Yevgenievich! It's about the certificate again. May I . . ."

And then something happened that Anya really had not foreseen. Igor Yevgenievich, the student's friend, was shaking with rage, turning purple in the face, and shrieking, "Dishonoring the university! Bringing us into disrepute! How dare you come back! Why, you should be grateful you are being allowed to complete your studies! And you talk about the Foreign Ministry! Over my dead body! Never! Away with you! Get out! Out of my sight! Never!"

He bellowed the last words as he walked down the corridor, without even looking at her. The door of the dean's office slammed shut and there was total silence. Anya looked around: the students about her had frozen like statues. This lasted a few moments, after which they suddenly came to life and very quietly slipped away and went about their business.

Anya went home too, her diplomatic career over before it had even begun.

*　　*　　*

"Wow! You're quite something," Katya said when Anya finished telling them the tale.

Diana, who was sitting next to her, looked groggy and spaced out from the hash, but she too nodded enthusiastically. Even Natasha, who had turned away at the beginning of the story, was lying on her back by the middle, and by the end had turned over to face Anya, propping her head up on her hand.

"And yet you seem so quiet, so calm," Katya went on. "But see what you get up to! It's the truth when they say demons lurk in still waters."

"I'm not very into still waters," Anya said with a smile.

"No, but it's clear now! How about that, I would never have guessed you were into girls."

"I would have," Diana said smugly. She stretched her hand out in front of her and looked at it, wiggling her fingers. In her present state she seemed pleased not so much about her powers of insight as just generally about herself.

"No, she d-doesn't look like one," Natasha muttered grumpily above them. "That sort usually do it because they are young and s-silly. Experimenting. Were you experimenting?"

"I was not experimenting!" Anya said indignantly, puzzled as to why she should have to justify her sexual orientation.

Natasha looked at her, unconvinced.

They had finished smoking the hash long ago, and gradually the agreeable laid-back sensation began to wear off. They threw the windows wide open and Katya, Diana, and Natasha smoked cigarettes "to kill the smell." The bottle was carefully squashed and thrown in the garbage pail, buried as deeply as possible to be safe. When the policeman came to take them to exercise, the cell looked as idyllic as a Russian prison cell possibly can.

During the exercise period Diana immediately began reaping her harvest. Anya saw her head for the farthest window, talk to some prisoners who were behind the bars, and then reach out to the window and take something. She repeated the operation at each cell in turn and came back to her cellmates looking pleased.

"What'd you get?" Katya asked lazily. She was sitting on the bench, leaning against the wall and screwing up her eyes against the sun.

Diana looked through the slips of paper in her hand.

"Eight phone numbers," she summarized. "Even one from a Tajik called Ikram."

"And what are you going to d-do with them?" Natasha asked disapprovingly.

"I'm not going to do anything with them. I just do it to make sure I don't lose my touch."

Natasha was not letting up: "And does your husband let you d-do that sort of thing?"

Diana raised her chin defiantly.

"It's not for him to tell me what I can or can't do. I'm an adult. Besides," she added after a moment's thought, "I shan't be telling him."

Have you ever been unfaithful to your husband?" Katya asked. "Any of them?"

"Only the first. With the man who later became my second."

"And you met the third one at the funeral of the second?"

"Correct. So you see, I'm very conservative in these matters. I once read about some aged Hollywood actress who married all her lovers. I like her style."

"But it must be sad to be getting divorced all the time, isn't it?" Anya mused.

"I wouldn't know. So far I've only ever gotten divorced once," Diana said with a shrug. "It didn't feel particularly sad. But when husbands die, that's different. There's certainly nothing good about that."

At lunch they had Uzbek-style pilaf, but after the hash Anya and her cellmates had the munchies and would have been glad to eat anything, even dry bread. As lunch was late, they had already devoured all of yesterday's gifts while they were waiting. Natasha eyed Diana and Katya, who were spooning food into their mouths at lightning speed, with an expression of supreme contempt.

Unlike the others who had been released that week, Natasha showed not the slightest enthusiasm at the prospect. She did not pack up her belongings, did not express regrets, did not ask what the time was, and displayed complete indifference to whatever fate might have in store for her. Anya noticed, however, that a couple of times she went over to the mirror and fussed with her curls. Only that gesture suggested that, in reality, Natasha was as keen as the others to be set free.

The cell door finally opened, and the cop told Natasha she had fifteen minutes to get her belongings together. She jumped down from the top bunk, not forgetting, however, to look displeased.

"You would almost think you didn't want to get out!" Diana said testily. "I'm counting the hours to my release, but you don't even seem pleased!"

"I am p-pleased," Natasha answered in a tone which suggested the exact opposite. "What do you expect me to do now, jump up and down?"

She started tossing her belongings into a plastic bag.

"Well, you could at least stop looking so grumpy!" Katya said, supporting Diana.

"You all seem to imagine getting out of here is some great blessing," Natasha said through gritted teeth. "Getting released from the camps certainly is a great relief, but this place is p-practically a holiday resort. It's felt like a break from being stuck at home."

Diana whistled.

"I wouldn't want to be in your home."

"There's nothing wrong with my home! It's just that you lot never stop whining about 'When will we get out, when will we get out!' You have nothing to whine about!"

Natasha took her bag by the corners, gave it an angry shake, and laid it on the bed. If she had had a suitcase, this would probably have been the moment she slammed down the lid. As she was leaving, Natasha grunted, "So long," to them all and practically skipped out of the cell.

"She's an odd one," Katya commented when the door had closed behind her.

"Everybody else in here was odd. We three are the only normal ones," Diana said.

Anya had serious doubts about her own normality, or indeed that of her cellmates, but, needless to say, kept her mouth shut. For the past day she had been unable to find the right moment (in reality, she had not found the courage) to ask Katya a direct question, and after so many hours it no longer seemed so urgent. It was easy to be brave during the day, but what might await her during the night, Anya preferred not to think about.

Their less populous cell was noticeably quieter. Diana and Katya sat on their own bunks saying nothing. In the absence of an audience they seemed less eager to talk. Anya became absorbed in her book. The radio was tuned to Like FM, which made this seem almost a good day, because it played only English-language songs, which, unlike songs in Russian, were easier to ignore.

A couple of hours later they were taken to make phone calls, then to dinner. In addition to Viktor Ivanovich and the mousy server, a new person was making waves in the kitchen. He was wearing black trousers, had short black hair, and an extraordinarily pale face. He was evidently a new arrival but seemed already completely at home, bossing around the hapless Viktor Ivanovich. He talked playfully to Anya's cellmates as he dolloped food into their bowls with a show of nonchalance. As soon as the girls were seated, he was out of the kitchen and joined them at their table. He ate nothing but chattered endlessly, asking them all what they were in for, bad-mouthing the cops, offering the girls tea or bread. Anya took an instant dislike to him but said nothing. Nobody noticed, because Katya and Diana were only too pleased to be chatted up by the new arrival.

In the evening the three women talked about what they had all been afraid of when they were little. Katya said her mother was forever threatening to give her away to the gypsies if she behaved badly, with the result that when one day they actually met gypsies on a train, little Katya had such a meltdown that the head steward on the train came running.

Diana said she too had a story about gypsies, though it was much more recent and hence all the more embarrassing. Diana was coming back after a short meeting with her husband in a prison camp. The camp was near Bryansk, so Diana took the train there and traveled on by bus. The buses did not line up with the train times, so on each occasion she had three hours to spend at the railway station on her way back. Diana was less than thrilled about having constantly to drag herself out to the back of beyond with heavy bags of supplies for her husband, and this long holdup every time on her way back home only fueled her bad mood.

At that moment she had just two thousand rubles left in her purse to last her to the end of the month, which was a few days away. That did not allow any high living, so Diana did not even go to her usual nearby café but took a seat in the waiting room. It was here that a passing gypsy woman latched onto her. She was off-putting—old, toothless, wearing a greasy headscarf, but her gypsy magic was in full working order. Despite the woman's unprepossessing appearance, Diana held out her palm to have her fortune told, and then handed over her two thousand rubles.

When she recovered her senses, Diana rushed to find the station cop. At first he could not believe what he was hearing. Had she really voluntarily handed her the money? Did she not know what she was doing? Diana, in tears, assured him she must have been hypnotized. She had heard a hundred times about gypsy talents of that kind but had never believed it, and now, incredibly, she had fallen victim herself. The cop sighed and promised to go in search of the gypsy, although with obviously little enthusiasm. Diana went back to her seat, sniffling and cursing herself for being such a fool. She mentally added up how many days her home stocks of buckwheat and pasta would last and came to a disconcerting conclusion.

Twenty minutes later, however, when Diana's natural optimism had returned and her disillusionment with the Russian law enforcement system was on the verge of becoming terminal, the cop reappeared. He was holding the gypsy woman by the elbow. She looked angry and frightened but was coming quietly, not trying to break free. "Is this her?" the cop asked Diana. "Yes!" Diana exclaimed delightedly. "Give her the money back," said the cop. The gypsy woman, muttering under her breath, extricated the two thousand rubles, rolled up into a tube, from beneath numerous skirts. Greatly relieved, Diana took the money and thanked the cop profusely. He assured her it was nothing and laughed it off, but went away pleased with himself. The gypsy woman was released and beat a hasty retreat, but stayed only a short distance away. Diana saw her standing by the opposite wall of the waiting room and scowling at her every now and then.

After the cop had disappeared from view, the gypsy woman waited a few minutes before again approaching Diana.

"Would you like me to show you a trick?" she asked suddenly.

"Are you crazy? Just go away before I call the police again," Diana retorted.

"I really will just show you a trick. I won't do anything bad, why would I? You've never seen a trick like this in your life."

Diana found it difficult to explain what happened after that. Whether it was that same gypsy magic or her own incorrigible curiosity, but she was drawn into conversation, and when the gypsy asked for five hundred rubles to show her the trick, she opened her purse and gave it to her. The gypsy turned the bill in front of her nose as if sniffing it, then whistled softly and made some magical passes with her hands. The five hundred rubles appeared to dissolve between her fingers. Glancing derisively at Diana's long face, the gypsy turned her back on her and very smugly, very slowly went on her way.

"And what? You just let her go?" Katya shrieked. She had long since moved to Diana's bunk and was now leaning forward, taking in every word.

Diana had gotten up from her bunk a while ago and stood in the center of the cell, acting out her story in character. She was so convincing and entertaining that Anya, as usual, could not take her eyes off her. She moved about, acting the part of the cop, then of the gypsy woman. She waved her arms, mimicked the voices, and treated them to a stage performance.

"Well, what could I do?" Diana said with a laugh. "Run back to the cop again? He would have thought I was out of my mind to give her money a second time."

"So why did you give her the money?"

"I really don't know! I was curious. After all, who would have thought that she could be so brazen as to take me for a ride a second time?"

Diana threw up her hands in despair and laughed again, her sincerity so bewitching that Katya laughed along. So did Anya, still full of admiration for Diana herself. And then, out of the corner of her eye, she noticed something strange on the wall. She looked over, still not fully aware of what had surprised her.

The shadow cast by Diana was an impossibility.

It definitely belonged to her. It had the same figure, the same silhouette of hair—but it was huge, extending almost to the ceiling. And yet, there was no light source that could be casting it. Anya saw that quite clearly. While Diana was speaking to Katya and gesticulating wildly, the shadow behind her was almost motionless, frozen in one position. Its left hand was raised, its right lowered, and there was a thread stretched between them. The thread was being wound onto something thin that expanded at the base. The shadow was deftly twisting this object around its axis with its lower hand. Despite the fact that Diana was not only waving her arms about, but walking around the cell, the shadow remained glued to the wall and only made very small rotating movements with its hand.

Anya slowly turned to look towards Katya. She was listening avidly to Diana and had obviously not noticed anything. Desperately hoping that when she looked at the wall again she would see nothing on it, Anya looked back. The huge, almost motionless shadow was still very, very swiftly winding the thread around the strange object. An unexpected thought came into her mind: *It's a spindle.* She had never seen any spindles, and the only associations the word had for her were from the tale of *Sleeping Beauty* and one of Alisa's songs called "The Spindle." The association with the hard rock group almost made her laugh out loud. She was not frightened, but that seemed to be largely because her emotions had dried up completely. She continued staring at the shadow on the wall as if it were a holographic picture such as she had seen in books when she was little. If you brought them up to your nose and focused your eyes the right way, three-dimensional objects like castles and ships would appear out of the flat pattern. Anya had a feeling that if she looked at the shadow on the wall for long enough, it would yield and also reveal its hidden essence.

"And that is where he died," Diana concluded, and Anya came back to her senses.

"Who died?" she asked.

"My husband, of course." Diana walked a few steps and sat back down in her bunk. The shadow followed her down the wall and disappeared. "Didn't you hear? I just said."

"I got caught up in my own thoughts. So how did he die?"

Diana looked at her in bewilderment.

"On New Year's Eve. I told you. He only had a month left before he would have gotten out, and I was making him this present. And no sooner had I finished it than I got a phone call, the very next day, to tell me it was all over."

"So what was the present you were making for him?" Anya asked. A feeling was taking hold of her that any moment now everything would become clear. It was as if she were running down a dark, deserted alley but could already hear the buzz of voices from around the corner. When she turned the corner she would see a great, noisy square spread out before her.

"It was a scarf. He kept moaning that he wanted something I had made with my own hands. In my life I had never held a needle and thread, let alone knitting needles or, you know, a crochet hook. But I had such a lovely time when I went in September for a long visit. That is when he fell ill for the first time. I felt so sorry. I really wanted to do something nice for him. So I started knitting this godforsaken scarf. I kept cursing it. There was always something going wrong. I had to unpick and totally unravel it and start again. And he kept getting more and more sick. When he was feeling better, everything seemed to work out all right, but when he was feeling worse I just wanted to give up. I did manage to finish it in the end. Ugh! I flung it out as soon as I heard. I couldn't bear to look at it. I had put my heart and soul into it."

Diana's voice broke as she spoke these last words, and when she finished she started to cry. Katya awkwardly sat closer and stroked her shoulder.

"There, there," she said, clearly having no idea how to console someone who is crying. "You're not to blame for anything. Some things just happen. It was fate, nothing to do with you."

"Why did I have to remember this now," Diana sobbed. "Today is my birthday, I am supposed to be happy, but here I am crying my eyes out."

"There, there," Katya said, continuing mechanically to stroke her shoulder.

Anya said nothing. She looked at the girls sitting there in front of her but seemed not to be seeing them. She had turned that corner, but the square had been dead. All the doors were locked and barred, there were no lights on anywhere and not a living soul to be seen. The truth, which Anya had been trying to catch by its tail, had eluded her. She looked at the wall and now saw no shadows. How could she have, when the lights were shining down vertically from the ceiling?

There was a tiny shadow from the locker, a strip three centimeters wide at its base; there was a shadow from the empty plastic bottles.

Despite the fact that there could be no doubting the unreality of what she had seen, that the evidence was clear and that any sane person, including herself, would screw a finger at their head if anyone insisted otherwise, Anya began for the first time seriously to wonder—what if all the things she had seen here in cell number 3 were real?

DAY SEVEN

Anya woke up because Diana and Katya were talking loudly and rustling plastic bags.

"I'll call you this week and we can arrange something," Katya was saying. "We could get hammered this weekend."

"I may be out in the country this weekend. But call anyway. If not this weekend then next."

"Do you have a dacha?"

"Yes, but it's not mine. It belongs to my husband. In Tver province."

Anya pulled the blanket up over her head but sleep proved elusive. She carried on listening to the excited voices and the sounds of her busy cellmates. One went to the washbasin and made the soap dish squeak, not managing to fit the lid back on the first time. The other shook her sneakers out of the bag and they bounced on the floor. Anya felt envious: not so much because her cellmates were being released, but because they would be getting out together. The two of them seemed now to have moved a step ahead, while Anya trailed miserably along in their wake.

Giving in to their energy, Anya stopped pretending to be asleep and sat up in her bunk.

"Packing your things?" she asked rhetorically, looking at the belongings strewn over their bunks.

"I seem to have so much junk," Diana said, peeping into another bag. "Would you like me to leave you my flip-flops?"

"No, thanks."

"I can leave you some shampoo and hand cream."

"Just the hand cream. Thanks."

Katya, meanwhile, had changed into jeans, put a cap on her head, and plonked herself down on a stripped bunk. Diana gave her a sideways glance and remarked,

"You still have two hours to go."

"I'm helping it to come as soon as possible."

The morning inspection was at nine o'clock or so, and Katya was due to be released at nine fifteen. She hadn't been sitting on the bunk for five minutes before she jumped up and started pacing around the cell like a caged tigress. Every time the gate creaked, or there were footsteps in the corridor, or a jingling of keys, Katya quivered and stared at the door, but no one came in. The morning hours usually went by quickest, with everybody half-asleep, chatting together, without the irritant of the radio. Today even Anya felt the time before inspection was dragging on forever.

Finally, from the corridor came the sound of doors being slammed and loud voices, a sure sign the rounds had begun. Katya, having just sat back down on her bunk, immediately leaped up. The door opened, and in two bounds Katya was standing in front of it.

"What time is it now?" she yelled.

The fat-cheeked duty officer, who had already put one foot inside the cell, hastily stepped back.

"Eight thirty," he said uncertainly, looking at Katya apprehensively. She wailed, "Forty-five more minutes! I don't believe it!"

She trailed back to the bunk and the duty officer, recollecting who was in charge here, drew himself up to his full height and came into the cell.

After reading out their names and recording something in his notebook, he said, "So, Vilkova, you are due for release today."

"Yes!" Katya responded.

"And I'm due for release today too," Diana chimed in, looking worried. "You aren't forgetting me, are you?"

"We'll let everyone out," the duty officer reassured her. Anya recalled he was not usually the most talkative of the guards, but he seemed to be in a good mood today. "So, you will be the only one still staying with us?"

Anya shrugged.

"Don't be sad," he said. "We'll find someone to keep you company. Tee-hee."

The duty officer left, and Anya gloomily reflected that finding herself in solitary confinement had become the thing she most aspired to in recent days. The detention center certainly taught you how to be content with little.

For the next half hour Katya was whining endlessly. No sooner had the door closed behind the cop than she was asking her cellmates how many minutes they thought had passed. She lit a cigarette, asked them to guess the time again, changed into sneakers, then back into flip-flops, then again into sneakers. She asked them again, smoked another cigarette, turned around in front of the mirror, asked them again to guess the time, squabbled with Diana when she refused to answer anymore, and was finally silent. But not for long. She again began pacing around the cell, and complained bitterly about the absence of a clock. When the door to their cell opened and the blonde who had taken Anya's fingerprints nodded to Katya that it was time for her to leave, all three cellmates breathed a sigh of relief.

Katya rushed to Diana and gave her a bear hug, murmuring that she would call her later that day. Then, with noticeably greater reserve, she hugged Anya. Just as she was reaching out towards her, it seemed to Anya that her recent nightmare was about to recur. Katya's face seemed to ripple, and for a fraction of a second it seemed to become menacing again, but the impression passed as swiftly as it had come. Katya wrapped her arms around Anya and stepped back. When she turned away, Anya gave a tiny shrug. It was not from disgust or fear, but Katya's touch provoked some strange emotion inside her.

With the departure of her friend, Diana became much more serious. Settling herself on the bunk, she started, stern-faced, writing something in a notebook.

"What time do you get out?" Anya asked. In the stillness her voice sounded diffident and almost plaintive. She felt angry with herself.

"At ten."

"You are waiting very patiently."

"What's the point of fussing? It won't get you out any sooner."

Anya waited for her to say something else, but she didn't, and carried on moving her pen over the paper. Anya took her book and settled down to read.

Diana maintained her aloofness until the peephole in the door opened and the blonde yelled, "Orlova! You're out in fifteen minutes!" At that, Diana jumped up and started getting things together—or rather, shifting them from one place to another, because she had already packed everything early that morning. Anya watched from behind her book. When the key rattled in the lock, Diana beamed.

"Goodbye, then!" she said excitedly, rushing over to Anya. Anya stood up, they hugged, and Diana immediately ran to gather up her bags. "I left the hand cream on the washbasin for you!"

"Thanks!" Anya called hurriedly in her wake, but Diana had already darted out of the cell and the door was immediately closed behind her. Anya was finally alone.

Looking around, feeling lost, she took a few steps and stopped in the center of the room. She had mixed feelings. On the one hand, she was conscious of the emptiness. All these days the cell had been full of other detainees. It had been noisy and alive. Now she was suddenly aware of her solitude. She had felt something analogous when she left the summer camp; even if she did not miss particular people, she missed the time that was now past. On the other hand, in her solitude Anya had suddenly become much more expansive. Everything here was hers. She could lie on any bunk, sit on the windowsill because now there was no one smoking there. She could open and close the windows as she pleased. She did not even have to run the taps while using the toilet. Anya walked contemplatively around the cell, inspecting her realm. On reflection, she decided Diana's place next to the wall was the most desirable, and dragged her bedding over there. She fluffed each pillow and chose the plumpest one. She reviewed her food supplies: she had one package of instant noodles left, a bag of crackers, some candy, and a whole lot of tea. She was feeling hungry. Anya automatically went over to the bed on which the bottle of hot water was kept under a pile of blankets. There was a bottle but it was empty—no one had gone to breakfast that morning. Anya could see that for her two remaining days she would have to organize such matters herself. There was something pleasing about that as well. Sitting in the bunk in her new position, she opened the packet of crackers and carried on reading.

Soon the radio came on. Being in a placid state of mind, Anya decided simply to ignore it. Half an hour later, however, she found she had turned only two pages. When her cellmates had been in the cell, the radio was easier to endure, but now every word emanating from it was pushing itself into Anya's consciousness. She got up, walked over to the speaker, and examined it carefully. It was high up above the door and almost impossible to get near. Not that that would have helped much. The mesh shield protecting the speaker looked firmly screwed in place. Anya went back to her bunk and lay down with her ear tightly pressed against the pillow. She was distressed to find that her other ear was still hearing clearly. Anya took a pillow from another bed and put it on top of her head, which made everything darker and quieter, but less comfortable. There was no way a person could read in that position.

Rummaging through her belongings, Anya found a pack of cotton makeup pads. These had been brought by her friends but the cosmetics they were intended for had not been allowed in because the packaging was not transparent. She rolled the disks into homemade earplugs, stuffed one in each ear, and took up her book again. Sitting with your ears plugged also turned out to be less than ideal, because now she could hear nothing except for sounds produced by her own movements. These were muffled and seemed to come from inside her. Given the choice between this inconvenience and the incessant noise of the radio, Anya made her decision without hesitation.

Soon, however, she tired of reading. She was really hungry and the crackers had only whetted her appetite. For the sake of having something to do, Anya paced around the cell, washed her hands, and used some of the hand cream. She stood in front of the washbasin and looked into the cloudy film of the mirror over it. It reflected back nothing other than her own face.

Anya did not know where her new confidence came from, but had a feeling that her hallucinations had vanished along with her cellmates. It was as if a brain fog had lifted, and this brought such a blessed feeling of liberation that even being stuck in a detention center became easier to bear. Her idea yesterday that her visions were not visions at all but real was obviously a symptom of mental desperation. Few people, after all, are able to accept calmly the fact that they are having a psychotic break, so she had been looking for some other explanation. Today, however, thanks to this unexpected clarity in her head, Anya could see that in the last few days her nerves had been shot to pieces, and that was why she had been imagining all sorts of weird stuff. It was, of course, nothing to do with her cellmates, but the stress caused by her arrest. She had now come to terms with that, and would in any case soon be released. She was feeling so much better.

Smiling to herself, Anya turned away from the washbasin but immediately recoiled with a scream and crashed backwards into the washstand. A dark figure was standing a meter away from her. This figure, however, also shied away and Anya belatedly realized that it was just the police boy. Her hands trembling, she pulled out her earplugs. The police boy looked at her wild-eyed.

"What are you screaming for?" he asked hoarsely.

Anya blushed.

"I'm so sorry," she mumbled. "I couldn't hear anything. I was trying to block out the radio."

She gave it a dirty look and the boy followed her gaze.

"Actually, I just came to ask you for some tea," he blurted out, still looking at the radio.

"What?"

"To ask for some tea. If you have some to spare. If you don't, we won't take it from you. It's Anatolievich's birthday. The duty officer. We've got him the cake but nobody has any tea."

The police boy finally turned to face her and gave her a watery smile. Anya continued to stare at him in astonishment until she came to her senses.

"Oh, yes, of course. Here." She hurried over to the locker and gave the boy their box of tea.

"We really don't need that much," he assured her. "I'll just take a few tea bags!"

He carefully pulled out six tea bags one by one and placed them in the palm of his hand.

"There, that's plenty. Thanks. We would bring you a piece of the cake, but it's against regulations."

"Perhaps then you could just turn off the radio."

The boy shook his head guiltily.

"That's against regulations too."

Anya gave a heartfelt sigh.

"Is it nearly lunchtime?"

"Yes! It is!" the policeman said happily. "I'll be sure you're the first person I take up!"

Watching him depart, Anya went back to her bunk and lay down on her stomach, resting her chin on her fist. She should at least have asked them for some hot water. Although perhaps giving someone boiling water was also "against regulations." But that cake! She was hungry, and the thought of it—a cake with buttercream frosting, white, with little pink buttercream roses—was more than she could bear. There were only two days now before she would be released, but they were clearly going to be the longest days of her life.

By the time she was finally taken to lunch, Anya had sat on the windowsill, read some more of her book, sorted through all her belongings, done push-ups on her bunk, and investigated the contents of the locker. She found it contained last December's issue of *Liza*, and Anya entertained herself by reading recipes for a New Year's party, until that turned from entertainment into torture.

"Oh, who's this then?" yesterday's pallid server sang out. With difficulty, Anya refrained from scowling back at him. "Where are all your friends?"

"They've been released."

"And what about you, are you all alone now? You must be feeling sorry for yourself. Don't worry, I'm here to keep you company."

"What's the first course?"

"Borsch."

Anya groaned inwardly.

"And the second?"

"Meat patty and buckwheat."

"Just give me the second."

The guy scooped buckwheat out of the tub and slopped it into a bowl.

"They brought it up five minutes ago so it's still hot," he boasted, as if he had some direct input to the temperature of the buckwheat. "Let me give you some extra. Would you like two patties?"

"But then someone else won't get any, will they?" Anya asked suspiciously.

"Well, big deal if someone doesn't get any! Some alky, some junkie, or whoever else we get in here. Who cares, I'd sooner feed you up!"

"I don't need two meat patties," Anya cut him short, practically snatching the bowl from him. Walking around the table, she sat down at a place where she could keep him in sight. She would have felt uncomfortable with her back to him.

No matter—the guy skipped out of the kitchen and sat down opposite her.

"What's your name?" he asked slimily.

"Anya."

"What a beautiful name. Anyuta. I'm going to call you Anyuta. And I'm Sergey."

"Don't call me Anyuta."

"Well, what would you like me to call you? Nyuta? Nyusha? Anita?" He giggled as if he had just cracked a brilliant joke.

Anya gave him a drop-dead stare.

"Have you got a boyfriend?" Sergey asked, going on the attack. Anya choked on her porridge.

"Mind your own business," she said, more rudely than she had intended.

"You just look so beautiful," he said. "We're going to fall in love, you and I."

Sergey gave her a big smile that made him look like a well-fed cartoon tomcat.

"We won't be falling in love," Anya advised him, just in case this was really in need of clarification.

"Don't be like that," Sergey urged, continuing to smile and quickly moving round to sit beside her. "Don't you like me?"

Anya was taken aback by this forwardness. Pausing for a moment, she moved herself and her bowl half a meter away from him.

"Correct. I don't like you."

"Never mind, you will," Sergey replied nonchalantly and moved very close to her, slipping an arm around her waist.

Anya jumped up and looked helplessly at the door out of the cafeteria. There was usually a cop sitting on a chair beside it, keeping an eye on everyone, but not today. Either Anya was in very good standing, or everyone was busy celebrating the guard's birthday, but having brought her there for lunch the cops had melted away into the depths of the detention center. For the first time in her life, Anya regretted the absence of the police.

Fortunately, at this moment Viktor Ivanovich emerged from the kitchen with a bowl of borsch, followed by the mousy server. Anya did not know his name and had yet to hear him say anything.

"Hey, Ivanovich, grab me some borsch," Sergey ordered.

"Get lost!" Viktor Ivanovich muttered. "Get it yourself. I'm not your effing waiter."

"Don't get all riled up. I only asked. Okay, I'll get it myself. Can't you see I'm talking to a pretty girl?"

Sergey ambled off to the kitchen, while Anya sat back down at the table. The presence of other people, and especially the familiar Viktor Ivanovich, restored her confidence.

Unfortunately, a minute later Sergey plonked himself down on the bench next to her. She pointedly moved away from him.

"Are you the only one left now?" Viktor Ivanovich was asking her in a kind voice. "How much longer do you have to sit it out here?"

"Listen, granddad, don't talk to her," Sergey interrupted rudely. "She doesn't want to talk to anyone other than me. Isn't that right, sweetie pie? We're in love."

Anya stared at him aghast. She had never been confronted by a situation anything like this, or if she had it was so long ago she had forgotten how to react. She found Sergey's behavior beyond belief. She felt like an aristocratic lady on whose table a cockroach has landed, leaving her so flustered she doesn't know whether it is acceptable to scream and squash it with a slipper, or whether she needs to muster all her willpower and merely pretend it is not there.

"I am not your sweetie pie," Anya mumbled, regretfully reflecting that this was the worst possible response.

"What are you, then?" Sergey immediately wheedled, raising his eyebrows, as if greatly amused. "My little fish? My pussycat? I will call you whatever you tell me to."

"You don't need to call me anything," Anya snapped. "In fact it would be best if you would just stop talking to me."

"Oooh, you are a serious girl, made of stern stuff. Just what I like!" Sergey said in delight, and again moved in, pressing his thigh against her.

Anya jumped up and moved to the opposite side of the table where Viktor Ivanovich and the other server were sitting.

"Leave her be, will you," Viktor Ivanovich muttered. "Can't you see she wants nothing to do with you?"

"Keep your nose out of our relationship, focus on your bowl," Sergey said and, turning to Anya, again switched on his well-practiced smile. "So what has brought you to this place, my lovely?"

Anya was about to snap back at him, but changed her mind, thinking a truthful answer might scare him off.

"Politics. I attend protest rallies."

"Politics? Wow! That what I'm in for too!"

"You are?" Anya asked, surprised and almost horrified.

"Sure am. The fuzz caught me without my license, and my dad refused to pay the fine. That's his politics!"

Sergey sniggered. Anya crammed the last spoonful of porridge into her mouth and stood up without more ado.

"Could you pour some hot water, please?" she asked Viktor Ivanovich.

"Of course, give me the bottle," he said, immediately coming to her aid.

"I'll do it!" Sergey intervened and rudely grabbed the bottle from him. "I'll do anything for you, my lovely, just you see," he gushed.

While he was off in the kitchen, Anya felt a sense of relief. She heard the water gurgling into the bottle and looked forward to finally taking refuge in her cell on her own.

Sergey put the bottle on the ledge of the serving hatch and gave Anya a meaningful look. She walked up to him reluctantly and held out her hand.

"Oh, no," Sergey said playfully, placing his hand on top of the bottle. "You can only have it in return for a kiss."

"What?" Anya said, flabbergasted.

Sergey turned his cheek to her and tapped his finger on it twice.

"You're crazy!" Anya exploded. "Just lay off, will you, creep? Give it here!"

She grabbed the handle of the bottle. It made an arc in the air but she had it in her hand. Luckily, the lid was screwed on tightly and it did not spill. With a glint in her eyes, Anya was out of the dining room, hearing Sergey behind bidding her au revoir "till exercise time."

Heading down the stairs, Anya found the exit to the cell corridor was locked. She angrily rattled the bars, afraid deep down that the limpet-like Sergey would come after her and she would have no escape.

"Aren't you supposed to be on guard when I go to lunch?" she snapped at the police boy when he finally appeared at the grating. Anya's complaint evidently took him by surprise.

"Do you need to be guarded against?" he asked, confused.

Anya wanted to be indignant, to complain that in their absence some idiot had accosted her, but at the last moment she stopped herself. It would be ridiculous to tell tales on another prisoner. With her nose in the air she stalked past the police boy, waited while he hastily unlocked the cell door in front of her, and disappeared inside.

On her own again, Anya made some tea, settled herself on the bunk, and picked up her book. She could not, however, get Sergey and his harassment out of her head. It might have seemed strange for her to attach such importance to it, but the gulf between what she regarded as offensive behavior and what a majority of people nowadays seemed to do all the same was only too plain.

Anya had begun consciously considering herself a feminist around the same time she began taking an interest in politics. Now she was inclined to explain her feminism by saying she was constantly wanting something to fight for. Whether that was a free Russia or women's rights made little difference. It could not be said that in the past she had been particularly conservative, rather she had just not thought at all about such matters. It was now, when she unambiguously identified herself as a member of the social category "women," that she believed in militantly defending her rights. Back when she hadn't put herself in any particular category, she had not felt especially oppressed.

There seemed to be two kinds of women's rights problems, Anya observed: those it was customary to condemn, and others which it was customary to laugh at. The former included domestic violence and female circumcision, while the latter were less obvious and more controversial. Was it permissible at work for a man to compliment a woman on her appearance? Was it okay to use the word "prostitute" as a term of abuse? Was it appropriate to advertise cars using semi-naked models? This was discussed on Facebook, and Anya read all the posts with great diligence. In the course of such debates someone would invariably appear to reproachfully remind everyone that while a well-fed public in Moscow was discussing the permissibility of the word "slut," in the rest of Russia women were being raped and murdered. This angered Anya. She entirely disagreed that one problem should be seen as more real than the other, but also knew very well that she herself was privileged. She was at the top of a pyramid, where she was allowed to engage in educated discussion and concern herself with subtle issues of language. It was a tiny peak, like the point of a needle, and below the pyramid rapidly broadened into a backward realm of horror where women had to fight for the right to retain their integrity, to remain undamaged and alive. Anya was conscious of this, but could not help feeling relieved that those were not the circumstances in which she found herself.

Stomping around on her peak for many years now, Anya had almost ceased to be afraid she might fall down the mountainside. Her family, the friends and acquaintances who surrounded Anya were a wall behind which she could feel safe and not imagine she might ever find herself in a less pleasant environment. The detention center was a reminder of how easily that could happen. It was not the case that there was anything particularly dreadful about this specific place. Anya reflected grimly that most places were pretty dreadful if you judged them on the way women were treated there. It did not matter how educated or successful people were, or even what gender they were, the idea that men were preeminent was firmly fixed in the heads of nearly everyone.

Anya thought back to the internship at the Foreign Ministry in her last year of study. The contingent there was markedly different from the prison population, but sexism was if anything more prevalent. The segregation of people by gender had developed into an immutable law. Men worked as diplomats and were the higher caste; women occupied technical positions and were the lower caste. In the department to which Anya was assigned there was only one female diplomat. She looked older than her years, spoke little, wore spectacles and, in winter, an old-fashioned fur hat. Anya kept out of her way, and even felt something akin to sympathy for her, since she gave the impression that she was unsociable and unhappy.

All the other girls around Anya were accountants, typists, and secretaries. They were young, smartly dressed, invariably went around in groups, and reminded Anya of shoals of small, brightly colored fish. Nearly all of them worked in one large office. There was also a mysterious department of special women who read and summarized the foreign press, but they only worked until two in the afternoon, so were regarded as outsiders even by the technical staff. The Ministry of Foreign Affairs came to life after four in the afternoon, when the end of the working day began to glimmer and everyone became more relaxed and playful.

Most of the time, the tropical fish-girls sat in their big office behind a closet, where they discussed various domestic problems, drank tea, and ate chocolates. Occasionally they did something connected with work, but it was considered almost bad form: good form was to slip through the nets of their work obligations. Some of them were smokers. The smoking area was on the stairs beside a huge floor-to-ceiling window, which made it very cold in the winter. Anya was also a smoker, so she went out to the stairs with the rest of them. The fish-girls very soon accepted her as one of their own. Sitting with them behind the closet and listening to their chitchat was the most enjoyable part of Anya's working day. She was enchanted by the simplicity of the everyday things they talked about.

Most of the girls in the department were unmarried, so the conversation revolved around two main goals: how to marry a diplomat or how to get a posting abroad and marry a diplomat out there. Day after day they discussed whether there might be a position free in an embassy and how close to Second Secretary Ivanov one of them had stood in the elevator.

One problem was that the average age of eligible bachelors in their department was around fifty, and this markedly reduced the pool of desirable men. Another problem was that age did not correlate with playfulness in any way, and older diplomats loved flirting with the fish-girls, who were obliged to flirt back. It was difficult to keep your standards up when the work ethic was based on flirtation.

There were only four diplomats in the department who were not middle-aged, and the interest of the fish-girls focused predominantly on them. The most eligible bachelor was considered to be the mentor of Anya's internship, a promising young diplomat who at the age of thirty-three was already a first secretary. By the standards of the Foreign Ministry that was seen as a meteoric ascent. The next in line was a serious man with dark curly hair who reminded Anya of an aging version of Lensky, a romantic hero in Pushkin's *Eugene Onegin*. The third was a plump, good-natured fellow about whom Anya knew only that he had spent several years in Zimbabwe and contracted malaria. The fourth was the youngest and most mysterious. There were rumors that he had done something so impermissible that he had actually been demoted from second secretary to third, which by ministry standards was a truly terrible sanction. He looked at the fish-girls so lasciviously that they instantly blushed and giggled. Anya felt uncomfortable in his presence. She constantly had the impression something about her must be wrong. Was her hair sticking out? Was her blouse not tucked in properly?

Anya's job was to sit in a tiny semi-basement room and answer the telephone. It rang incessantly. Most of the time the callers were people who had not been able to get through to the help desk. Anya always talked to them courteously, and sometimes at considerable length. Other than these phone calls and her get-togethers with the girls in their office, she had nothing to entertain her. In her room there was a stone-age computer with dial-up internet that took several minutes to load any site, but at least she had internet access, which was something nobody else could boast of. Given that Anya was interning in the Information and Press Department, that seemed a questionable corporate policy.

In addition to answering telephone calls, Anya helped diplomats with the accreditation of foreign journalists. This was a cushy job that only involved filling in a couple of forms. Nearly all the diplomats just did it themselves (the flow of documents was completely minimal), except for one. From the first day Anya appeared in the department, he clung to her like a burr. His name was Boris Borisovich, he was elderly, distinguished-looking, brimming with far more wisdom than he could use, and was therefore always keen to share it with Anya. When he brought her accreditation documents, he would not leave them on her desk but stand behind Anya, a hand resting on the back of her chair, and watch intently as she filled them out. Sometimes he would lean over (always too close to her) and, with a stubby finger, point out an error. He made endless calls from the telephone in her office, and often called Anya to his own office. Once, sternly looking Anya up and down, he said didactically that it was not appropriate for her, as a future diplomat, to be walking around in jeans. Another time, he passed her an invitation to a celebration at the Indian Embassy. (Anya puzzled for a long time afterwards whether this was hinting at a trip they might make together.) On a third occasion he suddenly lapsed into reminiscence and, looking nostalgically out the window, told Anya that Mrs. Thatcher had once sat on the leather sofa she was presently sitting on. He had told her to sit there himself, rather than on the chair placed in front of his desk.

After two weeks, Anya began avoiding Boris Borisovich, and a month later she was balking at the sight of him in the corridor. In an attempt to escape his unwelcome attentions, she began making mistakes when filling out accreditation documents in the hope he might become disillusioned and leave her alone, but this had the opposite effect. He began calling her in to his office ever more frequently and clearly enjoyed telling her off.

During one of these moralizing sessions, the mystery diplomat came into the office. He showed up in the department so rarely that Anya, a month after her arrival, still did not know his name. Leaning against the door frame, he listened for a while to Boris Borisovich coaching her on how to live life until, unable to stand it any longer, the latter turned and asked him irritably, "Was there something you wanted?"

"I'm looking for Fyodorov," said the mystery diplomat, nodding toward one of the empty desks. Fyodorov was Anya's mentor. He did not come in this early, like indeed the rest of the diplomats who had desks in this office. Only Boris Borisovich was there at the crack of dawn, which was another thing she had against him. If she was late, he would call her in for a lesson on ethics.

"Not here," Boris Borisovich informed him curtly.

"So I see," the mystery diplomat replied, without budging. He folded his arms and observed Anya and Boris Borisovich with a grin.

"Anything else?" Boris Borisovich asked with an edge of hostility in his voice. The spectator was clearly inhibiting his enjoyment of administering a reprimand, and he wanted rid of him as soon as possible.

"I need her," said the mystery diplomat, and nodded, with apparent reluctance, at Anya. Anya felt her cheeks flare up instantly. It was excruciatingly embarrassing to be the focus of his attention.

"As soon as I finish what I have to say to Anya, she shall come to you."

"I need her now," the mystery diplomat said, continuing to smile nonchalantly.

Boris Borisovich turned pink with indignation, but turned to Anya and said through gritted teeth, "Well, as you are needed 'now,' you had better go."

Anya slipped out of the door after the diplomat and stopped in the corridor, looking at him expectantly. He studied her with an expression of amused interest but said nothing. Anya involuntarily looked down and nervously pushed some hair behind her ear.

"Well," he finally prompted. "Say 'thank you.'"

"Thank you," Anya muttered.

"Are you the new intern?"

"Yes."

"From the Institute of Foreign Relations?"

"Yes."

"What's your name?"

"Anya."

"Well, I'm Andrey."

"And your patronymic?" Anya murmured, raising her eyes and immediately lowering them again. The eyes of the mystery diplomat continued roaming over her. She felt like an item in a shop window.

"Why? Am I really that old?" he laughed.

"No, but I can't address you without your patronymic."

"Pavlovich. But please do so address me. Who is your mentor?"

"Fyodorov."

"An excellent mentor. He will teach you only good things." Andrey Pavlovich said this so playfully that Anya imagined there had to be a subtext to the words.

She shifted uncomfortably from one foot to the other.

"I'll go now, if that's all."

"So how do you like working here?" Andrey Pavlovich asked, ignoring her remark.

"Fine."

"Actually, the guys and I were going to have a party this evening. Want to join us? Do you drink at all?" Anya's eyes widened. She was not sure whether to be more surprised by the invitation or that she had given the impression of being a teetotaler.

"Yes, I do."

Andrey Pavlovich gave her a very broad and very cynical smile.

"Then I'll call for you. You'll be in your little office? Well, see you tonight."

Anya spent the rest of the day on tenterhooks. For the first hour she was pleasantly excited by having attention paid to her. Later, though, the excitement faded and was replaced by doubts. The mystery diplomat had invited her, but what about the rest of them? They might be far from thrilled by her company. And what was the point of it for her? Sitting with a lot of older gentlemen and not daring to say a word? Her doubts grew as evening approached, until Anya finally made a considered, adult decision not to go. She started waiting for Andrey Pavlovich to come for her, so she could apologize and go home. But no one came. The longer Anya waited, the more agitated she became. What if they had forgotten about her? It was an unsettling feeling. It is one thing to turn down an invitation, but quite another to sit in pointless expectation.

The day seemed terribly long, but perhaps that was all for the best. Every time Anya glanced at the clock in the corner of the computer screen and reassured herself that it was still too early for a party, she calmed down a little. She listened constantly to voices in the corridor and tried to deduce from them what was going on out there. But whatever it was, no one came into her cubbyhole. Losing patience, Anya sternly told herself she would wait until precisely 6:30 p.m. and then just leave.

No sooner, however, had she made that vow than Andrey Pavlovich materialized in her doorway.

"We're just going to the store. What are you going to drink?"

"Wine," Anya blurted out before she remembered she was going to make her excuses.

Half an hour later she was sitting in Boris Borisovich's office with a plastic cup in her hand and looking bashfully around at the partygoers. Boris Borisovich had left long ago, and there were only the "eligible bachelors" and a couple of diplomats she did not know, presumably from a different department. Anya was either completely ignored or treated with impersonal goodwill, and that suited her fine. Only Andrey Pavlovich paid her any attention, not forgetting to top up her wine and periodically asking her half-joking questions about her work.

When the party was in full swing, the office door opened and Anya's diplomat mentor Fyodorov, one of the eligibles, came in at considerable speed. She cringed on the couch, almost crushing her plastic cup in embarrassment. Anya could hardly have been less horrified if it had been her parents bursting in on her drinking at work. Her mentor, although young, was always so strict and humorless with her that Anya found him intimidating. What would he think, discovering her here? What would he say? It did not bear thinking about.

He walked over to the table and put his briefcase down on it with a thump. Then he looked around the gathering and, noticing Anya, gave a surprised chuckle. Everything went dark in her eyes. Someone offered him a glass, but he shook his head in a dignified manner. Anya glanced fearfully at Andrey Pavlovich, who was sitting nearby. It was he who had invited them all into Boris Borisovich's office, where her mentor's desk was too. Drinking was obviously not allowed here. Andrey Pavlovich, nevertheless, was calmness itself, as if everything was just as it should be.

At this moment, Anya's mentor decisively threw back the flap of his briefcase. Sticking out, gleaming, were two bottles of Arsenal Extra.

Thanks to Andrey Pavlovich's tireless attentions, Anya got completely hammered that evening. By the time she left there was almost no one in the office. Her mentor was slumped at the far end of Mrs. Thatcher's sofa, looking with his crimson cheeks like a cross-eyed Renaissance cherub.

Despite Anya's feeble protests, Andrey Pavlovich insisted on seeing her off. When the taxi arrived, he kissed her on the cheek with his dry lips, which would have surprised her more if she had been less drunk.

The next morning, Anya woke up half an hour before she was due to be at work and with the mother of all hangovers. Only half-awake, she hastily got herself together and rushed to the Foreign Ministry, grimly picturing what a torture Boris Borisovich's sage advice would seem to her today. On the way, she agonizingly recalled everything that happened yesterday: how she had agreed with her mentor that from that moment on they would call each other by the intimate *ty* rather than the formal *vy* (an unimaginable liberty today); how she had downed a huge tankard of beer without coming up for air (no wonder she was feeling so awful); and how she had discussed details of her personal life with Andrey Pavlovich. When she recalled the memory of that, Anya was overwhelmed. Why on earth would she have talked about that with him? Last night one of her admirers in the dorm had called her several times, and Andrey Pavlovich, seeing a male name on the display, commented on it with jokey enthusiasm. But why on earth had she herself, instead of letting it pass or making a joke of it, started sharing all sorts of personal details with him?

In the metro Anya clutched her head in both hands. Never again must she cross Andrey Pavlovich's path. Or drink so much as a gram of alcohol, especially with diplomats. She could only hope they would forget all about her behavior, and at the end of her internship she would show a clean pair of heels and flee the department.

The first person Anya met when she ran into the Foreign Ministry was Andrey Pavlovich.

"Oh-ho-ho," he said, delight in his voice. "How are we today?"

He looked more crumpled than usual and was pushing a shopping cart from Crossroads (the store's name was printed on the handle) with a mountain of files in it.

Anya had only one desire: for the ground to open up and swallow her, but there is no room in the world for such wonders. Trying to adopt her most nonchalant and casual air (and succeeding only in twisting her face into a hideous grimace), Anya shrugged. She was desperate to keep her mouth firmly shut, so as not to poison him with toxic alcoholic vapors.

"We overdid it a bit yesterday," Andrey Pavlovich admitted. "You should see Dima, he's quite ill. We need to fix that. Do you drink beer?"

In a daze, Anya nodded.

"Great. I'll come and fetch you."

Staggering into her mini-office, Anya asked herself in martyred tones how she had just managed to fall into this trap a second time.

Self-flagellation yielded, however, to a sense of tranquility: if she was being invited out again, she could stop beating herself up over what had happened yesterday.

This time, not only did Andrey Pavlovich not keep her waiting, he appeared in her office in the middle of the working day.

"Okay, shall we go?"

"Where to?" Anya asked in alarm. "And what about work? They'll be looking for me."

"I've already asked Fyodorov to give you time off," Andrey Pavlovich said with a nonchalant wave of his hand. "After yesterday he's desperate for a beer himself but can't get away yet."

Distraught, Anya gathered up her things under the close scrutiny of Andrey Pavlovich. For some reason, she felt very uncomfortable at the thought of his asking her mentor to give her the time off. What would he have said to him? How would he have explained? "I want to go out for a beer with Anya"? Surely not. "Let her have some time off: she's got a hangover that needs to be attended to"? Eek! However he had phrased the request, the situation showed there were major questions about her moral standards.

"Where are we going?" Anya asked, realizing they were heading for the Foreign Ministry exit.

"Oh, there's this place not too far away."

They walked along Arbat and turned into a beer bar named Zhiguli.

"I often meet up here with the guys after work," Andrey Pavlovich explained. "Or during work, like now."

He laughed, and Anya yet again caught herself thinking that even the most apparently friendly actions—a smile, a laugh, a considerate question—all felt cynical coming from him.

Inside the bar Anya looked in vain for "the guys" Andrey Pavlovich often met up with here. There was no one in sight.

"Where is everyone?" she asked uncertainly.

"Everyone who?"

"Well, all the others."

"Oh, the others are working right now. It's you and me who are the slackers. Take a seat and I'll bring the beer."

Anya sat down cautiously at the sticky table and looked around once more. There were very few people here, and those that were seemed quite improbably drunk. The light of day outside the window imparted a sense of total degradation to the place. On the wall directly in front of Anya hung a huge photograph of Brezhnev in a fur hat and with a glass of vodka. Anya felt very uneasy. In her head she quickly ran through all the possible reasons for her anxiety and could not find a single true cause. She had not deserted her workplace, but left with a senior member of staff. He had not abducted her, he had asked her boss for permission. She was doing nothing reprehensible, just having a drink with him in a bar. So what was gnawing away at her? Andrey Pavlovich came back with two mugs of beer on a plastic tray. Anya hesitantly took a sip. The alcohol hit instantly, reactivating everything she had drunk yesterday. It was not a good feeling. She had never cared for the hair of the dog as an antidote to a hangover: the promised relief did not come, and re-intoxication was much swifter. It was all the more unwelcome right now, because Anya was determined to keep her mind as sober and leave as soon as possible. She did not want Andrey Pavlovich thinking that getting drunk was a normal state of affairs for her.

All the same, Anya's concern for her reputation coexisted with a sense of profound satisfaction. It hardly seemed likely that Andrey Pavlovich could have a bad opinion of her if, for the second day in a row, he was seeking out her company. Anya was very flattered by his liking for her. A real, grown-up diplomat wanted to go drinking with her, a snot-nosed nonentity. Which of her friends could boast of any such thing? Sitting in the Zhiguli bar, Anya felt closely involved in affairs of state and international relations. She found the diplomatic status of Andrey Pavlovich a little intimidating, but consoled herself with the thought that someday she would herself start work in the Foreign Ministry, and then would be on an equal footing with him and the rest of them.

There was, however, something else she found intimidating. Andrey Pavlovich continued to scrutinize her. It was not just that he was looking at her—they were, after all, sitting at a table opposite each other—but how he was looking. It seemed to Anya that the lower and upper halves of his face led a separate existence: his lips extended into a smile and carried on coherent conversation, but his eyes looked at her in a cold, hard way. When he laughed, they failed to become warmer even for an instant and continued to appraise her. This perpetual examination made her very jumpy. She was grateful to Andrey Pavlovich for his attention and did her best to appear especially sweet, intelligent, and interesting, so as not to disappoint him, but felt that all her efforts were futile. She could not change his eyes. He asked her lots of questions, but did not seem to listen to the answers. Anya began to wonder what it was in her that was so attracting him. She sensed clearly that their conversation was of no interest to him, but why, then, had he invited her for a drink?

Meanwhile, he was emptying one beer mug after another and urging Anya to do the same. This time, however, she was determined to resist temptation at all costs. After she firmly rejected his proposal to drink a third beer, he seemed suddenly to lose interest, and after a time he suddenly looked at his watch and announced that he had to return to the Foreign Ministry. They left the bar and he immediately said goodbye. He strode swiftly off towards the ministry, and Anya wandered distraught towards the metro. It was obvious that she had disappointed him in some way, but how exactly remained a mystery.

For the next two months, Andrey Pavlovich did not appear. Someone told Anya he was on a work trip, someone else said he was on vacation. He had not, of course, been overgenerous with his visits to the department previously, so there was nothing particularly surprising about his disappearance. At first Anya was upset, but then she was relieved. His absence was preferable to his deliberately not inviting her to diplomatic drinking sprees—she knew she would get no further invitations.

Andrey Pavlovich showed up again a week before the New Year, scandalously suntanned and as playful as ever. The fish-girls had only to spot him in the distance for them immediately to start giggling. When Anya first encountered him again in the corridor, she was dismayed. He looked at her with the smugness of a cat eyeing a bird. Anya had forgotten how awkward he made her feel.

He came into her secretarial cubbyhole a couple of times to send a fax. Each time he struck up a meaningless, cheery conversation with her, and Anya immediately started speaking, joking, and laughing in a louder way than usual. In his presence, she constantly wanted to appear more attractive and intelligent, and the more strained her attempts appeared, the more desperately she tried.

The final Friday of 2011 was Anya's last day interning at the ministry. A New Year's party was planned for the evening, but the festive mood was spoiled, because it turned out that somewhere near Murmansk a submarine with nuclear warheads had been ablaze for two days, and this was greatly disturbing Norway. The Information and Press Department was performing its customary function of blocking all information, so that Russia should not learn about the threat of a second Chernobyl on New Year's Eve. All day diplomats were scurrying up and down the corridors, looking intense and worried.

They started drinking to calm their nerves around midday, and by evening the problem of the burning submarine had receded significantly. Anya sat at first behind the closet with the fish-girls. As they got more drunk, the girls smoked more and more and, consequently, were hanging around on the stairs for longer periods. There they soon met up with men with flushed faces emerging from one of their meetings in Boris Borisovich's office and it was instantly agreed they should join forces. Grabbing their mugs with what remained of the champagne, the shoal proceeded en masse to the other office. Here there were a lot of drunk, noisy people, a smell of tangerines, and empty bottles sticking up like missiles out of every trash can. Their arrival was greeted with ribald enthusiasm.

Time passed, the conversations became more animated and the laughter louder. People got tired of going out to the stairs and someone suggested smoking in the office and opening the window. A mug got broken. A man Anya did not know passed out and was taken away. The office was very bright, the electric light reflecting off the polished tables and glass bottles, and then it got very cold. Even though everyone was smoking in the office, Anya slipped out to the stairwell several times. There the lights had been shut off, the only illumination came through the window, from streetlamps. She smoked in absolute silence, listening to muffled bursts of laughter from the office and immersing herself in waves of alcohol-induced happiness. The Garden Ring Road shimmering with headlights, the people in the office, flushed and merry, the pearly outline of the window on the stairs . . . everything around her seemed festive and wonderful. She had long since lost track of how much champagne she had drunk.

Neither did she notice the moment when she was the only girl left in the office, or later, when it was almost empty. The last few hours were hazy, but suddenly everyone seemed to have left. She found there were just the four of them sitting there—Anya, Andrey Pavlovich, the other diplomat, who was looking particularly like Lensky that day, and her mentor, who by now looked like a totally degenerate cherub. The

311

men were talking drunkenly among themselves. Andrey Pavlovich was sitting very close to Anya on Mrs. Thatcher's sofa, almost touching her.

She reached for her mug. It was empty. Andrey Pavlovich gracefully picked up a nearby bottle and poured what remained of its contents for Anya. "That's the last of it," he announced, shaking the bottle. Lensky and her mentor immediately prepared to leave, as if on cue. Anya knew that she too should be getting ready to leave, but her head was buzzing and she could not be bothered to move. She did not want the party to be over. Somewhere in the outer reaches of her mind she suddenly detected a secret, bold thought that it might really be very pleasant just to be all alone with Andrey Pavlovich. The champagne was finally making Anya feel attractive, and she felt like squandering her allure. Not, of course, on all of them. Neither Lensky nor her mentor were able to appreciate her, but Andrey Pavlovich definitely could. That was why he had paid so much attention to her in the past, and that was why he was looking at her so intently now. Anya looked on as Andrey Pavlovich got up when the diplomats left and locked the door behind them. As he turned the key in the lock, Anya's heart leaped. For a moment she came close to panic, but she was also feeling excited and reckless, like before a sharp descent on a roller coaster. He walked unhurriedly over to a cupboard and took out another bottle, more wine, presumably. He showed it to Anya with a question in his face and she nodded. He poured it into their mugs and they slowly sank down on the couch. Anya could smell his cologne. Half turning towards her, Andrey Pavlovich put his arm on the back of the sofa. The slowness of his movements and the coldness in his eyes were so unambiguously menacing that Anya shrank back, instantly losing all her ardor.

"So, today is the last day of your internship?" Andrey Pavlovich observed. Anya nodded. "Are you coming to work for us?"

"I hope so."

"That is good. We need people like you."

"What kind of people?"

"Bold people," Andrey Pavlovich said with a smirk. Raising his mug, he clinked it with Anya's and drank.

Anya straightened herself and took a gulp. Her confidence began to return. She decided there was nothing frightening about what was happening. They were, perhaps, sitting a bit too close, but that was just teasing. No more than that. It seemed to Anya that Andrey Pavlovich was looking approvingly at her. She squared her shoulders. It was nice to feel she was again the center of attention.

The next moment Andrey Pavlovich was on top of her, biting rather than kissing her, and pushing her backwards on the sofa. That first moment, Anya was numb with surprise and limply slid down. Then she made a movement to resist, as if she wanted to break free. It was more instinctive than deliberate, but Andrey Pavlovich pressed down on her with all his weight, kissing her and pulling her blouse out of where it was tucked into her skirt. Shoving his hand under it, he clutched at Anya's skin and she even cried out weakly at the pain. So many thoughts were running through her mind. This could not be happening, it was impossible—but it *was* happening. She was on her back on a sofa on which Mrs. Thatcher had sat, in the Ministry of Foreign Affairs, and somewhere off the coast of Murmansk a submarine was on fire, and Andrey Pavlovich's hand was already fumbling somewhere low. Anya again felt panic and recklessly excited. After all, she had nothing to lose, she owed nobody anything. It would have been naive to doubt things would go further. She had sensed from the outset that something was afoot. And there was the way he had invited her to come with him . . . Was this not, actually, what she herself wanted? Had she not actually planned it all herself?

Andrey Pavlovich broke away from her for a moment, hurriedly undoing the buttons on his shirt. His gaze was unyielding, as if he was continuing to hold Anya down with it. But she was not planning to run away. As she watched him it occurred to her he was looking at her as if trying to estimate her value. She hated that feeling, and leaned forward and kissed him, purely to stop him looking at her like that. Andrey Pavlovich did stop looking. He again piled on top of Anya, roughly pulling her clothes off. The weight of his body was uncomfortable, her leg began to go numb. The sofa was too short and proving less than accommodating. Anya wondered abstractly what they must look like, and then reflected that there probably were closed circuit cameras installed in the offices of the Foreign Ministry.

She suddenly went completely off the idea of having sex with Andrey Pavlovich. His rudeness and fussiness, the sticky leather sofa, the fact that they might be seen did little to bolster her enthusiasm.

Anya felt strangely remote from her body. It was lying here on a sofa, something was happening to it, but her mind was elsewhere. Anya pictured herself just getting up and walking out. The idea brought such a sense of relief that she had no doubt it was absolutely the right thing to do. That was what should be done. Only she could not do it. It would be such a disgrace to chicken out halfway. What would Andrey Pavlovich say? Even more to the point, she knew she would regret it the moment the door closed behind her.

She would not regret the sex she had missed, she would regret having missed out on a really funny tale to tell, she would regret an experience she had not had, an opportunity missed to learn something new about herself.

She stayed where she was.

Late that night Andrey Pavlovich took her back to the dormitory. The sleepy watchman did not want to let Anya in: the entrance was closed between midnight and five, but Andrey Pavlovich irritably thrust his Foreign Ministry pass under the watchman's nose and stated that Anya had been helping him with his work late into the night. Anya was grateful to him, but once she was inside the dorm she was also very glad to be rid of him. What had happened left her feeling awkward.

She was luckily spared any further embarrassment because she never saw Andrey Pavlovich again. As for what had happened, for Anya it was in fact very soon reduced to anecdote. "Sleeping with an intern—really!" she said with a laugh to Sonya and Sasha. It was not difficult just to laugh about it now. She really had not lost anything, though the memory of Andrey Pavlovich peering at her and appraising her as if she were an object he was about to use still made her shudder. The more time passed, the more clearly she saw that her value to him was determined solely by her availability. Although she did not feel she was a victim, there was little to be pleased about in that realization.

Anya got up and walked around the cell. Unable to think of anything better to do, she climbed up onto the windowsill and stared out the window. A pack of cigarettes was lying there. Anya automatically opened it. It was empty.

The sun beat down through the transparent roof; the leaves of the poplars gleamed, fluttering in the wind.

The door in the courtyard clanged.

"You, my lovely, are already waiting for me I see!" a cheery voice immediately resounded from below.

Startled, Anya looked down into the yard to see Sergey the server grinning up at her. Without a word, she jumped down from the windowsill and shut the window

The second half of the day passed more quickly. Anya was first taken to make phone calls and, seemingly, forgotten. Entirely on her own, she was able to enjoy the internet for no less than twenty-five minutes. Then she was taken on her own for exercise. Anya marched, with her head held high, into the yard carrying a book and a cup of tea. It was a misnomer to describe it as exercise. If before she had been reading on a bunk in her cell, now she was reading on a bench under a transparent roof. However, in the courtyard the radio was not playing, and that in itself made life much more agreeable.

She went to dinner, firmly resolved to put Sergey in his place if he tried pestering her again, but there was no sign of him in the canteen. A stern-faced woman she had not seen before was standing next to the serving hatch.

Anya went over, wondering who the woman could be. If she was a new prisoner, how come she was here for dinner without first having been set up in the women's cell? The woman looked to be in her forties. She seemed very tired, with bleary eyes and pale, chapped lips, but she was still beautiful. She was exotically dressed, in a long mauve skirt, a sweater, and a chunky knitted shawl in which she wrapped herself despite it being a warm evening. When Anya approached, the woman regally held out her hand to her. Her fingers were long and bony, and hot to the touch.

"I'm Alisa," the woman said.

Anya duly introduced herself.

The mousy, taciturn server placed a bowl of food on the ledge. Alisa picked it up with both hands—which were visibly trembling—and glided smoothly over to the table. Her hair was pulled back in a long plait. With her skirt, shawl, and long pigtail, she looked to Anya like a real Russian beauty from a classic movie, someone who might at any moment burst into song.

Anya took her dinner and sat down opposite. Alisa ate with great caution, carefully getting her food onto the spoon before very, very slowly raising it to her mouth.

"Are you also in custody here?" Anya asked diffidently. Alisa nodded.

"What for?"

"I am a conditional," Alisa said without looking at her, and again carefully spooned her food.

"Oh . . ." Anya mumbled vaguely, baffled. "For how many days?"

"Seventy-five."

Anya choked on her pasta.

"How many?!"

"Five times fifteen."

"But don't they run concurrently?"

"No, the court specifically ruled that they should be consecutive."

"That will take you through to the end of summer."

Alisa made no reply. She took a piece of bread with her bony fingers, tore it in pieces over the bowl and popped it in her mouth.

Viktor Ivanovich came out of the kitchen with a tray of tea.

"Here's your tea, girls," he said, as if he were the master of the house regaling his visitors. Alisa, still not saying a word to him, took a mug and placed it tidily beside her, moving the handle to align with the bowl.

Viktor Ivanovich sat down at the table with them.

"What's the time now? About seven o'clock, would you say?" He looked out the window and explained, "I'm being released today at 10:35. I should just be able to make it to the store. The main thing is to get out on time."

"Viktor Ivanovich, doesn't the radio in your cell get on your nerves?" Anya asked.

"Oh, we glued it up long ago."

"How did you do that?"

"Uh-oh," Victor Ivanovich responded. "You've been stuck with the radio on all the time? Why didn't you ask before? Anyway, look: you take a lot, but a lot, of toilet paper, wet it, you can add soap but it works without, and then you plaster it on the radio."

"What, you mean it stays in place?" Anya was amazed. "And that makes it quieter?"

"You better believe it!"

"And when it dries out, it still holds?"

"Sure does! You have to add more sometimes, of course."

Through the door leading to the stairs Sergey came into view, panting and gasping and looking sorry for himself. He was single-handedly dragging a huge can. The blonde policewoman was following behind him.

"You might give me a hand, grandpa!" Sergey yelled. The smile instantly left Viktor Ivanovich's face, and for a moment he did not budge, but then, after observing Sergey dragging the can for a moment or two, he got up with a sigh and went to help.

Anya also stood up and looked inquiringly at Alisa, but she carried on silently sipping her tea without raising her eyes.

The policewoman came to escort Anya back to her cell.

"Which cell is she in?" Anya asked, nodding in the direction of the canteen as they left.

"Oh, she's in with you. They're just taking a long time to fill out her forms so they let her go for dinner."

"Has she really been sentenced to seventy-five days?"

"Indeed she has."

"And what does she mean when she says she's a 'conditional'?"

"It means she has been released from the labor camps but with certain conditions. They check that she's at home at night, and doesn't attend mass events. If she does they sentence her to days in a detention center. They can even send her back to the camps."

"That doesn't seem fair," Anya remarked. "A person has already served their sentence, and then they get another punishment slapped on them."

"It doesn't apply to everyone who's served time," the blonde reassured her. "Only to those who were in for something serious."

Anya suppressed a groan.

At the door the blonde fiddled with the keys for a long time, and Anya looked around. Her eyes fell once more on the strange, waist-height pipe with a trumpet-like opening that was attached to the wall by the door to her cell. All the other cells had the same arrangement. Anya had noticed them on her first day, but at that time the strict police boy had refused to explain what they were for. Noticing that the blonde seemed to be in a particularly talkative mood today, and since Anya was herself feeling particularly inquisitive, she asked, "And what is this for?"

The blonde gave the pipe a quick glance and carried on sorting through the keys.

"It's in case there's a riot," she said, finally arriving at the right key in the bunch.

"A riot?" Anya asked, baffled.

"Well, yes. The keys to the cells get thrown in there so the rioters can't get them."

Anya looked at the pipe with new awe and respect: it was evidence that the detention center could sometimes be a far less dozy and boring place than it seemed.

Back in the cell, she decided her first priority was to try out Viktor Ivanovich's advice. She unwound some toilet paper, folded it in layers, wet it, poured liquid soap on it for good measure, and created a sodden mess. Doubtful of success, she jumped up and plastered it over the mesh on the front of the speaker. The sound from the radio was instantly quieter, as if filtered through a pillow. Anya was so delighted she put her hand on her heart and mentally sent her thanks to Viktor Ivanovich.

She went back to her bunk and opened her book, but still found it difficult to concentrate. She was tired of reading all day, and besides she constantly listened to the sounds in the corridor, waiting in some trepidation for Alisa to be brought along. Being imprisoned together with this stern, taciturn woman seemed even more of a pain than being locked up with five restless prisoners. All the more so after her recent blissful hours of solitude.

By the time Alisa entered the cell it was completely dark outside. She was clutching a small plastic bag so worn you could not even tell what color it used to be. She still had the shawl around her shoulders, although Anya was certain there was some absurd prison regulation prohibiting such a thing.

Alisa glanced over the premises and asked, "Where may I sleep?"

"Choose any bunk," Anya said with a shrug.

Alisa took a few steps and sat down on a bottom bunk two along from Anya. Then she carefully placed her bag against the wall and slowly, as if afraid an abrupt movement might cause injury, raised her legs onto the bed and leaned her back against the headboard. In this position she sighed, closed her eyes, and began running the fringe of the shawl through her fingers.

"Would you like some tea?" Anya asked in the hope of establishing at least a minimal level of contact. Alisa did not move or even open her eyes, continuing to braid and unravel the threads of her shawl.

An hour later, Alisa was brought her bed linen. She placed it on the bunk next to her but did not lay it out. Anya almost felt sad that the cops immediately went back out. At that moment even they struck her as more agreeable, lively company than her new cellmate.

When it came to lights-out, Anya had no option but to go to bed. Alisa continued to sit on the bed like an idol, faintly visible in the semidarkness. Pulling the blanket up over her head, leaving only a small gap for air, Anya felt relief that she only had one more day and night to endure.

A few hours later something woke her but, opening her eyes, Anya could not immediately tell what. It was quiet and dark, and only the bulb above the door gave out a dim light.

Nothing seemed to have happened, so Anya rolled over on to her other side to make herself more comfortable, and was startled to see Alisa sitting on the bunk next to hers. At the same moment, Anya realized she had woken because Alisa had said something to her.

"What?" Anya asked, alarmed.

"Can you see it?"

Alisa was sitting on the bunk, leaning towards and staring at Anya.

"What?" Anya whispered, feeling a chill run from the top of her head down her back.

"That!"

Anya propped herself up on her elbow and looked around, trying simultaneously to inspect the cell and not let Alisa out of her sight.

"I can't see anything."

Alisa very slowly freed one arm from her shawl and, still peering straight at Anya's face, pointed a long, thin finger at the wall opposite. Anya obediently looked in the direction indicated. There was nobody by the wall.

Alisa suddenly burst out laughing, throwing her head back, and then sat bolt upright and switched off her laughter. A tress of hair escaped from her plait and fell across her face.

"I'll show you," Alisa said, unexpectedly calm.

She quietly got up from the bunk and walked over to the wall. Pausing beside it, she moved her hand forward and made several passes in the air as if stroking a dog. Anya could not tear her eyes away. She could feel a rapidly rising sense of panic, an emotion with which she was already well familiar, except that now Anya could have no doubt at all that what was happening was entirely real.

Alisa walked unhurriedly around the empty space by the wall and stood facing Anya. She looked almost cheerful. She put one foot forward and began tapping it softly on the floor. She pinched the fingers of both hands together and began to cast something away from herself. Anya watched her strange dance as if spellbound. There was a distinct crazed energy in the cell. Anya was afraid to move. Alisa was smiling but not uttering a sound and continuing to look merrily at Anya.

She finally stopped, took two steps to one side, and asked, "Want to try?"

Anya was afraid to open her mouth in case her voice betrayed her fear, which she felt it was best not to bring to Alisa's attention. She silently shook her head.

Alisa suddenly leaped forward to within a centimeter of Anya's face. There was madness in her eyes, and a light seemed to be burning deep inside them.

"You must try," she whispered excitedly. "It is for you it is standing here!"

She is out of her mind, but they must be seeing us through the camera, Anya told herself, trying to back away in the bunk without Alisa noticing. *They'll realize there's something wrong and come to check. Everything is going to be fine.*

Alisa suddenly seized her wrist. Her fingers were unbelievably hot.

"You must touch it," she whispered menacingly, peering first into one of Anya's eyes then into the other, which made her own eyes look like the pendulum of a metronome. "I'll show you how!"

She tried to drag Anya after her. Anya finally got up, afraid that if she resisted it would only make matters worse. As soon as she saw Anya was going to follow, Alisa seemed to relax. The expression of menace vanished and she was looking merry again, even a little wicked. Clutching Anya's wrist tightly, she led her over to the wall and pulled her hand forward, as if she wanted to force her to touch something. There was only emptiness in front of her.

Anya again felt the energy, and pulled her hand back. Alisa's face was contorted with fury. Anya retreated. It is one thing to be locked in a cell with a madwoman, quite another if the madwoman has turned violent. There was no time left to wait for the police to finally notice what was going on. Anya glanced over her shoulder and saw the panic button by the door. She had noticed it on her very first day, but tried not to attach any importance to it, unwilling to believe it might ever be needed. Right now it offered salvation. Rushing over, Anya slammed the palm of her hand on it as hard as she could.

Nothing happened. Total silence reigned in the detention center. Anya hammered the button, hoping it might suddenly come to life, but with each hysterical blow the silence seemed only to deepen.

Alisa again tightened her fingers on Anya's wrist, and she was overwhelmed by horror. No one was going to hear her, no one was going to help. Stricken by that thought, she felt her strength drain away and she turned defenselessly to Alisa. Whether from the heat radiating from her, or because of the soft glowing of her hair in the dim light of the lamp, Alisa suddenly seemed to Anya to be a living flame, a candle that at any moment was going to melt.

"Touch it," Alisa repeated.

Anya obediently took one step after her, then a second, then watched as Alisa raised her inert hand and seemed to place it on something.

Anya felt it touch a wooden surface.

Panicking, she jerked away as if she had been scalded, but Alisa was unrelenting. She grasped Anya's wrist and again pressed her hand down on something invisible. Anya felt a smooth curve under her fingers. Alisa again pulled her forward and Anya, who a moment before

323

had been trembling like a frightened bird, without understanding why, suddenly lowered her other hand onto the invisible object.

It was a wheel. Anya could feel its roundness and, sliding her fingers over it, she felt its smooth polished spokes. Not sure why she was doing it, she tried giving it a slight spin. It barely moved, as if something were holding it back. Her unseeing eyes wide with horror, Anya slowly ran her fingers along the wheel and felt a thread going off to one side. Very slowly Anya turned to Alisa. She was unmistakably visible. Together they were standing next to nothing, but Anya knew her eyes were deceiving her.

She could bear it no longer. Pulling her hands away as if they had been burned, she rushed to the door and started pounding on it with her fists. The metal door responded with a muffled trembling. Anya began kicking it with her slippered feet and shouldering it with all her strength. She felt like smashing her head against the door if only that would ensure this nightmare never recurred, that she would never again experience such overwhelming horror.

The door burst open and the police boy ran into the cell.

"What's happened?" he yelled. "What's going on here?"

But Anya could not speak, she could only point her finger toward where Alisa was standing.

Alisa had been watching in silence as Anya pummeled the door a second before. Now she screeched and rushed at her. The police boy grabbed Alisa at the last moment. She thrashed about in his arms, shrieking something incoherent and trying to break free. The police boy dragged her to the door. There was a commotion in the corridor as other people came running. Anya saw the sleepy, frightened face of the duty officer in the doorway. Alisa was dragged away along the corridor. She had not stopped her shrieking for an instant. Anya heard stamping in the neighboring cells and voices from inside asking what was happening.

Anya slid down the wall of the toilet to the floor. The cell door remained open. Alisa's shrieking grew fainter and was drowned out by other voices, a nervous rattling of keys, and the slamming of doors. One more door slammed before there was silence, and only in the neighboring cells did any noise continue.

Anya was still on the floor when footsteps were heard in the corridor.

"Quiet! Quiet!" the duty officer shouted. "Everything is fine! Go to bed!"

He stopped at Anya's doorway.

"Go to bed," he told her, sounding annoyed.

Anya didn't move.

"What happened?" she murmured.

"The shakes. Bad case of it she has. We'll call an ambulance and send her off to the hospital."

Anya looked up at him. The stern duty officer relented.

"Gave you a scare, eh? Bad thing, like I say. Anyway, everything will be fine now. Go to bed. We won't put her back in here with you anymore."

He closed the door and locked it. Anya heard his footsteps moving off down the corridor. For a while she sat on the floor, and then she got up and marched resolutely over to the place where the invisible wheel stood.

DAY EIGHT

Anya did not close her eyes again that night. She met the morning sitting on her bunk and staring into the emptiness in front of her. The detention center did not sleep either. All night she kept hearing footsteps in the corridor and saw the cops opening the peephole in her door and peering inside. That simultaneously irritated and calmed her, bringing an illusion of security to the awful situation. She was fully aware, however, that it was no more than an illusion.

The wheel was not there. Anya made a point of walking along the wall several times, probing it, waving her hands in the air in the hope they would bump into an invisible object. There was nothing. For a moment, Anya was tempted to believe that and to say that her mind had once more been playing tricks, but, after some vacillation, she firmly forbade herself to think that. She knew in her heart that what had happened to her in the night was real. Alisa really existed, and what she had forced Anya to feel was no less real. It was just that without Alisa she could not break through all the layers behind which the truth was hidden, and now all she could do was sit here, wakeful, aware that there was still something ineffable and unreachable in the cell. She just needed somehow to get used to the thought, and although it made her hair stand on end, she forced herself to think it all through in order to overcome the fear.

The more she thought, the more the events of the past week began to make sense. Several times Anya reached for her phone to research her suppositions, only to remember that she did not have a phone on hand. Even in her first days in the detention center, that had not frustrated her as much as it did now. Anya felt that she was on the verge of solving the riddle, but did not want to draw hasty conclusions. She needed other people's knowledge as backup, needed their words in black and white to confirm her own thoughts. Sitting on the bunk during the night, she had replayed over and over in her head everything that had happened, until she felt nauseous from monotonous thoughts that led nowhere.

Breakfast was a tremendous relief. She almost ran up the steps into the cafeteria. Anya announced she would be having breakfast, took a bowl of porridge, and sat down. The porridge was very sweet, so Anya agreed to drink the tea her cellmates had always warned her against. They had been right: the liquid flowing out of the battered teapot really did taste more like boiled twigs, but Anya was now prepared to endure anything to delay having to go back to her cell.

The sounds in the dining room seemed to be filtered to her through a quilt. At first, she did not think it was anything serious, but when Sergey plonked himself down on the bench opposite her and said something, she was surprised to find she could hardly hear him. One ear seemed to be bunged up.

"What?" Anya asked.

"You are here all alone. Where is your cellmate, still asleep?"

"My cellmate got the shakes last night and was sent to the hospital."

"That's bad luck," said Sergey, feigning sympathy. "So again you'll have no one to talk to."

Anya tugged at her earlobe, as if that might help her hear better but it did not. Returning to the cell, she viewed the outside of her ear in the mirror, then poked about in it with a cotton swab. There was no immediate effect, although as the cell was so silent it would not have been easy to tell.

She had no desire at all to sleep. The only thing Anya could think about was her phone. She had a feeling that if she could not go online for a few more hours she would burst. Walking around the cell several times, she noticed the chain Natasha had filched from the duty officer lying on the floor beside her bunk. She picked it up, fingered it, and then hung it on the frame of the bunk above hers.

She needed to find something to do to keep herself busy. Anya opened her book and started reading, but soon realized she was just turning pages without seeing the words. She gave up and buried her face in the pillow. An unexpected drowsiness, of which there had been no trace five minutes before, suddenly came over her, and she fell asleep almost instantly.

Her sleep was uneasy. She dreamed she was running away from someone, chasing after someone. She felt someone pat her back and, when she quickly turned around, saw Alisa's face with her blazing eyes, very close to her. Anya recoiled, and plunged deeper into the darkness. Someone shook her shoulder roughly. She opened her eyes and jumped up in her bunk.

The duty officer with the empty eyes was leaning over her bunk. She was angry, but even so, her face remained impassive. Unlike most people, whose faces can register several emotions when they are displeased, the face of the duty officer seemed capable of showing only one single, inadequate expression, which left it looking half-empty. Anya had completely forgotten today was her shift.

"Get up!" the officer said. "Or do you expect a special invitation? I've been calling and calling."

Anya reluctantly crawled out of bed, regretfully noticing that one ear was still not hearing properly.

"Surname!"

"It's Romanova, for heaven's sake," Anya said with a scowl. Now that she was the only person in the cell, this formality seemed even more pointless.

"Complaints, requests?"

"Yes. When does the doctor get here?"

"What doctor would that be?" the officer demanded, staring at her blankly.

"The one for this detention center, of course. I've got something wrong with my ear."

"You want to see the doctor?"

Anya sighed.

"That's what I'm trying to say. And don't use *ty* with me, if you don't mind."

The officer paused, staring at her with those empty eyes.

"You'll have to wait," she finally muttered, and didn't so much walk as wobble slowly out of the cell.

Left alone, Anya went to the washbasin. After her short, restless sleep, her head was as heavy as if she had a hangover. "Tomorrow. This will all be over tomorrow." That single thought reverberated in her head. It seemed to Anya that she was apart from reality. Outside the window summer seemed finally to have arrived. She could hear water gurgling in the pipes, calm voices in the corridor, but she herself was being attacked by a chilling feeling of anxiety. All these material, familiar phenomena were stage props, put in place to blunt her vigilance and leave her feeling confused. She needed to keep her defenses up and not be lulled by the apparent tranquility of things.

She tried to go back to sleep, but then the radio was turned on. The paper muffler she had stuck over it meant it was barely audible, and Anya's deaf ear proved a small unexpected bonus. But she discovered that poor hearing produced a constant urge to listen more intently. Within a few minutes she could stand it no longer and again started pacing around the cell.

Kirill's red head popped up at the window.

"Are you in there all alone now?" he asked, trying to get a glimpse of all the bunks from his position behind the grille.

"Any cigarettes?" Anya asked jumpily, almost running to the window. Kirill grunted, retrieved a cigarette from behind his ear, and placed it on the windowsill.

Anya hurriedly lit up from the lighter Kirill held out to her, and coughed almost immediately. He looked at her condescendingly.

"I haven't smoked for a long time," she explained. The first few puffs left her feeling giddy. "I don't suppose you'd have anything else to smoke?"

Kirill looked at her suspiciously.

"No. I already gave you a third of what I had."

Anya was eager not to be left alone with her thoughts, and glad of any company. For the first time in these past days, she actually wanted to talk.

"Tell me something interesting," she said.

Kirill raised his eyebrows in surprise.

"We have a man in our cell with a metal jaw," he blurted.

"Can you actually see it?"

"No, of course not. There's some kind of plate in his face. He was involved in an accident."

"Does it set off metal detectors?"

"I didn't ask. He has a wife, though, and a mistress, but he's only allowed one visit. He kept wondering which one to ask to come. He thought about it and thought about it, but in the end the mistress was the first to come running. Now he has to make excuses to his wife, tell here there's no need for her to come or bring anything because the food is really good here."

"The food here really isn't that bad, is it?" Anya commented. "I was expecting worse."

"Yes, I was hospitalized once and the food was really shit. Of course, that was a long time ago. Shall I leave you another cigarette?"

"Please."

Kirill pushed a crumpled pack through the bars, nodded a quick goodbye, and jumped down from the bench.

Her sleepless night was making Anya feel today had already lasted forever. In her situation, it was a mistake, of course, not to sleep at night. At least when you are asleep you are not conscious of time passing. Now her nervous tension was again keeping her from falling asleep, although she conscientiously tried several times. Whenever she heard footsteps in the corridor, she held her breath and listened. Her impatience was making everything worse. Her ear was too. After a couple of hours of futile waiting, Anya felt drained, as if she had been working hard. She tried to console herself with the thought that this was her last full day here, but it seemed she would never get through it. She was not convinced the day would ever end. Taken together, all the days since her arrest seemed to have passed faster for her than this one, and it wasn't yet even time for lunch.

With nothing better to do, she smoked another of Kirill's cigarettes. There were two in the pack. It again made her head spin and she decided to lie down, but when she did it only made matters worse and she had to sit up straight. How do people ever start smoking if, on the way to addiction, they first have to overcome these hurdles? Anya could not remember what she herself had thought the first time she smoked. Perhaps she supposed that reconciling yourself to suffering was the price you had to pay for growing up. Adults seemed often to behave very oddly in forcing themselves to get to like stuff that tasted bad, like beer or olives.

Although Anya had no recollection of what she might have thought when she started smoking, she fully recalled the day she quit. It was quite by accident. She, Sonya, and Sasha were on their way back from the conference in Novosibirsk to Moscow. It was a very long journey. They had to first take the local train from Sasha's village to the city, then go by minibus to the airport, and then, of course, return by plane. On top of that, Sasha had things to do in Novosibirsk, so they had to be off at the crack of dawn.

The train swayed through forest. The rails had been laid along the narrow ridge of an embankment, and Anya felt the train moving along it like an acrobat on a tightrope. There were pine trees all around. They did not pass any large settlements and each platform was no more than an asphalt rectangle in the middle of a thicket of trees. "At the next station we pass very close to a reservoir," Sasha said, looking at the map. Sonya decided she wanted to get out and take a look, but Sasha was in a hurry to get to the city to pick up some documents. "Why don't the two of us get out, and catch up with you in Novosibirsk," Anya said.

Getting off at the next stop, they walked deep into the forest. There was no grass growing there, only sandy soil underfoot. Gnarled pine roots spread out over the ground. Sonya said she had always liked sand and pine trees because they remind you of the seaside. They went down a slope and, sure enough, found themselves on a shore. The reservoir was vast, and sparkled so dazzlingly in the sun it hurt their eyes to look at it. They strolled down to the water's edge. Scooping up the sand with her feet, Anya thought that walking on it in sneakers was as unnatural as getting into a bath with your clothes on. They were alone. Colorful beer bottles were scattered everywhere and sparkled in the sun. Against a backdrop of white sand, they were almost pretty. Sonya reached the water first, dipped a hand in it, and pronounced it icy cold.

They sat for a time on a fallen tree, looking out at the reservoir and exchanging occasional words. Then they walked along the side of the water. Anya took out her stone-age cell phone and surreptitiously took a photo of Sonya, who was walking ahead and did not notice. The photo was overexposed. The sand and the water were ashen, and even the bottles had lost their vividness. Only the figure of Sonya in her coat stood out like an inkblot. Anya could not help staring at the photograph: for some reason it seemed to show not just Sonya walking by the reservoir, but Sonya leaving her. The weather was perfect, the sun warm. There was a refreshing breeze and the time went by as they talked. They boarded the next train just as planned. It had been an idyllic two hours, during which Anya finally, irrevocably realized that Sonya did not love her anymore. Later she could even find it amusing that she had succeeded in photographing the very moment when Sonya, perhaps without knowing it herself, had finally left her for good.

On the train, Anya realized that her cigarette pack had fallen out of her pocket, most likely when they were sitting on the tree. Time was short and they were in a hurry to get to the airport, so there was no time to go to a store. At the airport, after they had entered the security zone, their flight was delayed for several hours. As a result, they landed at Moscow in the morning and had to rush to their English exam. Then, when the scandal over the *Afisha* photos was just beginning to take off on the porch of the university, Anya was in such a hurry to get away that she quite forgot to smoke. Later, when she remembered, she reflected that if she had not smoked for over a day, which was longer than she had managed for several years, now was as good an opportunity as any to quit completely. And she did.

In the wake of the *Afisha* scandal, the dormitory management came to inspect their room and were predictably appalled. Sasha was instantly evicted back to his all-male room, and Anya and Sonya were obliged to put theirs to rights. Sonya magnanimously did her bit restoring the beds and painting the walls and then, after the commotion had died down, wordlessly moved in with Sasha. She came to spend the night in her own room only every few days.

Despite the fact that all these days Anya had impatiently been awaiting her return, as soon as Sonya appeared in the doorway she started harassing her with small grievances. Anya's reproaches were as absurd as they were tactless: she did not like what Sonya ate, how she relaxed, how she was studying for her exams, or how she behaved with Sasha. Sonya treated all these complaints with the same aloof courtesy. She never defended herself or squabbled, and at times the horrifying thought occurred to Anya that Sonya might just be feeling sorry for her. Unsurprisingly, Sonya began returning to their room less and less frequently.

Left to her own devices, Anya vacillated between impotent rage and utter dejection. At one moment she might be cursing Sonya and venomously hoping she would break up with Sasha, but then the next she would lapse into self-pity and promise herself that she would always fight for Sonya's well-being and happiness.

But as the tension mounted between her and Sonya, her relationship with Sasha grew ever more amicable. They went no farther than chatting on the porch or heartfelt hugs when they met, but Anya was grateful. Sasha made it clear he wanted to stay out of someone else's conflict, but was also trying to compensate for the cooling of relations with Sonya.

One day they ran into each other in the doorway of the store. Anya was going back to the dorm with some bags, and Sasha literally took them off her to afford her some practical help. The bags were not heavy, it was no distance, but Anya did not deprive her friend of the opportunity to display his considerateness. When they got to her room, Anya invited him in for a glass of tea. Neither of them actually wanted tea, because it was the beginning of summer and incredibly hot outside, but Sasha unexpectedly accepted. Neither of them had anything pressing to do, so they decided to watch something. They sat on the bed and put the laptop on a chair opposite. Sasha wanted to show her an American comedy he had loved as a boy, and Anya had no objection. Ten minutes later he put his arm around her, and Anya rested her head on his shoulder. She thought how great it was that they had known each other for so long and been through so much together that they could afford to sit like this without any sense of awkwardness. Sasha kissed the top of her head and she gave him a grateful hug in return. She was still feeling great about their special relationship even when he kissed her on the lips, and it was only when she felt his hand under her T-shirt that she finally realized she had been greatly overestimating its specialness.

She said no. Sasha said fine. Five minutes later everything was repeated. Five minutes after that, it was repeated again. Each time Anya was just a little slower in saying no. It's only a game, she told herself. There is nothing wrong with it until you cross that final red line.

Anya could not have pinpointed the exact moment she tired of playing. She did not even know straight away what exactly had swung her decision. Certainly it was not Sasha. Despite his direct participation, he exerted little influence. The battle was between Anya and the outright evil she could visit on Sonya, and the evil won.

Secretiveness is what transforms sex into infidelity. After Sasha left, Anya reflected for a long time. With bated breath she waited to be overcome by repentance or an urge to immediately go and confess, but instead she felt something quite different. The sheer nastiness of her behavior paradoxically raised her in her own estimation. She felt she had been promoted to the status of a complete villain. Up till now Anya had been just like everybody else, floundering in a gray zone of subjectively good and bad deeds. Now for the first time she had done something that moved her out of that gray area and into a different part of the spectrum. The unambiguousness of her new situation was almost comforting.

Anya enthusiastically threw herself into mastering her new role. When, soon afterwards, she again found herself alone with Sasha and the situation repeated itself, she no longer had any hesitation. It gratified her to assert her criminal nature over and over again. She found it no less pleasurable to keep the secret, to hide, to be scared of being caught.

Sometimes Anya wondered if Sonya had seen through them, from the way Sonya looked, when the three of them were together, at her and at Sasha, and from vague hints Anya imagined she detected in what Sonya said. If Sonya did suspect anything, though, she did not talk openly about it. Their relations actually improved: by betraying her friend Anya could give her the luxury of no longer finding fault with her all the time. Sometimes, as a mental experiment, she would speculate as to what would happen if she told Sonya the truth. Probably nothing too terrible. Anya was fully confident that Sonya would forgive her. She enjoyed toying with these fantasies. She was not fully satisfied by wallowing in her own nastiness, she wanted also to be able to brag about it. In fact, though, she did nothing of the sort.

After graduating from the institute and moving out of the dormitory, Anya and Sonya moved in with Sonya's brother. He occupied one room in a communal apartment and the three of them were unbelievably cramped in there, but at least it gave them time to search for more permanent accommodations. Anya and Sonya were not looking together. Sasha, who had another year of study to complete, was able to carry on living in the dormitory, but the expectation was that, as soon as Sonya found an apartment, he would move in with her.

Because of the lack of a proper place to stay that summer, the three of them met up far less often. That particularly applied to Anya and Sasha, who of course had something to hide. One time they even decided to rent a hotel room. From what she had seen in films, Anya felt there was something especially sordid about shacking up with a mistress in a hotel room. On the other hand, she felt that if she never knew for sure what it was like, her fall from grace would be incomplete. As in the episode with Andrey Pavlovich, she was not going to stop halfway.

They decided to go ahead on the spur of the moment and, leaving a bar in the city center, wandered off randomly, confident of finding some suitable place around the next corner. There were no hotels around that corner nor the next, and the first one they tried had no vacant rooms. They ended up close to the Foreign Ministry and saw, across the road from it, two identical skyscrapers that looked very much like hotels. They exuded Soviet chic and appeared expensive, which the jobless Anya and Sasha could ill afford. By now, however, they had not enough stamina to carry on looking. One hotel was called The Golden Ring and the other was called The Belgrade. They opted for The Belgrade as having the more exotic name and went inside.

Shifting uneasily in front of the reception desk, Anya endured several minutes of humiliation. She felt everyone was looking at them suspiciously and disapprovingly. She was not sure whether this was because their shameful intentions were obvious, or because of their obvious lack of creditworthiness. The room cost nine thousand rubles, practically all the money she and Sasha had between them. They paid. Not a muscle twitched on the face of the girl at the reception as she watched them count out the bills. Anya found it excruciating.

Their room was on the tenth floor, with views of The Golden Ring Hotel and a bit of the brightly illuminated Ministry of Foreign Affairs. They had a high bed, with tightly tucked-in sheets. Anya could not remember the last time she had stayed in a hotel, and was impressed by their dazzling whiteness. Hotels evidently seemed sordid only to people who could afford to stay in them regularly. Anya was finding this quite an adventure.

They hardly slept at all that night. Anya and Sasha left the hotel at eleven o'clock the following morning and, staggering slightly, walked down the Arbat to the metro station. It was September first, and every now and then they encountered smartly dressed children carrying flowers and balloons for the start of the new school year. Bracing music gushed from loudspeakers on poles and a festive, almost carnival, atmosphere was all around. They went home to Sonya's brother's.

He was out at work but, as it happened, Sonya was home. As they went in the door, Anya thought, this must surely be the end of everything. A single glance at her and Sasha would suffice to make it clear how they had spent the night. At the same time, Anya felt so tired she was not sure she had even enough energy to lie.

Sonya asked if they had had a good time yesterday. She knew they had been planning to meet some mutual friends at a bar. She herself had decided to stay home because she had an interview in the morning. Anya readied herself to emit monosyllabic answers and wait for the next question, but suddenly Sasha started speaking. Anya gaped in surprise. He lied with such inspiration, it was an art form. Anya perked up and, for some reason, helped out. To her own amazement, she spent the next ten minutes vying with Sasha to invent all manner of new details about last night, which included an attempt to get into the dorm, a quarrel with security, and spending the night on a bench; also a morning trip to the institute to celebrate the holiday. Their story was replete with so many improbable and totally uncalled-for details that it was impossible to believe and, seemingly just for that reason, Sonya believed it. At least she heard them out, wide-eyed, and did not ask a single other question.

The relationship between Anya and Sasha fizzled out after a couple of months. Quite simply, one time they met in private suddenly turned out to have been the last. They kept in touch just as before, the three of them together or in company. Anya suffered no guilt pangs, reasoning that if Sonya had suffered no ill effects from their relationship, then there was nothing to worry about. On that basis, close but at a polite distance, they lived for another couple of years.

Everything came to light in the most ridiculous way imaginable. Sasha got drunk, started accusing Sonya of infidelity, and threatened to leave her. This immediately awakened the spirit of Don Quixote in Anya, who decided to even the scores. She was, indeed, pleased to have a legitimate opportunity to tell Sonya the truth, because it would also enable her to demonstrate conclusively to her that Sasha was unworthy of her. Although Anya's own relations with Sasha remained as positive as ever, and she no longer had any amorous claims on Sonya, she found it infuriating that Sonya refused to see the obvious. Telling Sonya the whole truth gave Anya a smug feeling that she was heroically sacrificing herself so that the scales might fall from her friend's eyes, but deep down she felt she had nothing to worry about. She was confident there was nothing in the world that Sonya would not forgive her for.

And Sonya did forgive her. She listened to Anya in silence, and when Anya wept (cathartic tears of joy rather than of repentance), Sonya put her arm around her and patted her back. They talked for a full three hours, but the longer they talked the more uneasy Anya began to feel. She had supposed that when she dropped the bomb of realization on Sonya, she would finally feel deeply wronged and would, without asking a single question, instantly dump Sasha.

Instead of which, Sonya questioned her in detail. She wanted to know when this had started, how long it had lasted, and why it had ended. Although she did not look at all angry, with each fresh question, Anya felt more unsettled.

They gave each other a final goodbye hug and Sonya left. Anya would have been perfectly at ease but for a tiny feeling of doubt. She did not know where that was coming from. She did not know how things would develop, but was confident that, for the first time in many years, she was being completely honest with herself and those she loved, and that the future was out of her hands.

They did not see each other for a couple of months, although they texted several times. Sasha carried out his threat and did indeed walk out, not so much on Sonya as into binge drinking, although initially the two things overlapped. Sonya was unhappy and tried to get him to come back. Reverberations of the drama reached Anya, and she watched passively from the sidelines: she no longer had any trump cards to play that might influence the outcome. Then Sasha invited her to a dacha near Moscow where he had been drinking for the last several days. When Anya arrived she was horrified: it was a dark, ramshackle building, dirty and uncomfortable, and with a nauseating smell of apples. Apart from the owners and Sasha, it transpired that Sonya was also there. Anya immediately suspected Sasha had invited her purely to raise the temperature. There was, however, no big scene. Sasha soon fell asleep, and Sonya and Anya made polite conversation until evening. Very drunk, the owners drove Anya to the train and Sonya came to see her off. She herself would be staying the night. When they got to the station, Anya gave her a hug and got out of the car. She would have been lying if she said that at that moment her heart sank. It did nothing of the sort but, after slamming the door, she looked back to see Sonya's pale face in the dark rectangle of the car window. She did not know then that she was seeing Sonya for the last time, and later wondered why she would even have looked back.

Sonya and Sasha made up, and Anya received a message from her to say that, having thought everything over, she realized she could not forgive Anya. This was something Anya could never have imagined, and at first she was not upset, but irate. She did not believe Sonya could have been that hurt by the infidelity—Sasha constantly cheated on her anyway. Anya little doubted that Sonya had other grudges against her, but decided not to point them out. She would hide behind wounded pride. After politely leaving enough time to pass for Sonya's anger to subside, she messaged her again, but received only a polite dismissal. Months passed which, to Anya's amazement, turned into years. Thinking back to their last day at the dacha, she asked herself many times how she would have felt if she had known then that she was seeing Sonya for the last time. Probably she would have had the same feelings as now. After years, that image of Sonya's face in the car window still weighed crushingly on Anya's mind. She also wondered whether, if she could turn back the clock, she would still tell Sonya about her disloyalty, and concluded that she would not. No one benefits from being told that sort of thing. But the deed was done. Whatever Sonya's real motives might have been, one thing was for sure: it was Anya's fault. She had created all these causes by her own efforts.

The radio in Anya's cell suddenly turned itself up to maximum volume and immediately turned itself down again. In her bunk, Anya started in surprise. The worst of it was that she was again reminded about her ear. Making a point of stamping her feet, she walked to the door and banged on it as hard as she could.

The peephole opened.

"When are you going to take me to see the doctor?" she demanded.

"You'll have to wait," a male voice replied crossly from behind the door. The peephole cover was dropped back in place and swung to and fro.

"And what about phone calls?" Anya shouted after him, but got no further reply.

Seething with rage, she went back to the bunk.

An hour later, the door opened and the scared police girl appeared.

"Are you going for exercise?" she asked timidly.

"When do I see a doctor?" Anya replied sternly.

"I don't know," the girl said, even more frightened. "I wasn't told. I was only told to take you for exercise."

Anya sighed. Exercise was the last thing she was interested in right now, but it was a blessed hour of silence that Anya was not going to miss.

It was hot and windless outside, but through the gap under the roof downy poplar seeds drifted slowly into the yard. On the ground in the corners, clinging to the grass breaking through the asphalt, white tufts were gathering. Anya sat down on the hot bench, tucking her feet under her, leaned her back against the wall, and started reading. Here it really was quiet, the stillness broken only occasionally by voices coming from the cells.

It seemed to Anya that not twenty minutes had passed before the stony-faced cop came into the yard.

"Lunch!" he announced.

"What?" Anya asked, not hearing.

"It's lunchtime, I'm telling you."

"What do you mean, lunchtime? I've only just been brought out here for exercise."

"Well, now it's lunchtime."

"I don't want to go to lunch. I want to go to see a doctor, so if you you're not going to take me to the doctor, I'll stay sitting here for the regulation hour."

The cop shifted uneasily.

"Are you really not coming?" he finally asked.

"Right now? I'm really not coming," Anya stated.

She had read only another fifteen pages when the cop was back again. Anya tried making a fuss but this time he was adamant. She gave up and trooped after him into the canteen. As they went past the doctor's room, she said, "Well, perhaps I could just finally drop in now, since I'm already here."

"Against regulations," the cop replied. "I can only take you when the duty officer gives the word."

"And when will that be?"

"I don't know."

"Will it soon be time for phone calls?"

"I don't know."

As the day wore on, Anya's exasperation grew. She had no doubt the duty officer was deliberately withholding permission to take her to the doctor to get back at her for her morning impertinence. She imagined the woman was not having her taken to make her calls on purpose, having sensed that Anya could not wait to get her hands on her phone. Now she was also worried that she would not even be allowed to take a shower. That seemed to be a right everyone got the day before they were released, but she was sure the duty officer would not miss that opportunity to spite her.

Sitting on the windowsill, she smoked her last cigarette. Oddly enough, this one did not seem as unpleasant as the earlier ones, and Anya almost regretted she had no more left. It was at least something to do. Outside the window the light had changed. It was not yet sunset, but gradually getting darker. This was the last evening she would spend in this cell, Anya reminded herself, but for some reason the thought gave her no joy. When you finally get something you have long wanted, it always turns out to be a disappointment.

Anya was still finishing her cigarette when the key rattled in the lock. She leaped down from the windowsill and stood waiting in the middle of the room.

The fairylike prosecutor came into the cell and the duty officer ambled in after her. Today the prosecutor was looking no less chic than last time, with high heels and a flowery sundress so ridiculously summery and casual it made Anya jealous.

"Hello," the prosecutor said gently. "Are you here on your own? Do you perhaps have any complaints or requests?"

Anya narrowed her eyes and, sizing up the duty officer, said, "Yes. I want to complain. I've been asking since morning to be taken to the doctor and nothing has happened."

"That is because the doctor hasn't been here since morning," the officer hastily intervened. And although she was clearly trying to suck up to the prosecutor, all emotions seemed to register on her face only half as clearly as they would on the face of anyone else.

"But the doctor is here now, is she?" the prosecutor asked sternly.

"Oh, yes, yes," the officer again hastily assured her.

"You will be taken to see the doctor shortly. Is there anything else?"

"I'm being released tomorrow and was hoping to take a shower today," Anya blurted out. She very much doubted that the provision of showers fell within the purview of a prosecutor, but was anxious not to miss an opportunity.

The prosecutor turned to the duty officer.

"We have showers on Thursdays, and today is Monday," the duty officer said, grim-faced.

"A shower outside the regulation day is only at the discretion of the staff," the prosecutor said, spreading her arms regretfully. "Anything else?"

"No," Anya reluctantly admitted after a moment's hesitation.

The prosecutor fluttered off out of the cell, trailing clouds of her exquisite perfume. The duty officer followed, without looking at Anya. She waited.

This time, however, she was not kept waiting for long. Barely ten minutes later, the frightened police girl appeared at the door and Anya was taken to see the doctor.

The canteen seemed oddly lifeless when no meal was being prepared. In the stillness you could hear a faucet dripping in the kitchen. Anya went to the door of the first-aid post and hesitated. Her fear of such places, where everything gleamed ominously and smelled disagreeable, was impossible to eradicate. Sighing, Anya gave a cursory knock and opened the door.

Inside, everything was surprisingly white and new, as if there had been a recent refurbishment, but she was not fooled: underneath, it was exactly as she had imagined. By the entrance stood a white coat stand with protruding rods and hooks, and next to it there was a brown oilcloth couch, sitting on which promised humiliation. Then there was a white cabinet, inside which medicine bottles glinted. The window was open and outside it the sun was shining warmly, but the room itself was cold, as was only to be expected. The most characteristic, and at the same time most alarming, feature of the setting was crouched in the center of the room at a table that looked like a school desk: a diminutive crone with skin like tree bark, short henna-red hair, and a face filled with such malice and contempt that Anya took a step backwards. She remembered having seen her, when she was dispensing Lyrica to Ira. Anya felt a shameful urge to lie and say that everything had sorted itself out, but it was too late.

"There's this girl here," the police girl said tremulously, and Anya could not help feeling some sympathy for her. Confronted by such an alarming old woman it was understandable she felt scared. "Says she's got a sore ear."

"Ear!" the doctor said indignantly through gritted teeth and got up with difficulty from the table. Even standing at full height she came to just above Anya's elbow, but it cost Anya an effort of will to stand her ground. "Need to keep your ears clean!"

"I do," Anya said, offended.

The doctor grunted grumpily and hobbled over to her. She most closely resembled a doddery spider.

"Sit down!" she commanded, nodding at a chair by her desk.

Anya meekly sat down. Snorting, sighing, and muttering something under her breath, the doctor started rummaging through the medicine cabinet.

She finally took something out of a drawer and shuffled over closer to Anya, who cringed. Tilting Anya's head, she inserted a small, shiny funnel into her ear. Of course, it was cold. Even though the doctor could barely move herself around the office and seemed hardly able to lift her feet off the floor, her hand movements were unexpectedly definite, almost rough. Anya winced, not from pain but from dislike of the woman.

Without a word, the doctor took the funnel out and shuffled back to the cabinet.

"Well, what is it?" Anya asked tentatively.

The old woman did not reply, but irritably threw the funnel into a kidney-shaped white bowl and again fussed about in the cabinet.

"Ear hurts?" she muttered.

"No, it's blocked."

The doctor snorted again, took a bottle from the cupboard and set off on her way back to Anya. She had such difficulty traversing a distance of a meter that Anya wondered whether she was really up to an expedition of that length.

Roughly tilting Anya's head again, the doctor, without preamble, poured a fluid, ice-cold, of course, into her ear. Anya jerked back and liquid ran down her neck.

"What is that?" Anya gasped.

"Boric acid. Sit still, stop moving. Well, has that unblocked it?"

Anya straightened herself cautiously and shook her head, like a bather coming out of the sea. She still had a noise in her ear.

"No."

"Well, wait for a bit," the doctor said. "Go and take a shower. Rinse it and that may make it feel better."

Crawling back to her desk, she grunted as she sank back into her chair and began filling out forms, thereby indicating that the appointment had ended.

Going down the stairs with the police girl, Anya remarked with a grin, "At least now we can say the doctor has prescribed a shower for me."

"That's for the duty officer to agree," the police girl stammered.

Back in the cell, Anya stretched out on her bunk and began staring at the ceiling, which in her case was the upper bunk. She was not thinking about anything in particular, and had long since noticed that she found the mornings here much more unsettling than the evenings. By evening she was simply tired of worrying. Reaching for the chain, which was hanging from the rails of the upper bunk, she began to wind it around her finger, and found the action curiously soothing.

Anya dozed off and in a viscous sleep, which felt quite unlike her sleep in the morning, she dreamed she was winding a thread as thick as a rope onto a gigantic spool.

When she opened her eyes, it was dark outside.

Anya jumped up in horror, with no idea how long she had slept or what the time was. The radio was still barely audible through its paper muffler. She turned her head this way and that, trying to figure out what time it was. The reassuring thought occurred to her that if it were really late, she would have been called to dinner by now. But what if she had and had not heard it in her sleep? Anya strode to the door and banged on it with her hand.

"Who's knocking?" the scared police girl cheeped in the corridor.

"3," Anya yelled.

"What's happened?"

"What's the time?"

"Quarter to eight."

Anya took a quick look at the sheet with the daily schedule on the wall by the door. You could make calls "up to 21:00 hours."

"When are you going to take me to make calls?" she asked severely through the door.

"After dinner."

"What about the shower?"

"I spoke to the duty officer, but she didn't answer."

Anya wandered morosely back to her bunk. Just before she got there, she wondered why, when it was summer and not yet eight, it should be so dark outside. Climbing up onto the windowsill, she looked out into the exercise yard and immediately understood. While she was sleeping, the weather had taken a turn for the worse: the sky was dark, a storm was brewing. The wind had picked up, and a breeze was blowing poplar fluff past the window like snow.

Anya went back to her reading, but at the same time carried on listening to herself and, as her internal clock counted down the minutes, she became steadily more anxious. What if the duty officer deliberately delayed taking her for dinner, so she could say it was too late for phone calls? Running out of patience, Anya put down her book and began pacing up and down the cell. She was hungry. There were still a few crackers in the bag in the locker. Anya went over to it and from beneath it cockroaches scattered across the floor in all directions, instantly seeping into the cracks between the floorboards.

Anya jumped back, and completely went off the idea of crackers. While she had been here with all her cellmates there had been never an insect in sight. Perhaps they had been hiding from so many people. Reflecting on this, she felt very alone and defenseless against these vile hordes.

It seemed an eternity before she was finally taken to dinner. In the canteen, Anya wolfed down her rice and meat patty and got up from the table. When she was allowed calls depended wholly on the mood of the duty officer, but she could not help trying to speed things up. Her internal clock had stopped ticking and was now ringing like an alarm clock. She had the feeling that if she could not immediately get her hands on her phone, something awful would happen.

When, ten minutes after dinner, the policeman came to take her to make calls, Anya was filled with both relief and dread. All day she had been focusing on the importance of this moment, so that now she felt an almost unbearable sense of responsibility. What if she did not have time to read everything she needed? What if everything was not as she thought? Or what if everything proved to be *exactly* as she thought?! Letting her breath out very slowly, Anya followed the policeman.

After going through all the customary formalities: surname— phone in striped bag—signature—waiting for the grating to be unlocked—she hurried into the room, turning on her phone as she went. It was cold in there: the window was open and an unseasonably chilly wind was blowing in. Anya could see a branch of cherries swaying outside the barred window. She sat down, threw off her flip-flops, and tucked her feet up under her. The ceiling light hummed quietly.

Anya entered three terms in the search box: "spinning wheel," "thread," "fate," and started reading.

Penelope, unpicking the shroud at night, Slavic deities keeping watch over newborn babes, Sleeping Beauty pricking herself on a spindle, Scandinavian sorceresses spinning destinies, Roman goddesses, Greek. Anya remembered the Greek goddesses from school. They were called Moirai, but she was struck by the number of analogues. Suzhenitsas, Rozhanitsas, Norns, Parcae; one goddess, three, more—from Homer to the Brothers Grimm, from pagan to ecclesiastical texts, the notion of higher powers determining fate with the aid of a spinning wheel and a pair of scissors seemed universal.

Anya studied the pictures of spindles, and even more closely what spinning wheels looked like. She skimmed through the Wikipedia article about Moirai and their foreign sisters. She browsed images on Google. She had a distinct and by no means uncanny feeling that she already knew all this. However, for some reason, she felt a real thrill as she looked at their images and read their names, as if the truth she had been groping for all these days lay not in the notion, but the detail.

She looked up from her phone and gazed at the branch outside the window. Even though her head was full of scraps of information, she was conscious that deep inside herself she had already known everything. All that remained was to collect her thoughts and let the knowledge rise to the surface.

The grating clattered and the duty officer came into the room.

"Time to return the phone," she said dryly.

"Will you let me take a shower?" Anya asked, surprising herself by the steady tone of her voice. The duty officer looked at her levelly for a while before finally saying,

"Today is not the day for showers."

"Oh, come on!" Anya flared up. "Everyone gets to take a shower the day before they're released. Are you really that mean?"

The duty officer was silent again.

"Very well," she finally announced. "Before lights-out. And now return the phone."

Anya shoved the phone across to her and walked out of the room.

Back in her cell, Anya again walked first in one direction, then in another. She was going to make tea, and went to take a cup from the locker, but remembered the cockroaches and thought better of it. Climbing onto the windowsill, she gazed into the darkness outside. Her suspicions had been forming for a long time, and when Diana had told them about her knitting, they finally gelled. All her cellmates had similar stories, in which someone's life depended on threads, ropes, laces, anything that could be cut or torn. Diana knitted and unraveled a scarf for her husband, and he duly became more ill or improved. When she stopped knitting it, he died. His life was so clearly dependent on the yarn in her hands that it could have seemed like a joke, were it not for all the other coincidences.

Katya tore the cross off that cop, and soon after that he had an accident. In other words, she ruptured the lace on his neck and then he died. That too could, of course, have been an accident, but Anya had already ceased to believe in pure chance.

Something had been acted out in front of her eyes. Andrey, the server in the canteen, had accidentally broken the homemade string Natasha had meshed around the bottle and was duly scalded. He, however, had not died, so there must be a difference between his case and the earlier ones. Anya wanted to figure that out.

Ira and Maya, though, remained a mystery. In Ira's case there was at least a death, and also a pair of scissors. But had Ira cut anything with them? Anya remembered her saying she found them in a closet, and later threw them to the floor just before she jumped out the window. Anya closed her eyes and tried to focus, to remember everything Ira had told them about what happened to her that night. She had been promised money. They had gotten her drunk. They took her to a dacha. They were going to rape her. She tore herself free. What did she tear herself free from? She was tied to a bed. Anya opened her eyes. Ira had said she was tied to the bed, but when she came to she began gnawing at the rope to get free.

Filled with energy, Anya jumped down from the windowsill and again began pacing the cell.

Well, okay, so Ira had gnawed through a rope she had been tied up with, and soon after that a man died. But what about Maya? She hadn't had anyone die on her. She told a funny story about a guy who cheated on her. She had her driving license canceled. Never a death in sight.

Anya stopped in front of the washbasin and looked at herself in the foil mirror. She shifted a few centimeters to one side to see the reflection of the cell. It was the same perspective as when she saw that other dreadful Maya with the spidery fingers and live cascade of hair. Anya shuddered at the memory even as something inside her seemed to respond. She remembered Maya, sitting on the bed, constantly playing with her hair, plaiting it, unplaiting it. She turned this all over in her mind.

"*My sister wanted to get pregnant but couldn't, and she thought I must have jinxed her. So then I pulled out a single hair of hers, tied a knot in it, and said, 'There, wait and see. You'll get pregnant now.' And she did.*"

It seemed to Anya that this had all been whispered to her just above her ear. Frightened, she turned around, but the cell was empty.

Of course, she had thought nothing of it when Maya told them that story because, out of context, it made no sense. But now it had deeper meaning. While all the others had been involved in someone's death, Maya had been involved in a birth. The goddesses of Fate were, after all, responsible for human life from beginning to end.

The wind blew the window open with a loud bang. Anya jumped. Shivering with cold, or perhaps in excitement, she closed it and sat down on a bunk.

Did she really, seriously believe the women who had been imprisoned with her in this cell were endowed with magic power to give life and take it? That was ridiculous. She could not imagine five more earthly beings. She got quite annoyed with herself. Ira stoned out of her head or toothless Natasha—which of the two of them looked more like a goddess?

Anya looked at the neighboring bunk bed that had belonged to Ira, and remembered their recent pot-smoking session. Goose bumps ran over her skin as she remembered opening her eyes and not being able to take her cellmates in with a single look. She had felt then that, although they were sitting in front of her, they seemed to occupy all imaginable space, and what she could see of their individual features was not human.

She jumped up and started pacing round in circles. The only way to be done with all this weird stuff was to find an obvious flaw in it, which would confirm that there was nothing at all behind these coincidences. Why, for example, had the other victims all died but not Andrey? Anya knew from her internet research that the Fates were only implementing a higher law and felt neither compassion nor malice. They were a blind tool, devoid of any will of their own.

If one were to assume for just a moment that the women imprisoned with her were indeed Fates (or Moirai, or Norns, or Suzhenitsas), did that mean they only killed people whose hour to die had come? And helped to be born only those who were due for birth?

Katya certainly wished harm on the policeman who beat her up, just as Ira was probably glad to escape from the dacha even at the cost of someone else's life. But Diana had said she loved her husband. If she could choose her victim, would she have killed him? The same was even true of how Andrey had been scalded. Natasha had absolutely no reason to harm him.

Why, when Andrey had broken the string, did he not die? She was, of course, only hypothesizing that her cellmates might have had special powers. Anya felt ashamed of even entertaining such an idea, though she knew nobody could overhear her thoughts.

Diana's husband, the policeman with the cross, the man who tied Ira to the bed—all dead. In all these cases, the "Moirai" themselves cut, tore off, or even gnawed through the fatal thread.

Anya's thoughts turned to Maya and her sister. The fact that Maya had plucked a hair from her sister's head was a fairy-tale touch. In fairy tales witches usually ask those who turn to them for help to provide some personal item, so that the spell hits the right target. Here Maya had not only knotted the "thread," but had plucked the hair from her sister's head. Katya too had torn off a cross that belonged to that policeman. Ira had obviously gnawed her way through a rope that her failed rapist owned and had kept at the dacha. Even Diana had not just been knitting a scarf: she had been knitting it as a gift for her husband, so in a sense, it was already his, even though he did not yet know that.

Natasha had not made the mesh bottle holder for Andrey, and she did not tear it herself. Moreover, as Anya now recalled, Natasha had been far from happy about what happened. Could it have been that Andrey suffered because with his own hands, which had absolutely no magical power, he had accidentally intervened in fate? Did he not die because that was not the day he was destined to die, but had suffered anyway because the magic was too strong?

Anya glanced around the cell. Outside the window it had started to rain. She could hear the drops pattering on the roof in the yard. I have gone mad, Anya decided. I've been seeing hallucinations for days on end, and now I'm talking seriously about magical beings.

It really was too ridiculous to believe in such nonsense. Magic did not exist, there were only tricks played by the brain. Schizophrenia, on the other hand, did exist. Perhaps she had bad heredity in her family in terms of mental illness and just had not known about it.

Anya stopped in front of the place where yesterday she had imagined the wooden spinning wheel.

What about Alisa? She was indisputably real, albeit mentally ill. She had not been in the cell earlier, had not heard the stories of the other prisoners, and yet, nevertheless, in the grip of withdrawal symptoms, had begun spinning on a nonexistent spinning wheel. Could that really be explained as coincidence?

Very tentatively, Anya moved her hand forward, expecting at any moment to feel smooth wood under her fingers. Her hand passed through thin air, meeting no resistance. She went back to her bunk. Despite this failure and her common sense, she had no doubt in her mind that yesterday she really had felt something. How could she have imagined such a thing as a spinning wheel? She had never even seen one, and was still unclear as to how they worked. Whatever had happened yesterday had been real.

She groaned and collapsed onto her bunk, her hands still covering her face. Why was this happening to her?

"It is for you it is standing here!"

At this unexpected recollection, Anya removed her hands and stared into the space in front of her. Something in her chest tensed, as if before a reckless jump.

What if she was one of them too?

Anya sat up in bed again and shook her head, in case that might bring more order to her thoughts. Her hopes were disappointed, so she got up, went to the washbasin, and turned on the water. The water hissed as it hit the sink. She washed her face and took a look at herself in the mirror. She appeared perfectly normal, only tired. A minute before, she had been trying to convince herself she had made all this magical stuff up, yet now here she was, auditioning herself for the role of goddess.

She wandered around the cell, not knowing what to do with herself. She climbed back onto the windowsill. It was still raining, with water streaming down the transparent roof of the courtyard.

But what if it was in the nature of Moirai to learn of their abilities only at a time appointed? And how many goddesses were there in the world determining fates? In Greece there had been three, but in ancient Russia there seemed to be whole hordes of them. How would she know whose fate she was to decide? How long did Fates live? Could they recognize from their external appearance who was a goddess like them and who was an ordinary human being? Anya gave a nervous giggle. She had so many questions and nowhere to go for answers. What an unhelpful coincidence that, as soon as she seemed to be starting to understand everything, there was not a single Fate left in the cell. And why, in any case, had they all ended up in this cell?

She had no answer to that question either.

Anya jumped down from the windowsill. She needed to distract herself from these thoughts. One good thing was that while she had been thinking them she had not been thinking about her blocked ear. She had not yet been taken for her shower. Anya went to the door and kicked it with her slipper.

First, as usual, the peephole opened slightly, then a lock rasped, and the hatch in the door opened. Anya leaned forward to see who was at the door and immediately recognized the dumpy figure of the duty officer. Her fat belly was visible through the hatch, accentuated by her blue shirt. She did not lean forward to speak to Anya.

"Are you going to take me to the shower?" Anya asked.

There was a pause.

"It's almost time for lights-out. You should have gone earlier," the duty officer finally replied.

Anya froze, unable to believe anyone could be so sly. She could not see the policewoman's face, but could tell just from her intonation how much she was enjoying saying no. Without waiting for Anya to respond, the duty officer slammed the hatch shut.

Anya wanted to rush and beat on the door with her fists. She was enraged. The issue was not, of course, the shower, but the humiliation of her situation. She had to beg to get what was readily granted to others, and this repulsive woman had, for some reason or other, the right to decide whether or not Anya should get what she wanted. Anya clenched her fists in fury. She was held back from actually banging on the door and making a scene by the awareness that this would only compound her humiliation. The duty officer clearly had the intention of giving her as hard a time as possible, and the more noise Anya made over her demands, the greater the pleasure the woman would derive from denying them. Grinding her teeth, Anya collapsed onto the bed and burrowed under the blanket. And as for the Fates—what on earth was she thinking of? There was no such thing, and she herself most certainly did not possess any magic powers. Anya closed her eyes tight and ordered herself to go to sleep. For a while that seemed impossible because she was seething with rage. She turned to lie on one side, then back to the other, and then, quite unexpectedly, fell asleep as if someone had pressed a button on her.

DAY NINE

Anya's first thought when she opened her eyes was—I'm getting out today.

She immediately sat up in her bunk and looked around. The cell seemed suddenly cozier than ever. It wouldn't be too bad to be imprisoned in a cell like this for another ten days, Anya thought charitably. She liked everything about it: the peach-colored walls—such a nice shade. And spacious. The bunks were really not that bad—she had never had backache here. Anya looked out the window. It was overcast, but today even that seemed good news—at least it was not hot. She swung her legs off the bunk and felt for her slippers. She had slept soundly, was well rested and, for the first time in ten days, since she first landed in the police department, she was in a really good mood. She was just about to stand up when she happened to glance at the metal bars of the headboard.

The thin chain was lying next to her pillow. Last night before going to sleep she had again been twisting it absentmindedly in her hands.

That one glance was enough for all of Anya's positive thinking to dissipate in an instant. Yesterday's thoughts came flooding back. Had she imagined it all or had it all really happened? Had the women in her cell really been Fates? Was she one? Her troublesome ear, which

Anya had quite forgotten about, seemed suddenly to be fully deaf, despite the fact that it was quiet in the cell. She could hear nothing with it.

She got off her bunk, feeling like a decrepit old woman. There remained not a jot of her earlier cheeriness. Shuffling to the washbasin, Anya washed and for a long time looked at herself in the square of foil, hoping to discern visible evidence of her divine nature. Alas, she found none. From the makeshift mirror, a completely ordinary face looked back at her: brown eyes, pale lips, a smattering of freckles on her cheeks. Can goddesses have freckles? Anya wondered about that and snorted. There were no goddesses, with or without freckles!

And yet, although she kept reminding herself that magic did not exist, she could not stop speculating if there might not be something magical about herself. Wandering back to her bunk, Anya tried to recollect whether anything magical had happened to her before. Perhaps she had been controlling other people's destinies since she was little and had just not realized it. She did not know what exactly she was looking for, so she jumped from one memory to the next as if they were plaques of ice on a fast-flowing river.

University. School. Her friend Sveta in fifth grade . . . she had hair like the golden fleece and one time, out walking with Anya, she picked a rose and tucked it behind her ear. Anya thought at the time it was the most beautiful thing she had seen in her life. There had been a classmate who teased her about her spectacles. Once when he was being really objectionable, she hit him, and then she was so scared she ran away and cried for the rest of the day. When she was nine, she woke in the night and heard her parents talking. Her mother was asking her father to change a light bulb in the corridor, but her voice sounded like someone else's. Anya quickly went back to sleep, and in the morning her parents told her they were getting divorced. Then, when she was ten, she was watching a play for children. Her feet were terribly cold, despite her fur boots, and Anya wanted to pull them off and put her arms around her legs, but you can't do that at the theater, so she put up with it. She was nineteen, and one summer evening she and Sonya climbed out onto the hostel roof to look at the sky, which in Moscow even at night was a smoky pink color because of light from all the advertising. These images flashed through Anya's mind like slides in a projector, precious but empty, yielding no answers.

Then she decided she should try thinking about something more relevant—death, for example. It was the case that everyone around her cellmates had died, so perhaps that might offer a clue.

When she was thirteen, her parakeet died. Anya went out onto the balcony one morning and it was lying on the floor of its cage with its wing sticking out at an unnatural angle. She remembered studying it for a long time and being afraid that her mother would catch her at it. For some reason, Anya thought it was indecent to show such interest in death, even of a parakeet, and she was sure she would be told off.

Then she remembered her grandmother's death. In her last few days the old lady had been unconscious, only wheezing hoarsely as she lay in her mother's bedroom. Then one morning Anya woke up and was amazed how quiet the apartment was, and that was how she understood her grandmother was gone. She thought that she would then feel pain and a great emptiness in her heart, but instead she felt the presence of something new, as if death had not taken away but actually added something. Before she died her grandmother had been an ordinary person, but now she had entered a new state, and the attitude toward her had become more complicated. Anya tried to make sense of it and failed. How can someone just stop existing? Anya was fifteen, she was going through a period of adolescent nihilism and did not want to deceive herself with false consolations. She did not grieve or cry, but lay in bed, angry with herself for her lack of imagination, for not being able to imagine what it was like to die. She could picture her grandmother going off to Africa forever. She could picture her flying off into space. Anya could come up with any number of circumstances that would prevent her from ever seeing her grandmother or talking to her again, but she simply could not imagine her not being alive at all.

These two deaths were the totality of Anya's experience of death, and she had had no involvement at all in either of them. She knew for a certainty that she had not wished for anyone to die and, frankly, found it hard to imagine how anyone could wish such a thing.

Feeling hopeful, Anya switched to reminiscing about births, but things proved no better with babies than with the deceased. There were two births—a brother and a sister on her father's side but, given that Anya had been unaware of anything out of the ordinary for the nine months prior to their birth, she could hardly have exercised any influence on it.

She could only admit that, if indeed she had a divine essence, it was so sound asleep that the most she could hope for was to hear it snoring.

Anya was taken to breakfast by the stony-faced cop. This morning he was, for some reason, particularly stern, did not respond to her greeting, and looked only at the floor. Sneaking a sidelong glance at him as they went up the stairs, Anya reflected that one of the joys of being released was that she would never see this horrid shift again, and in particular its duty officer.

The server Sergey seemed also to be treating Anya more coldly than usual. She was even rather hurt. Her mood had begun to improve again (not least because this was the last time she would see Sergey), and Anya would even have been prepared to gladden Sergey's heart with a conversation, but he looked half-asleep, and doled out her porridge without the usual jokiness.

Almost everything Anya did today brought her some pleasure. Slowly eating the cloyingly sweet porridge, she thought joyfully that she would never see its like again. Suddenly, everything that had previously aggravated her began to acquire a patina of nostalgia. Even the lethargically squabbling servers, even the scary door of the first-aid post. But not the tea brewed from twigs. That was still revolting.

When she got back to the cell, Anya began thinking about how she could kill time. It was still too early to be gathering her belongings together, although she could not wait to do so. She looked at her unfinished book, but recognized she would not be able to read now. Her sense of anticipation was slowly but steadily mounting. She walked around the cell several times, eager to remember every chipped tile, every crack in the floor, so as to be able to tell her friends every detail later. She pictured her evening in freedom. Everybody would come to visit her, drink wine, and listen to her stories.

Would she tell them about the hallucinations, Anya wondered, and immediately answered that, of course, she would not. Quite apart from the question of how real they were, talking about such things was an embarrassment.

Unable to bear the inactivity, Anya did in the end start gathering her things. She told herself she was just tidying up, but in fact she was carefully laying things out on the bed, and throwing out what she did not need in the process. She did not want to take anything from the detention center with her. Its cloud was on everything. Anya would have preferred to depart with next to nothing, but guessed that she would not get away with "forgetting" all the stuff she had here. So she just tried to get rid of anything she felt could be classed as trash. Her eye again fell on the chain. She twiddled it in her hands and, unable to think of what else to do with it, put it in her pocket.

Her activities were interrupted by the morning inspection. Standing with her back to the door, Anya heard the familiar rasping of the key, turned around and was astounded.

Into the cell, notebook in hand, waddled yesterday's duty officer. Behind her came two women, one with a stony face, whom Anya had not seen in the previous shift, and the other the blonde woman who had fingerprinted her. Stopping in the middle of the cell in her favorite posture—legs wide apart like a goalkeeper—the duty officer gave Anya a hollow look and said, "Surname."

Anya's daze suddenly gave way to loathing, which flared up somewhere in the region of her stomach and shot instantly to her head, like a fire in a mineshaft. Anya looked at the duty officer and could hardly believe she was really seeing her. She had just been rejoicing at the thought they would never meet again, yet here she was, standing there and asking her what her name was!

Restraining herself with difficulty, Anya said, "I am the only person left in this cell. I would have thought you might have learned my name."

The duty officer continued to survey her glassily, then slowly blinked and said, "Surname."

"Romanova," Anya answered through gritted teeth. The palms of her hands turned cold with rage.

The duty officer half turned and nodded, and the stony-faced policewoman immediately headed for Anya's bunk, taking the metal detector from her belt. Pushing Anya aside, she started rummaging through the bedclothes. All the things Anya had carefully laid out were instantly piled in a heap.

"Complaints, requests?" the duty officer continued, as if nothing was up.

Her face was frozen in its usual expressionlessness and Anya felt a great urge to go over and punch it, just to bring it to life.

"What's going on? Is your shift on duty twice in a row?" Anya asked. The duty officer did not reply but the blonde policewoman piped up.

"We're standing in for Yury Alexandrovich," she said. Rather regretfully, Anya thought.

The duty officer again turned her head slightly, seemingly to silence the blonde, all the time keeping her eyes on Anya. The stony-faced policewoman finally finished searching the bunk and stepped away. The three of them stood silently looking around for a while, as if hoping to spot something illegal, until the duty officer finally turned on her heel and walked out, waggling her fat thighs. The others followed.

Anya watched them depart, before throwing herself down right on top of her crumpled belongings. In the morning she had been so pleased that she would never see this foul old bag again, and now she felt cheated and wronged, although it was difficult to say by whom. She thought back to how yesterday the woman had so sneakily prevented her from having a shower. Recollecting the unfairness of it made Anya's eyes prickle with tears.

When she had calmed down, she again started getting ready for her release, but it was no longer the same. This whole day was supposed to be a leave-taking. Anya had been mentally checking off what she was doing for the last time. She had one trip to the canteen left, one session of phone calls, one final exercise period. But now the duty officer had spoiled that, because Anya believed she had seen the back of her yesterday and now she had shown up again and profaned the ritual.

The radio came on. In spite of her deaf ear, it seemed to be at full volume. Evidently its paper covering had dried out and was no longer effective. She jumped up, trying to dislodge it, but realized she couldn't reach it. She had to take the mop and rub it over the mesh to get the paper off. The ossified mask fell at her feet, and it was immediately clear that the radio had, in fact, been sounding quieter with it in place. Anya tossed the lump of paper into the bucket. At least her torment would not last that much longer.

As if to spite her, this station endlessly played '80s disco music, which Anya detested, and it also meant there were no news breaks, which meant she had no way of knowing the time.

For the sake of something to do, Anya tidied. She threw out half-eaten candy, unused cups, and empty bottles. She sat down on her bunk and looked around to see if anything was out of place. Apart from her own nook, the room looked empty and lifeless. Anya felt as if she were on a train arriving at its destination. Forest gives way to low houses, which rise and rise as the train comes towards the city. Roads, bridges, and cars appear. Your fellow passengers busily fold up their bed linens and take them to the conductor. Anya felt a great urge to fold up and get rid of her bed linen in order to complete the preparations for leaving this cell, but still had several hours of waiting ahead and did not fancy sitting on a bare mattress. She would have to put up with it.

She heard voices out in the yard. Someone was being taken out for exercise. Hoping it was Kirill's cell, she moved over to the window. She could at least try begging cigarettes from him. Unshaven, sleepy men were wandering listlessly around the yard. Kirill was not one of them. Disappointed, Anya was about to move away, but accidentally caught the eye of a short, dark-eyed man who immediately headed in her direction.

"Lovely lady!" he said with an accent and gave a broad grin, displaying gold teeth. "How are you doing, my lovely?"

"Fine," Anya replied but, to indicate she had no wish to talk, moved away from the window and sat on a bunk.

This did not discourage the man. He climbed onto the bench and, panting, climbed almost up to the window and hung on the bars.

"Are there many of you lovelies in there?" he asked, trying to see into the cell.

"No, there's only me."

"You are alone?" the man asked, clearly dismayed. "Are you bored?"

"No."

"But what are you doing?"

"I'm reading."

"Do you have a husband?"

"What?" Anya asked in astonishment.

"Such a lovely lady cannot be without a husband," the man said with a beaming gold smile.

"I do not have a husband, and I really don't want to talk."

"Why not, when you are sitting all alone! And how do you not have a husband? Did he die?"

"I *never* have had a husband!"

The man was visibly upset.

"How can this be!" he said, deeply saddened. He would have thrown his hands up in dismay but for the need to continue clinging to the bars. "And how old are you, my lovely?"

"Twenty-eight."

His face fell.

"Twenty-eight . . ." he repeated, distressed. "And never had a husband! So you cannot have had children?"

"No."

"Do not be upset," he said with a weak smile, although his voice was so funereal it was clear it was already too late for Anya to think of being upset. "I have three wives. If you still have not married in a year's time, call me. I will marry you. Never mind that you are twenty-eight. You are very lovely. What is your name?"

"Anya," said Anya, who by now was finding the conversation entertaining.

"My name is Ikram. Here is my phone number for you." The man gasped, trying to hold on to the grating with one hand and reach into his pocket with the other. He failed and disappeared from view. A moment later, a piece of paper landed on Anya's windowsill and the man reappeared in the window. "Call me when you get out. I will take you to Tajikistan. Can you think how lovely it is there?"

"Thank you," Anya said, by now almost laughing. "May I read now?"

"Read? Yes, of course. But how can it be . . . twenty-eight!" Ikram muttered, crestfallen, under his breath and jumped down.

Anya waited for him to leave and closed the window.

After an endless succession of songs from the '80s, during which Anya considered disabling her other ear, the blonde policewoman came to take her for exercise. It proved to be much colder outside than it had seemed from her cell. Anya buttoned her sweatshirt up to the throat and paced from one wall to the other. Those afflicted by nicotine deprivation immediately reached out to her appealing for cigarettes, and as soon as she replied, thereby divulging her sex, it transpired that many more were so afflicted. Tired of their shouts of "Girlie!" and "Pretty one!" Anya took refuge on the bench under her own window where she was out of sight. Her slippered feet were soon cold, and she hugged her legs, glad she was not in a theater.

A cold wind was blowing through the gap in the roof, whirling the poplar fluff. Anya brushed it off her face. *Could there be any way to test your divinity,* she wondered. However absurd that notion might seem, the thought lodged in Anya's mind and tossed and turned there, giving it no rest. Why could she not have figured this out sooner! She could just have asked her cellmates straight out. Anya imagined herself asking them, and cringed. She could not picture herself doing that.

On the other hand, she could certainly have asked Alisa. She was so crazy herself that there would have been no shame in it. Well, maybe not crazy. Maybe she was just a goddess.

That was my last exercise period, Anya thought as she went back to the cell. If she could not measure the wait in hours, she would measure it by activities undertaken for the last time.

"Will you take me to make calls?" Anya asked the blonde police-woman as she was already locking the door.

"But you're leaving today," she said in surprise.

"So what? Can you imagine how boring it is, especially when there is so little left."

The blonde laughed.

"What time are you getting out?"

"Supposedly at three," Anya said. "That's the time I was arrested."

"Well, we'll certainly have time to take you before three," the blonde reassured her. Anya noted with regret that three was evidently still far in the future.

Even though waiting was no fun, time seemed to be passing faster today than yesterday. Or was it just because today all her prison distractions were being concentrated in the first half of the day? She managed to settle down to read, but shortly afterwards was taken to lunch. First there was pea soup, followed by the most exotic dish on offer here—pasta with sauerkraut. Anya drank the soup and ate the cabbage, but left the pasta. She felt like a child who, because it is a holiday, is allowed not to finish something she does not like. Actually, she did not really need to eat lunch at all, because soon she would be free and able to eat whatever she fancied. Where would she start? Anya remembered her cellmates sighing for McDonald's. Could Fates really care about such things? What Anya was most hankering after was regular plain kefir.

That was my last meal here, Anya thought as she went downstairs.

Back in the cell, she sat again to read. She had bookmarked the page with the chain and now, as usual, was twining it around her finger. She found that this had such a calming effect on her that she decided to take it with her as a talisman.

When she was taken to make calls, her heart began beating faster. This was the last event in the daily prison routine that stood between her and freedom. Anya quickly came out of the cell behind the stony-faced policewoman, and did not even make a fuss about giving her name and the number of the striped bag to the duty officer. The latter waddled off and brought her phone out of the office. Without looking at her, Anya grabbed it and dashed into the room for phone calls.

First she called her mother, to remind her she was getting out today. Her mother did, of course, remember. Then she called a friend to remind him to come and meet her at the entrance. He, too, hadn't forgotten. She did not feel like going onto the social networks. It would have seemed like a false start. Anya again reflected that one good thing about a special detention center was that, when you got out, even the most ordinary life would seem full of interest.

That was my last visit to the phone call room, Anya mused as she walked down the corridor.

Once back in the cell, she began to pack things in her bag in different ways, trying not so much to put them in better order than to kill time. A couple of days ago she had been laughing at her cellmates doing this, and now she had fallen into the same trap. Sweatpants. T-shirts. Books. Slippers. No, books first. Then sweatpants. T-shirts. Slippers. Why take the slippers at all? Leave them under the bunk. Put on jeans. Sneakers. Do your hair.

Anya looked at herself in the mirror and could not believe the time had finally come. She had been picturing this moment for so many days—not actually being released, but the moment before—that getting out seemed almost unimaginable. Her hands were trembling with excitement. She smoothed her hair, then sat on the bunk. Finally those idiotic bedclothes could be pulled off and thrown to one side, which she did with special pleasure. The bare mattress looked cheerless, but Anya felt real satisfaction that everything had now been sorted, gathered up, thrown away, and there was nothing between her and freedom.

Lying back against the pillow, she considered the cell, waiting for her train to finally arrive at its destination. When she was released, she would have more time to sort all this business of the Fates out. She would be able to read a proper book or two on the subject, or even try to find one of her cellmates and get something out of them. She knew their names and surnames, which meant she would be able to find them on the social networks. If she asked the right questions, she should be able to learn a lot. If only she had asked Alisa something!

She could also try an experiment. To weave a thread and give it to someone to break was probably too bloodthirsty. You could never be sure: one person had been scalded, another might be even more seriously maimed. But you could certainly try to begin a life. Anya imagined hunting for a hair from her friends to tie a knot in, and giggled. This truly was beginning to sound like schizophrenia. She wondered how, if she really were a Fate, she would select her victims. Would you just wake up one morning and feel, *it is time for this person to die*? Or that it was time for a new person to be born? And how could you be sure the time really had come for someone? Anya found that the most difficult thing to imagine. How would you deal with doubts? What if you killed someone by mistake? Anya closed her eyes and tried to imagine what it would be like to have the power to take someone's life. Somehow, she found that much easier than trying to imagine death per se. Lying back with her eyes closed, Anya imagined breaking a thread.

To start with, she tried remembering someone she would not mind killing, but no one came to mind. With her eyes still closed, Anya frowned and imagined a theoretical person whose hour had come. She found that easier. If she really was given the godlike knowledge that such was someone's fate, she thought she probably would be able to see it through. Lying on the bunk, Anya pictured in detail how she would take a pair of scissors and cut the thread. She even seemed to hear the sound of the blades snipping, and see the cut thread slowly falling at her feet. And then someone would die? No, that she could not imagine.

She mechanically wound the chain around her forefinger. Her next thought chilled her for a moment. She could check everything out right now, before her release. She already possessed something that belonged to a person—the duty officer.

Anya looked in fascination at the chain on her finger. Here it was, someone else's fate, already in her hands. Should she tie a knot? But even if the duty officer became pregnant, which Anya had some difficulty imagining, she would not see her again after today, so she would not know the result. That approach was not valid.

What else then? Break it? The chain was very thin, it would not be at all difficult. Anya took it off her finger and held it up to her eyes. It twinkled faintly in the semidarkness. Break it—and the duty officer would die. Anya shuddered. She hurriedly clutched the chain in her fist and tucked it under her. No, she was not prepared to bring about anyone's death, even that woman's. With a mixture of relief and annoyance, Anya concluded that she would never make a worthwhile Fate. Anya simply could not have any godlike gift, because she could never force herself to try it.

The door rasped open and Anya jumped up, hitting her head on the top bunk. Rubbing the top of her head, she missed what the blonde policewoman had said to her.

"Three o'clock," she repeated. "Out you come."

Wincing in pain and continuing to rub her bump, Anya picked up her bag of things and hastened to the door. The blonde policewoman watched her with a smile. Anya went out into the corridor and the policewoman closed the door. *That door is closing behind me for the last time*, Anya thought.

They went to the reception area.

"Sit down," the blonde said, nodding towards a chair. "There are some forms you need to fill in."

She brought some notebooks out of the office and placed them in front of Anya. There was no sign of the duty officer.

"Where is she?" Anya asked, nodding towards the office.

"With the director. She'll be here in a moment. She will have to issue you the certificate of release. We'll have to wait a bit. Meantime, you fill in these and I'll bring you your phone."

Without sitting down, Anya obediently signed several times across from her name. The blonde took out her phone, opened the storage room and helped pull out her bag. There was still no sign of the duty officer. Anya was bubbling with impatience. *Where's she gone off to?* she wondered, but she was so happy she could not get angry.

Several minutes passed. Finding her shoelaces in the bag, Anya began threading them into her sneakers, bending over. This task did not distract her for long. Footsteps were finally heard in the corridor and Anya jumped up.

The grating screeched and the duty officer emerged from the depths of the detention center. Taking two steps into the room, she stopped in her tracks, peering at Anya with her empty, birdlike eyes. Anya looked at her in response, feeling almost squeamish.

"What is she doing here?" the duty officer demanded.

Anya did not yet understand what was going on, but felt her heart sink, while her stomach tightened.

"She's being released," the blonde replied.

The duty officer moved her foot back and folded her hands on her rotund belly.

"No, she is not," she said, pronouncing each word crisply. "This is not the date for her release."

"What?" Anya whispered, or perhaps only thought she did.

"What?" the blonde asked with a frown.

The duty officer smirked. Anya saw only the corners of her small mouth creeping in opposite directions.

"I have just been talking to the director," the duty officer announced smugly. "The court did not include her day in the police department. So she stays another day."

It seemed to Anya that everything inside her broke, and at the same time, fury, pure, blinding fury, engulfed her. She felt like hurling herself at the duty officer, seizing her by the throat, kicking and punching her. She staggered, but did not take a step. Everything inside her was raging but her body felt numb. The duty officer continued to smirk, and Anya could not take her eyes off that mouth. All the hatred she could feel was focused for her on those stretched lips. She tried again to take a step but suddenly felt so weak that she sank into the chair instead.

Everything around her suddenly moved into action. The table scraped on the floor as the blonde, abruptly standing up, bumped it. The registers she had just been made to sign flitted into the hands of first one policewoman, then another. Papers rustled, somebody gasped, her phone slipped back into the striped pouch, her bag was lifted off the floor and floated out of sight. Anya herself was picked up. She wanted to break free, to scream, but had no strength. She was dragged down the corridor. One door, another. The third stopped right in front of her, chomped on its key, and opened up.

Anya was standing in the middle of her cell. Barely audible, water was dripping from the faucet. Eighties music was still playing. The poplars were still swaying outside the window. It was unbelievable that this could be happening. What of all the farewells she had taken of everything?

Anya put her hands in the pockets of her sweatshirt, still not moving from where she stood, and only looking from the bunks to the window to the wall, and back. She felt something in her pocket. Mechanically she took out the chain and stared at it. All the thoughts in her head lay like a shipwreck. In front of her she saw only the face of the duty officer with that smug smile.

Not daring to breathe, her head blazing hot, Anya looked at the chain. *Nothing will happen if I break this anyway*, she reasoned. *But what if something did?* Her heart was pounding. The smirk of the duty officer floated up before her eyes, and Anya was suddenly ablaze from head to toe. The chain was stretched taut between the forefingers of both hands. Just one second and Anya would know the truth. She froze, clenching her fists. Of course she was not capable of doing such a thing. Of course she would never do it. Of course she . . . Without another moment's hesitation, Anya closed her eyes and tugged with all her might.